D1076758

Also by Yvonne Lindsay

Honour-Bound Groom
Stand-In Bride's Seduction
For the Sake of the Secret Child
Tangled Vows
Inconveniently Wed
Vengeful Vows

Also by Yahrah St. John

At the CEO's Pleasure
His Marriage Demand
Red Carpet Redemption
The Stewart Heirs
Cappuccino Kisses
Taming Her Tycoon
Miami After Hours
Taming Her Billionaire
His San Diego Sweetheart

Discover more at millsandboon.co.uk

BLACK SHEEP HEIR

YVONNE LINDSAY

INSATIABLE HUNGER

YAHRAH ST. JOHN

MILLS & BOON

First Published in Great Britain 2020
by Mills & Boon, an imprint of HarperCollinsPublishers,
1 London Bridge Street, London, SE1 9GF

Black Sheep Heir © 2020 Harlequin Books S.A.
Insatiable Hunger © 2020 Harlequin Books S.A.

Special thanks and acknowledgement are given to Yvonne Lindsay for her contribution to the *Texas Cattleman's Club: Rags to Riches* series.

Special thanks and acknowledgement are given to Yahrah St. John for her contribution to the *Dynasties: Seven Sins* series.

ISBN: 978-0-263-27928-3

0720

BLACK SHEEP HEIR

YVONNE LINDSAY

I dedicate this book to the memory of our darling aunty Joy, who will be forever missed but carried in our hearts forever.

One

"Vultures!"

Miles Wingate balled up the newspaper in his hand and tossed it across the dining room in a controlled burst of fury. The crumpled ball bounced on the polished wooden floor and skittered to rest against the molded baseboard. Even then, he could still see the glaring headline that had destroyed his appetite for anything remotely resembling breakfast.

WINJET FAILS SAFETY INSPECTION!

The syndicated article had cut far too close to the bone, exposing serious flaws in safety procedures at the WinJet aircraft manufacturing plant in Texas. At the very least, the fines would be massive. At the worst, the entire plant could be shut down. The fact that his late father's cost cutting measures and often-underhanded tactics had come home to roost didn't cause Miles much surprise. But when it meant his elder twin brothers, who headed Wingate Enterprises, and the rest of his family had to bear the brunt of it? That infuriated him in ways that he hadn't experienced since long before he'd turned his back on the family business and moved to Chicago.

Still, his dad had been dead and buried for two years. Surely his brothers, Sebastian and Sutton, should have picked up on the discrepancies, which had led to the fiery disaster at the plant last month. Three workers had been seriously hurt. The lawsuit that had followed could easily be handled, but the subsequent internal investigation findings that had now led to a joint OSHA and FAA investigation becoming fodder for the media? That meant serious trouble for the company.

"Not my circus, not my monkeys," Miles ground out.

And, because he couldn't tolerate mess, he strode across the floor and picked up the balled-up paper and tossed it in the recycling bin. Even without the reminder there in front of him, he knew he had to do something to get this irritating itch out of his system. He shouldn't let it bother him that his family name was being dragged through the mud. After all, he'd made his choice to step away from everything associated with Wingate Enterprises a long time ago.

He'd used his knowledge and his contacts to establish his own company, Steel Security, and he had a team of employees that he valued and respected. People who took security, both personal and cyber, as seriously as he did himself. He would never let anything happen to any of them, if he could help it, and if something did occur, you could bet your last dollar that he'd hold himself accountable until proven otherwise. As far as Miles was concerned, his responsibilities began and ended right here, in Chicago, with his team.

But that didn't stop him from feeling as if he

shouldn't do something for his family. Wingate Enterprises had enjoyed many years of escalating success on the backbone of the employees who worked for the company. His family had a duty to look after those people. That they hadn't, and that it had come down to something as basic as safety, stuck in Miles's craw like a dry husk. The injured workers were well within their rights to sue. Everyone deserved to come home safely at the end of their shift. But something about the whole matter didn't sit right with him. He knew his brothers were nothing like their dad. They didn't cut corners, and they respected people. He should call them, at least.

"Not my problem," he reminded himself.

He had to get out, clear his head. It was the start of the new month and a Wednesday morning, his work-from-home day. His usual routine meant he'd go for an hour-long run, come home, shower and lose himself in his work with no interruptions. If he didn't go for that run, he knew he'd never be able to settle. The phone calls could wait. Already dressed for exercise, he grabbed his earbuds, strapped his phone to his upper arm and headed out the door.

Pounding the pavement between his town house and Lincoln Park, he finally felt his body begin to relax into a calming rhythm. And with every yard he covered, he could feel the distance between the disturbing news back in Texas and the life he'd chosen here in Chicago widening. Yeah, this was exactly what he needed.

Today was set to hit the low nineties but the temperature right now was still comfortable. Despite how things had started, this was going to be a good day.

Chloe Fitzgerald checked her watch again. He was late. Every Wednesday at exactly 8:00 a.m. Miles Wingate ran in the park. Every Wednesday but this one, by the looks of things, she thought ruefully. It just went to prove, even with the best-laid plans, there was always something that could throw a wrench in the works. She strode back and forth on the pavement, debating whether or not to give up on her idea for today and to regroup. Find another way to engineer that *chance* meeting with the man who would ultimately lead her to the vengeance her family so richly deserved.

She'd waited so long for this. Years, in fact. Tears of frustration suddenly pricked at her eyes. Why had he changed his routine today of all days? Was it because of the story that had been plastered all over the news? Reading the report that the illustrious Wingate family were under investigation for unsafe practices had given her so much satisfaction. After all, it was past time they got their just desserts. It wasn't fair that her family had suffered while theirs had prospered—especially when the late Trent Wingate had built a generous proportion of WinJet's success on the back of her father's own business after driving her poor dad to take his own life.

Growing up with the stigma of having a parent who'd committed suicide had left its scars. Scars that had deepened with her mother's bitterness at having to pack up the life she'd known in Texas and accept charity from distant family here in Chicago to get them where they were today. No, their life had not been easy. And there'd been plenty of time for Chloe to think about the Wingates and what she'd do if she ever got the chance.

Discovering that the younger Wingate son lived and worked in Chicago, versus being enfolded into the Wingate Enterprises umbrella, made him more accessible. And, as a Wingate, Miles was no less culpable in her book. Yes, she was all about visiting the sins of the father onto the sons and daughters of that callous bastard, Trent Wingate. His progeny had taken their privileged lives for granted for long enough. It was time they saw their sainted father for the scoundrel he truly was.

The family could ill afford more bad press, and Chloe had plenty to dish out. All in good time of course. To get the ball rolling, she'd contacted the reporter who'd broken the first story about the fire at the WinJet plant with an offer to give him more information about the family at grass roots level. She'd given him her background and told him about what Trent Wingate had done, but the reporter had said the story lacked immediacy. He could maybe use it in conjunction with something else—something more current. So she'd created her campaign.

First, she planned to get close to the family. Then, when she was well entrenched, she'd show them, through the media, exactly what their father had done to hers. And, ultimately, teach them how much it hurt to be betrayed. But first, she had to get close to the family, and if Miles Wingate didn't turn up for his regular Wednesday morning run, her plans would fall apart.

Which was *unacceptable*.

She'd spent hours and hours on this. Scheming and waiting to be able to implement her plan until she was on summer break from her job as an elementary schoolteacher. Now it seemed foolish to have pinned all her strategy on an initial chance meeting during his regular Wednesday morning run. But it had made so much sense to her at the time. Bump into him. Strike up a conversation. Let the conversation lead to a drink or dinner, maybe. She wasn't ugly and she knew Miles wasn't in a relationship right now. Surely he'd take her bait?

He was a creature of routine. She'd taken heart from

that. Except today he'd varied that routine. Normally Miles would have passed this section of path by now and been heading up toward the monument. Chloe ceased her pacing and stood still, searching the area around her for the tall, familiar figure she'd been scoping out for the past couple of weeks.

Maybe she should just start running. Maybe he'd taken a different route today for some unknown reason. Maybe she'd bump into him somewhere else on the many paths that lined the park. So many maybes. She hated anything to be unsure. She'd had quite enough of that in her life. Miles Wingate's routine had reassured her—underscored that she was doing the right thing.

Routine was the backbone of her existence, too. It was one of the reasons why she'd become a teacher. The sweet young faces in her class might change with the start of each school year, but the basics remained the same. Structure was everything. Planning was everything.

She needed a new plan.

Chloe spun around and started to head back toward her car, at the exact same moment as a tall, blond-haired, male figure came toward her and barreled straight into her. The impact knocked her clean off her feet and drove the breath from her lungs. She landed smack on her bottom on the path and uttered a startled "Oh!"

"I'm so sorry," the man began. "Are you okay? Are you hurt? Can you stand?"

She looked up. The morning sun was like a halo behind him and she couldn't quite make out his features, but there was something in his deep, masculine voice that she recognized from the online video clips she'd seen about him and his company.

Miles Wingate, in the flesh.

Her jubilation at tracking down her quarry was tempered with the fact she could still barely draw in a breath.

"A minute," she managed to squeak out, and raised a hand with her forefinger up.

He knelt on one knee in front of her. At this angle she could now see his face, and she felt as if she'd been sucker punched all over again. The man, in person, was so much…*more*… than he was on-screen or in news bulletins.

"I'm okay," she said eventually, even though her heart continued to race in her chest. Due more to his proximity than to their collision. "Look, I'm sorry. I got in your way. I didn't hurt you, did I?"

He smiled. "I'm fine. I'm more concerned about you. Are you sure you're all right? That was quite a fall."

She shifted gingerly. Her butt was tender but there was no way she was admitting that.

"I was more winded than anything, I think," she said with a smile. "Again, I'm really sorry about all of this. I should have been looking where I was going."

"You did kinda change direction all of a sudden, but I should have been more careful, too." He straightened and extended a hand. "May I help you up?"

She hesitated a second, caught by the old-fashioned courtesy in his Texas drawl. She and her mom had lived in Illinois so long now, she'd almost forgotten what that sounded like.

"Thank you."

Chloe placed her hand in his and allowed him to help her to her feet. His hand was warm and strong, and despite her intentions, she felt a zing of awareness travel up her arm. He let her go the minute she was upright. A gentleman to the core. It would have been so easy to have allowed their contact to linger, but he hadn't. There was absolutely nothing inappropriate in his touch, although a curl of curiosity in the back of her mind made her wonder if he'd felt that same electric charge that she had.

"Is that blood on your hand?" he asked, jolting her out of her reverie.

Chloe turned her hand palm up. She *was* bleeding a little. Must have been from when she put her hand out behind her, to try and stop her fall. Actually, now that she came to think of it, her wrist was a bit sore, too.

"It'll be okay. It's nothing serious."

"May I look?"

Again, that courtesy. She proffered him her hand and caught her breath as he cradled it in his own.

"Is that sore? Me touching you like this?"

"A little," she admitted.

Actually her wrist was now beginning to hurt a lot, and to swell, too.

"I don't like the look of this," Miles Wingate said. He looked up at her with a small frown furrowing between his sharp green eyes. "You need to get this seen to. Let me take you to a medical center."

"No, seriously, I'll be fine. A bit of ice, a compression bandage—that's all I need."

"Look, I feel responsible for your injury. Let me help you."

Chloe chewed her lower lip. She knew exactly who he was, but he had no idea of that. What would a regular woman do in this situation? She certainly wouldn't instantly act as if she trusted him. Would she?

"No, it's okay," she forced herself to say, and reluctantly pulled free of his touch. She winced a little and cradled her wrist in her other hand. "My car is parked nearby. I'll be fine."

Miles straightened. "Look, I know you don't know me from Adam, and despite having bowled you clean off your feet, I really mean you no harm. Let me introduce myself properly—Miles Wingate, at your service. And you can trust me. I actually work in security, so I totally get why you don't want to accept my help. Thing is, I feel bound to offer it to you and to see that you accept it. But not in a creepy way, of course."

He smiled at her then and looked so earnest she couldn't help but smile back in return.

"Chloe Fitzgerald," she murmured. "And thank you for your honesty."

"Will you let me walk you to your car?"

"That would be lovely. I just need my—" Chloe looked around for her cell phone. She'd had it in her hand when she'd fallen. A few moments later she spied it lying on the path a couple of yards away. The screen was a maze of cracks. "Oh no," she cried.

Miles picked it up and ruefully studied the smashed screen.

"Look, this is entirely my fault. I'll replace it for you. It's the least I can do."

Chloe didn't quite know what to say. She felt like she ought to protest, but she certainly couldn't afford to buy a new phone right now.

"I—" she started, but Miles cut across her protest before she could fully form the words.

"Ms. Fitzgerald, allow me to replace your phone. Believe me, it's no bother."

There was something in the way he said the words that rankled. It was a combination of the expectation that she wouldn't dare to refuse, blended with the fact that the purchase of a new device for her would hardly be a blip in his budget. She swallowed the bitter retort that immediately sprang to mind and forced herself to smile.

"Please, call me Chloe. And, thank you. I wouldn't normally accept such a generous gift but I'm totally lost without my phone."

"As are we all," he said with another drop-dead gorgeous smile.

Like an idiot, she felt herself automatically smiling back again. Oh, he was too much. Too good-looking, too polite—just too *everything*! And every cell in her body that wasn't currently throbbing in pain was reacting to him in ways she hadn't anticipated.

"Where are you parked?" Miles asked, oblivious to the turmoil she was going through.

Chloe mentioned where she'd left her car, and together they walked along the paths.

"Do you run here often?" Miles asked after a few steps.

Chloe giggled.

"What? What's funny about that?"

"Oh, just a new take on an old line, don't you think?" she quipped, looking up at him.

Doing so, unfortunately meant she wasn't fully looking where she was going and her foot caught on an uneven section of pavement. Miles was quick to reach out and steady her and, she noted with reluctance, just as quick to let her go again. Even so, the warmth of his hand and the gentleness of his touch had left her wanting more.

Ridiculous, she told herself. She'd only just met him. She wasn't the kind of girl who reacted like this to anyone. Her mostly tame relationships to date had been few and far between. Juggling the responsibilities of teaching with supporting her mom, who was prone to depression, Chloe usually didn't feel as though there was much of her own self left to go around. Most men didn't understand her relationship with her mother and, until that one special guy did, she was happy to wait. Besides, being in a relationship would complicate her plans for vengeance.

A shiver of apprehension prickled along her spine. *Vengeance*. It was such a deliberate and often cruel word. Did she have what it took to go through with it?

Two

Miles walked beside the slender woman he'd sent flying. How could he have been so careless? He wasn't in the habit of bowling over blue-eyed petite blondes any day of the week. At least not literally. And she was definitely the kind of woman he would normally notice. Even now he was deeply aware of the lightly sunkissed tone of her skin, the gentle curves of her body beneath her running clothes and the way her lips parted slightly on a sharply indrawn breath. Not that he should be looking, he silently castigated himself, nor reacting he realized, as he felt his own physical awareness of her sharpen. He really felt he owed her a great deal more than a new phone—and he wasn't too pleased with how her wrist was looking now, either.

"This is me," she said.

She'd stopped by an old model sedan that looked as though it had seen better days. He peered inside, noting the stick shift.

"Are you going to be okay with that?" he asked, pointing to the gear lever.

"Oh. I didn't think of that."

"The pain is getting worse, isn't it?" he pressed.

She looked reluctant to admit it but eventually nodded.

"I'll drive you to get it checked out. Last thing you need is another accident today."

"I don't want to impose. I'm sure you have better things to do."

"Better than rescuing a damsel in distress?"

She laughed, just as he'd intended.

"Okay then. Thank you."

He didn't realize, until she agreed, just how much he didn't want to say goodbye to her.

"Keys?" he asked, holding out his hand.

"On top of the front wheel."

"You're kidding me, right?"

She gestured to the tight-fitting running pants she was wearing. "No pockets."

"Those things usually have a pocket at the back, don't they?"

"Budget version," she said with a light shrug of her shoulders.

"As a security consultant, I can't begin to tell you how risky this is," he grumbled, retrieving the keys from their not-so-hidden spot. "You're lucky your car is still here."

"I know, but I figure it's so old, it's hardly likely to attract trouble."

He opened the passenger door for her and it gave a loud creak of protest. "I can see why," he commented wryly.

She laughed again, and the sound made something

begin to unravel at the center of his chest. He closed the door once she was inside the car and got in on the other side.

"I guess your mother told you never to get into a car with a stranger when you were little, right?"

"She did. Are you suggesting I'm not safe here with you?"

Her words made every protective instinct bloom from deep inside of him.

"I want to reassure you that you are completely safe with me."

"Good to know," she said before awkwardly fastening her seatbelt. "I'd hate to have to hurt you."

His lips tweaked into a smile. "Hurt me?"

"My mother also sent me to self-defense classes. You'd be amazed at what I can do with one good hand."

He nodded slowly and turned on the ignition. "Good to know."

After he drove to the nearest urgent care center and parked the car, Chloe turned to face him.

"Look, I really don't want to take up too much of your time. You don't need to stay with me. I'm sure once my wrist is bandaged up, I'll be okay to drive."

"No problem, and, as to your wrist, we'll let the doctor decide. Okay?"

Two hours later they were back at the car with Chloe protesting every step of the way.

"You didn't need to pay for me, Mr. Wingate. I have insurance."

"Miles."

"What?"

"Call me Miles," he said with a smile. "And, yes, I *did* have to pay. If it wasn't for me, you wouldn't have been hurt in the first place."

"It was my own silly fault," she reminded him half-heartedly.

She was looking pale. The examination of her wrist had been painful, but they'd both been relieved when the X-ray had shown nothing was broken. But clearly she was tired now.

"How about we call a truce on whose fault it was? I'll see you home and then I'll arrange your new phone to be delivered."

"No, I have to draw the line at the phone. I'm sure I have an old one somewhere I can charge up until I replace my other one."

"I won't hear of it. Look, Ms. Fitzgerald—"

"Chloe. If I'm to call you Miles, you must call me Chloe."

"Chloe." He liked the way it tripped off his tongue. In fact there was an awful lot he liked about this woman. "One thing you're going to learn about me is that I am a very determined person."

She quirked a brow. "Does that mean you don't listen to other people?"

"Oh, I always listen. It's how I work out what people really need. In my line of business it would be a mistake not to listen."

"You said you're in security?"

"Yes, both personal and online."

"Just you?" she asked.

"No, I have a team of experts working for me."

"So, you're the boss of everything?"

He felt a grin pull at his lips. "Well, maybe not *everything*. But I am the boss of Steel Security, so trust me, paying for your medical bills and for a new phone won't cripple me financially."

She looked him straight in the eyes. From here he

could see her pale blue irises were flecked with gold. They were the kind of eyes he could stare into for quite some time and happily get lost.

"Based on your experience as a security expert, would you advise a woman on her own to allow a stranger, like yourself, to take her home?"

Miles laughed. "Not under normal circumstances, no. In fact, I would advise against it most strongly. However, if you would like to speak to my assistant at the office, I'm sure they could vouch for my identity and, I hope, my trustworthiness."

She continued to stare at him, then gave a little nod. "As a schoolteacher, I've learned to be a pretty good judge of character, and I think I'll be okay with you. I accept your kind offer."

"Excellent. Now, I'll take you home so you can rest up."

"And what about you?" she asked. "How will you get home?"

"I'll call for a ride. Honestly, it's no bother. So? Where to?"

She gave him her address and he raised his brows.

"Midlothian? You came a fair distance to run in the park."

She shrugged and looked out the window. "I like the park."

Miles continued to look at her, but she kept her gaze firmly outside. He couldn't help but admit it. She intrigued him in a way that he didn't want to ignore, but there was something about her that made his senses prickle, too. Something he couldn't quite put his finger on. Something that made him curious on a professional level as well as a personal one.

Miles turned on the car and backed out of the parking space before heading toward Midlothian. This time of day the trip would probably take around forty minutes. Again, he wondered why she'd chosen to come to Lincoln Park this morning, since it was so far away from where she lived.

She shifted her gaze from out her side window and back toward him. "I'm always looking for places to take my class on day trips. The Lincoln Park Zoo is one of my favorite places to go. That's why I was at the park this morning."

"Hey, no problem," he said, wondering why she sounded a little defensive.

"Did you want to come in for a coffee or something cool to drink before you call your ride?" she asked unexpectedly, changing the subject.

Miles was on the verge of refusing but then thought better of it. "Sure, that'd be great. Thanks. Although, as a security expert, I would advise against it."

She laughed. "I'm pretty sure you're safe."

They got out of the car, and he followed her down the path to the small single-level house. She let them into the house, which looked neat and tidy, and was furnished with the bare minimum. A couch and an armchair in the living room, together with a wall-mounted TV and a small coffee table. They went into the kitchen, where Chloe one-handedly filled the carafe on her coffee maker and then tried to measure out the coffee.

"Here, let me do that for you," Miles said, stepping forward.

Their hands brushed as she passed him the scoop, and his eyes flicked to hers. Her pupils had dilated, and that tiny fact made him more than a little curious. He was definitely attracted to her, and it gave him no small measure of satisfaction to see that attraction reciprocated. He knew right then and there that, one way or another, he would be seeing more of Chloe Fitzgerald.

Chloe leaned back against the kitchen counter and watched as Miles moved around the compact space while he made their coffee.

"You're pretty good at this knight in shining armor thing," she teased as the machine spluttered, signaling the coffee was done.

Miles grabbed the carafe to pour out their coffee. "I try to be good at everything."

"I've had a couple of kids over the years like that." She looked at him, noting the intent way he concentrated as he did everything. "Challenging kids. Does that make you a challenging adult?"

He barked a short laugh. "You'd have to ask my family about that. Or maybe my staff. I'm sure there'd be any number of them happy to fill you in."

"I'll bear that in mind."

She accepted the mug he passed her and walked through to the living room. He followed soon after and sat beside her on the couch. Chloe took a sip of her coffee.

"Good coffee, thank you. I'm sure I do exactly the same thing as you and yet mine never tastes as good."

"Ah, it's an old Wingate family secret," he said with a slow wink.

And just like that, the easy camaraderie they'd been building shattered. Chloe forced herself to keep a smile on her face, but it was difficult when she'd just been so soundly reminded of exactly who it was that was sitting here in her house with her. She'd allowed herself to be lulled by his care of her after her fall, but she had to keep her wits about her.

"So, I guess that means you're not sharing your secrets?"

"I'm an open book. I don't have any secrets. Seriously, though, it's all about how you measure the coffee."

She laughed. "And that's it? No magical ingredient hidden up your sleeve?"

He held out his arms in his short-sleeved T-shirt. His biceps and forearms were beautifully shaped, and muscles rippled beneath his tan as he turned his hands up then back again to show her he had nothing hidden anywhere.

"As you can see, nothing," he said.

Oh, there was no way there was "nothing" about Miles Wingate. He certainly was *something* and, despite her throbbing wrist and sore palms, she was completely and utterly aware of him as a man. A very attractive man at that.

"You mentioned being a teacher," he said. "Do you work near here?"

"Yes, at a school a few blocks away. It works well living here. I can walk to school during the semester when the weather's good. A bunch of kids often walk with me."

"I bet you're popular."

She pursed her lips. "Oh, how so?"

"Let's see. From my first impression of you, you're warm and friendly and don't want to cause a bother. You listen well and you're not demanding or pushy. How's that for starters?"

"You discerned all that from just this short time?" she queried.

"It's my job to read people and situations. I know there's also a lot about you that you're holding back.

You choose your words carefully, as if you don't want to accidentally give anything away."

Chloe felt her eyes widen. Did he read her that well? Maybe this whole idea of hers was about to head to hell in a handbasket.

"You're good," Chloe admitted non-committally, taking another sip of her coffee.

"I make it my business to be good." Miles drained his coffee mug and stood up. "I'd better call that ride."

"I feel terrible to have taken up so much of your day. I am sorry."

"Hey, no need. I wanted to make sure you'd be okay. And, now I know where to have your new phone sent to."

He gave her a smile and went through to the kitchen, where he washed out and dried his mug and returned it to the shelf where he'd taken it from originally. So far, he'd done nothing to be faulted on, Chloe realized. He'd been friendly, chivalrous, and he made a darn fine cup of coffee. And she wanted to bring his family's world down around their ears? Her conscience pricked at her.

She knew this wouldn't be easy, but she had to remain committed. Chloe thought about the family portrait of her parents and her that she kept on her nightstand. It was a constant reminder of what Trent Wingate had destroyed. Three lives irrevocably changed because of Wingate's greed. And that greed had continued to fester as his fortune had grown. Nothing had ever been enough.

Chloe needed to keep that truth in the forefront of her mind because no matter how charming Miles Wingate was turning out to be, he was, first and foremost, one of Trent Wingate's children. Much of the privilege he'd grown up with and taken for granted every day of his life was due to his father stomping all over hers.

All her life she'd witnessed her mother's deep unhappiness, and she would give anything to see her mom genuinely smile again. Maybe, just maybe, if Chloe succeeded in hurting the Wingates, even if it was just a little, it would be enough to break her mom free of the miserable state she'd lived in over the last nineteen years.

They'd both suffered long enough.

Three

Miles parked his Audi e-tron quattro at the curb outside Chloe's house and looked at the sad little building. She didn't belong there. The sagging guttering, the peeling paintwork on the clapboard exterior and the general air of neglect to the rental home told him more about her landlord than he wanted to know. The house could best be described as a renovator's dream.

His fingers tightened on the leather-wrapped steering wheel. Yes, he knew his feelings about Chloe's living conditions were irrational. They were also none of his business, if he was being totally honest with himself. But, and it was a *big* but, he wanted to make it his business.

From the moment he'd knocked her over this morning, he'd wanted to make sure she was okay. And the more time he'd spent with her, the more he wanted to ensure that things went right for her. Sure, he'd been taken by her pretty face, her blond hair and the clear blue of her eyes. Her figure was pretty damn fine, too. Hell, he was a heterosexual male and she was absolutely his type. He'd have to have been blind not to notice her—although, in hindsight he hadn't noticed her soon enough not to cause her hurt.

But there was more to it than just that. He'd seen the vulnerability in her gaze when she'd looked at him. Sensed the reserve behind the words she'd so carefully chosen before she'd allowed him to help her. Caution was a good thing. His entire business plan revolved around it, after all. But there was something about Chloe that made him want to slay dragons for her. She drew on every protective instinct he'd never known he'd had. And that surprised him.

Every relationship he'd had, to date, had been based on equal footing. Women as strong mentally and, occasionally, even physically as he was. None of them had needed his care or protection in the same way he sensed that Chloe might. Not that she was a complete damsel in distress—in fact she was probably far from it.

She was a schoolteacher. He had no doubt she could control a room of potential delinquents with a smile or a frown—she had that air about her. But there was something else, something that lingered beneath the surface. A sadness. A sense of something broken. Something that called to him to fix it.

Miles had never experienced this kind of attraction before. An intriguing blend of physical awareness together with that special something else that made him want to know everything about her.

The aroma of the Thai takeout he'd picked up on the way here teased his nostrils. Enough thinking. Time to do. He got out of the car and grabbed the takeout bag and tucked the box with the new phone under his arm.

Oh sure, the store had offered to courier it out to Chloe for him, but he'd wanted to make the delivery himself.

Miles could hear the sound of music from inside the house as he strolled up the path to the front door. And was that singing? Well, he supposed it might be singing but it sounded like it had more in common with a nine-tailed cat in a room filled with rocking chairs. He raised his free hand to the front door and knocked firmly. Instantly the noise stopped.

A few seconds later, the door opened and Chloe stood there, cheeks flushed and eyes wary.

"Oh," she said. "You're back."

"I'm glad to see that fall today didn't affect your vision," Miles said with a grin. He held up the takeaway bag. "Dinner."

"I wasn't expecting you. I thought you were the courier."

"Tonight, I'm whatever you want me to be."

The flush on her cheeks deepened and a laugh gurgled from her throat. "Did that come out exactly as you meant it to?"

He laughed in response. "To be honest, not exactly. It sounded much better in my head."

Chloe stepped aside and gestured for him to come in. "I thought as much. You'd better bring that all in then."

He noticed she was still wearing her arm in a sling, but she'd changed from the plain white one she'd left the clinic with, to a large, multicolored silk square instead.

"I like the sling."

She half smiled. "White is so yesterday, don't you know?"

"How's your wrist?"

"Feeling a lot better, to be honest. I think the pain relief medication helps."

Miles went into the kitchen and spied some sandwich fixings on the counter. "Dinner?"

She rolled her eyes. "Well, it was going to be until you showed up."

He gave the stale bread and jar of peanut butter a disparaging look. "I'm glad I did, if that's what you call dinner."

"I wasn't really hungry." She sniffed the air appreciatively. "But what is that delicious smell?"

Miles opened the bag and removed the containers. "Green curry and vegetables with jasmine rice and a prawn pad Thai."

Chloe gave him a sharp look. "Are you sure you're not some kind of mind reader?"

"Not the last time I looked. What makes you ask?"

"Those are my favorites. I can never decide between them."

"Then you can have some of each," he told her. "But first, I thought we could set up your new phone. I've already charged it for you so it's ready to go as soon as you've transferred all your data."

"Miles, you really are too generous." She looked rueful. "I'm not sure I can accept all of this from you. After all, we hardly know one another."

Miles stilled. "Would you rather I leave? Have I come on too strong?"

"Too strong?"

"I'm going to be honest with you, Chloe. I know I never knew you existed before today, and it's going to sound strange, but I feel like we were meant to meet. I'd like to know you better and I'm not the kind of man who likes to waste time." He blew out a breath and looked her straight in the eye. "When I see something I want,

I go for it. Life is too damn short to spend it wondering what if. But that said, I'll go if you prefer."

Chloe caught her breath at the earnest expression on his face. From anyone else, that could have come across as stalkerish, but for some reason his words sounded just right. *And*, the little voice in the back of her mind reminded her, *it means he's falling into line with what you have planned without any hard work on your part. You were meant to meet today, after all. He just didn't know why—yet.*

"I…" She blinked rapidly, unsure of what to say. "Please stay. I'm just not used to people like you."

"Like me?"

"So sure of what you want," she clarified. "Most folks I know are too afraid to reach for what they dream of."

"Everyone has their reasons."

"And yours are?"

He'd been in the process of putting their takeout in the oven to keep warm, and he closed her oven door and straightened.

"My reasons are simple. I never want to be beholden to anyone for anything. I got where I am on a vehicle of my own making and I have dreams I'm still reaching for. Anyone can ride along with me if they want to and if they're prepared to work hard. I'm not into forcing compliance. I'm not into unreasonable expectations. I lay all my cards on the table and if people don't like what they see, they're free to go."

Chloe weighed Miles's words carefully. His outlook was basically the antithesis of everything she'd ever known about his father. The senior Wingate had been known for his ruthlessness. It must have been so galling for the senior Wingate to have been stricken by the first debilitating stroke he'd endured five years ago.

For a man so in control of everything in his life to be reduced to relying on others for even his most basic human needs? It would have been torture. And yet when Chloe had heard the news she'd found it difficult to summon even an ounce of sympathy for him. Knowing the man had died in his sleep two years ago had only served to stoke the fire of her anger. Her father had had no such luxury.

And now she had his youngest son in her crappy kitchen, espousing his live and let live policy on life. She'd always thought the apple didn't fall far from the tree when it came to family dynamics and the way people grew up. But it seemed that Miles was different. For starters, he'd made his success here in Chicago, far from the Wingate empire that was centered in Royal, Texas, and which had arms that reached out internationally through aviation, oil and hotels.

Had she made a mistake in targeting the closest, easiest option for her revenge? No, she decided, she couldn't think that way. Whatever Miles was like, it was his family she was after. She wanted them all to feel and know pain, like she'd felt and known it. To suffer like her mother had—and still did, locked as she was in her grief for the past.

Chloe forced a smile to her face. "Well," she said as brightly as she could manage. "That sounds fine to me. I have a small confession to make. I've done a little research on you."

There, it was out in the open. Not a lie, although the implication she made was that the research was recent, whereas in actuality it was of far longer standing. Miles began to grin and Chloe felt a twinge of some-

thing entirely feminine deep inside her body. The man
was far too attractive for his own good. And probably
hers as well.

"Research, huh? And what did you find out?"

"Enough to know that I'm intrigued by you, and I'm
wondering what the heck it is about me that's made you
come back tonight."

He took a step toward her and she felt a flutter in
her chest as he stood close enough for her to inhale the
fresh, crisp fragrance he wore. It was clean and enticing,
like a breeze off the lake on a summer's day. It made her
want to lean in a little, to lift her face, to see whether
he'd respond to the cues and do whatever came next.
When Miles lifted a hand to push an errant strand of
hair off her cheek she felt as if his fingertip had burned
a brand of ownership across her cheek.

"Y'know, I've been asking myself that same question. But it all comes down to me knowing what I want
when I see it. Like I said before—I know its early days,
Chloe, but there's no question that I want you. And I
want to get to know you better while you decide if you
want me, too."

His gaze dropped to her lips and she saw the flare of
hunger in his green eyes. Her body flooded with heat in
response, but then he turned away—leaving her standing there with her lips slightly parted and her brain and
body on overload. He'd been about to kiss her; she knew
it, and yet he hadn't. Had he decided it was too soon,
or had she been sending the wrong message? Or was
he just some kind of tease?

No, she doubted it was the latter and she knew for a
fact she'd just about had foot-high neon signs blinking
over her head shouting at him to do it. To close the scant
distance between them and to take her mouth with his.

And he'd been about to. Every feminine instinct in her told her that was so. Then, for some reason, he hadn't. If anything, it intrigued her even more.

She continued to watch him as he turned his attention to the box containing her new phone and knew she wasn't mistaken that he was as deeply affected by that short interaction as she'd been when she realized there was the slightest tremor in his hands.

"It's the latest version of the phone you had already," he said, looking up at her. "You should be able to transfer the information from your old one easily."

"That's great. Thank you. Like most people, I have my life on that device."

"Do you back up?"

"Yes, religiously."

"Good. And everything is strongly password protected?"

She nodded. "And changed regularly."

"Good. You'd be amazed at the number of people who aren't. They really ought to know better, too."

She shrugged. "I learned my lesson when I was in college. I had my notes for one of my courses on my phone. I dropped it in a toilet."

Miles laughed. "Uh-oh. Well, you'll be relieved to know this version is waterproof, to a certain depth anyway."

She really liked it when he laughed. The corners of his eyes crinkled and he had a twinkle in his eye that showed he really meant it. She moved across to stand by him as he passed her the phone.

"Here you are," he said. "Longer battery life on this model, too."

"It's great. Thank you. I really appreciate it."

"It's the least I could do after what happened. I had

them put additional antivirus and antiphishing software on the phone, too."

They set up her new phone and then had dinner together. Miles was good company and Chloe had to remind herself that she wasn't supposed to be enjoying him quite so much. One thing that did surprise her, as they kept their talk along very general lines, was that he never once mentioned his family. Then again, neither did she. It was as though, by some unspoken agreement, they'd decided not to discuss anything but the most peripheral of subjects. It was kind of refreshing, in a way.

After their meal, he helped her clean up and then she walked him out. For some reason, though, she felt awkward as she held the door open for him. She could see his car, the dark navy paintwork glinting under the streetlight, parked outside her house and the sheer luxury in every line of the vehicle reminded her of the gulf in their lives. Of him being a "have" and she having grown up a "have not." It firmed her resolve to see this through. She was scrambling to try to come up with a logical way to thank him for his help today and for his generosity with the phone and dinner, when he started to speak.

"I have tickets to a show in town tomorrow night." He mentioned the name of an up-and-coming blues musician she'd been hoping to be able to hear perform live. "Would you be interested in coming with me?"

"Tomorrow? Wow, that would be great! Thank you. I'd love to go."

He grinned. "Awesome. I'll pick you up about seven. We can have a bite to eat before the show."

"Oh, it seems silly for you to come all the way out here to get me. I can meet you at the club if you'd rather."

"It's no bother. Besides, my mom would whip my

butt if I expected my date to meet me at a function. She brought me up far better than that."

It was the first time he'd mentioned family. Interesting, she thought, that it had been his mom and not his dad who'd come up so casually in conversation.

"Well, then, I'd best let you make your mom proud."

He smiled. "Thank you. And thank you for tonight."

"Me? You brought dinner."

"Yeah, but you didn't have to share it with me."

"Oh? I didn't know that was an option. My mom always lived by the mantra that if you had more than you needed it was your obligation to share."

He winked at her. "She sounds like a wise woman."

"She can be."

She could also be bitter and trapped by circumstances. Circumstances created by the father of the man standing right there in front of her.

"Hey, we're all human, right?" Miles said. "I really enjoyed tonight."

"Me too," she murmured with genuine pleasure.

"I'm also glad you're happy to see me again."

And then he leaned in. Chloe's body, already wildly attuned to Miles, responded automatically,—closing the distance between them until his lips were on hers. In that instant, she lost all sense of where she was. All she could think about was the warm, firm pressure of his mouth on hers and how she'd been longing for it ever since that moment in the kitchen. Miles reached up with one hand and slid it under her hair to gently cup the back of her head. His fingertips against her scalp sent tiny zaps of electricity through her and she wondered what they would feel like on other, more sensitive, parts of her body.

She parted her lips slightly in invitation and Miles

deepened the kiss. Her mind went into overload. The taste of him, the scent of his cologne, the gentle caress of his fingers, all of it combined to make her want to sink into him and lose herself completely.

And then, just like that, the kiss was over and he was pulling back. Releasing her. Giving her space.

"Wow," she said on a rush of air. "Do you kiss all the girls you knock over like that?"

"Only the ones I really, really like," he replied. This time his face was serious. Not even an ounce of humor colored his eyes, which had deepened to the bottomless green of a lake at twilight. "See you tomorrow."

He turned and walked down her front path and she saw the interior light come on in his car as he unlocked it. He raised a hand briefly in farewell before getting in and driving away. Chloe closed and locked her front door and leaned against it, her fingertips on her lips, reliving the kiss they'd just shared.

She was playing with fire. She only hoped she wouldn't get burned.

Four

As he drove along the interstate toward the city, Miles couldn't help but savor the anticipation of seeing Chloe again. That kiss last night had knocked him sideways. He hadn't meant to kiss her just yet. In fact, he'd planned to make their first embrace something special, to be remembered for location and timing as well as for content. But need had overcome rationality and he wasn't a bit sorry about it.

He wanted to repeat the experience and this time he was going to ensure that it would be a moment to savor and that they wouldn't be framed in a well-lit doorway open to the street and any passersby. Miles pulled up outside Chloe's place and was halfway down the path when she came out the front door to greet him. He stopped in his tracks and let his eyes roam the loveliness that greeted him.

She'd gathered her fine blond hair up into a knot at the nape of her slender neck and delicate gold chain earrings hung from her earlobes. The dress she wore was black and beaded with fine black crystals and had a deep V-neck that exposed a great deal of lightly tanned skin. His eyes were drawn to the gentle swell of her breasts and the slight flush of color at her chest. Nerves, perhaps? Whatever it was, she was a vision and he felt a pulse of feral need beat in his veins at the sight of her.

"You look stunning," he said as he continued up the walk to meet her.

She ducked her head slightly before angling her neck and looking up at him.

"Thank you. Not too much? You didn't say where we were going and I've always been taught it's better to overdress than turn up looking like a slob."

He laughed. "You are nothing like a slob. This is perfect."

He looked at her again, noting the way the cocktail dress skimmed her hips and ended a few inches above her knees. Not so short as to cheapen the outfit, and not so long as to dampen desire. The dress looked as though it had been made for her. She wore heels that made her at least three inches taller, but he still topped her by inches. They'd make a very distinctive couple tonight, he thought as he offered her his arm.

"All locked up?"

She nodded and took his arm with her good hand.

"How's your wrist today?"

She held up the bandaged appendage. "Much better today, thanks."

"And the phone? It meets your needs?"

"Perfectly, thank you."

They were at the car and he reached for the door, holding it open for her as she lowered herself to the passenger seat and drew her legs in. He tried not to stare but the sight of those long, slender, bare legs sent another jolt of pure male appreciation spearing through his body. He wished he knew her well enough that he could suggest skipping the show tonight and cutting straight to dessert at his place instead. But he appreciated there was a process to follow when it came to courting.

Was he courting her? he wondered as he closed her door and walked around to the driver's side of the car. It was such an old-fashioned term. Certainly not one he'd ever considered in any of his previous relationships. But then again, he'd never felt about anyone the way he already felt about Chloe. The need to understand her and to share her thoughts and dreams had sneaked into his mind several times each hour of his working day. He'd always been able to compartmentalize before. Work life, personal life. They were two distinctly separate things. But when it came to this woman, everything was different.

By the time they reached the club, they'd covered every inane subject under the sun from Chicago's public transport system to the current state of public school education in Illinois. She was a passionate advocate for her kids, he noticed, and he envied her students in some ways. To be the recipient of her love of teaching combined with a keen interest in the world around her that he knew would light fires of curiosity in many of her students, would be a precious gift indeed.

Miles got out of the car at the valet parking station and went round to the other side. Chloe's door had already been opened for her and she was waiting on the sidewalk.

"I've heard about this place. Do you come here often?" she asked.

Miles nodded. "I love it. The atmosphere inside is

second to none, and they always have great artists. We're ahead of most of the crowd. I considered taking you somewhere else for dinner but they do great meals here, too."

"Good," she answered as she took his arm and they carried on inside the building. "'Cause I'm starved."

"You look like you hardly eat at all," he teased. "Or did you just save all your appetite for me?"

She stumbled slightly and he steadied her. She looked him square in the eye. "Oh, I've saved my appetite. I've learned never to let opportunity pass me by."

Miles couldn't help but wonder at the double entendre in her words.

"Is that what I am? An *opportunity*?" he probed.

"Well, that remains to be seen, doesn't it?" she replied coyly.

Miles decided to shelve that train of thought for another time as the hostess came forward to greet them. She showed them to a cozy, private table for two, which also had a great view of the stage.

"Can I get you both a drink before I send your waiter across with menus?" the woman asked.

"Sure, I'm in the mood to celebrate," Miles said, turning toward Chloe. "How about you? Champagne to mark our first date?"

A huge smile spread across her face. "Champagne? Really? We might hate each other by the end of the night."

"Somehow, I doubt that. Besides, I've learned that you have to take time to stop and celebrate every facet of life. I think tonight is a good place to start."

He'd surprised her. Again. She thought she'd done her background search on him quite thoroughly, but he continued to deviate from the type of character she thought he really was. She decided it was time to probe a little deeper.

After their champagne had been brought and poured, Miles handed her a glass, then held up his in tribute.

"To you," he said simply.

Chloe felt a blush rise on her cheeks and bent her head in acknowledgment. No one had ever toasted her before. Not when she'd graduated college, not when she'd secured her first permanent teaching position— never. It was quite a rush, she decided, having someone appreciate you so openly. She took a sip of the golden, sparkling liquid in her glass and enjoyed the fizz on her tongue as she swallowed a mouthful. Oh yes. She could get used to this. But then again, wouldn't she have been used to this if it hadn't been for the Wingate family in the first place?

She wondered when the last time was that her mother had enjoyed something as simple as a glass of imported wine. In fact, when was the last time her mother had enjoyed anything? Chloe racked her brain and was shocked to discover that she barely remembered the last time she'd seen her mother smile, let alone laugh or simply bask in the joy of a sunny day. Loretta Fitzgerald's entire life had become a bitter circle of distrust and regret. Which was precisely why Chloe was even here in the first place. She wasn't supposed to be enjoying herself, and yet she couldn't help but relish the attention Miles showed her, or the way he could coax a chuckle from her when she least expected it.

"Why so pensive?" he asked. "We're celebrating, remember?"

"Oh, family stuff. You know what it's like."

Oh no, she thought. Had she just let slip that she knew more about his family than she ought to know?

"Families. Can't live with 'em, can't live without 'em," he said with a tone of inevitability she hadn't heard from him before. "I chose to move away from mine. It was too hard trying to always live up to expectations that were unreasonable and didn't take into account my own dreams for the future. I guess that makes me the black sheep of my lot."

"Your lot? You have brothers and sisters?" she pressed, even though she knew the answer.

"Two of each, for my sins," he said with a rueful smile. "And a couple of cousins who are like brothers to me as well."

"Wow," Chloe remarked, putting her glass down carefully on the table in front of her. She didn't want to drink too much and potentially put her foot into what were undoubtedly treacherous waters. "I can't imagine being part of a large family like that. Were you close as youngsters?"

Miles shrugged. "When my father wasn't trying to pit us all against one another. Dad was a man driven to succeed, at any cost."

Yes, even at the cost of another man's life, Chloe thought bitterly.

"That must have been hard on all of you. Did your mom make up for that?"

"It had its moments," he said sparingly. "And, actually, Mom isn't too different. She's always been driven to succeed and expected the same of all of us. Not the most maternal type."

He cleared his throat, then went on. "Anyway, after college, I moved to Chicago to make my own way. And I have. Dad died a couple of years back. He never told me that he was proud of what I'd achieved. It wasn't until after he'd gone that I realized how important that was to me, to actually hear him say the words. Now I've decided that his opinion doesn't matter. I'm here for me. To live my best life. It's why I go for what I want when I see it and I make no apology for that."

"And why should you. Isn't that how we should all live? Striving for what we want? Honestly, as long we don't do harm to others, isn't that the way to live our best lives?"

Miles cocked his head and looked at her carefully. "I'm more and more convinced that fate put you on that collision course with me yesterday. Does that sound corny?"

Oh, it was *fate* all right. A fate that had begun with his father's ill treatment of hers. She tamped down the bright flare of hurt and anger that burned inside her and painted a smile on her face.

"Maybe it would to anyone else, but it doesn't to me."

Of course it didn't sound corny to her, because she'd orchestrated their meeting so carefully. She'd plotted and planned and it had almost gone awry. But out of nothing had come this growing connection with Miles Wingate. He was not the man she'd thought he was. After reading all the articles that had talked about how hardheaded he was and how successful his security business had become—she'd tarred him with his father's brush. Chloe knew that success always came at a cost. Was she prepared to pay the price for hers?

She was powerfully drawn to Miles. It was there in the way her heart raced when she saw him. It was there in the way her body reacted with the age-old pull of desire that drew her insides into a knot at his touch. And that kiss of his? Well, that had stimulated a long-dormant libido that had sent her subconscious into over-drive during last night's sleep.

If their circumstances had been different, she'd be able to allow herself to enjoy his company more. She wouldn't have to remain on tenterhooks all the time, wondering if she was going to say or do something that might reveal her true intentions. And what were those exactly? She asked herself the question simply to re-mind herself to remain on track.

She wanted the entire Wingate family to feel the shame she'd been forced to grow up with. It had started already in the media, with the family's jewel in the crown, WinJet—their private jet manufacturing com-pany—in the headlines for all the wrong reasons. The scandal would be hurting them, even Miles. They were, historically, a family that couldn't bear to be seen to be less than perfect. But the cracks were beginning to show, and when she uncovered new information about the family to give to the reporter and he took it—and her father's story—public, that would blow those cracks wide-open.

Revealing that the patriarch of the Wingate family had driven a business colleague to suicide, then swept in and bought up what was left of that friend's company in order to consolidate WinJet's early entry into the avi-ation industry, would confirm to all the world that the recent incident at the WinJet plant was merely proof that the rot in the family and their companies was systemic.

"You're not drinking your champagne. Is it not to your taste?" Miles asked, interrupting her reveries.

"It's delicious. I just want to make it last so I can enjoy it longer."

"I can make sure you enjoy it all night long. Just say the word."

Chloe was saved from saying the word that hovered on the edge of her lips by the arrival of a waiter with menus. She took her time poring over the available selections. Her mind was so scattered by Miles's comment, and her own willingness to say a categorical "yes" to whatever he suggested, that she had to get herself back under control. None of this was turning out how she expected it to.

She sighed. Wearing the vintage cocktail dress she'd picked up in a charity store near one of the more affluent suburbs in Chicago had been a calculated risk. He could have turned up in jeans and a T-shirt, geared up for a casual evening, but the moment she'd spied him through her living room window and seen the cut of his suit and the polish to his shoes, she'd known she'd done the right thing. The dress accentuated her good points and she'd seen the way he'd looked at her when she'd come out to greet him.

It did a woman's soul good to feel appreciated. And he'd made her soul sing. Not just when he arrived but when he'd made that toast, too. From any other man it might have come across as orchestrated or false, but from Miles it felt right on an entirely instinctive level. She was wildy attracted to him. From his short, dark blond hair and green-eyed gaze, to the way his large, masculine hands so capably did whatever he set out to do.

She looked at those hands now. Remembered the punch of awareness that had rippled through her at his touch. Sex with him would be incendiary. She knew it as well as she knew the sun rose each morning. That pulse of lust deep in her lower belly pulled stronger. She dragged her gaze from his hands. What the heck was she doing thinking about sex with a man who was virtually a stranger to her? A man who was part of a family she'd loathed and envied for nineteen years of her life.

Things aren't always as they seem.

One of her father's favorite sayings slid through from the back of her mind, prompting her to wonder why on earth she had thought of that right now. Was it that Miles was not as he seemed? Or maybe it was that he was exactly as he seemed and her perception of his family was the part that was tainted.

Chloe had heard that revenge could be a double-edged sword but she never expected the execution of that revenge would cause her so much confusion. The waiter returned for their orders and she dragged her thoughts back to the menu in her hands.

"Look, I'm hopeless when I'm given too many choices. What do you recommend?" she asked of the young man standing patiently beside her.

"The lobster is always good, ma'am," he said deferentially.

"Fine, I'll have the lobster."

"Make that two," Miles said. "If we're going to get messy, it may as well be together."

There he was again, with a comment that was perfectly innocent, and yet not at the same time. Chloe involuntarily pressed her thighs together, the movement increasing rather than relieving the demand building in her core.

And so the evening went. A little conversation, the sharing of the occasional anecdote from childhood, the mutual enjoyment of their meals and the champagne that accompanied it. By the time the band began to set up for the show, Chloe was feeling relaxed and happy. Two states she didn't usually indulge in.

She glanced across the small table at Miles, who

was slightly sprawled on his chair and looking toward the stage.

"Thank you," she said with a depth of feeling that made him sit up straight and look at her with a question in his eyes and one brow raised. "Tonight is perfect."

Miles reached across the table and took her hand, his thumb brushing back and forth over her knuckles.

"Good. You deserve perfect."

Just like that, he stole her breath away and, she suspected, a piece of her heart as well. The band began to play and the featured artist began to sing a smooth, slow bluesy number that spread from her ears to her muscles, making her feel lissome and sensual and craving a fulfilment that she knew would only come with total capitulation to her desires. Miles continued to hold her hand throughout the performance. The slow touch of his thumb across her knuckles just made her want more of him touching more of her. By the time he tugged her to her feet and led her onto the tiny dance floor and drew her close, she was primed for anything.

Dancing with him was an exercise in restraint— and temptation all rolled into one. When he bent his head and whispered in her ear, she felt his warm breath on her skin and suddenly the music she'd been aching to hear all day was replaced with a deeper ache that she knew only this man could assuage.

"I like the feel of you in my arms," he said huskily.

She nuzzled the side of his neck and, suddenly emboldened, nipped the skin just beneath his ear.

"I like everything about you," she replied.

She felt the shock of his reaction shudder through him and he stopped moving. Another couple on the dance floor bumped into them, but he was oblivious to anything but her. She discovered that she really liked being the center of his universe. Even if it was only for this moment.

"Let's get out of here," Miles ground out.

"Yes."

Her response was short and sweet and thrilling all at the same time. Miles took her by the hand back to their table where she retrieved her evening bag and he went to settle their check. She met him by the front door. There was a fire burning in his eyes. Eyes which locked on her as she approached him. He smiled at her and she felt her entire body react at the promise reflected there in his face.

She knew they'd only met yesterday. She knew that she had an ulterior motive. But right now all she could think about was how much she wanted him. *All* of him.

The valet had brought his car to the door and they drove in a tense kind of silence for what seemed to be a very short distance to his town house. She barely noticed the pretty facade to the three-story building and didn't, in fact, realize it was one house until they stepped through the ornate front door and into the spacious foyer and she saw the flights of stairs curving to the floors above.

"This is all yours?" she asked, looking around her at the quality furnishings and the high ceilings.

"Is that a problem?"

"No, not at all. It just seems like a lot of house for one person. That is, if you're living here alone."

Oh heck, she was messing everything up. The atmosphere that had enveloped them back at the club had cocooned them in a cloud of sensual promise. And now she was discussing his real estate?

"Yeah, it is. One day I hope to share it with a special someone and maybe fill it with kids, too."

A deep sense of longing threaded through his words, and she felt an answering tug from deep in her chest. Those were the things she wanted most, too. That special someone. A family of her own. Growing up as an only child hadn't been so bad, until her father had died. After that she'd been so afraid and felt so insecure. Having a sibling to share her feelings with would have meant the world to her. Instead, she'd had to be her mother's support person, which, at eight years old, had forced her to grow up way too fast.

Miles reached a hand for her and she slipped her palm in his. Instant warmth flooded her. She liked the way his fingers curled around hers, infusing her with his strength and purpose. He turned to the stairwell and she followed him as he ascended to the next floor. Then he led her down a thickly carpeted corridor to a room at the end where he pushed open the double doors and led her inside.

A large master suite spread before her. Heavy drapes hung in the tall windows overlooking the back of the property and a massive bed dominated the center of the room. She looked from the bed to Miles. There was an unspoken question in his eyes. In response, she turned in his arms and lifted her face to his.

He groaned in what she hoped was relief and then his lips were on hers and he kissed her, hard and deep and with a longing that mirrored her own. Sensation poured through her body as he wrapped his arms around her and held her close. The hard muscles of his chest pressed against the softness of her breasts, and she felt her nipples stiffen at the pressure. Deep in her lower belly, need throbbed with an insistent demand, and she pressed her pelvis against him, rocking gently and moaning into his mouth. She felt his hands searching for the zipper of her dress and forced herself to tear her mouth from his.

"It's on my left-hand side," she murmured before kissing him again.

His fingers found the zipper, and she felt the fabric loosen around her body before he lifted both hands to her shoulders and gently eased the fabric down her arms, taking care not to tug on her injured wrist. He eased the gown over her hips and let it drop in a pool at her feet. She hadn't worn a bra tonight and he gave a sharp intake of breath when he realized she was standing there dressed in nothing but a lace thong and a pair of high-heeled shoes that showcased her long lean legs to perfection.

"You're a dream come true," he said with a slow smile.

"And you're wearing entirely too many clothes," she replied, and reached up to help him off with his jacket.

Her fingers were a little clumsy as she reached for the buttons of his shirt and slowly slid each one from its buttonhole and yanked the tails from the waistband of his trousers. She pressed her palms against his bare chest and splayed her fingers over his muscles. Her wrist twinged at the movement, but she ignored it because for some weird reason, it felt as if by skin-to-skin contact he was sharing his energy with her and she ached to feel more of him.

Chloe placed a wet kiss at the base of his throat and then trailed a line of kisses to one of his nipples while her fingers traced a circle around the other. Miles didn't remain a disinterested party. His hands were at her waist, then sliding up over her rib cage to cup her breasts. She wasn't heavily endowed in that area but he didn't appear to be complaining. And nor was she as ripples of delight spread through her as he gently cupped and squeezed her breasts and rolled her tightly budded nipples between his fingers.

He was still overdressed, she decided, and she reached for his belt buckle. Her hands shook a little as she undid it and then loosened the fastening at the top of his zipper before pulling his zipper down and pushing his pants down past his thighs. Formfitting boxer briefs wrapped around his hips, and there was no doubting he was as turned on as she was. She grasped his length through the stretch cotton, relishing the hardness and the heat of him.

Miles kissed her again before saying, "Let's move this to the bed, hmmm?"

Chloe stepped out of the glittering black circle of fabric pooled at her feet and walked across to the expansive bed, while Miles quickly divested himself of his shoes and socks and kicked his trousers to one side. He shrugged his shirt off, letting it fall on top of the rest of his clothing, and followed behind her. Then he reached past her to yank back the bedcovers and coax her onto the high thread count sheets that felt silken soft beneath her buttocks.

Miles knelt between her legs and removed her shoes, pressing a kiss into the arch of each of her feet as he did so. The sensation of his mouth against her incredibly sensitive skin sent spirals of pleasure up her legs and to the apex of her thighs. She was already wet for him, wet and ready and aching for his possession but he seemed to want to take his time. He trailed small kisses on the inside of her ankles, up along her calves, then the backs of her knees. She had no idea she had so many erogenous zones on her body, and she dropped back against the sheets, focusing solely on the pleasure he offered.

The feeling of his lightly stubbled jaw and the warm, wet heat of his mouth on her inner thighs made her moan again. And at her core she felt an insistent, pounding demand for more. His lips and hands drew inexorably closer to her center, and when his mouth closed over her and he pushed a warm breath through the lace of her thong she felt her hips lift off the bed in a desperate involuntary thrust.

She felt his fingers at the edges of her thong, and she fought the urge to beg him to move faster.

"You like that?" Miles rasped.

"Oh yes, please don't stop."

"What about this?" he asked as he brushed a finger around the entrance to her body, coating it in her moisture before encircling her clit.

"Yes! That, too."

He kept up the motion, pressing incrementally more firmly and driving her closer and closer to climax.

"I think we can get rid of these now, don't you?" he said and withdrew his hand to ease her thong down her legs and off completely.

She felt totally exposed, lying there with her legs splayed, but there was no embarrassment or discomfort. Instead she was mesmerized by the look on his face as he gazed down on her.

"You are so beautiful, Chloe. I want to give you so much pleasure you can barely think."

She wanted that, too. "Yes," she whispered, incapable of saying more.

He traced the inner edges of her hips and his fingers trailed down, down, down to her aching center. And then he bent his head and pressed his mouth to her clitoris, his tongue sweeping against the sensitive bud in a firm rhythmic motion, driving her absolutely wild.

He slid a finger inside her body, murmuring in appreciation as she clenched around him. The stroking of his tongue combined with his deep, probing touch pushed her even higher until, in a rushing crescendo of pleasure, she tumbled off the peak of anticipation and into a breathless maelstrom of marvel as pulse after pulse of pleasure racked her.

Her entire body continued to tremble as her climax slowly faded, leaving her limp and sated at the same time. Miles rose to his feet, lifted her from the edge of the bed and lay her fully onto the middle of the mattress before he slipped off his briefs and joined her. The heat of his strong body alongside hers was searing, and Chloe could feel his erection against her hip. She reached for him, stroking the silken skin of his shaft all the way to the tip and then back down again.

"If you keep that up, things are going to get intense around here," he rumbled in her ear.

"Intense? I think I like intense. Don't you?"

"Oh yeah."

Chloe forced herself to move and straddled him in a lithe movement. Her entire body still felt sensitized by the heady satisfaction he'd given her. Now it was his turn.

"Condom?" she asked.

"Top drawer of the nightstand."

She reached over, letting her breasts brush against his naked torso as she did so, and retrieved a strip of condoms from the drawer. She held the strip up in front of her as she settled back down over his thighs.

"Hmm, impressive," she teased. "Good to see you're prepared."

His eyes glittering, he looked up at her and chuckled.

"You don't find that intimidating?"

She smiled in return. "Not at all. I'm a girl who enjoys a challenge. Let's see how many of these you have left by morning."

Chloe quickly tore a packet open and sheathed him before lifting her body higher and positioning herself over his erection. She slowly lowered herself, taking him deeper and deeper. The sensation of his shaft against her still-tingling and sensitive core made her insides clench and she relished the sound of his groan as she tightened around him. Miles slid his hands along her thighs and up to her hips. She tilted her pelvis so his length slid a little deeper and rocked there.

"Oh, you're a torment," he said on a harshly blown out breath.

"You haven't seen anything yet," she crooned, then proceeded to show him exactly what she meant.

By the time he was shuddering into his own climax, Chloe was a beat away from another spine-tingling orgasm, and as she gave herself over to the sheer joy of it and collapsed against his body in paroxysms of delight, she knew that as far as Miles Wingate was concerned, revenge was the last thing on her mind.

Five

Physically, he was exhausted, and yet he'd never felt more energized in his life. Miles turned his head on the pillow and looked at the woman responsible for his current state. Blond hair tangled against the pillowcase and a sweep of lashes lay on her flushed cheeks as she slept deeply. *And so she ought to*, he thought. They'd spent the better part of the night discovering exactly what brought one another pleasure and, since there was only one condom left, he'd have to make another trip to the drugstore, he noted with a wicked grin.

"What are you smiling about?" she asked with one blue eye open.

"Your willingness to take on a challenge," he answered, rolling onto his side so he could better appreciate the view of her naked body.

The top sheet and comforter had hit the floor somewhere around 4:00 a.m. and the warm glow of the morning sunshine gilded her skin like a lover's caress. Like *his* caress, he realized. They'd become lovers in every sense of the word last night. And here she was, still in his bed. No sneaky dawn exit. No regrets. Nothing but a sense of well-being he'd never known before.

He'd thought she was special from the moment they'd met, and he hadn't wanted to leave her to her own devices. But during the night he'd begun to grasp just how special she truly was. He'd heard of people embarking on whirlwind romances before, but he'd never thought it would happen to him. He was far too focused, too pragmatic to fall for flights of fancy. So if this wasn't a romantic whim, what was it?

"Well, I think even I have hit my limit when it comes to challenges," she said on a yawn.

"It's always good to know your limits," he drawled, tracing a finger over the delicate curve of her shoulder and down her arm. "How's your wrist today?"

"A bit achy to be honest."

"Then let me take care of you."

And he did, slowly, deliberately and carefully as if he was making love to a figurine made of spun glass. There was something to be said for fast and frenzied, but then again taking it slow made everything all the more poignant and special. Every breath shared, every touch, every ripple of sensation through their bodies was experienced a thousandfold times deeper—as if they were making love on an emotional level as well as the physical. As if they were irrevocably bonding together in a way he'd never known with another.

When their climaxes came, they were in total sync. And instead of the intense rocket of satisfaction that was normal for him, he felt his pleasure spread through his entire body, growing stronger and deeper with each beat of his heart before ending on a starburst of sensation that almost brought tears to his eyes. He spied a telltale trail of moisture leaking from the corners of Chloe's eyes and knew it had been equally special for her. Gathering her into his arms, he rolled them both onto their sides as they waited for their heart rates to return to normal.

"Spend the day with me," he said.

Oh sure, he knew he should have phrased it as a question—that would have been the polite thing to do—but it would have given her a choice.

And he couldn't bear the thought of her saying no.

"I don't have any clothes, or are you suggesting I won't need any?"

He laughed. He really loved the way Chloe responded to him. Then he realized, in her own way, she'd acquiesced to his demand and a burst of sheer joy ballooned in his chest.

"We can go back to your place. Maybe you could pack a bag. Stay the whole weekend with me?"

This time he made it sound like a question and it wasn't until she nodded and said yes that he realized just how much he'd hoped for her affirmative answer.

"Why don't you go shower. There's a robe behind the bathroom door you can borrow. I'll make us some breakfast and then we can head out to your place."

"Sounds good. You don't want to join me in the shower?"

"I have the feeling that if I do we might both not be capable of walking afterward," he said with a grin. "Besides, we're out of condoms."

She laughed and got out of the bed. "There are other options," she murmured slyly.

Despite having just made love to her, Miles felt his libido begin to stir to life again.

"Tempting, but I'm starving. Food first, then clothes, then other options," he said.

"Sounds good to me."

He watched her as she crossed the bedroom and went into the en suite bathroom. Every cell in his body urged him to follow her, but he overrode the impulse and got up, pulling on a pair of sweatpants and a T-shirt and heading downstairs to the kitchen. He'd just poured two glasses of juice and put beaten eggs in the pan to scramble when Chloe entered the kitchen dressed in his robe.

Seeing her in his clothing gave him a sucker punch to the chest and a sense of pride he never imagined he was capable of feeling.

"You were quick in the shower," he commented as he forced his attention back to the eggs.

"My mom was very much into saving while I was growing up. I learned to be frugal in everything, including my showers."

Miles let her words sink in. He'd had no such boundaries placed on his life as a child. There was always an abundance of everything. If you were hungry, you went to the kitchen, and Martha, their cook, would always find you something. If you were thirsty, you helped yourself to a drink. If you wanted a shower, there was no one beating on your door to hurry up because in their home there were more bathrooms than bedrooms. He had no response for Chloe because he could not fathom what her life must have been like.

She sat on one of the stools at the kitchen's central island.

"Scrambled eggs! Yum. My favorite kind of breakfast."

At the end of the counter, the toaster popped.

"I hope you like toast with your eggs?"

"Sure, would you like me to butter it?"

"Yep, butter is in the fridge. Plates are warming in the oven"

She went and retrieved the toast, buttered it and put the slices on the two plates in the oven.

"I wasn't sure if you preferred tea or coffee at breakfast, but I have poured you juice."

"I'm a tea in the morning kind of girl. I can make it."

He told her where to the find the tea and cups and watched her as she moved confidently around the kitchen. He liked having her here, working alongside him. And it made him look forward to the rest of the day and the weekend following that they had before them. He plated up the eggs and put the plates at the place settings he'd made on the kitchen island, then poured himself a coffee before joining Chloe.

"This looks great, thanks," she said, tucking straight into the creamy scrambled eggs. "Mmm, and it tastes great, too. What kind of herb did you use?"

"Dill," he replied. "I wasn't sure if you'd like it but eggs are so plain without embellishment."

"I haven't tried it before but I really like it. What made you become so adept in the kitchen?"

He took a mouthful of his own eggs and chewed and swallowed before answering. "I used to watch our cook, Martha, a lot. She would always give a running commentary while she was cooking, whether anyone was listening or not. I am lucky enough that I have a very good auditory memory and I picked up most of my cooking skills from her. The rest I've learned along the way. Living on your own, it's a challenge to keep things interesting when it comes to food, don't you think?"

"Yes and no. I've been lucky enough to have a roommate most of the time. You haven't had anyone living with you here?"

He heard the probing note in her voice. The question about whether he'd lived with another woman hanging on the air—there, yet not quite verbalized.

"I've had this place for five years and, no, I've never had a roommate or any other kind of mate stay here before."

"You mean stay, or move in? Oh heck, I'm sorry. I shouldn't be so darn nosy. It always gets me into trouble. You don't have to answer that."

Her cheeks had flushed a charming shade of pink and she refused to meet his gaze, finding refuge in lifting her cup of tea and taking a great big swig of the liquid instead.

"I'll answer it because I think it deserves to be said. No, I've never had anyone stay over before, or move in."

Silence stretched between them. Eventually Chloe replaced her cup in its saucer and faced him.

"So I'm your first?"

"So to speak, yes."

She let out a long breath. "Wow. Thank you, I think."

"No need to thank me. I always knew the right person would come along at the right time. I just never expected that to be on the path at Lincoln Park, is all."

She laughed but he could sense a restraint in her that wasn't there before. Miles reached out and took her hand in his.

"No pressure, Chloe. We can take this at your pace. You can even tell me you never want to see me again. I'll accept it. Not happily, but I will survive. But I think that what we have is something special. Something worth exploring. I feel like I have a connection to you." He shook his head. "Listen to me, I sound like something out of a romantic movie. I don't want this to come across as clichéd, but I mean what I said. And I hope you still want to spend the next few days with me."

This was the time to do it. The time she needed to come clean and tell Miles exactly why they'd bumped into one another. The thing was, she didn't want to destroy this incredibly special and potentially fragile thing they had going. It was clear he had nothing to do with the Wingate fortune and, from what she'd seen so far, little to do with his family, either. They didn't come up in general conversation in the way of people who actually spent time in their siblings' company. So, even if she did tell him, would that damage what they had going?

She stared into Miles's intense green eyes and asked herself if she could risk shattering their fledgling relationship, and the answer was a resounding no. He was different than any other man she'd ever dated. And he wanted her. *Really* wanted her. That was a feeling she'd never experienced before. Most of the other men she'd gone out with had always kept themselves aloof, except if they'd wanted sex.

Maybe part of that had been her fault. Choosing men who were commitment-shy because deep down Chloe was afraid to trust completely, or to give herself to another without restraint. Losing her dad and seeing how his death had affected her mom had left deep emotional scars. Loving someone so completely was scary. There had always been something lacking in her previous relationships—whether it was her partners' fault, or her own. But now, even after this impossibly short time, she knew exactly what that something was. Intimacy and commitment. And Miles appeared to be prepared to give both those things to her.

"Don't think you can scare me away so easily," Chloe said, deliberately keeping her tone light even though what they were discussing was 100 percent serious. "I absolutely want to spend today and the weekend with you. And I hope our friendship won't stop there, Miles. Besides, who else is going to cook me eggs like these?"

She saw him visibly relax and realized, with some relief, that she'd struck just the right note.

"Well, aside from Martha, who retired several years ago and who lives in Texas, there isn't anyone who can cook eggs just like these, so it looks like we're stuck with each other. In the best possible way, of course."

She couldn't help the grin that spread across her face. She really liked how he spoke seriously one minute, then resorted to humor the next. This was going to be a very provocative weekend. But, it occurred to her, today was only Friday.

"Don't you have work today?"

He shrugged. "One of the perks of being the head honcho. I can delegate, and I did. I rang my office while you were in the shower. They'll manage just fine without me for a day. I want to give you my full attention, get to know you better. You know, the usual stuff people do when they like each other."

Like? She had no doubt she was in danger of more than liking him. And she suspected he felt the same way. The novelty of that was incredibly refreshing.

"That sounds like fun. I'd like that. Have you thought about what we might do today, aside from pick up a change of clothing for me, that is?"

She plucked at the lapels of his robe. When she'd put it on she'd caught the faint whiff of his cologne and it had done crazy things to her insides. She had felt like a giddy schoolgirl wearing her boyfriend's sweater for the very first time. It was ridiculous, really, and yet it had left her feeling as if her blood fizzed in her veins. She was looking forward to spending time with him far more than she'd anticipated.

"I thought we could go for a stroll around the aquarium then maybe head to Navy Pier? You up for that?"

"Fish followed by carnival rides? You bet!"

"So, did you want to think about that a little?" he teased with a laugh.

"Absolutely not. I hardly ever got to do things like that as a kid, so you can be sure I'll make the most of the day. How about I clean up here in the kitchen while you shower and get dressed. Then we can get started."

"Yes, ma'am," Miles answered. He leaned over and kissed her briefly on the mouth. "I really like your enthusiasm, but you're really bad for my work ethic. That's twice now this week I've played hooky to be with you."

She felt a dip in her tummy. "Is that okay? I mean, you said you're the boss and all, but can you afford to be away from work this much?"

He kissed her again. "Don't worry. I have an excellent team working for me. Sometimes I feel quite redundant around the place."

"Okay, then. If you're sure."

"I'm sure," he confirmed.

"Fine. Now hurry up and get ready so we can go and have some fun."

Miles rushed through his shower and got dressed. When he came out of the bathroom, he noticed that Chloe had already made the bed and picked up her clothing from last night. The girl moved fast, he thought, with approval. In fact, he liked the way she moved, period.

She was downstairs waiting for him in the foyer, dressed in her cocktail dress and heels again. He felt that now-familiar tug of attraction when he saw her. Man, it didn't matter if she was dressed to the nines or simply wearing his robe and fresh from a shower. The magnetic pull between them did not abate in any way.

"I feel strangely underdressed," he said, gesturing to his T-shirt and chinos.

"You look perfect," she replied, then blushed.

He cocked his head and looked at her. "Perfect, huh? You're good for my ego."

She laughed out loud. "Somehow I don't think your ego needs a lot of boosting."

He pulled a face. "Are you saying I'm conceited?"

"No, in fact, with someone with your level of privilege, you're refreshingly unpretentious."

He studied her again. "My level of privilege?"

She waved her hand to encompass the lavish entrance of his home. "Need I say more?"

"Okay, you made your point. Let's go get you into something more suited to a day out with an unpretentious man of privilege."

"Are you going to tease me about that all day?"

"No, I'm sure I'll find something else to tease you about," he said lightheartedly.

But her comment had stung just a little. He'd grown up in a family with immense wealth and privilege and a father whose sense of entitlement had made him a difficult man at the best of times. Miles had done everything he could, his entire adult life, not to become the man his father was. But did a man have to live in a hovel and dress like a pauper to make his point? Miles had never thought so. Yes, he was wealthy, but he'd earned that wealth based on sound business decisions and his own intelligence. And he'd held on to it and continued to build it in the same way.

As he and Chloe drove out to Midlothian, he wondered what had prompted her remark. Obviously she'd been burned somewhere along the line. But how badly, and would it make an impact on their chances of building a future relationship?

And was he putting the cart before the horse by overthinking this entire thing? They'd only just met two days ago, after all, and they'd been more intimate in that time than he'd been in any of his past three relationships. He'd brought her home, and he never did that. He'd always wanted an out, in the past. But with Chloe, he just quite simply wanted *her*.

He reached across and grabbed her good hand and gave it a squeeze. Out of the corner of his eye he saw her look up at him and smile. He smiled back, realizing he'd probably laughed and smiled more in the past forty-eight hours than he had in the past forty-eight days.

Yeah, he wanted her, and sure, they might not be financial equals, but he had no doubt that when it came to the things that were important to him, like honesty for example, he and Chloe were very much on the same page.

Six

He really needed to take time off more often, Miles realized as they left the aquarium and headed to the pier. Chloe had exhibited a genuine delight in all they'd seen so far, and he found her enthusiasm infectious. He couldn't remember the last time he'd really relaxed and simply been in the moment like this. And sneaking kisses when she wasn't expecting them was fun, too.

However, walking around in a state of semiarousal all the time was something to get used to. Especially if he was planning to spend more time with Chloe. When they'd arrived at her house, she'd suggested he come in with her while she packed her bag for the weekend so he could advise her on wardrobe selections. Of course, being in her bedroom with her like that—well, one thing had led to another, and while he hadn't yet replenished his supply of condoms, it turned out that Chloe had a healthy supply of her own. Less one, now, he thought with a deep sense of satisfaction.

When they reached the pier, she dragged him onto the Ferris wheel. They were stalled at the top while people loaded in a car at the bottom, when he felt his phone vibrate in his pocket. He'd already told work, no calls unless it was a life-or-death situation—and in their line of work with clients all over the world in difficult circumstances, that could actually happen.

He slid his phone from his pocket and checked the screen. Sebastian? The elder of his twin brothers rarely called, but in light of the news reports about WinJet failing their safety inspection, hard on the heels of the news they were being sued by employees hurt in the recent fire at the plant, Miles knew this had to be important.

"I'm sorry, I'm going to have to take this," Miles said to Chloe.

"No problem," she replied breezily. "I'll just remain enraptured by the view."

She gave him a look that went from head to toe and back again, and Miles couldn't help the pull of attraction that flared under her gaze. He answered the call.

"Sebastian, what can I do for you?"

"What? No hello, brother, long time no see?"

There was an edge to his brother's voice that confirmed to Miles that this was definitely not a social call.

"I've seen the news. I assume that's why you're calling?"

Miles was careful to keep his choice of words as vague as possible. While there was little chance of being overhead way up here on the Ferris wheel, he wasn't about to take any unnecessary risks, either. Through the phone, he heard his brother sigh heavily.

"I wish I was calling under better circumstances."

His lips firmed into a straight line and he waited for his brother to continue.

"Look, Sutton and I have been talking. Something's not right about the whole situation, and we need someone with very specific expertise to make sure that the rot hasn't spread to our other companies."

"Expertise such as?"

"Someone we trust implicitly who is capable of doing a full forensic sweep of our systems. You're probably aware that we're being charged with criminal negligence in the jet plant fire, which our legal team is working on now. But it gets worse."

"Worse?"

Sebastian sighed again. "Look, I'll cut straight to the chase. During the independent safety inspection, drugs were found on the WinJet premises."

"*What?* Like a personal stash?"

"More like a considerable quantity for supply and distribution. The DEA have been brought in and they've opened an investigation. I can't tell you how serious this is. Based on their findings, they could have a case to present against us for drug trafficking."

Miles felt as if he'd been dealt a physical blow. A string of curse words escaped his mouth, and Chloe looked at him in concern. He reached for her hand and gave it a reassuring squeeze before thinking carefully about his reply to his brother.

"And, of course, you guys knew nothing about it, right?"

"Of course not." Sebastian sounded deeply insulted. "Look, you might not want to be a part of this family in a commercial sense, but I'd like to remind you that dirt sticks. If we're going to be tarred with this brush, it will affect you, too."

"I'm aware of that, and I know that you'd never dream of going down that road so don't get on your high horse with me, okay?" Miles fought the urge to lay a few more truths at his brother's door. Things like better IT security and plant surveillance, just to name a few, but that would be akin to locking the stable door after their entire breeding stock of horses on the ranch had bolted. "What do you want from me?"

"Can you come home? We'll give you access to all systems. Look, with the fire, everything is in disarray but one thing has become very clear since the investigation. Corners have been cut, and Sutton and I think it has to be someone at a higher level who authorized or instigated it. That someone has to have left a trail somewhere. We need you to find it."

Miles tried not to allow emotion to rule over common sense, but hearing his older brother tell him they needed him—well, it was hard to remain dispassionate after a comment like that.

"When?" he asked.

"Ideally? As soon as possible. We can send one of the company jets to collect you today. Can you be ready in about four hours?"

He could, but that would mean leaving Chloe behind on what was supposed to be a weekend getting to know one another. Of course, she'd be there when he returned, but now that she was with him, he didn't want to leave her. But the pull of family was strong, no matter how much he tried to pretend otherwise, and what his family was going through right now was deadly serious with far-reaching ramifications.

"Look, let me confirm with you in about an hour or so. There's something I need to take care of first."

"Something?" his brother asked wryly. "Or some-one?"

And there it was, the usual big brother banter.

"I'll call you back," Miles said, deliberately ignoring Sebastian's question.

"I'll be waiting."

Miles disconnected and shoved his phone back in his pocket. Chloe was watching him carefully.

"Miles? Are you okay? You look like you've had a shock."

Yeah, he had received a shock. Hearing that the DEA were potentially preparing a case against his family for drug trafficking was hellishly serious.

"Family stuff," he gritted out without really saying anything at all. The car they were in on the Ferris wheel was nearing the exit point. "C'mon, let's go somewhere where we can talk."

Holding her hand, they exited the car, and Miles moved them through the crowd until they found a quiet spot on the edge of the pier.

"Chloe, I'm sorry, but our weekend plans are going to have to be put on hold."

"Of course, if your family needs you then they take precedence."

He felt the knot in his stomach begin to ease. He wasn't sure why he'd thought she'd object to the change in their plans. Maybe it was because the women in his experience to date, his mother and eldest sister included, had been the kind who disliked last minute changes in plans. Not that his mom or sister were princesses, far from it. They were sharp, intelligent and insightful women in their own right, but they also liked things their way.

"Thank you for understanding."

* * *

Chloe studied Miles's face carefully. He definitely looked conflicted by the news disclosed in the phone call. With the sounds of the pier and the music playing on the Ferris wheel, she hadn't been able to make out much of the conversation the two men had shared, but she'd seen the change in Miles's body language and his face had grown strained and serious. It still was.

She wondered what on earth had happened in the Wingate family that was so dire. That it had to do with the fire at WinJet was most likely. But even with the safety investigation and the bad publicity, they had more than enough money to make a payout to the injured parties and to ride out the storm until things settled down again. So what else could it be?

Chloe was suddenly reminded of her original plan with Miles Wingate. To get close, to find out secrets if she could, then to expose his family for the dirty, low-down scum they really were. She'd been distracted by the powerful physical attraction between her and Miles. Maybe this was the reminder she needed to get back on track and focus on the revenge she'd been planning for all her adult life. The revenge that she hoped would return her mother to being the woman she'd been back when Chloe's dad was still alive.

Dare she ask Miles what was involved in this sudden change to their plans? Of course she dared.

"What's wrong? Is there anything I can do to help you?"

He gave her a quick grin, but she noticed it didn't reach his eyes. Whatever this was, it had really done a number on him.

"This is something I need to take care of personally."

"Oh, secret squirrel stuff?"

That got a laugh out of him.

"Yeah, something like that. One of the family businesses had an accident. There's been an investigation into the cause, etc., but they need me to go deeper."

"Not something you can delegate, then?"

"Unfortunately, no. I'm really sorry, Chloe. I'm going to have to head to Texas later today."

"So soon?" She couldn't help the exclamation from spilling out. "Do you know how long you'll be away?"

"No. While that's not a problem for me with my business, it is a problem for us."

An idea came to mind. "It doesn't have to be."

"What do you mean?"

"Well, I'm still on summer break. Maybe I could come with you?" She deliberately hesitated a moment. "If you want me to, that is. Of course, I understand if you think I'm being ridiculous. After all we've only just met and—"

Miles kissed her into silence.

"That's the best idea I've heard all day! After all, you're already packed, right? We'd only need to stop by my place and then head out to the airfield. My brother said he'd send a plane. I just need to tell him when we'd be ready."

Chloe didn't know whether to sing for joy that her suggestion had been so willingly picked up, or to regret the rashness of it. Now it was out there, she needed to work with it.

"I'll need to make a few arrangements before we go," she told him. "Get my mail collected and someone in to water my plants. You know, the usual stuff. If you could run me back home, I could set all that up, add a few more things to my suitcase, then I can get a cab to the airport to meet you."

He nodded. "I'll tell Sebastian to send the plane to Midway. But I won't hear of you taking a cab. I'll wait for you to get your things ready. I'll get my assistant to pack for me and meet us at the airport."

She wasn't about to argue, not when he'd accepted her suggestion so willingly.

Miles looked around them. "It seems a shame to have to leave all this."

"What, screaming kids, tired parents and too much cotton candy?"

"Well, when you put it that way?" He smiled and grabbed her hand, lifting it to his lips, where he pressed a kiss against her knuckles.

Chloe felt it all the way to the center of her body. The sounds around them almost faded completely away as her every cell focused solely on this man and his gentle touch. A pang of regret shafted through her as she reminded herself that this was all supposed to be fake. That she was seeking retribution and the peace it would hopefully bring her mother—not for her own gratification and, while she would have loved to have remained connected to him this way forever, she forced herself to pull free of his touch.

"Come on then, let's go. The sooner you call your brother, the sooner we can be on the road—or, as the case may be, in the air."

They made their way back to where Miles had parked his car and then drove to her house. He called his brother using the Bluetooth feature in his car. Once they arrived at Chloe's place, she went to her bedroom to phone her mother, while Miles called his assistant from the living room.

Loretta Fitzgerald answered on the third ring.

"Hi, Momma, how are you?" she asked brightly.

"Oh, you know. The usual. Yesterday would have been your dad's and my wedding anniversary. Those milestones are always tough."

Chloe felt a burning shame fill her. How could she have forgotten such an important date? Since her father's death, her mom had marked every milestone without him. Not with joy or happy memories, however. Most likely her mom had barely moved from her bed or opened her drapes. Her depression was mostly managed well, but anniversaries were particularly hard for her. If there was ever a day when her mom had needed her, it had been yesterday. And where had Chloe been? Wrapped up in Miles Wingate.

But then again, she rationalized, maybe knowing that her daughter was stepping up her goal of revenge against the Wingate family would make her mom feel as if they were finally getting closer to gaining closure on the Wingate family's responsibility behind her father's death.

"Momma, I'm sorry. I genuinely forgot."

"Oh, it's okay, hon. I know you can't buoy me along every day. You have your life to live."

It wasn't even as if her mom was being passive-aggressive. She honestly expected nothing in her life because she'd schooled herself to believe that if she expected nothing, she'd never be disappointed again.

"We both have our lives to live, Momma. And I have news. You know how we've often talked about making the Wingates pay for what they did to Daddy? Well, I met Miles Wingate the other day and, surprisingly, we've quickly become quite close."

"Oh, honey. I hope you know what you're doing. They might smile and look nice on the outside, but deep down they're like a viper's nest."

"I'm being careful," Chloe reassured her with the fingers of one hand firmly crossed. "Really careful, I promise. I won't get hurt. But I need to tell you that I'm going to be away for a few days. I'm going back to Texas, with Miles."

"Are you sure that's wise? Someone might recognize you. In fact, I'm surprised Miles didn't recognize you. We did mingle with the family on occasion back then."

"Not often enough for any memory of me to stick, I'm sure. And I'm all grown-up now. Nothing like the scrawny tomboy who was more interested in riding horses and climbing trees than in petit fours and lemonade on the veranda."

"You still miss your pony, don't you?" her mom said softly.

Chloe felt the all-too-familiar clutch in her chest when she thought about Trigger. He'd been one of the first things she'd truly loved that they'd had to let go after her father's death.

"I've moved on, Momma," Chloe lied. "And we'll both be able to move on once I've exposed their father for his part in Daddy's death."

"Well, if you're sure you're doing the right thing…"

Loretta didn't sound sure at all that her daughter was doing the right thing but, Chloe noted, she didn't tell her not to stay the course, either.

"I definitely am, Momma. We've discussed this. You know Daddy deserved better."

"I do, honey." A more positive note began to creep into Loretta's voice. "And he'd be so proud of you, too. It won't be easy going back. So many memories."

"Well, less for me than for you, I'm sure, Momma. And don't worry, I'll do you both proud. I promise." Chloe could hear Miles moving about in the living room and hastened to end the call. "Look, would you be able to clear my mailbox and water my plants while I'm away? I'll call you when I can, okay? Keep your fingers crossed for me."

"Sure I will. It'll do me good to have a reason to leave the house, and I'll keep everything crossed for you, Chloe. I love you."

"I love you, too, Momma. Talk later."

She ended the call and quickly repacked her case, ensuring that she put in a few items that would do in case they had to attend any formal events, including the dress she'd worn last night to dinner. Under her mother's tutelage, she'd developed an eye for what best suited her figure, and shopping in charity stores nearest the more expensive suburbs of Chicago had given her some lovely pieces for special occasions.

"Chloe, I don't want to rush you, but we really need to get going," Miles called out from the living room.

"It's okay. I'm just about done."

She swept a few more toiletries into the bag and zipped it shut before wheeling it out of her room. She studied Miles's face. Lines of strain had become apparent at the corners of his eyes, and his mouth, which she'd been accustomed to seeing curved into a smile, was a straight line.

"Is everything okay?" she asked.

His features softened as she approached him.

"Sure, at least it will be once I'm back with my family."

His words felt like bullets to her heart. *Family.* At least he had one, which was more than she and her mother could say. She'd been worried that she was making the right decision to follow through on her plan for payback, but this had just sealed the deal. As much as she was deeply attracted to him, she needed to remind herself that it was purely physical and the magnetic pull between them was merely a means to an end.

Miles and the rest of his brothers and sisters took their position in life and their wealth for granted. Wealth that was created, in part, on the backbone of her father's hard work. After her father's business had begun to suffer financial hardship due to a client going bankrupt and not settling their accounts with him, Trent Wingate had offered his support. But the support had never been forthcoming. Instead, the man had simply sat back and waited until he could swoop in and take over her father's business completely at a steal of a price, thereby driving him to his death.

Her daddy had thought Trent Wingate was a good man—someone he could count on—but his judgment had been fatally wrong. Chloe uttered a silent vow that she would not forget just how callous and cruel the Wingates could be. They needed a mirror brought before them to see how their choices and behaviors affected others. She would be that mirror, and maybe, just maybe, her momma would start to smile again.

Seven

Chloe settled into the wide leather seat in the private jet and stretched out her legs.

"Comfortable?" Miles asked as he secured his seat belt.

"You know this is going to spoil me for regular travel anywhere, don't you?" she said archly.

"All part of my nefarious plan," he answered, wiggling his eyebrows like an old-time villain in a black-and-white movie reel.

She laughed. "Well, I have to say that so far I like the sound of your nefarious plan."

He took her hand and squeezed it gently. "Good." Then he sighed, and his expression became more serious. "I'm glad you're with me. I haven't been home since my father's funeral two years ago."

"Do you miss him?"

"He certainly was a force in my life. We didn't always see eye to eye, but he was my father."

Which told her everything and nothing all at the same time and gave her the perfect opportunity to do a little digging.

"Tell me about your family. You are so lucky to have brothers and sisters. And your mother, too, she's still alive?"

"Yeah, my mom's still alive and kicking. She was devoted to my father and nursed him for as long as she was able." A shadow crossed his face. "She took Dad's death hard. They'd been together since my dad was about twenty-two and it was her that helped him focus his energy on starting up Wingate Refineries. After Dad passed away, Uncle Keith, who is a family friend, took her on a tour of Europe, but now she's involved in the family business again.

"Not so sure Uncle Keith is thrilled with that. From what I hear from my siblings, he seems to expect more than friendship from Mom and wants more of her attention. He and Dad were rivals for Mom's affections back in the day. Dad won and he and Uncle Keith remained friends. Since Dad's death he's been a constant support to her but now she's back on her feet, she doesn't need him as much, I guess."

"She sounds formidable."

Miles chuckled. "Not sure she'd like that description, to be honest."

"Well, I'm intimidated already," Chloe said with a smile to soften her words.

She fought back a yawn.

"Hey, the flight is going to be about two and a half hours, once we reach cruising altitude. Why don't you put your seat back and have a bit of a sleep?" Miles suggested.

Chloe felt a blush of heat bloom through her body at the memory of exactly why she was so tired.

"Sounds like a plan. In fact, I may not even reach cruising altitude before I nod off. Must be something to do with the engine noise singing me to sleep."

Miles's lips curved into a smile. "Or something to do with last night."

"A lot to do with last night, I suspect," Chloe admitted aloud. "And if I'm to look anything near respectable when I meet your family, I'll definitely need that nap."

"I'll leave you to it," Miles said, dropping a kiss on her lips as he unclipped his seat belt when the pilot notified them that it was now safe to move around the aircraft. "I'm going forward to have a word with Sam, the pilot."

"Friend of yours?"

"We went to high school together."

"Well, don't distract him from flying the plane, okay?"

Miles laughed. "Duly noted."

When he came back to sit by Chloe, she was fast asleep. He'd noticed the shadows under her eyes this morning, but the sparkle in her eyes had offset that. He couldn't believe how much he enjoyed being with this woman, or how quickly they'd fallen into sync with one another. It had surprised him on so many levels. His business was security. He was a naturally cautious person. And yet, with Chloe, he hadn't felt his usual need to hold back or to run a standard background check like he usually did whenever he considered letting someone into his life.

He settled back in the seat and fastened his seat belt before leaning his chair back and closing his eyes. Being here, next to Chloe, felt right in a world that he knew—for his family, at least—was fast descending into chaos. He'd need his wits about him, going home. But he also knew he needed the quiet strength of the woman beside him to get through it.

When the plane landed in Royal, Texas and taxied to the administration building of the Wingate family's private airport, Miles could see his twin brothers standing on the tarmac, waiting for him. He felt that familiar tug of belonging to something far greater than just himself. The Wingates were a force to be reckoned with, not just in Texas but worldwide, too. But, to Miles, they were his family, and family trumped all things no matter how much he'd tried to distance himself from it.

To be a Wingate meant meeting very high expectations, and he knew his brothers were heartsick about the incident at the plane factory. He only hoped that he could do something effective when it came to studying the necessary data to find out where the security breach had come from.

Miles leaned over and woke Chloe with a kiss on her cheek.

"We're here."

"Oh, already? I feel like I only just closed my eyes. Heavens, I must look a sight. Do I need to freshen up before we get off the plane?"

He let his eyes drift over her face and he shook his head. "No, you look beautiful."

A hint of color tinged her cheeks. "Thank you. You're good for a girl's ego."

"I don't believe in lying and deception. I wouldn't tell you that you were beautiful if I didn't believe it."

Her gaze skittered away from his, as if his words had made her uncomfortable, and she caught her lower lip between her teeth. The action sent a bolt of lust straight to his groin as he remembered biting that same lip only hours ago and remembered, even more vividly, exactly how she'd tasted.

Chloe reached for her tote and gave him an apologetic grin.

"I'm going to need a minute to two, at least."

"If you don't mind, I'll head on out to my brothers." He gestured out the window. "They're obviously eager to see me."

"Oh, of course. And I really will only be a couple of minutes, I promise."

He kissed her again and watched as she got out of her seat and went to the compact bathroom near the rear of the plane. Then, he squared his shoulders and headed out the door.

Sutton, the younger of the twins by only a few minutes, came forward and clasped his hand before dragging him into a tightly held man-hug.

"Miles, good to see you. Thanks for coming. We've missed you." Then he released his younger brother and stepped back.

"Yeah, I missed you guys, too."

"But not enough to come home more frequently," Sebastian said, coming forward and hugging Miles, also.

"What can I say? All work and no play makes me a very dull boy," Miles countered.

He'd had to face his own demons about his lack of contact with the family since their father's death, but he wasn't about to hash all that out right now.

Sutton issued a low whistle. "Miles, it looks as though you've made some time for play if the lovely lady coming off the plane is any indication. You didn't mention you were bringing company."

Miles turned around and watched Chloe as she donned an oversize pair of sunglasses and slowly walked across the tarmac toward them.

"To be honest, you didn't really give me time to tell you anything. We can stay at the Bellamy if it's going to be a problem."

"Hell, no." Sebastian said quickly. "Mom would never forgive us if we drove you away before you even got to say hi. Besides, she'll be intrigued you brought a girl home to meet her. It's a first for you, isn't it?"

"Yeah," Sutton chimed in. "And since Beth and Cam have hooked up, Mom's got ideas about all of us settling down."

Miles laughed and turned away from his brothers so he could slide an arm around Chloe's waist and draw her to his side.

"Chloe, I'd like you to meet my brothers. Don't feel bad if you can't tell them apart. Each one is likely to be masquerading as the other at some stage of our stay anyway."

"Now, now, Miles. Don't go giving your guest the wrong impression," Sebastian said as he stepped forward and offered Chloe his hand. "I'm Sebastian. The good-looking one."

Chloe laughed, obviously charmed by his brother's foolishness. "And you must be Sutton?" she said as she shook hands with the other twin.

"Obviously Miles has been talking about us," Sutton drawled as he delivered a killer smile to Chloe. "Don't believe everything he tells you."

Miles felt a prickle of unease tug at the back of his mind. He didn't recall ever telling Chloe his brothers' names, and that was the kind of detail he didn't normally forget. But then again, nothing about his life had been normal since he'd literally bumped into her on Wednesday morning. Besides, it wasn't as if his family wasn't in the news from time to time. He decided to ignore the niggle of doubt and, once their luggage was removed from the plane, they all walked together to the large SUV waiting outside the airstrip to take them home.

Home.

It was quite a concept to most people but for Miles it left his shoulders tense and his mind full of memories of disappointing his father and hearing in no uncertain terms that unless he toed the family line he'd be written off as a failure. What Trent had never understood was that Miles was possibly more like him than any of his other children—strong-minded and determined to succeed on his own merits. Where they differed was that Miles was not prepared to succeed at any cost—even at the expense of others—and that, unfortunately, had been what had driven the permanent wedge between the two of them.

And, despite the warm welcome he'd received, Miles still sensed the invisible gulf between himself and his brothers. They, too, had been unhappy when he'd struck out on his own after finishing college. Not to say that the twins had agreed with their father 100 percent, either, but their methods had been to effect change from the inside. This being made easier, of course, after their father's first stroke, which had given them more of the necessary control to keep Wingate Enterprises at the top of its game. But now the company's position on the ladder was under grave threat.

Miles and Chloe settled into the back of the SUV, and Sebastian and Sutton took the front. As they headed toward home and passed through Royal, Miles noted the familiar landmarks and wished he'd thought to book a room at the Bellamy just so he and Chloe would have some space away from the rest of his family. Yes, the Wingate mansion was huge and the land sprawled over many acres, but he knew he'd be on tenterhooks until they were on a plane back to Chicago again.

He reached across the leather seats and took Chloe's right hand. Even she seemed tenser than he'd known her so far. Her gaze was fixed on the passing scenery and her entirely kissable lips had firmed into a straight line. He leaned over to whisper in her ear. "If you're not comfortable at the house, we can check in at a hotel. Okay?"

She turned her face to his and gave him a brittle smile. "I'll be fine. Just don't abandon me."

"I'll try not to but I will have to go into work with my brothers," he said, keeping his voice low. "If I have to leave you, I'll make sure you're in good hands, I promise. My sister Beth will welcome your company, I'm sure."

"And you have another sister, too, don't you?"

"Yes, Harley. She's living in Thailand at the moment. Both my sisters are heavily involved in charity work."

Sutton looked over from the front passenger seat. "Sharing family secrets, Miles? Or uttering sweet nothings?"

"I apologize. My brother thinks he's a comedian," Miles said as he straightened. He made a point of not letting Chloe's hand go.

Her smile became even more strained, and she turned her attention back out the window. He'd handled this all wrong, and she was clearly overwhelmed by his family's obvious wealth. He knew it made some people uncomfortable. They should have taken a regular flight out of Chicago and hired a car. That way they would have had total independence. Hell, he probably shouldn't have brought Chloe along at all. Talk about baptism by fire. Well, he'd do the job he came to do and that would be it. They'd be back in Chicago and back to discovering all there was to know about each other in no time.

Chloe felt her entire body cringe as they drove onto the Wingate estate. She'd been here once, as a child, the summer before she turned eight and her world, as she knew it, had disintegrated. Trent and Ava Wingate had hosted a massive picnic and invited all their local staff and business associates. There'd been bouncy castles and pony rides and a magician. It had been like a fantasyland and left her completely overwhelmed by everything, and she had clung to her mother like a limpet.

"Don't worry," she heard Miles say from beside her. "It's not as imposing as it looks and I have it on good authority that my family won't bite."

She dragged her thoughts from the past. "Good to know. And, as to imposing? I'll get back to you on that."

The road to the house began to rise slightly, and there on the highest point of the gently rolling hills, stood a large mansion. Oh, it was imposing all right. A mix of Southwestern and California ranch architectural styles, the cream stone and stucco building dominated the knoll on which it was built. It certainly wasn't your average family home.

Sebastian rolled the SUV to a halt outside the front of the building, and Chloe was quick to alight from the vehicle. She drew in a deep breath and was assailed with the scents of home. Pasture, animals, clean air. It was what she'd taken so much for granted growing up. Her family's home hadn't been terribly far from here, and while they hadn't lived anywhere near the grandiose scale of the Wingates, they'd been affluent enough. Until Trent Wingate had done the dirty on her father, she reminded herself and steeled herself for the welcome that was apparent on the face of the woman coming through the front door.

A few inches taller than Chloe, Beth Wingate had a thin but elegant build. Her dark blond hair hung long and straight and she looked amazing in the designer sundress she'd teamed with a matching pair of flat shoes that took a little of the edge off her sophistication.

"Miles! So good to see you!" She flew toward her younger brother and wrapped her arms around him in a hug. "It's been too long since you've been home."

"So y'all keep telling me," Miles answered, hugging her back with a wide grin on his face.

He seemed far more comfortable with his sister than he'd been with the twins, Chloe realized.

Another woman appeared in the doorway. Thin and looking a bit frail, Chloe recognized Ava Wingate immediately. Grief and time had tinged her hair, once the same color as Beth's and Miles's, with gray but her gray-green eyes were sharp and clear. Chloe felt a moment of anxiety. Would Ava recognize her? She'd changed a lot from the shy seven-year-old who'd been here last time. Maybe she should have stopped and thought about this a bit more before suggesting she accompany Miles. She could bump into anyone who'd once known her parents , and she looked enough like her mom that someone might actually recognize her. A sick feeling took up residence in her stomach.

"Miles, welcome home," his mother said as she moved elegantly toward her youngest son. "It's good to have you back. And you've brought company? What a surprise. Welcome, I'm Ava Wingate."

Ava extended a slender hand to Chloe, who took it automatically. The woman might look frail but that handshake was pure steel. Much, Chloe suspected, like the woman herself. She still remembered running away, frightened, from the magician show and straight into the skirts of Ava Wingate. The woman had placed firm hands on Chloe's shoulders and turned her around to face the magician before bending down to whisper in her ear, "Never show fear. Always face it down." Then she'd given Chloe a gentle push back toward the rest of the children.

The advice had stood her in good stead throughout her life even if it wasn't always comfortable. This was definitely one of those occasions.

"Hi, I'm Chloe. I'm sorry if my presence is an intrusion," she said apologetically.

"Well, I can't deny it would be nicer to have met you under better circumstances. However, you're here now. Please come inside. We can have iced tea and a snack on the patio by the pool while Miles and his siblings discuss what they need to."

Chloe went with her hostess, feeling somewhat like a calf that had been cut from the herd. She cast a glance back over her shoulder to Miles, who was handing their luggage to a staff member who had appeared. He caught her glance and gave her a reassuring wave. Chloe reminded herself that he had said no one at the house would actually bite, but she was going to have to stay on her toes nevertheless.

On the patio, Ava gestured for Chloe to take a seat in a delightfully shaded area. Shortly after, a woman brought out a tray with iced tea and warm, fresh cookies. Chloe's stomach gave an unseemly rumble and she apologized immediately. Miles's mom merely waved a hand in the air, dismissing the apology before Chloe had finished.

"Please, help yourself. These are fresh from the oven and they're always delicious. Dinner won't be for a couple more hours. Plus, if I know my son, he probably forgot that you need to eat at regular intervals to keep your stamina up. He's a lot like his father was. Driven and focused to the expense of those around them at times. Tell me, have you known each other long? And, how did you two meet?"

Ava's gaze locked onto Chloe like a laser, and Chloe sat a little straighter on the outdoor chair and fought the urge to nervously smooth her hair. She took a sip of her tea and was relieved to see her hand didn't shake.

"Oh, that's lovely," she commented, and gathered her thoughts together. She may as well stick as close to the truth as possible. Less chance of getting caught out. "To be entirely honest with you, Miles and I haven't known each other long. In fact, we only met on Wednesday."

She was pleased to see a flare of surprise in the older woman's eyes. "Tell me more," Ava coaxed. "It isn't like Miles to be spontaneous."

Chloe forced a laugh. "Well, the last few days have certainly been that. We met in the park. He, quite literally, swept me off my feet."

She went into a little more detail about her fall, how solicitous he'd been and how he'd looked after her afterward.

"Good to know he hasn't forgotten everything his family taught him," his mom said wryly. "So you've actually only known one another two days?"

Chloe felt a heated blush stain her cheeks. It might

only seem like a couple of days, but they'd been a very intense forty-eight-plus hours. She nodded and took another sip of her tea.

"Well, you certainly must have made an impression."

"She did," Miles murmured as he walked up toward them. He bent to kiss his mother on the cheek. "And we had plans for this weekend."

"Plans that we disrupted. I'm sorry about that, Miles, but we do need your expertise. There's no one else I trust more than you right now," the older woman said solemnly. "After what's happened, we're not sure who is telling the truth anymore."

"I'll do what I can, Mom. I'll go into the office with Sebastian and Sutton tomorrow. We'll need to work fast if the DEA is involved. They may shut everything down before we can—"

Chloe's ears pricked up. The DEA? So it wasn't just a safety issue anymore?

"Let's not discuss the finer points right now," Ava said, cutting Miles off quickly.

Chloe had no doubt it was because she was here.

His mother continued. "I've put you in your old room, Miles. Since you didn't see fit to tell us you were bringing a guest, I wasn't sure where I should accommodate, Chloe."

"She's with me," he said firmly.

Ava looked from her son to Chloe and back again. One finely plucked brow arched in acknowledgment. The older woman rose from her chair. "I'll let the staff know and have an extra setting laid for dinner tonight."

She gave them a regal nod and walked away, her back ramrod straight and disapproval pouring off her in waves.

"I don't think your mother likes me," Chloe said in a small voice.

"Then it's a good thing I do. Chloe, I'm sorry you had to face her so soon after we arrived. I wasn't expecting her to be home, to be honest. She's always at the office until late most days."

"It's okay. I'm not here to please her."

"Does that mean you're here to please me?" Miles's voice dropped an octave, and Chloe felt a shimmer of desire spread through her.

"Well," she replied, "that depends on how close your mom's room is to ours, don't you think?"

Miles laughed out loud. "Don't worry, we're on the second floor. She's on the first."

"Good to know," Chloe said, and grabbed a cookie from the plate on the table. "How about you show me our room. I really will need to freshen up before dinner."

"Sure thing. I could do with a little freshening myself."

Miles offered her his hand and she let him tug her to her feet. He drew her close and bent his head and kissed her deeply. When he pulled away, he said, "I'm glad you're here, Chloe. This would have been tougher without you."

She lifted a hand to his cheek and looked directly in his eyes, for a split second forgetting her real reasons for being here. "I'm glad I can be here for you, too."

He grinned. "Let's go shower."

Eight

Chloe woke alone to tumbled sheets and a sense of satiation she was fast coming to associate with Miles Wingate. Dinner last night had been strained, as if everyone there was on tenterhooks for a variety of reasons to which she was not allowed to be privy. But when she and Miles retired after dinner, all the tension of the evening swiftly dissipated.

She stretched against the sheets before rising from the bed and getting ready to head downstairs. After a quick shower and choosing a cornflower blue sundress she knew flattered her blond hair and blue eyes, she went downstairs.

Beth Wingate was in the breakfast room off the kitchen. She looked up with a friendly smile as Chloe entered the room.

"Good morning. Help yourself to breakfast from the buffet. Mom and the guys have already headed into work."

"Yes, Miles told me last night that they'd be going in early. Do you think he'll be able to help source the problem?"

A small frown pulled between the other woman's brows. "I sure hope so. Say, you'll be at a bit of a loose end today. Would you like to spend the day with me? I can ask Miles to call us when he's heading back to the house."

Chloe pushed down the automatic "no" that sprang to her lips. She wasn't quite sure how to take the friendly overture from Miles's sister, but it was an opportunity to learn more about the Wingate family, which could only help her cause.

"I'd like that, thank you."

"Great! I'm working on a masquerade ball fundraiser for the Texas Cattleman's Club and was planning on heading to the club after breakfast to discuss decorations. I'd appreciate another woman's input."

"I'm not sure how much use I'll be to you," Chloe said on a laugh. "My experience with decorating relates most to second graders in the classroom."

"Well, there's a child in all of us, right?" Beth replied with a warm smile.

"Do you do a lot of fundraising?"

"It's my role in life to part the wealthy from their money for worthy causes. Mom used to manage Wingate Philanthropies, but after my dad had his first stroke, she devoted most of her time to him so it was natural for me to take over. I have to admit I love it. There's a real satisfaction in knowing that what you do makes a difference for those less fortunate. The upcoming ball isn't for a few months yet, but I like to make sure that all my ducks are in a row early on. That way I always have contingencies should anything go awry."

Chloe filled a plate with scrambled eggs and a couple of strips of grilled bacon and sat at the table.

"Contingencies are always a good idea. I'll text Miles and let him know I'm spending the day with you, just in case he comes back here and wonders what I'm up to."

Beth made a face. "Oh, now Mom and the boys have their hooks into him again, I doubt they'll be letting him home early. They really need his expertise. I'm not sure how much Miles has told you, but things are looking pretty dire for WinJet at the moment. Safety is such an important issue."

"And the DEA?" Chloe pressed.

Beth's face froze. "He told you about that?"

"Just a little," she half lied.

"Mom wanted a lid kept on that."

Chloe felt a burst of irritation. "Well, I'm hardly likely to run screaming it from the rooftops," she said stiffly, even as she began to wonder what the reporter who'd written the safety investigation exposé could do with that information.

But did she dare feed that to him? It was exactly the kind of information he was looking for. Chloe's hands bunched into fists on the table. She started as one of Beth's hands settled on hers.

"I'm sorry. I didn't mean to offend. It's just that we're finding it hard to trust anyone right now. What with the safety issues leading to the fire and the hurt caused to our staff and now the DEA being brought in. Someone has betrayed us horribly."

Chloe withdrew her hand from beneath Beth's. "I understand. It's a difficult time for you."

"I'd still enjoy having your company today, if you can forgive me for what I said just now?"

It was clear Beth was trying desperately to make amends. Chloe forced herself to relax and painted a smile on her face.

"Sure, no offense taken."

But she *was* offended. This family took so much for granted and circled the wagons instantly when under threat. But she was on the inside of that circle now. She'd waited all her life for this opportunity, and she was exactly where she needed to be to make a difference to her mom's future. But could she go through with it? Could she deliberately hurt the man who was fast coming to mean a lot more to her than simply a means to an end?

"Well, can you see anything?" Sutton asked as he looked over Miles's shoulder.

Miles pushed back from the computer and huffed out a sigh of irritation.

"I'm not quite sure what you expect of me, Sutton, but trust me, it takes a whole lot more time and focus—*uninterrupted* focus—to look for what I believe you suspect has happened."

"So, nothing?"

Miles closed his eyes and counted to three before opening them again. "I didn't say that. It would seem that someone has tampered with the safety logs at the jet factory."

Sebastian uttered a string of curses while his twin merely paled.

"So it *was* deliberate," Sutton said grimly. "The accident was no accident at all." He swore. "I can't believe someone in our employ would put other people's lives at risk like that. No wonder we're being charged with criminal negligence. This should never have happened."

"What can we do to make sure it doesn't happen again," Sebastian asked.

"Well, we can put some short-term security measures in place, but frankly the entire Wingate IT system needs a major upgrade. Steel Security can do that for you, but it is going to take time and if the DEA—"

"Let's cross that bridge when we get to it. Organize what you can for us for now, and we'll take the next step as it comes." Sebastian rubbed a hand across his face. "Man, this sucks, doesn't it? Tell me, if we'd done the IT upgrade like you'd told us to, could this have happened?"

Miles frowned. "No system is 100 percent hack proof but, to be honest, what you have had running here is child's play."

"So we've been negligent on this as well?" Sutton pressed.

"I wouldn't say negligent. Your staff signs a code of conduct with their contracts, don't they? Whoever did this was in breach of their agreement with WinJet as their employer. If criminal charges need to be laid, it's against whoever did this. And, I suspect, more than one person. The digital footprints are all over the place." Miles rocked back in his chair and looked at his brothers before delivering his final judgment. "To me it looks like a deliberate attack."

"I don't like the sound of that," Sebastian said carefully. "How long do you think this has been going on? After all, we know Dad made some enemies. Is it possible it stems further back, to when he was still alive?"

Miles shook his head. "This looks a lot more recent than that."

Sutton growled. "So this is on us. We've got to find out who is behind this, but before we can do that we have to do right by the men who were injured. Forget the lawyers and trying to beat them down, it's our obligation to settle with the least fuss. We need to take responsibility and then make sure nothing like this can ever happen again."

Sebastian was nodding. "I agree. Mom's in her office. Let's tell her our decision. I know Uncle Keith was advising that we fight the claim and imply it was staff negligence that caused the fire, but the deeper we look into all of this, the less I like it. We tell the lawyers we'll take the hit and admit liability. After all, it happened on our watch."

Miles watched his brothers talk it out and felt a swell of pride grow in his chest. They were nothing like their father. Trent Wingate would have fought paying out until his last breath. He would never have had the grace to admit any level of failure. Maybe Wingate Enterprises stood a chance of being a better, more ethical employer under his twin brothers' guidance than it ever had before.

There was a movement at the door to the office they'd been using, and all three men swiveled round.

"I can't tell you how much it gladdens my heart to see all my boys working together like this," Ava said as she glided gracefully into the office and perched against the edge of Miles's desk.

"Well, don't get too used to it, Mom. I have a business I'm very happy running back in Chicago."

He smiled to take the sting out of his words, but he couldn't help but feel the burr of irritation that she continued, in her not-so-subtle way, to try to lure him back into the family fold. It had been the same way every time he'd come home. As if she and his dad had believed he'd come back eventually and that he just needed to get his misguided burst of independence out of his system. Forget that his company was now worth several hundred million dollars and that he had investors and clientele stretching to every corner of the globe as well as a staff of thousands. Not to mention the fact he'd started his business up, all on his own, without their input or advice or financial backing. One day they'd see him as the success he knew himself to be. At least he hoped so.

Right now, he knew he'd had enough of the cloying atmosphere of the Wingate Enterprises head office. He wanted nothing more than to get back to the house, back to Chloe, and to take her on a long walk or horseback ride far from the house and his family obligations.

"Look, I've done all I can for the time being. I'll get one of my IT security geeks to work on a quick fix for now, and have the team work on something for the entire system in the next couple of weeks."

"And you'll charge us accordingly," Sebastian said with a half smile.

"Of course. No free rides," Miles confirmed, quoting a phrase his father had used far too often while they were growing up.

Sebastian laughed and got up from his chair and clapped Miles on the shoulder. "Come on then, little brother. Let's head home. Mom, are you finished for the day? Can we give you a ride back?"

"No, Keith is coming to meet me. We have some matters to discuss, but we'll see you all at the barbecue tonight."

"You're still going ahead with the annual Fourth of July celebration tonight?" Miles asked.

"We may be in a state of flux, Miles, but we still have a responsibility to observe tradition. We've never canceled before, and we're not about to start now."

There was a vein of strength in Ava's tone that told him that the world could be ending and she would still keep up appearances. He wasn't sure if he admired her tenacity, or if he thought it more reminiscent of rear-ranging the deck chairs on the *Titanic*. Either way, he wasn't sure a showy display of wealth from the family was such a great idea right now.

"Well, before we go, let's get you up to speed with what we've decided," Sutton said before briefly outlining everything.

To her credit, Ava listened intently without interrupting. When Sutton was done, she nodded.

"Well, if you think that's best, although it's not what your father would have done," she said softly.

"Mom, we're in charge now. Dad and you have done great work building Wingate Enterprises to where it is today, but Sebastian and I are heading the corporation now. This is our decision and we both stand by it."

Miles could hear the note of frustration in Sutton's tone and wondered just how often their mom had voted the guys down on their decisions so far. She was an as-tute businesswoman and she'd guided their father for years, when he would allow himself to be guided, that was.

"I understand, Sutton. Look, before you take it to the legal team, how about I run it past Keith? Maybe we can talk about this some more tonight."

A trickle of unease skittered down Miles's spine. "Mom, I know I don't have a pony in this race, but for now I think it's best if we keep this decision between just the four of us until the offer is made to the workers who were hurt."

Ava looked shocked. "Are you suggesting Keith is less than trustworthy? I'll have you remember he is a valued and long-standing member of this company and he's been stalwart at my side since your father died."

"Even so, the evidence is right there. Someone with pretty high clearances tampered with the safety reports. Until we know who it is, nothing we've discussed here today should be shared with anyone. Am I clear?"

Miles held his breath. He'd never used that tone of voice with his mother before, but this was vitally important. No doubt Keith would be furious when he learned that major decisions were being made without his input, but he wasn't the only senior management or adviser being kept out of the loop. Someone had to be responsible for the damage that had been systematically done to Wingate Enterprises. They couldn't be careful enough until they had the information they needed to bring that someone to justice.

"I agree," Sebastian said in support.

Sutton murmured the same.

"Well," Ava said, her eyes bright with indignation. "I suppose I should consider myself fortunate that you've thought to include me in your findings."

"Mom, don't be like that," Miles said.

"Don't be like what? Don't be hurt that a man we've trusted and included as family for longer than each of you has been alive is to be cut out of this? I don't like it one bit, but I will concede to your directive. For now."

"Thank you," Miles rose from his chair and took his mom's hands in his before leaning forward to kiss her on the cheek. "I'm sorry. I know Keith has been your rock since Dad died, but I know what I'm doing."

He didn't want to add that it was always the people you least expected who could do the most harm.

Nine

Despite their rocky start, Chloe had enjoyed her day with Beth. Miles's older sister was very passionate about what she did, and her enthusiasm pulled Chloe along in her wake as they visited the Texas Cattleman's Club here in Royal and then met with Beth's fiancé, Cam, for lunch at the club. Initially Chloe had felt uncomfortable—as if she was intruding on the newly engaged couple's time together, but Cam had hastened to assure her she was welcome and had shown a great deal of interest in her teaching when he'd heard what she did.

Back at the house, Chloe had decided to make the most of the pristine swimming pool. Her wrist was feeling much better today, and she'd been busy doing laps when she felt a frisson of awareness that told her she was being watched. She glided to the edge of the pool and looked up.

"Oh," she said. "You're back."

A curl of sheer joy unfurled from deep inside as

she looked up at Miles. He was dressed for business in a light gray suit and a crisp white shirt that was open at the neck. A pulse of need rippled through her. She couldn't wait to take it off him. But then she noticed the lines of strain on his face and the tiredness in his eyes.

"Nothing wrong with your powers of observation," he teased, and with the light humor she saw some of the tension on his features begin to ease.

"Did you want to swim with me?" she invited.

"Actually, I came to find you to see if you'd like to go for a ride before tonight's barbecue."

"Do we have time? If it's going to be as formal as last night, I'll need plenty of time to get ready. I really wouldn't want to offend your mom."

"It'll be casual and out here on the patio and lawns. We have time."

"Then I'd love to go for a ride with you. I'm assuming you mean on a horse?"

That earned her a belly laugh, and the last of the strain fell away from his face. "Yes, on a horse, although I'm open to suggestions."

"Let's get away from here first and see what comes up."

He didn't miss the double entendre. "I'll make sure I pack a blanket."

He held out a hand to assist her in getting out of the pool and she dried herself quickly before wrapping the towel around her and hurrying upstairs to get changed. She didn't bother drying her hair, instead twisting it into a loose knot secured with a clip at her nape. Miles wasn't far behind her. He shed his suit and shirt and threw on a pair of jeans and T-shirt together with a pair of boots. Chloe searched her case for her own jeans and a light sweater. She hadn't brought boots so she pulled on a pair of socks and trainers that had seen better days.

"Will these be okay?" she asked, gesturing to her feet.

"Sure, unless you'd like me to see if Beth or Harley has a pair of riding boots lying around that'd fit you. There are always spares at the stables."

"No, it'll just mean it takes longer before we're out on our own. I'll manage," she said, slipping her hand in his. "Let's go."

At the stables she was mounted on a gentle-natured gelding, while Miles, predictably, rode a more spirited animal. Chloe leaned forward and patted her horse's neck. "I hope he's as gentle as you say. It's been years since I've ridden. I'm probably going to be hellishly sore tomorrow."

"We can take it easy," Miles said, urging his mount forward. "I just need to clear my head a little."

"Do you want to ride on ahead at your own pace?" Chloe suggested. "I'm happy to toddle on behind with my new best friend, here."

"No, I want to be with you. You remind me that life shouldn't be all about work."

Chloe fell silent as they walked the horses away from the stables and down the hill toward a small lake on the property. Miles had sounded serious. Very serious. It was a reminder to her that her reasons for being with him were not entirely altruistic, and it left her feeling more confused than ever. When she was with Miles, she wanted to be truly with him, heart and soul. It was easy to forget about the sins of his father and her long held dreams of revenge when they were together.

He only had to be within ten feet of her for her entire body to crave him. And when he spoke she found herself genuinely wanting to listen to what he said.

Whether he recited a grocery list or the Declaration of Independence, it would make no difference to her. The timbre of his voice was as alluring to her as his physical attributes. And, of course, those were outstanding. He seemed to know exactly what she needed. She'd never had a lover like him before.

Of course, it wasn't just his physical presence or bedroom prowess that drew her like metal filings to a magnet. He was genuinely good, from what she could tell. In his case, the apple had fallen far, far from the tree. The way he'd treated her from the moment they'd met was a case in point. She had no doubt that he'd feel utterly betrayed if he knew of her ulterior motive in meeting him and inserting herself into his family gathering.

She was beginning to doubt her own motives, too. It was one thing to grow up in a household infused with her mom's desperate unhappiness, which was fueled by anger and a desire to seek recriminations, but quite another to come face-to-face with the perpetrators of those emotions and find they were, in fact, for the most part anyway, decent people. The jury was still out on Ava, Chloe thought to herself. But the woman hadn't been rude or unkind. Instead she'd been deeply protective of her family, not wanting their current dirty laundry to be aired amongst anyone she didn't know she could trust.

Would Chloe have been any different under the same circumstances? She doubted it.

"Are you planning to ride to the border?"

Chloe drew her horse to a halt and looked around, realizing that Miles had dismounted some way back. She laughed and turned her mount and trotted back toward him.

"Sorry, I was away with the fairies."

"Should I be worried you could forget me so easily?"

Miles came over to stand beside her horse and helped her dismount. As she slid from the saddle, her body grazed against his and bursts of heat ignited at each point they touched. She turned and found herself wrapped in his arms.

"No, not worried. I can't remember the last time I felt this relaxed, and that's all because of you. Thank you."

She spoke from the heart and she could see her simple words had struck him, too. He leaned forward and kissed her. At first a simple touch of lips, as if he wanted no more than that for now, but then it was as if he couldn't hold back and his hold on her tightened, crushing her to him as his kiss became more demanding, the pressure of his mouth on hers firmer than before. Chloe welcomed his hot, hungry possession and returned his kiss with equal fervor.

She raised her hands to his shoulders, and beneath her touch she could feel the tension in his body ease and relax a little. Well, most of his body anyway. There was no doubting his arousal, and she felt an answering need beat steadily within her as his tongue dipped and delved into her mouth. Eventually, Miles pulled back and loosened his hold on her.

"I so needed that," he said before letting her go completely.

"Bad day?"

"Helluva day, to be honest."

"Then I'm glad I could help in some way," she murmured.

"Oh, you have no idea how much."

Chloe looked up at him under half-closed lids. "You want to show me?"

"Let me secure the horses and grab the blanket."

He was back at her side in seconds and, taking her

hand, he led her to a secluded nook where they would not be immediately visible to anyone. Over his shoulder, Miles had a leather saddlebag, and from it he pulled a blanket and two long-stemmed glasses together with a bottle of champagne.

"We're celebrating?"

"Hell yes, we're celebrating," Miles said with a smile as he tossed her the blanket to spread out on the ground.

"Care to tell me what, in particular?"

"Is the fact that we've managed to get some quiet time to ourselves not enough for you?"

"Sure, I'll drink to that." Chloe laughed and smoothed the blanket out on their patch of privacy at the edge of the lake.

"And, I'd like to show my appreciation to you, too."

She arched a brow. "Your appreciation? For what?"

"For not running straight back to Chicago when I had to abandon you today." He poured two glasses of the sparkling golden liquid and handed her one. "You're quite a woman and I am very glad I met you."

Chloe's mouth and throat dried, and she found it hard to speak. He was being so lovely. In fact, he was being everything she always told herself she ever wanted in a man. And she was deceiving him. Or was she? She hadn't actually taken any steps to disclose their family secrets, yet. Not that she truly knew anything in any detail, but she had the feeling that it wouldn't take much digging to find the kind of dirt she needed to steer the media in the right direction with respect to the DEA involvement with the family's business. It wouldn't take much to overturn the necessary stones that would do the most harm. And then her mother would be vindicated, wouldn't she?

No.

She couldn't do it.

She couldn't cheat on the trust this man had placed in her. She couldn't destroy the family he loved. She couldn't destroy *him*. And it would surely decimate their growing relationship if she followed through on her plans. She didn't want to do that. She'd felt as if she had been alone for the last twenty years or more. Oh sure, she'd been with her mom, but her mom had depended on her so much and had been so wrapped in grief that Chloe had learned from a young age to shelve her own needs and wants and desires. Now it was her turn. Her time. Hers and Miles's.

She clinked her champagne glass to his and took a long sip, letting the fizz travel over her tongue and down her throat. Imbibing the liquid as though it was her new truth. The seal on her new direction. This thing with Miles, it may not go anywhere, but she owed it to herself to find out, didn't she?

"This is such a beautiful spot," she said, looking out over the water.

"I find it is much improved with the current company."

She smiled coyly. "You really do say the nicest things. It makes me feel special."

"Good," he answered simply.

They sat for a short while, sipping their champagne and watching the birds land on the water, leaving a gentle wake in their stead. With her free hand, Chloe traced small circles on the back of Miles's neck. His skin was warm beneath her touch and she felt connected to him in a way she hadn't experienced with another man before. When their glasses were empty, she took his from him and set them both down in the grass away from their blanket.

"That was delicious, but I find myself craving something else," she said in a low voice as she straddled his legs and gently pushed him back to lie down on the blanket.

"Tell me more."

"Well, technically you were going to show me, remember? But it's a good thing I'm an equal opportunity kind of girl."

A smile spread across his lips and his hands settled at her waist, sliding beneath her sweater to burn like a brand against her bare skin. She sighed a little and leaned down, brushing her lips across his, again and again. Just lightly, teasing. One of his hands slid up her back and cupped the back of her head, drawing her to him and encouraging her to kiss him properly. And, because she wanted to, she did.

She loved kissing him. Loved the taste, the feel, the texture of him. He moved his hand again, clearly enjoying what she offered and happy to take it. She shifted slightly so she could kiss a trail across his cheekbones, then along his jaw and down his throat until she nipped the skin at its base. He groaned in response. Emboldened, Chloe pushed his T-shirt up, exposing his chest. Miles helped her by lifting his torso slightly, and she slid the shirt off him completely and dropped it beside them.

She ran her hands over his shoulders, his arms. Then skimmed across his belly and back up over his ribs and his chest.

"You are magnificent," she whispered with a reverence that would leave him in no doubt as to just how true the words were that she spoke.

She kissed him again, then. Firmly on the mouth. Taking her time to dip her tongue to duel with his as her hands continued to touch and follow every curve and hollow of his body. Her fingers glided to the waistband of his jeans and his hips bucked beneath her touch.

"Impatient, are we?" she asked, smiling against his lips.

"For you? Always."

She moved her hand over the now-bulging denim of his jeans and gripped him firmly through the fabric.

"We need to do something about this," she whispered, and moved lower on him.

Her fingers dealt with the button at the waistband of his jeans before slowly, carefully, lowering the zipper. Miles lifted his hips as she tugged his jeans down, together with his briefs, exposing his arousal to the warm air and her even more heated gaze. She traced his erection with her fingers, letting her nails graze ever so lightly over his sensitive tip before she lowered to him and took him into the warm, wet cavern of her mouth.

He groaned again and his hips thrust upward, as if he couldn't get quite enough of the sensation of her mouth and tongue on him. Chloe encircled the base of his penis with her hand and slowly let her fingers glide up and swirled her tongue gently over his swollen flesh as she did so. She kept up her momentum, subtly increasing the pressure of her hand and her tongue until she felt him fall apart beneath her.

This was what she wanted for him. Complete abandon. No cares. No stress. No worries. Just the deep satisfaction of knowing someone else could, and would, give him what he most desired. She took her mouth from him and moved to lie with her head on his chest. Instantly his hands were on her and began stroking through her hair, which had begun to slide free from its knot. Then his fingers drifted lower, rubbing circles on her back. She felt him kiss the top of her head.

"I think that from now on this will forever be one of my favorite places in the whole world," he rumbled.

His voice was thick, and beneath her ear she could hear his heart still hammering in his chest.

"Mine, too."

They lay like that for some time—just being in the moment. Listening to the sounds of the birds in the trees and the lazily buzzing insects around them. Reveling in the whisper of the breeze in the trees and shrubs that wrapped them in their own cocoon and the gentle lap of the water on the lake's edge.

And then Miles rolled her onto her side and sat up to kick off his boots and socks and completely remove his jeans.

"I feel overdressed," Chloe said as she stretched out on the blanket.

"You most definitely are. Thankfully, I'm just the man you need to solve that particular issue."

"You are, are you?"

"Indeed. Solving problems, all kinds of problems, is my forte."

"I don't think I've ever met a man with a forte before," she mused.

Miles laughed out loud. "I've never met a woman who could steal the breath clean out of my lungs, send me to heaven and make me laugh all within the space of a few minutes."

"Perhaps that is *my* forte," she teased.

But even though her tone was light, her heart was bursting with the realization that she wanted to be that woman for him. Every day. And, as he began to worship her body, the way she'd worshipped his, Chloe was forced to acknowledge that she was fast losing her heart to Miles Wingate. She could only hope he wanted it as much as she wanted to give it to him.

Ten

They were late back to the house and there was a great flurry of activity around the property as they approached.

"What's happening?"

"That'll be the guys finishing the setup for the fireworks display tonight."

"Fireworks *display*?" she asked. "You mean, like a big display or just the family setting off a few rockets and firecrackers?"

Miles laughed. "A proper display. Family tradition. And heaven knows you can't buck tradition. Mom always invites anyone she knows who isn't attending the Cattleman's Club celebrations to come along. She takes it quite personally if they choose the club over her."

"Um, so how many people are we talking, here?"

"A hundred or so."

"A hundred? That's hardly a casual barbecue," Chloe

declared, feeling flustered. "I thought it was only going to be family."

Miles looked at her across the back of his horse as he dragged the saddle off. "I'm sorry. I thought I had told you that the July fourth barbecue and fireworks was an annual thing. Given what's happening with WinJet, I suggested axing it but Mom insisted it was a better idea to keep things running as usual so as to avoid any unnecessary attention."

"Well, I'm certainly going to need more than five minutes to get ready, if I'm going to be suitable for public consumption. I hope I've packed something appropriate."

Chloe lifted a hand and pulled a piece of grass from her hair. Miles put his saddle up on its stand and came over to her, and tugged a couple more pieces from her hair for good measure.

"You look beautiful in anything. Honestly, this is just casual. Just think of it as a family get-together— just with a really big family."

He bent down and gave her a kiss as Ava walked into the stables.

"Well," his mother said with a definite snip in her voice. "So glad you two decided to return on time. The rest of the family is gathering in the living room before our guests arrive. Perhaps you could join them when you're ready."

Without awaiting a response, Ava turned around and walked back to the house. Chloe chewed her lower lip. Anxiety roped through her stomach, tightening like a boa constrictor. Her eyes met Miles's.

"She really doesn't like me."

"It's not you. She's still mad at me for not joining the family business, and she is mad at whoever has caused the problems at WinJet. Obviously she's really worried, because I've never seen her be so openly rude before. I apologize for her behavior, Chloe. You can be sure I'll call her on it when I get the opportunity."

"Oh, please don't. I don't want to cause any more friction."

"Oh, there's friction aplenty without dragging you into her nest." A muscle ticked in his jaw. "You're a part of my life and I won't have her treat you like that. Not now, not ever."

They finished with the horses and tack and made their way quickly up to the house. After another quick shower, Chloe sorted through the items she'd brought with her and chose a fitted pair of white jeans together with a black sequined tunic and a cute pair of silver ballet shoes. Her hair was a mess so she did what she could to brush it into a bun and used a set of diamanté studded pins to secure it in place. She was quick with her makeup, choosing to accentuate her eyes and not to wear foundation. The blush of warmth from the sun and Miles's lovemaking had given her a glow that made makeup almost redundant. A quick slick of lip color and she was done.

Miles smiled as he waited for her by the bed. "You're wasted on this crowd, Chloe. Right now, I don't particularly want to share you with anyone."

She smiled back at him, feeling that inner glow expand by several notches.

"You're too good for me," she murmured.

As the words fell from her lips she realized she wasn't being trite. She truly meant it. What would it be like to come clean with Miles—tell him the truth about why she'd inserted herself into his life? He deserved to know, but telling him would mean giving up on all her plans—giving up on finally seeing her mom vindicated and genuinely happy again. Even if she wanted to, Chloe knew she couldn't do that, and it was beginning to tear her apart.

There was a knock at their bedroom door.

"Yeah," Miles called out.

Sebastian's voice floated through the door. "You better hurry on down. Mom's getting antsy."

"Well, we can't have that, can we?" Miles muttered to Chloe with a liberal dose of sarcasm. "We'll be right there," he called back to Sebastian.

"Come on," Chloe cajoled him. "This is obviously important to her. Let's not be any later than we already are."

"I like you more and more every minute, you know that?" Miles said, taking her hand and leading her out of the room. "Mom was outright rude, and you're still prepared to play nice and soothe her sensibilities?"

"Miles, I'm a guest in her house, and I'm here with her son. I don't want to do anything to upset her."

"And I won't stand for her upsetting you, either. You know that, right?"

"I don't deserve you," she whispered, and squeezed his hand tight.

They were at the bottom of the stairs and people were pouring through the front door and being directed by additional staff out through the back to the patio and pool area where the barbecue had been set up.

"Looks like we're right on time," Miles remarked as they moved through the crowd and headed in the same direction.

Outside, the entire area had been converted with a patriotic and festive scene. Red, white and blue bunting hung from the veranda overhang and the uprights were wound with ribbons.

"Your family really goes all out, huh?" Chloe said, looking around her.

"Yes, we do," Ava answered, drawing up from behind.

Chloe started in surprise. She hadn't even seen the woman coming nearer.

"Mrs. Wingate, the decorations look wonderful."

"Thank you." Ava inclined her head graciously. "I don't think you've met our good family friend, Keith Cooper, yet, have you? Keith, come on over and meet the young lady Miles brought down from Chicago with him."

A tall man, with the remnants of an athletic build, extracted himself from the people he'd been talking to and walked over to Miles and Chloe.

"Keith, this is Chloe Fitzgerald. Chloe, this is Keith Cooper."

Cooper offered his hand to Chloe and gave her a quick handshake. He only took the tips of her fingers, not even offering her the courtesy of a proper handshake. It was something that always bothered her when she met certain men. As if they thought the little woman couldn't handle a full-on palm-to-palm grasp. Personally, she found it disrespectful.

When Mr. Cooper let her hand go, he snaked a possessive arm around Ava's waist. Chloe felt Miles stiffen beside her at the familiarity.

"Keith is an old family friend. He and Dad went way back. In fact, they were rivals for Mom's hand in marriage," Miles pointed out quite deliberately.

Chloe could feel an undercurrent vibrating in the air between the three others.

"And the better man won the fair maiden," Keith said with a wide smile.

But Chloe could see the smile didn't quite reach his eyes.

"If you'll excuse me, I need to speak to the caterers for a moment," Ava said, smoothly extracting herself from Keith's touch.

The man turned his attention to Chloe.

"Fitzgerald, name sounds familiar. You're from Chicago, you say?"

"Yes, I teach elementary school there."

"Hmm, and we've never met? You kind of look familiar."

Chloe felt her blood turn to ice in her veins. She'd been told often enough that she looked like her mother. Had this man ever met Loretta Fitzgerald? Had he known her dad? If so, he could potentially expose her right now. Here in front of everyone. That wasn't how she wanted to do things. When she told Miles the truth of her identity, she wanted that to be in privacy.

"I'm sorry, I've never had the pleasure," Chloe forced herself to respond as smoothly as she could. "And Fitzgerald is a fairly common name. Those Scots travelled far and wide, didn't they?"

The man laughed. "They certainly did. Still, I'm sure if I know you from somewhere it'll come back to me. It always does."

Someone from over by the oversize barbecue hailed him, and he turned and waved to them before making his excuses and leaving Miles and Chloe to themselves. She watched him walk away, feeling as though a ticking time bomb had been activated inside her. Keith Cooper must have known her parents. If he was as close to the Wingate family and as entrenched in the business as he appeared to be, he probably would have known about Trent Wingate's offer to her father, too. And he'd have known what had happened next when that offer had failed to materialize.

A bitter taste flooded her mouth, and she gladly accepted the glass of champagne Miles took from a passing waiter and offered her. She downed half of it in one desperate gulp.

"Thirsty?" Miles asked with a quizzical look on his face.

"I probably should have started with water," she said, forcing a laugh. "I promise I'll go slower with the rest."

He leaned forward and kissed her cheek. "I don't blame you for reaching for a little liquid courage. My family en masse is quite enough, but with all of the hangers-on as well? It makes a good case for drinking. Come on. Let's go check out the buffet."

Chloe nodded and tucked her free hand in the crook of his arm and fought the sensation that she was rapidly losing control of the world around her. It was clear that she really hadn't thought things through properly. While her mom had severed ties with everyone back here in Royal when they'd moved to Chicago, people could still remember her and a gathering like this was bound to prompt memories. Chloe could only hope that no one connected her to the late John Fitzgerald, and she also wanted to distract Miles from possibly pressing her more about how Cooper might have known her.

"Miles, I got the impression you're not all that happy about Mr. Cooper and your mom?"

He firmed his lips before replying.

"He and Dad were cut from the same cloth. Maybe I just see too much of my father in him. I can't help feeling he's just been biding his time until the coast was clear so he could win Mom back, and I think the way he is around her now, a little too familiar. He—" Miles paused for a moment choosing his words carefully. "He doesn't have the best track record with women. Keith's been married and divorced three times, and he's known to have a temper."

"You know, watching them, I don't think you need to worry. Your mom isn't as into him as he is into her."

"Let's hope you're right."

Miles looked up as Sebastian joined him for breakfast. His brother looked tense. In fact, it had been a tense week all round. Everyone had been walking on eggshells, waiting to see whether the DEA would lay charges against WinJet or not. Tempers had been frayed, and even family dinners in the evenings had failed to create the bonhomie that his mother had so prided herself on.

"Any news?" Miles asked, putting his coffee mug down on the table.

"Yeah, I heard just now. They're preparing the case to officially charge us with drug trafficking."

"What? No. There's been a mistake."

Sebastian looked as if he'd aged ten years overnight. "No mistake. A large supply of drugs was found concealed in cargo holds of three planes nearing completion. They say the street value is estimated at millions of dollars."

Miles let out a long, low whistle. "What happens now?"

"We tell our very expensive team of lawyers to fight the charges for us and fight hard. Oh, and if the charges aren't bad enough, WinJet's assets are tainted by what the DEA have deemed probable drug trafficking. They're freezing the company's assets with a view to forfeiture if we're found guilty."

"They can't actually seize property until you're found guilty, though, right?"

Sebastian nodded. "But when the asset freeze becomes public knowledge, there won't be enough damage control in the world to save us. WinJet can't continue to trade under the freeze. All the company's real estate and accounts will be inaccessible to us. I'm not going to lie to you. This, and the roll-on effect, is going to hit us hard."

"Have you told Mom and Sutton yet?"

"No, and I'm not looking forward to it. Miles, I really need you to up your game on finding out who is behind the safety report tampering. I can't help feeling the fire and the drugs are somehow tied together."

Miles shook his head. "I'm doing what I can but I have to be careful, too. If the DEA discover me poking around in your systems, especially now, they're going to think I'm trying to hide something. Aside from what that might do to my own company, it wouldn't be a good look for the family if we're not seen to be doing the right thing from the outset."

Sebastian sighed. "You're right. We'll have to issue some kind of preemptive announcement—make it abundantly clear that we're innocent and that we're assisting the DEA in any way we can."

"What's this?" Ava asked as she joined them in the breakfast room. "Of course we're innocent. As to assisting the DEA—"

"Mom, we will be assisting them inasmuch as we're capable. They've decided to file charges." Sebastian quickly filled her in on the details. "To be obstructive would only make everything worse."

"Of course it would," she said, coming to stand by her firstborn and putting a hand on his shoulder. "I—"

His mom halted what she was going to say as Chloe came into the room.

"Good morning, everyone."

Miles watched as Chloe halted in her steps and looked at each of them in turn. It was obvious she could feel the tension in the air.

"I think I might have my breakfast on the patio, today," she announced with a forced smile.

"Thank you, Chloe," Ava said graciously. "The boys and I have some business to discuss."

"Of course," Chloe replied brightly. She made up a bowl of cereal and milk and grabbed an apple from the bowl on the sideboard. "Let me know if you need me," she directed at Miles.

He nodded in response. He wished, more than anything, that he could join her outside in the morning air. Summer mornings like this had always been his favorites when he still lived at home.

"We won't be long," he said firmly, letting his mother and brother know that he wasn't about to be dragged into a day-long discussion about the whys and wherefores of what they were going to do next.

After Chloe had left the room, he faced them both. "Look, there's nothing more I can do from here. I can support you just as well from my office in Chicago. I think Chloe and I should head back. Today, if possible."

"No, please reconsider," Ava pleaded. "Zeke and Reagan's engagement party is tomorrow night. At least stay until then. You know Zeke would appreciate it, and it's vital we continue to show a united front as a family."

And there it was, his mother's not-so-subtle form of pressure when it came to family obligations. With everything that had been happening, Miles had forgotten about his cousin's recent engagement.

"I'll speak with Chloe and let you know what we decide."

"Surely you can answer for the girl."

Miles pinned his mother with a look. "I wouldn't be so presumptuous. She was kind enough to travel here with me, and I will be courteous enough to check with her about our plans for our departure home."

"This is your home."

"It might have been once, Mom, but it isn't anymore. I made another life for myself in Chicago a long while ago. One you're actually welcome to see if you'd come to visit. I have a guest room for you, should you ever decide to do that. We're quite civilized up there, you know—hot and cold running water and all that. We even have theaters."

He smiled to soften his words but he could see his words had struck the right chord. His mom was too used to calling the shots with her kids the way she called the shots in business. There were times in the past when they'd all wanted a bit more motherly compassion from her. Thankfully, they'd had that from their aunt Piper, who was nineteen years Ava's junior. Piper had been raised by Ava after their parents died and was far more maternal than her older sister. But Ava's stubborn belief that the fact Miles had made a new life for himself away from the family was merely a temporary aberration drove him crazy. Would she ever accept he was an adult capable of making his own choices?

"Maybe I'll visit when things settle here a little," Ava hedged.

"And if things don't settle?" Sebastian asked bluntly.

"Let's not borrow trouble. We're a strong family and

we have powerful connections. Don't ever discount that. We'll get through this, and we'll be even better than before."

Miles could only hope she was right. Wishing for it was one thing, but with the writing on the wall and no way to conduct their own investigation without drawing unwelcome attention to their activities, he had the feeling she was clutching at straws.

Miles finally extricated himself from the meeting with Ava and his brothers and went outside to find Chloe. He was relieved to see she was still out on the patio by the pool. He plonked himself down on the chair beside her and sighed heavily.

"Everything okay?" she asked, reaching out to put her hand on his arm.

Beneath her touch he felt himself begin to calm. He was learning to appreciate that about her. Her touch could do so many things to him and for him. Incite his senses or soothe them, as she was doing now.

"Yes and no."

"Care to explain?"

"Yes, because I'm with you now. No, because my family is facing a truckload of trouble."

"To do with the fire?"

"Among other things." He shook his head. He didn't want to discuss it but understood that Chloe might be curious, and he didn't want to shut her out completely. "This is going to be made public at some stage, but for now I can't tell you more than this. The WinJet plant won't be operating for a while. The investigation has led to it being frozen until certain factors have either been proven or otherwise."

Chloe looked shocked. "But what about the staff? The customers?"

"Exactly. We have a lot to work out." He realized he'd used the word "we" and immediately amended it. "At least my mom and brothers do. As to the rest of us, we're needed for support. Mom asked if we can stay on to attend my cousin Zeke's engagement party tomorrow night—show a strong family front and all that. I'm happy to do whatever you prefer. We can head home right now, or stay a few extra days."

"Miles, you know I'll do whatever makes you happy."

He smiled at her response. "And you do it very well."

She slapped him lightly on the shoulder. "That wasn't what I meant. Look, if you need to be with your family, then we'll stay. Family is important. Everything, really. Sometimes you do things you'd rather not have to do, just to keep them happy. Which reminds me, I need to report in to my mom."

That was a strange choice of words, Miles thought as Chloe rose and left to make the call. And there'd been an odd undertone to her voice. Maybe it was wistfulness, but his spider senses suggested there was more to it. Miles shook his head slightly to rid himself of the sensation. Clearly, he'd been around his family too long already—he was beginning to see discord in everything and Chloe had nothing to do with it, did she?

Eleven

Chloe made her way slowly upstairs. She wasn't looking forward to making that call. Her mom had been so excited when she'd learned that Chloe was going to Royal with Miles so she could get closer to the Wingates and find the leverage she needed to really do them some harm. By the way things were going, though, they didn't need any help in that regard.

She'd heard far more than she was meant to this morning, thanks to an untied shoelace that she'd attended to before entering the breakfast room. Sebastian's words about the DEA and the company asset freeze had been shocking. Chloe hated seeing the strain on Miles, too. This entire issue had ballooned beyond everyone's imagination.

But were they innocent? It was hard to tell. Surely, with the volume of drugs involved they must have known something. And the DEA—they weren't in the habit of laying charges without a solid basis for doing so. Someone in the family had to know something and that would make them just as heartless as she'd always thought they all were. And, as much as she was drawn to Miles and as much as she didn't want it to be true, maybe he was exceptionally good at lying and projecting a false facade. Heaven only knew his father had been—after all, her father had trusted Trent Wingate implicitly. Maybe the apple hadn't fallen far from the tree at all.

A deep ache started in her chest at the thought. She was on the verge of giving her heart to the man, despite her initial intentions. And he'd confounded her at every turn. He'd been solicitous, kind and the type of lover women usually only read about in novels. She didn't want to believe that he was complicit in this in any way. But, she reminded herself, the second his family had crooked a finger, he'd come running to help.

Of course, that didn't tell her anything other than the fact that he was essentially a good man, one part of her argued. Or maybe it told her that he needed to be here to cover his bases regarding his own involvement in whatever was going on. So, what was she to do? Her mom expected her to take action and Chloe had the contact details of the reporter at the paper. All she had to do was send a text or an email to him about what she'd overheard this morning and the Wingate's privacy would be blown wide-open before they had a chance to do damage control.

She picked her phone up from inside her handbag and stared at the blank screen. All her life she'd been bitter about this family, but flawed as they were, were they any different to her own, or any other family? Sure, they had more money than most—a lot more, and much of it amassed on the misery of others—but did she have the right to stomp all over them and expose this latest scandal to the press?

Chloe jumped and nearly dropped her phone as the screen lit up with her mother's face and her mom's special ringtone split the air.

"Hi, Momma," she said, accepting the call. "I was just going to call you."

"Since you hadn't called me, I thought I'd better phone you and check in."

There was no doubting the unhappiness in her mom's voice.

"I'm sorry," Chloe hastened to say. "It's been...busy here."

"I wish I could say the same. Here it's still the same old, same old. I got my utilities bill today. I don't know how I'm going to settle it or how much longer I'm going to be able to support myself."

The ache that had started in Chloe's chest earlier hardened into a painful knot. She knew her mother's financial position better than anyone.

"We'll find a way, Momma. I promise." She thought about the credit card she kept only for emergencies and which she'd painstakingly just paid off. "And you know you can live with me if you can't afford your apartment anymore."

Her mom sighed. "I'll manage, just like I always have. Anyway, I don't want to talk about it. How are things in Texas? Has Royal changed much?"

"I guess it must have, Momma, because I haven't seen anyone I recognize yet. But then again, I was so young when we left."

Her mom sighed down the line. "It was wrong what they did to us, Chloe. So wrong. We deserved so much better. Your *father* deserved so much better."

And with those words Chloe knew she had to do something, even if it wasn't directly. She could give her mom the ammunition. Loretta then just needed to aim and send it in the right direction. Her mom had lost everything she'd ever held dear, aside from Chloe. Now she had the power to actually give her something back that might bring joy back into her life even if it destroyed the untried bond that was growing between her and Miles.

"Momma, I'm going to tell you something I learned today. Something about the Wingates."

"You are?"

For the first time in a long time, Loretta Fitzgerald sounded thoroughly animated. Chloe swallowed against the bitter taste in her mouth.

"Yes, I am. But I want you to think carefully about what you want to do with this knowledge. This could change things for the Wingates forever."

"The way they changed everything for us?"

Chloe closed her eyes against the sting of tears that suddenly burned there. "Yes."

She repeated what she'd overheard this morning. At the end of the line, her mother gasped.

"So why aren't you giving that information to the reporter that you told me about?"

"Because it's not my fight anymore, Momma. I'm handing it over to you. I can't do it. I'm too close…" Her voice trailed off as her throat thickened, making it hard to speak.

Understanding began to filter through her distress. She'd said it wasn't her fight anymore, but maybe it never had been. And it certainly didn't need to be now. Especially not when she realized her feelings for Miles were genuine. She'd passed the baton to her mom, what

Loretta did with it was entirely up to her. For herself, Chloe would explain everything to Miles when they got back home to Chicago and then she'd accept the consequences of her actions. She could only hope that he could see what had driven her to do this—and forgive her all the same.

"Chloe, I warned you about getting hurt. Those people are ruthless."

"No, Momma. They're just people. Yes, Trent Wingate let Daddy down when he most needed support. But he's gone now."

"You're falling in love with that Miles Wingate, aren't you?" There was a definite accusatory tone in her mother's voice. "What about me? What about what they owe me?"

"I've given you the information you need to take your revenge, if you're prepared to go through with it. But I'm not doing it, Momma. I can't. It's just not right." Tears were flowing down Chloe's cheeks now. She couldn't take anymore. "I'm hanging up now. I'll be home by the end of next week. I hope that's okay."

"It'll have to be, won't it," her mother answered snippily.

"Don't be angry with me, please."

"I'm not angry—just disappointed. We've talked about this for so long. You've been just as determined as I was to take revenge if the opportunity came along."

"I know, and that's my cross to bear. Look, I have to go. I'll talk when I can."

She ended the call and threw her phone on the bed before going through to the adjoining bathroom and washing her face. Man, she looked a wreck. Every one of the emotions tumbling through her—sorrow, regret, guilt—was evident in the blue eyes staring back at her. Chloe started as Miles's reflection appeared next to hers.

"What's wrong?"

Chloe scrambled for a valid reason to be standing in the bathroom, crying. "Mom had some bad news."

"Oh no. I'm so sorry. Do you need to go her? I can arrange it for you."

He was already sliding his phone out of his pocket, but she turned and put a hand on his to stop him.

"No, it can wait until we're back."

"Are you sure? I can book a ticket back to Chicago for you right now. You only have to say the word."

"Please, don't. I'm staying with you, okay? Besides, there's nothing she can do right now."

Nothing except destroy the growing hope Chloe had for a future with Miles.

Miles watched from near the bar as Chloe chatted with Beth and Cam. He could barely take his eyes off her. She was wearing the same beaded black dress she'd worn to the blues evening, and it brought back some darn potent memories right now. He wondered just how long they'd have to stay here before they could slip away and create some new ones. There was a faint smile pulling at his lips as he contemplated just what those memories would entail.

"Penny for them?"

Miles straightened and held his hand out to his cousin Zeke. The son of Ava's late brother, Robert, and his also deceased African American wife, Nina, Zeke and his brother, Luke, were both tall, handsome men who embraced their biracial heritage with pride and confidence. Zeke was the Vice President of Marketing at Wingate Enterprises, and he'd been none too pleased about the revelations in the family meeting Sebastian called late yesterday afternoon. He had his work cut out for him trying to find a way to put a positive spin on the company going forward.

Despite the fact this was a family celebration and the guests were supposed to be family friends, there'd been murmurs and finger-pointing about what had happened with the fire at the jet plant already and he could feel the divide beginning to grow. It wouldn't be long before the asset freeze was being bandied about, too.

"I was contemplating the job you have ahead of you, spin-doctoring Winjet out of this mess," Miles said with genuine sympathy.

"We have our work cut out for us," Zeke said with a heartfelt sigh. "But we'll get through it. Maybe not exactly unscathed, but hopefully close to it."

Despite the positivity in his cousin's words, Miles couldn't help but feel things were beginning to teeter on the edge of a dangerous precipice. But then he gave himself a mental shake. They were here to keep up appearances and to celebrate Zeke's engagement to Reagan. He needed to chill out a bit. His eyes tracked across the room, back to Chloe.

Zeke turned to follow Miles's gaze.

"She's pretty. Luke and I were surprised you risked bringing her home to meet us."

"Risked?" Miles asked with a raised brow.

"Well, you know what Aunt Ava's like. Has she checked Chloe's pedigree and breeding options yet?"

Miles laughed out loud, earning inquisitive looks from many of the people milling around them. "No, but there's still time. We're staying on an extra few days."

"Well, good luck, cuz. If she's worth it, look after her."

"Oh, I plan to, for as long as she'll let me."

Across the room, Chloe had begun to work her way over toward him and Zeke. A few people smiled or nodded to her, but there were equally as many who turned their backs. Watching it made Miles's hackles rise. Chloe was his guest. Under normal circumstances, that meant she should be welcomed with open arms, but with everything that was going on, she was being treated by some as a rank outsider.

She had a smile painted on her face as she drew closer to them, but he could see that it wasn't reflected in her eyes. In fact, her gaze showed just how angry she was.

"I can't believe the nerve of some people," she fumed.

"Oh?"

"Outside of your immediate family everyone here is a stranger to me, and yet several people tonight have warned me not to trust y'all and to run for the hills. And they're not kidding, either. If it had been said in jest I wouldn't have minded, but these people, these *leeches*, are standing here eating and drinking what your family has provided and they still have the audacity to speak to me like that?"

All of a sudden, she realized that Miles wasn't alone.

"Oh heavens, look I'm sorry. That was very rude of me, and here I am complaining about your guests. Hi, I'm Chloe, and you're Zeke, right? Congratulations on your engagement."

"Don't apologize to me," Zeke said smoothly. "I'm just as annoyed as you are. But I guess this is high society, right? The loyal and the not-so-loyal rubbing shoulders and all playing as if they're friends in the same sandpit."

"Well, I wouldn't mind kicking a bit of sand in a few eyes tonight," Chloe growled. "But, enough of that.

How exciting to be engaged and how lovely to have something cheerful, like a wedding, to look forward to in amongst all the turmoil. Have you two set a date?"

Miles felt Zeke shift a little, betraying his discomfort with the question. Was Zeke having second thoughts? Last month, Zeke had shared the surprising news with his cousins that his and Reagan's engagement and their forthcoming marriage were purely born of convenience to help Reagan access her grandmother's inheritance. But Chloe wasn't to know that and it wasn't Miles's secret to share.

"Reagan's mother has stipulated a six-month engagement so it gives her sufficient time to organize the wedding on their property. We're happy to go along with that although we had hoped to marry sooner."

After a little more small talk, Zeke excused himself to go mingle further with the crowd, and Chloe sneaked in close by Miles's side. Slipping an arm around her waist, he smiled down at her as she took a small sip of the champagne she held in her hand. But there was a brittle air to her, which he'd noticed since yesterday after she'd talked to her mother. Obviously, something was worrying her, and equally obviously she wasn't prepared to share that with him just yet.

It frustrated him. He wanted there to be no secrets between them, but he could hardly complain when he hadn't been fully forthcoming about what his family were dealing with. Chloe had been a breath of fresh air in his life right from the beginning, and he was starting to think that he'd like to keep her there, maybe even forever. He turned the idea around in his head. Yeah, *forever* had a nice ring to it. Clearly, they still had so much to learn about one another, but if the way he felt about her and the way he believed she felt about him were any indicator, it wasn't impossible to think that they could have a future together.

He splayed his fingers across her hip and pulled her in even closer.

"You okay?" she asked. "I hope no one's been rude to you, too."

"Not to my face but I've heard a few things here and there. I guess all of us have. In a place as close-knit as Royal it's only to be expected. Some have been jealous of the Wingate family's success and sought to pull us down a peg or two, and something like this is bound to bring out both the best and the worst in people."

She stiffened at his words. "Jealousy?"

"Sure, a lot of people say my dad built his success on the misery of other people's failures. I'll admit, he wasn't perfect all the time, but he was a darn hard worker, and so is Mom. In fact, the entire family has a strong work ethic no matter what they're doing."

"No matter what?"

"Obviously I don't mean at the expense of anybody else, but business is business. Sometimes you have to be ruthless to get ahead. Anyway, we're not here to talk business. We're supposed to be celebrating my cousin and his fiancée's happy future."

A small frown furrowed her brow. "Miles, do you think you'll all have a happy future? I mean, with everything that's going on and all? I don't know exactly what's going on, of course, but it doesn't take a genius to figure out that something is really upsetting your family."

"We'll get through it," Miles said firmly. "We Wingates always do."

Twelve

Later that night, after they'd made love and Miles had drifted off to sleep still holding Chloe in his arms, she played his words over and over again. Yes, there was that air of entitlement she'd always expected from the Wingate family. But it hadn't rankled with her as much as she'd anticipated. She'd seen for herself this past week how hard everyone worked and how strongly they pulled together when the chips were down.

Being an only child, she'd had to be the sole emotional support for her mom. Yes, her mom had the distant family members who'd provided a roof over their head after they'd relocated to Chicago, and provided the hand-me-down clothing that had been Chloe's and her mom's sole source of wardrobe for the first five years after the move. But there'd always been a sense of being beholden to them—that they were a charity case, not family. There hadn't been the extensive network of siblings or cousins to share her troubles with.

Watching Miles and his family pull together toward a common goal, even though there was clearly some tension between them, was something she kind of envied. Although she certainly didn't envy them the storm of negative interest that was about to deluge them soon.

She wondered if her mom had followed through on sending what Chloe had told her to the reporter. She truly hoped not. Of course, she might just be indulging in false hope. Loretta had sounded pretty darn mad on the phone. She wanted her pound of flesh. Even if she never saw any financial compensation, she wanted the Wingate's name to be dragged through the mud and back again. She wanted them to know shame. After all, hadn't that been what had happened with Chloe's family?

She sighed and turned away from Miles, suddenly unable to bear the turmoil of the double life she'd been living since she'd met him. This wasn't her. Not deep down. Yes, she'd had her plan for revenge, but that was before she began to know the family and understand them a little better. She now knew with certainty that she was falling in love with Miles. Deeply and truly.

He was everything she'd ever dreamed of in a man. But she honestly couldn't hope for a future with him until everything was open and honest between them. She'd told herself she'd tell him the truth when they got back home—she had to wait until then. He was dealing with so much right now with his family. Laying out her own motivation for meeting him now would be another burden for him to bear and she simply couldn't do that to him. Not yet, anyway. Eventually, listening to Miles's steady breathing, she drifted off to sleep.

The next few days were quiet around the house. Everyone appeared to be waiting for the next ax to fall.

She and Miles made the most of the quiet, heading out riding each morning and spending part of each afternoon lazing around the pool.

Chloe was relieved, the following Wednesday, when Beth invited her to lunch with Gracie, her personal assistant. Beth and Chloe drove to the Texas Cattleman's Club and met Gracie in the foyer outside the restaurant. Beth and her assistant were obviously close, and the warmth in their greeting to one another was a balm to Chloe's soul. No fear of veiled insults or snide remarks to be expected here, she realized. She felt herself physically relax as the tension in her body dissipated.

Gracie was gorgeous, but seemed to be totally unaware of the looks her glossy, long, brown hair and perfectly balanced features drew from passersby. And the way she held her slightly taller than average frame was incredibly elegant. Gracie was effusive in her greeting to Chloe, putting her instantly at ease and treating her as if she'd always been a part of Beth's extended family.

After they were shown to their table, Gracie and Beth briefly discussed Beth's plans for the upcoming masquerade ball.

"I know it's months away, yet," Beth said. "But, with all the rumors flying around, I'm worried about the impact my family's involvement may have on the success of the outcome."

"Beth, don't worry," Gracie said, putting her hand on top of her friend's. Chloe could see the genuine concern in her eyes. "People won't boycott the ball. It's for a great cause."

"But we're associated with the money trail and with the way things are going—"

"No. Stop that. The gala is going to be a great success. We'll make sure of it. Okay?"

Chloe looked up as a tall and very handsome man walked over to their table. He had jet-black hair, closely cropped to his well-shaped head, and his muscular build sat comfortably beneath a distinguished suit that hugged his shoulders like a lover's caress. Beth saw Chloe staring and followed her gaze.

"Ah, Grant," she acknowledged as he drew closer to the table. "It's good to see you. Chloe, I don't believe you've met Doctor Grant Everett, yet? Grant, this is Chloe Fitzgerald. She's visiting with Miles at present."

"Ladies," he said with a nod. "Look, I don't want to take up your time but, Beth, I just wanted to say that your family has my full support, and I know there are many other club members who feel the same way. You guys do great work and you're well respected for what you give back to the community."

Chloe saw tears spring to Beth's eyes.

"Thank you, Grant. That means a lot to me."

He nodded again. "Please pass on my regards to the rest of your family."

"I will."

The three women watched as the doctor moved away from the table.

"It's a sin," Gracie said solemnly.

"A sin?" Chloe asked, confused.

"That a man should be that good-looking and single."

The three women laughed at Gracie's comment, but then Gracie got serious.

"Beth, see? That's what I mean. You have the support of so many people. You seriously don't need to worry about the fundraiser. And if every person in support of your family makes it clear they won't listen to the lies or speculation, it'll soon die down."

Beth gave her assistant a weak smile. "Well, I certainly hope so. Cam has thrown his full support behind us, too but I still worry that we won't be welcome in Royal society for much longer."

"Anyone who turns their back on you, turns their back on me, too. We don't need them in our lives."

"Bless you, Gracie. You're my rock."

"And speaking of rocks. How's Sebastian coping?"

Chloe noticed there was more than a little interest in the tone of Gracie's question. Maybe there was some exasperation there, too? She wondered what that was about.

"You see him as a rock?" Beth said with a giggle.

"Yup," Gracie said lightly. "He's strong, reliable and generally immovable once he's on a course of action. This business will be tearing him up inside."

"He's doing everything he can to get to the root of who's responsible. Together with Sutton and Miles, they're constantly having meetings. Not having access to the WinJet offices and computers anymore is frustrating them intensely."

Chloe flitted a glance to Beth and then across to Gracie. Did Gracie know the full extent of what was happening? Chloe had the impression from Ava and from Miles's reticence to discuss the matter with her in much detail, that the family had closed ranks on talking about what was going on with outsiders. But then again, as Beth's assistant, maybe Gracie wasn't considered to be an outsider. Not like Chloe was.

Beth must have noticed the concern on her face because she said, "It's okay. Gracie is up to speed on everything. I trust her with my life."

"And Mrs. Wingate, how's she managing?" Gracie asked with obvious concern.

"Well, you know my mom. Always presents like a

swan gliding along the surface without a care in the world, while all the time she's pedaling flat out beneath the surface of the water. I have noticed, though, she's leaning more and more on Uncle Keith. I can't say I'm happy about it. Aunt Piper assures me that Mom just sees him as a friend. I can only hope she's right, because as a partner, Uncle Keith is all wrong for her."

Beth shook her head. "Look, we didn't come here to talk about Wingate business. We came here to celebrate you. So let's celebrate."

"Good, I'm in a mood to celebrate. Shall we have champagne with our lunch?" Gracie suggested.

"Champagne for lunch. I'm in! What are we celebrating?" Chloe asked.

"Gracie recently had a healthy win in the lottery," Beth disclosed quietly. "She's just received her check and I'm expecting her resignation any day now."

"*Healthy* win? It was an obscene amount of money," Gracie confirmed with a broad grin. "And as to my resignation, I haven't decided what to do yet, so you're stuck with me for a while longer."

"Wow, congratulations, Gracie! How does it feel to be a winner? I don't know if I could even comprehend how to manage something like that, although I'd probably start with sending my mom on a fabulous vacation," Chloe said with a happy smile.

Gracie grinned back. "Well, I'm doing something like that. I'm sending my mom and baby brother to Florida to live near my aunt. I'm buying them a beautiful house and sending my brother to an exclusive private boys' school, where he'll get the opportunity to really make something of himself."

Chloe could feel the enthusiasm and joy pouring off the other woman as she shared her plans. "That sounds fantastic. They must be so excited. And will you go down there, too?"

"Right now I'm undecided. What with the ball and everything, I don't feel like it's a good time to abandon Beth."

"For which I'm grateful, Gracie, but you can't put your life on hold for me. You need to follow your own heart. Find a man to love and want to settle down with. Have a family."

Gracie's eyes grew misty, and Chloe couldn't help but feel that she was very probably thinking of one particular person. Was it Sebastian?

"You know I've always wanted kids, but with all the guys suddenly turning up in my life since the lotto win, I'm not sure if I could trust anyone not to be with me just for my money. Sometimes I think it might just be easier to make an appointment with our friend Doctor Garrett at the fertility clinic and have a baby on my own."

The ladies laughed together, but Chloe couldn't miss the note of seriousness in what Gracie had said. It made her pause for thought. Ever since she and her mom had left Texas, they'd lived on the bare minimum. She'd dreamed of having enough money one day to be able to go shopping for groceries without having to count every penny. To live like a Wingate, basically. But it seemed money brought its own problems, too. It was a side of things she hadn't really considered before.

It was late afternoon when she and Beth returned to the Wingate estate after what had turned into a truly lovely afternoon with Gracie. The longer she spent with the women, the more she realized, all differences in their upbringings aside, they could truly be friends.

Chloe had never had a large group of friends growing

up. Her mom had been relying on her to make something of her life, so she had done whatever she could academically and on the track to ensure she'd be eligible for scholarships, which meant she hadn't had the time to socialize like her peers. But an afternoon like this one? Well, it had served to remind her that her life hadn't been as balanced as it probably should have been. As they started up the long driveway, Chloe turned to Beth, who was driving.

"Thank you so much for including me today. It was really lovely to meet Gracie and to spend time with you both."

Beth gave her a big smile in return. "You're welcome. I know your visit with us hasn't been under the best circumstances, but I can see how much you mean to Miles. You're important to him. I want you to feel included, and I look forward to getting to know you better. You can never have too many friends in this world, right?"

Chloe smiled in return and looked out the front window of the car feeling a whole lot lighter than she had since she'd arrived here. She was fitting in. She was being accepted as a part of Miles's life, and it felt marvelous. There was one dark spot on the horizon, though. The way she'd engineered their meeting. She had to come clean with him and face the consequences of that. She owed it to him. He'd been nothing but up-front with her and he deserved her honesty.

As they neared the house, she spied a different car parked out front. The vehicle was dusty with road grime, as if it had done some miles before getting here.

"That looks like my aunt Piper's car. We weren't expecting her," Beth mused aloud as she pulled up next to the other vehicle.

They got out of the car and Chloe immediately spied

the infant car seat secured in the back. Just as she did so, the front door opened, and a young woman holding a small boy, who couldn't have been more than about four, stood in the doorway.

"Oh my! Harley! Daniel! You're home!" Beth cried.

Chloe watched as Beth ran up the stairs and enveloped her little sister and her nephew in a big welcoming hug. The two women greeted one another with genuine affection. Another, slightly older woman joined them, and Beth squealed with joy and hugged her warmly, too. Chloe spotted the newcomer's resemblance to Ava almost immediately. She must be the aunt that Beth had mentioned lived in Dallas. When she'd spoken of her, it had been with much warmth and love. More so than when she spoke of her own mother. Beth turned back to Chloe and gestured for her to come on and meet everyone.

"Chloe, come up and meet Harley and her son, Daniel. And this is my aunt, Piper Holloway."

Chloe proffered her hand and smiled at each of the women as she drew up in front of them. "Hi, I'm Chloe Fitzgerald. A friend of Miles's. Lovely to meet you."

"Does Mom know you're back?" Beth asked her little sister.

"Not yet, and I'm not in a hurry to cross paths with her, so our visit here is short. Piper picked me up in Dallas and brought me down, but I'll be staying with an old friend back in Royal."

Beth wore a small frown on her face. "It would have been wonderful to have you here."

"I know, but you know what things are like between Mom and me. I don't want to expose Daniel to that any more than necessary. But I hope to see a lot of you, though. I'm going to need your help."

"Anything," Beth said quickly. "I'm just so thrilled to see you. You've heard about the mess that's going on."

"Yes, I gathered things were bad when Mom called me in Thailand to tell me the income stream from Win-Jet to Zest had been frozen. It's why I came straight back. I need to find alternative donors and quickly before it starts to impact on the work Zest does. But we had a good flight back to the States and then on to Dallas, didn't we, Daniel?"

The little boy shyly nodded, then turned his face back into his mother's neck.

"He's a little jet-lagged," Harley explained. "Or he'd be talking all our ears off."

"And I was overdue a visit so I offered to drive them from Dallas. It made for a good opportunity to catch up." Piper said. "Besides, there's a new artist just outside of Royal I'm hoping to persuade to give me an exclusive showing at my gallery."

Beth turned to Chloe with a laugh. "Piper has an art gallery in Dallas. We like to tell everyone it's her substitute husband."

Piper chuckled. "Hey, with my gallery I have everything just the way I like it. No crumbs on the breakfast bar in the morning and no socks on the bedroom floor. I'm quite satisfied with my life just the way it is, thank you."

Chloe could see the genuine affection that wove these women together and felt a pang of envy. Even though she wasn't estranged from her mom, they'd never had the kind of relationship the Wingate sisters appeared to have with their aunt. While none of the Wingate children appeared to be emotionally close to their mother, it looked as though they had a strong surrogate in Piper Holloway.

They all went inside and gathered in the family room. There were a few toys already scattered on the floor, as well as a couple of children's books on the coffee table that hadn't been there before. Chloe could see the other women were itching to catch up together, so she suggested she mind Daniel for a bit so they could spend some time alone. At first, Harley looked a little dubious.

"Chloe is an elementary school teacher," Beth filled in for Harley. "Daniel will be quite safe with her, I'm sure."

"Honestly, I miss my class kids so it would be a delight to spend some time with him," Chloe said.

Once Harley had explained she'd just be in another room nearby with his aunts, Daniel accepted that he was being left with Chloe. She kicked off her shoes and joined him on the carpet, helping him put together a wooden track on which he could roll the toy cars he'd brought home with him. She lost track of time and was startled to hear the front door slam closed and the sound of footsteps coming toward them. Chloe looked up to see Miles with a quizzical expression on his face.

"Uncle Miles!" Daniel shouted.

The little boy scrambled to his feet and launched himself at his uncle from about six feet away. To his credit, Miles dropped the briefcase he'd been carrying and caught his nephew in his arms and whirled the giggling child in a circle. Chloe watched him with the boy and felt something shift inside her. What would it be like, she wondered, if the scenario was different and it was *her* child running to his or her daddy. And just like that, Chloe knew she had fallen even harder in love with Miles Wingate.

Thirteen

Miles looked over his nephew's head at the woman sprawled on the floor amongst the toys. She looked just as comfortable there as she had at his side at the engagement party last weekend. More so, in fact. Seeing her like this made him appreciate that there were so many more facets to Chloe than he realized. He'd never gone out with anyone before who didn't think twice about getting down to a child's level and simply having fun with them.

"Miles!" Harley squealed from the side door and came rushing through the room to give her brother a big hug.

Miles flung an arm around his younger sibling and squeezed tight. He'd seen Harley six months ago when he'd been on a business trip to Bangkok.

"Hey, I didn't expect to see you back home, too," he said.

"Piper brought me through from Dallas. She's here, also."

"You didn't mention anything about coming home this year when I saw you last. Is everything okay?"

"Just this wretched business with WinJet. You know they're the primary donor to my charity, Zest. With the freeze, Zest's funding has been locked up, too. I need to drum up new funding to tide us over until this whole mess is cleared up. Is that what you're here for, too? To help with the WinJet crisis?"

Harley looked up at Miles in adoration, and he felt the old familiar twang of pride she'd always managed to imbue in him. His other three siblings were all older, and the twins had always been tight-knit as they all grew up. But Harley had always seen Miles as her knight in shining armor. Cute most of the time. A little less so when he'd started dating and she'd taken it upon herself to start vetting his girlfriends.

"Something like that," he acknowledged. "Although my hands have been tied with the freeze, much like yours back in Thailand, I imagine."

"It's so darn frustrating, isn't it? We're just trying to do good things, make a living, help others to make theirs. I don't know why anyone would be working so hard to discredit us."

"Well, hopefully that will become clearer soon." Miles set Daniel down onto his feet and ruffled the little boy's hair. "He's grown since I saw him last. But you haven't. Have you lost weight? Are you looking after yourself okay?"

"Don't you start," Harley said with a laugh. "I'm doing just fine. C'mon Daniel, let's go to the kitchen to find something to eat. Are you hungry?"

"Yes, please!" the little boy answered and put his

hand in his mother's. As he passed Chloe, he gave her a shy smile and a wave with his free hand. "Thank you for playing with me."

"Anytime, Daniel. I enjoyed it," Chloe answered with a warm smile.

There was definitely something about her that made everything in Miles ease and relax. He flopped down next to her on the carpet.

"Nice job on the racetrack," he said, gesturing to the convoluted road Chloe and Daniel had obviously built together around the furniture in the room. "I had no idea you were so adept at playing with boys' toys."

Chloe arched a brow at him. "Toys are toys. Gender doesn't enter into it."

"I consider myself duly chastened," Miles answered playfully.

"As your punishment, you can help me tidy this away. I'm sure when Ava gets back, she'd prefer to see her family room looking its usual pristine self."

Chloe went on all fours and began to disassemble the train track and stack it into the box it came from. Distracted momentarily by her pert derriere, Miles was slow to join her.

"Well, come on!" she said in exasperation.

"Yes, ma'am."

Once the room was back to its regular condition, they went up to their bedroom. Miles flopped down backward on the bed and heaved a big sigh.

"Bad day?" Chloe asked.

"Not a great one. I'm still parsing through the data I put on a hard drive prior to the freeze, but it hasn't revealed much, so far. I feel like I'm this close." He held his thumb and forefinger close together in the air. "But something is eluding me. Whoever did this knows the

Wingate business systems inside and out. I've got my team in Chicago working on improving overall security for the entire corporation. It just frustrates me because this all could have been avoided if they'd listened to me earlier about their IT security."

Chloe sat down next to him on the bed. "I'm sorry this is proving so tough for you."

"Hey, it's not your fault. How about you? Did you have a good day?"

She smiled down at him. "Yeah, I did. I got to know Gracie a little better. She's quite a woman. I'm glad Beth has her support. And your aunt Piper seems lovely, too. And she's so close to Beth and Harley."

"Yeah, Piper is the mother figure we never had growing up. We all love her to bits. And Beth is brilliant at what she does and even better at choosing people to help her who are equally as strong. Hopefully she can pull some magic out of a hat for Harley, too."

"Harley seems nice," Chloe commented as she lay partway down beside him and started stroking his chest with one hand.

"Harley is one of life's truly good people. I think that by the time she was born, all the snark had been bred out of us, leaving her only what was sweetness and light."

"That's such a cute way to portray her. You do know she's a grown woman with a child," she teased him.

"Yeah, I know. We were all shocked when she announced she was pregnant with Daniel. She was only nineteen when he was born, and she refused to tell any of us who his father is. I think Sebastian and Sutton were on the verge of organizing a lynch mob. But she's done an amazing job of raising him on her own, and she's taught him a lot about compassion and sharing, too."

"He's a darling kid. I really liked being with him."

Miles rolled onto his side and looked Chloe in the eye. "Have you ever thought about having kids?"

"Of course. I love kids. I always hoped I'd have two or three of my own one day. When I was with the right man, of course. I know a lot of strong women, like your sister, tackle raising a child on their own, but having spent most of my life without a father figure, I would prefer to have an involved and present father there for my children."

Miles knew it was still early days in their relationship but it gave him a deep sense of satisfaction to hear that Chloe's views on parenting were so similar to his own. Wanting a family and raising that family with a woman he considered his equal and enjoyed having by his side was part of the reason he'd bought the three-story town house he had back in Chicago. There was a yard out back; they'd be close to the Park for bike rides and walks. And for everything else they could always come back to Texas.

This business with WinJet and his family was a temporary thing, he was sure. While it looked bad right now, he had no doubt that eventually they'd be cleared of the charges that had been laid against them. Until that happened, though, he was bound to support his family. And, while his own personal wealth and his business wasn't affected by this, yet, he couldn't honestly think of or plan for a future until the present was more secure. But when it was, he was looking forward to exploring that concept of the future with the woman lying here with him on the bed.

And speaking of the woman lying on the bed, her hand, which had been massaging the muscles of his chest had begun a slow, but determined, trajectory to the waistband of his trousers. Instantly his flesh leaped to attention. It seemed that no matter the external stressors in his life, one thing remained constant. His powerful attraction to Chloe Fitzgerald.

"Is that linen you're wearing?" he asked her.

A puzzled frown appeared between her eyes. "Yes, why?"

"That stuff creases badly—you should probably take it off."

"Is that right?" she purred.

Chloe withdrew her hand and sat up on the bed, reaching for the tab of her zipper.

"Here, let me," he said, also rising to a sitting position.

He brushed her hand away and reached for the tab, then ever so slowly lowered it, inch by inch exposing smooth honey-colored skin. Then he bent forward, and with his other hand, brushed her hair off her neck and placed his lips at her nape. He felt the tremor that rippled through her body in response to his touch. Emboldened, he lowered the zipper farther, placing kisses on each vertebra of her back as he did so.

It only took a moment to push the garment off her shoulders and down to her waist. Miles stood and pulled her to her feet, letting the dress slip to the floor in a heap and leaving her standing there in pristine white lingerie that was anything but innocent. Behind the sheer lace of the cups of her bra he saw her sweet pink nipples tighten, and he reached for her, thumbing those taut peaks through the fabric.

"Stay there," he directed as he swiftly undid the buttons of his shirt and tugged it free of his waistband before shedding it and throwing it down beside him.

He stepped forward and wrapped her in his arms,

bending his head to hers. She lifted her lips in response and he kissed her, his tongue gently probing past her lips to dance against her tongue before withdrawing. The taste of her, hell, everything about her, intoxicated him on every level. And he couldn't get enough.

He reached for the clasp of her bra and, with the deft fingers of one hand, unsnapped the hooks. The confection of fabric fell free and he gingerly tugged it off her, exposing her small perfect breasts to his gaze. He didn't waste another second. He bent his head to her breast, taking one nipple in his mouth and rolling the tight bud with his tongue. Chloe moaned and clutched at his head, holding him there as he kissed and licked and sucked her. He could spend an eternity with Chloe and still never have enough of her.

He carefully walked her backward to the bed and guided her down on the covers before tugging her panties off and tossing them on the growing pile of attire on the floor. Then, he shucked off the rest of his clothes and joined her on the bed. He lay beside her, propped up on one arm while he traced the glorious feminine lines of her body with his other hand.

"You know, these past couple of weeks have really opened my eyes."

She writhed beneath his touch and her eyes met his. "They have?"

"Yeah. I can see that being with the right person can make anything bearable. I think you could be *my* right person, Chloe."

For the briefest moment she looked conflicted and she briefly averted her gaze. When she looked back at him, her eyes shone with unshed tears. "Oh, Miles. That's a beautiful thing to say. Thank you. I feel honored that you feel that way about me, and I have to be completely honest with you and admit I never expected to want to make your world right or to need you as much as I do. But I do."

He didn't know how to tell her what her words meant to him. Instead, he showed her with his body just how much *she* meant to him. He moved over her and settled between her legs and relished the feel of her hands as they stroked his back and clutched at his buttocks, urging him to take her and drive them both to the pinnacle of their need for one another. So he did, and as he entered her body he knew he'd found the place he needed to be—not just now, but forever—and it was with her.

It was a couple of days later, and Chloe had gone riding with Harley and Daniel, when his mother asked him if he could meet with her and Keith Cooper for lunch at the club. Ava, it seemed, was determined for everyone around them to see that things within the family were strictly business as usual and even though the news had not yet broken about the asset freeze at WinJet, Miles knew it wouldn't be long before it was front page news.

The family had spent many hours in meetings discussing the best ways to manage the impending fallout. To that end, Zeke had been working overtime with a trusted handful of staff in the marketing department. Miles could only hope his cousin's preemptive damage control would do its job.

He'd been catching up on Steel Security business from the estate today, and as he drove out to the club, he decided there was little he could still do from here that was any concrete help to his family, other than showing a united front. He'd discuss it with Chloe, but he felt it was definitely time for them to head home. He knew she had classroom prep and shopping to do for the rapidly approaching start of the school year, too.

Miles smiled a little to himself as he parked his car and sauntered to the club's main entrance. In the last two days he'd felt closer to Chloe than ever. Admitting to his feelings for her—it was something he'd never done before with another woman. In fact, he'd begun to wonder if he'd ever find the right gal for him, but there she was and all because of an accidental meeting in the park.

He spied his mom and Uncle Keith at their usual table in the restaurant and walked toward them. They were talking earnestly, heads bent together. Miles didn't quite know how he felt about the development of his mom's relationship with the man who used to be his father's best friend. He knew Beth wasn't completely happy about it, either. But his mom wasn't easily fooled, and if she found comfort in Keith Cooper's almost constant presence by her side, then so be it. Goodness only knew she'd been faithful and loyal to her husband for all the years of their marriage. Maybe it was his own newfound joy in love that was coloring his way of thinking, but if Uncle Keith made his mom happy, then Miles could accept it, even if he'd never been particularly fond of the man. Besides, if anyone could keep a rein on the man's temper, it was Ava.

His mom looked up and gave him a brief wave, beckoning him over to join them. At the table, he shook hands with Cooper and bent to place a kiss on his mother's cheek before sitting down.

"You two look as if you're in cahoots about something," Miles said as he picked up his water glass and took a long pull at the icy liquid.

"Miles, darling, Keith has brought something to my attention that I think you really need to hear."

It was the use of the word *darling* that did it. His mother wasn't the kind of person to use terms of endearment.

"Oh?" Miles said and looked straight at the older man across the table. "And that would be?"

"No need to get your hackles up, boy," Cooper said. "Your mother and I are merely looking after your interests."

His proprietary tone when he mentioned Ava and calling him a boy irritated Miles on a level he didn't want to study too carefully. Instead, he put his game face on. The one he used when he was about to deliver serious news to one of his clients about their safety.

"Perhaps you'd like to enlighten me?"

"Now, Miles, don't be defensive. Keith, tell him what you told me about Chloe."

Chloe? What did she have to do with Cooper?

"Yes, Uncle Keith, How about you tell me."

Miles kept his barely banked irritation firmly under control.

"Well," Cooper started, reaching out a hand and taking hold of Ava's as if to comfort her. "Your dad wasn't always the best kind of man when it came to business."

"Tell me something I don't know," Miles bit out.

His father's approach to business and Miles's ethics had never been on the same page. It was what had driven him to make his own place in the world thirteen hundred miles away from where he'd been born and bred.

Cooper nodded his head in acknowledgment. "There was a situation a little under twenty years ago where Trent behaved particularly badly. He entered into a verbal agreement with an acquaintance of his who was in the business of making aircraft seats and supplying them to private jet manufacturers."

Miles began to feel a creeping sense of uneasiness at the tale.

"Sounds like a reasonable thing to do."

"Well, yes, it would have been. Except when this acquaintance of his invested heavily in the materials to supply WinJet exclusively, Trent decided to pull the plug on the arrangement. As they'd never entered into a written contract and only agreed to their partnership on a handshake, the poor guy didn't have a leg to stand on. His suppliers started demanding payment for the stock he'd bought in anticipation of the WinJet job, which he obviously couldn't pay for and he went bankrupt.

"Trent just stood by and watched a man, who'd trusted him, dig himself deeper and deeper in debt, and when the guy was forced to walk away from his business, your father swooped in and bought the remains of the company out from under him and amalgamated it into WinJet, where it remains today."

Miles pursed his lips and considered what Keith had told him. None of it came as any surprise. It was just the kind of underhanded thing he knew his father was capable of. The man had always wanted to win at any cost and damn the consequences. Miles had long believed his father was devoid of any social conscience and had often wondered how his mother, who'd once been heavily involved in philanthropic works, had coped with that. But then again, he rationalized, maybe that's why she'd worked so hard for charity—to offset his father's less stellar attributes.

"I don't see what that has to do with Chloe."

"I'm getting to it. Just listen. After being let down by

the very man who'd promised to grow his business and being made bankrupt, then seeing his company sell to the one person who could have prevented his downfall, the poor guy committed suicide." Keith sighed heavily. "I went to his funeral. I'll never forget seeing his wife and daughter. They were bereft. They'd not only lost their husband and father, they'd lost *everything*. He'd cashed up life insurances and cleared out his bank accounts all in a desperate attempt to keep his business afloat and to pay back his creditors. His name was John—" he paused before continuing "—John Fitzgerald. And his daughter's name is Chloe."

Miles felt his stomach drop and the chill of arctic waters ran through his veins. His father had cheated Chloe's dad?

"Why didn't you say anything sooner?" he ground out when he could trust himself to speak. Miles looked at his mother, who looked equally shocked.

"I didn't know," she uttered in a strangled whisper. "I would have done something, anything. I had no idea Trent had done something so vile. He never told me about the initial agreement, but I remember him being very smug about acquiring the aircraft seat manufacturing plant and absorbing it into WinJet."

"And I wasn't certain until now," Keith said, patting Ava comfortingly on her hand. "I thought Chloe looked familiar at the Fourth of July barbecue. You even heard me say as much. But she denied ever meeting any of us before she met you. Remember? So my questions to you, Miles, are, what's her agenda and why is she keeping her family's earlier involvement with us a secret?"

Fourteen

Chloe was rubbing her horse down and laughing at something Daniel had just said when she heard footsteps approaching the stables. The smile was still on her face when she looked up and saw Miles in the doorway, but it soon died away as she saw the expression in his eyes. He was angry. Furiously, undeniably angry. So much so that he barely even acknowledged his sister or his nephew, who both looked nervously between him and Chloe before making their goodbyes and heading up to the house.

"Is something wrong?" Chloe asked, her fingers clutching tight around the currycomb in her hand as if her life depended on it.

"Who are you? Really?" Miles demanded.

Waves of rage billowed off him, and Chloe swallowed against the knot of fear that now constricted her throat.

"I… I'm Chloe Fitzgerald. Just like I always told you. I never lied about who I am."

"Chloe Fitzgerald. Daughter of Loretta and John Fitzgerald of Royal, Texas."

Her legs began to shake. *He knew?* How? What had happened?

"Miles, please. I was going to tell you. I wanted to tell you so many times."

"Really? We've been virtually glued at the hip for the past two and a half weeks. Living side by side, sleeping together, making love—"

His voice broke on the last two words, and Chloe felt her heart begin to shatter into a million tiny pieces. He dragged in a breath and continued.

"I trusted you. I brought you here. To my family home. And you—" His voice broke off and he shook his head. "I don't even know what kind of agenda you had. Can you imagine how it felt to have someone else inform me as to your true identity? You violated every level of trust I placed in you. I can't believe I was that blind. Did it give you a good laugh to deceive me? And, tell me, our first meeting—it was a sham right from the start, wasn't it?"

"Miles, I'm sorry—"

He put up a hand, halting her in whatever she'd been about to say next.

"Don't. Just don't bother lying to me anymore. I want you out of here. I've arranged a car for you to the airport and a charter flight to get you home. After that, you're on your own."

He turned to leave and she shot across the short distance that separated them and grabbed hold of his arm.

"And you're just dumping me like that? Without

hearing me out? Without trying to understand any of this from my point of view?"

"Sure looks that way," he said harshly, and shook off her hand.

"Miles, I love you."

"Oh, don't go making this any worse than it already is. I think we've already established you're a liar."

"But I haven't lied to you. I might have omitted to tell you everything about my family's background, but I haven't lied."

"So you're saying our meeting was a coincidence?"

"No." She shook her head. "I'm not. I did force our meeting. I had this ridiculous idea that I could somehow insert myself into your life and learn what I could about your family with a view to using what I learned to somehow help my mom get her life back on track. She's lived with the misery of knowing your father's actions drove my father to suicide all these years. She wanted some kind of payback. And me? Well, I wanted my mom back."

"Payback? Why not call it what it is. Revenge." His voice was cold, and the expression on his face told her it tasted as bad in his mouth as admitting it to him had tasted in hers. "I can't believe I was so stupid as to fall for you."

She felt each word as if it was a stab to her heart.

"Miles, I never expected to fall in love with you, either."

"Oh, so that makes what you did better? I don't think so. You've not only betrayed me, you've betrayed my whole family. I've said my piece. The car will be here in fifteen minutes. Make sure you're in it when it leaves."

He started to walk away from her again, and she

knew she had only one last chance to try and make this right.

"You have no idea what it's like. To see your father crumble from the strong and healthy man who loved and supported you to someone who just sat in a chair and wept constantly. I was eight years old. Eight! It terrified me. And when he decided it was easier to take his life than to face rebuilding it with my mom and me, I was the one who found him. It was…horrifying.

"And then my mom fell apart. She'd held it together through the worst of the company stuff, but after he died she lost it. She still hasn't recovered. Yes, she's bitter and, yes, that bitterness transferred to me. Have I spent every day since my father killed himself wondering if one day I'd come home and discover my mom had done the same thing? Of course, I have."

Chloe paused and dashed away the tears of anguish and grief that stung her eyes before taking a deep breath and continuing in a fiercely controlled voice. "And did we see your family lose anything while we lost it all?" She shook her head. "You lost nothing. Your father could have reached out at any time and helped us, or, here's an idea, honored his original agreement with my father. But he chose not to. So I grew up hating your family—all of you. And when the news came about the fire and the failed safety inspections, well, I saw an opportunity to exploit your misery and I took it.

"But I never expected to discover you were not like your father. I never expected to love you."

Miles stood there—immovable, expressionless—as she spoke so passionately. As she laid her heart bare to him.

"Are you done?" he gritted out.

She could no longer speak. Her eyes flooded with

persistent tears, and her throat completely closed as a massive sob rose from deep within and choked her. And then he walked away.

Chloe couldn't remember how she traversed the distance between the stables and the house, but she found herself in their room, her suitcase opened on the bed, and piling the items she'd brought with her into it. The tears had stopped, but the raw pain of loss clawed at her from deep inside. It couldn't end this way, she kept telling herself. But it had.

She didn't even bother changing her clothes. She knew he wanted her out of here and that's what she had to do. Once she was packed and had double-checked she hadn't left anything behind, she grabbed her handbag and her suitcase and went downstairs. Ava was just coming in through the front door with Keith Cooper as Chloe reached the bottom of the stairs.

"Chloe? You're leaving us?"

"Miles has asked me to go," she said stiffly. "But before I do, I just wanted to apologize to you. To your whole family, really. I didn't disclose who I was, and by omission I have lied to you all about my intentions toward your family. I didn't expect to like you all so much, much less fall in love with Miles. But I can't deny that I had an agenda when I met him. My feelings for Miles, now, are true. I only hope that someday he can forgive me for what I've done."

"Oh, Chloe."

Unexpectedly, Ava rushed toward her and enveloped Chloe in a brief hug. Chloe held herself stiffly. Unable to accept the solace Miles's mother offered because if she did, she would crumble into a thousand pieces and not be able to move again. She had to say her goodbyes. She had to leave. Not to do so would be in direct contradiction of his wishes and, above all else, his wishes were paramount.

Thankfully, Ava let her go and, with a nod to Keith Cooper, Chloe continued out the front door and to the car that had just pulled up in the driveway.

"Ms. Fitzgerald?" the driver asked as he got out of the car to open the back door for her and take her case.

"Yes."

She got in the rear of the car and the driver closed the door. The dull thud a final knell to the hopes she'd begun to nurture that she could have a future with Miles. Once the driver had stowed her case in the trunk, he took his seat behind the wheel.

"To the airport, right?"

"Yes, to the airport."

She didn't even bother looking back. This was the last time she would leave Texas. The first had been painful and full of uncertainty, but this was so much worse. Because this time she felt as though she was leaving a vital part of her behind. A part that she would never recover again.

By the time she landed in Chicago it was getting late. She texted her mom from the airport to let her know she was back. It took her just over an hour and a half, using public transport, to get to her home. Despite her mother's frequent visits, the house smelled musty, but Chloe locked the front door behind her, dropped her bags in the hallway and then went straight to her bathroom and turned on the shower.

She could still smell the scent of her horse on her clothing as she stripped off and stepped into the shower stall. And there, she let go of all the pent-up misery of the past several hours. It was ages later before she could summon the energy to wash her body and her hair. Even longer before she had the strength to turn off the water and dry herself.

Exhausted by grief, she tumbled naked into her bed and closed her eyes, willing herself to sleep, but all she could think about was the shock and betrayal she'd seen on Miles's face. Knowing she'd hurt him so badly was like being flayed with a whip and left her entire body sore and aching. She thought she was done crying but as she flipped and flopped on the bed, she realized that her pillow was now sodden with the steady stream of tears that simply would not let up.

So she curled into a ball and she let herself cry and wail and howl. And in the end, none of it made any difference. She was still alone. And she'd devastated the only man she'd ever truly loved.

"Chloe? I know you're in there, honey. I'll let myself in if you don't come to the door."

Chloe woke to the sound of her mother's fist battering on her front door. She dragged herself from her bed and wrapped herself in a robe before staggering to the door and opening it. Bright sunlight streamed through the open portal, temporarily blinding her, and she put a hand up to shade her eyes.

"Oh, honey. What happened?" Loretta asked, stepping across the threshold and kicking the door closed behind her while enveloping her daughter in her arms.

Chloe tried to hold herself together, the way she always had for her mom. Since her father's death she'd learned that her role was to comfort her mom, not the other way around, but right now she lacked the energy to hide her hurt. Instead, she leaned right into Loretta's softer frame and put her arms around her mother's waist.

"I fell in love, Momma. And I broke his heart and then he broke mine."

"Oh, my darling girl. I'm so sorry."

Her mother hugged her tight and didn't move, didn't say a thing. Just held her. The tears cleared more quickly this time and, once she'd stopped, Loretta led her into the sitting room and pushed her down onto the couch.

"I'll go make us some coffee and get you something to eat."

"I'm not hungry, Momma, truly."

"I'm going to fix you something and you're going to eat it. Then you're going to tell me everything."

"I don't have any food in the house," Chloe protested.

"And why do you think I came around this morning?" Loretta asked as she moved around the room opening windows. "I got you some groceries. If you'd given me notice that you were coming home, I'd have aired the place out and had some food in the fridge for you for when you arrived. But as it stands, I'm glad you didn't, because you'd have just borne this alone, wouldn't you?"

Chloe couldn't deny it. She'd spent the last nineteen years learning to suck up whatever bothered her and, while this was more monumental than anything she'd endured before, she would have tried to shield her mom from this, too.

"It makes no difference. Telling you won't change the outcome."

"A problem shared is a problem halved, honey. Remember that."

Chloe cracked the weakest of smiles as her mom espoused one of her dad's favorite sayings. He also used to say that happiness shared was doubled, but Chloe didn't know if she'd ever feel happy again. She sat back on the couch and watched as her mom put away a couple of bags of groceries and then put a pan on the stovetop. Soon the air was redolent with the aroma of fresh coffee, toasted bread and fried eggs with bacon. The scents of her childhood, she realized as Loretta loaded everything on a tray and brought it through to her.

Despite her protestation that she wasn't hungry, Chloe did her best to eat the simple meal her mom had prepared for her. To her surprise, once she started, she couldn't stop until it was all gone. She was on her second cup of coffee when her mother sat down next to her and patted her on the leg.

"Now, tell me everything," she urged her daughter.

So Chloe did. She unloaded everything—well, the G-rated version anyway—that she'd said and done with Miles right up until he'd ordered her out of his life. To her credit, Loretta didn't once interrupt, and when Chloe was finished speaking she merely shook her head.

"It was like that with your daddy and me. Falling in love hard and fast. High emotions. They're exhilarating and exhausting all at the same time, aren't they?"

Chloe just nodded. She knew her parents had had a whirlwind courtship, but she hadn't wanted to ask her mom too much by the time she was old enough to show an interest, because doing so would only cause her mom more pain.

"I'm sorry, Momma. I failed you."

"No, don't you dare say that! You haven't failed me at all."

"But I didn't get the revenge we'd both talked about for so long. When it came down to it, I couldn't do it."

"And I'm glad you didn't, to be honest. When you called me and told me that you weren't going forward,

I'll admit I was mad at you for not following through with your plans, and I was determined to finish off what you started." Releasing a pent-up breath, Loretta admitted, "But then I got to thinking, and I realized it shouldn't have ever been your fight. It was mine. Realizing that made me see I'd failed you as a parent all these years. I put unrealistic pressures and expectations on you your whole life and, you know, to be totally honest, it's all credit to you that you're the incredible human being you are.

"I also realized that I've been selfish for quite long enough."

"No, Momma, never selfish," Chloe protested.

"Yes, honey. I can see that now. I was so wrapped in my own grief and all we'd lost with your daddy dying, and I harbored a fair amount of anger toward him, as well, for leaving us to deal with it all on our own. I just didn't see how much you needed me, too. I took all the support you gave me and I expected more. That was wrong—and that's going to change from here on in. I promise.

"When you told me about the drugs and the DEA, I knew that making that news public would be crippling to the Wingates. I wanted to do that more than anything, to bring them to their knees the way Trent Wingate brought your father to his. But I also realized that doing so would hurt you, too, and I've hurt you enough, my darling girl. It's time I stopped living in the past. Time I took control of me and my life and let you live yours."

"Oh, Momma, I don't ever want to be without you," Chloe said fervently.

"And you won't be. But *I'll* be the mother from this moment forward. You will be able to depend on me as should always have been your right. And I want you to reach out to your young man once he's had a few days to calm down. You both deserve a bright future together."

Chloe shook her head slowly. "I don't think he'll ever forgive me for this. I betrayed him in the worst possible way."

"Keep the faith. If your love for one another is as strong as you believe it is, it'll work out eventually."

"I hope so."

"Believe it, honey. True love never dies. It takes a hit sometimes, but it *never* goes away."

Chloe watched as her mom stacked their cups on the tray together with her breakfast plate and took it through to the kitchen. She wondered if her mom was right.

Fifteen

Miles was like a dead man walking. A snarly one at that. Everyone, even Daniel, had kept a wide berth since he'd sent Chloe home. Miles had been back in Royal for three weeks now, and they'd been both the worst and the best of his life. Heavy on the worst, he told himself.

Chloe had been gone only three days, and while he told himself, frequently, that was a good thing, he found himself missing her so badly it had become a physical ache. He'd avoided his family over the past weekend and had spent most of his waking hours at the head office of Wingate Enterprises working on running the beta version of the new IT security system his team back in Chicago had designed for the company. So far it had been running perfectly and at this rate, in another few days, he'd be able to head back to Chicago and be satisfied that any surprise glitches could be managed remotely from there.

But that didn't stop the hurt that reverberated through his every waking moment. He let himself back into the house and headed for the stairs up to his room. It was late and the house was quiet, but he was surprised when he saw his mother come from the main sitting room.

"Miles, we need to talk," she said firmly.

"Not now, Mom. I'm tired and I need my bed."

"What you need is a good talking-to, and you're going to get it whether it's down here in the sitting room or up in your bedroom if I have to follow you there. And don't think you can lock the door on me. This is *my* house, remember? I hold all the keys. So, which is it to be?"

Ava put her hands on her hips and stared at him, awaiting his response. Miles sighed in frustration, knowing she'd darn well follow him upstairs and to his room if he tried to avoid her.

"Fine," he said with ill humor. "Let's get it over with."

"Thank you," Ava murmured, preceding him into the sitting room.

She settled on one of the leather wingback chairs by a picture window that looked down the hill and toward the lake, although it was pitch-dark out now and even under the scant moonlight there was little to be seen. Ava gestured for him to take the other seat, and he threw himself down and leaned forward, forearms resting on his knees, hands clasped together and head bowed in acquiescence. He was startled when he felt his mother's hand on his hair. Even more so when her fingers shifted to his chin and forced him to raise his face toward her.

"Miles, I hate seeing you like this."

"What? Tired? Once I'm satisfied with the new IT system I'll get plenty of rest again. But it's vital everything is running properly before I leave because I don't plan on being back anytime soon."

"I'm sorry to hear that. I had hoped, in these years since your father's death, you would come to see this as a place you are always welcome to come home to. That you might even consider moving back to Royal, even if not onto the estate."

He shook his head, staring at her in disbelief. "No, that's not going to happen."

"I know your father was hard on you, but—"

"*Hard* on me? He took every opportunity to let me know I was a disappointment to him. Hardly the actions of a good man or a good father."

"Everything he did, he did for us," Ava said in fierce defense.

"Everything? Really, Mom? Even driving a man to suicide? I don't know how it made you feel to hear that the other day, but it made me sick to my stomach and ashamed to even bear the name Wingate. I can't believe that even now, knowing what kind of man he truly was, that you still continue to stand by him or that you continue to mourn him."

His mother's face bore a mask of pain for a moment, but she pulled herself up straight and her features cleared.

"One can forgive much if the love is real, Miles. I want you to think about that. I know you sent Chloe away after discovering her background but I'd like you to consider just how different you are from your father right now. Isn't that exactly what he would have done in the same situation?"

Miles flinched as if she'd slapped him. "Don't go there, Mom. I'm nothing like him. *Nothing!*"

"Don't you realize it, yet? The harder you try not

to be like someone, often the more like them you become." He stared at her in stony silence but allowed her to continue.

"You have all the good of your father. Be careful you don't develop the bad along with it." She released a quavering breath, and when she spoke again, her voice rang with emotion.

"Yes, I know he wore two masks. I know he could be ruthless at times, and while your father capitalized on another man's unhappiness, he did everything he could to ensure that you children always had everything you ever needed whether it was the roof over your heads or the educations you undertook. He used to watch you sleep at night, when you were babies, and he'd share with me his dreams for our future, for the empire he wanted to build so that none of us would ever want for anything. He loved you all in his way."

Miles wanted to refute his mother's words. To tell her she'd viewed her late husband through rose-colored glasses and that the man had been a monster, not some gallant hero forging a life for his family. But deep down, he knew that, faults and all, that's exactly what his father had done. It didn't mean that Miles's feelings toward him changed one iota, and he could live with that. What he couldn't live with, however, was his mom thinking he was just like the man who'd fathered him.

Ava continued. "Miles, I need to be honest with you. I wasn't thrilled when I saw you'd brought someone home with you, especially under the circumstances we're facing. But I could see that she was special to you and, the longer you two stayed, the more I could see how right Chloe is for you. She brought out a softness I haven't seen in you since you were a little boy. Softness your father drummed out of you. Yes, he shouldn't have done that, but you're an adult now. You make your choices. You decide how you treat people, how you'll let them treat you.

"I know how hard you've worked to build your own empire and you've done an outstanding job. But—and you have to admit I'm right here—it's a lonely life managing everything on your own. Chloe loves you. Even a blind man could see that. Give her another chance. Don't let the fact she hid her true identity from you banish her from your life forever."

"I trusted her," he said bitterly.

"I know. We all did. And, when you look at the bigger picture, whatever her initial intentions were, she didn't betray that trust. People make mistakes, but I believe she loves you, Miles. The way you deserve to be loved. Wholeheartedly. You need to make this right between the two of you."

"I don't know if I can do that."

"Then maybe you're your father's son after all," she said quietly.

Ava rose from her chair and placed a gentle hand on his shoulder before leaving the room. A cascade of thoughts tumbled through his mind. He thought back to the moment he met Chloe, to his instant visceral reaction to her. To his need to ensure she was okay, and not just medically okay but safely home and fed and cared for. Those weren't his usual reactions on meeting someone. He'd taken her at face value and he'd acted accordingly. Why? She'd admitted she set up the whole thing. Goodness knows how many times she'd lain in wait for him, trying to force a meeting.

But there were no guarantees that even if they'd met that he'd have fallen for her bait and wanted to see more of her. She'd taken a risk but he had the feeling that for all the years of unhappiness she'd endured, she really hadn't thought the whole thing through. And even if Chloe had released any of the information she'd gleaned from his family during her time here, how much damage could that have done to any of them, anyway? Every dirty, nasty, fact would come out eventually. In fact, he was surprised that nothing had leaked already.

Whoever had been trafficking the drugs stood to gain more by besmirching the Wingate family and falsifying their involvement in all this than whatever Chloe could possibly achieve by sharing details with the media. Which she hadn't done in the end, anyway. Not even after he'd sent her back to Chicago. A truly vindictive woman bent on revenge would have been on the phone to the papers, selling her story to the highest bidder, the moment she was off the property. Maybe even before that. But Chloe hadn't.

Miles got up and faced out the window at the darkness, staring at his reflection in the glass. Right now, he didn't particularly like what he saw. Yes, he was still the same man who always stared back in the mirror when he shaved each day. But his eyes were empty. His soul bleak.

He missed her.

He wanted her.

He had to know if she'd been telling the truth about her feelings for him.

Acknowledging those things didn't make him weak. It made him strong. And what he decided to do about it could make him even stronger.

The next morning, Miles went into the office before dawn. He ran a final check over the beta security system and decided it was time to hand it over. Just to be certain everything was covered, he contacted one of his best analyst/programmers back in Chicago, apologizing for waking her.

"Steph, I need you here on the Texas job. How quickly can you pack and get on a flight?"

He heard her sheets rustle as she obviously got out of bed, soon followed by the sound of fingers clicking on a keyboard.

"Well, I've missed the red-eye but I should be able to be there by three this afternoon. Is that soon enough?"

It would have to be. "Great," Miles said abruptly. "I'll have a car and a driver waiting at the airport for you when you arrive."

"Sure, boss. Um, is everything okay?"

Miles allowed himself to smile for the first time in days. "It's going to be."

Chloe closed her classroom door behind her and made her way out of the building. Normally, she loved this time of year. The anticipation of the classroom filled with new faces. Of the bright young minds waiting to be filled with enthusiasm for learning. But today her feet dragged and her heart lay like a lump of concrete in her chest. She had to pull herself together in the next couple of weeks or she wouldn't be bringing her best to her students or to her love of teaching. But how was she supposed to find joy when, no matter what she did, she couldn't stop thinking about Miles Wingate?

Her mom was doing her best to cheer her up, but there were only so many mother-daughter dates you could fit into a week. Loretta had even suggested Chloe give up the lease on the house and come and live with her again. After relishing her independence all these years, she was shocked to find herself considering it. Yes, the commute to the elementary school where she taught would be longer, but she wouldn't be so darn alone all the time.

She could tell her mom was deeply worried about the cloud of sorrow that hung around Chloe's shoulders. It worried Chloe, too. Even after her father's death she'd managed to keep putting one foot in front of the other. She'd needed to, for her mom's sake. But now it was Momma that was the strong and supportive one, and all Chloe wanted to do was take to her bed, hide under the covers and not come out until her heart didn't hurt so much anymore.

She'd walked to school today, hoping the much-needed exercise might help to lift her mood, but now, it was growing dark out and the idea of walking home didn't hold a great deal of appeal. Still, she squared her shoulders and, with her house keys firmly lodged between the fingers of her right hand, she headed for home.

Chloe hadn't been walking long before she became aware of a vehicle driving toward her. Dark and sleek and all too similar to the one Miles had driven, she felt her stomach lurch as she wondered if it was him. But the car continued on down the street, away from her, and she felt the sharp sting of tears in her eyes as she realized she'd have to be dreaming to think that a man like Miles Wingate would ever forgive her for what she'd done, let alone come and find her.

She dashed the tears away, firmly telling herself to get a grip. She couldn't spend forever moping about. She had a life to live. Kids to teach. Maybe even someone new to fall in love with.

At the thought of allowing herself to get close to anyone else, her stomach did that weird lurch again. No, she definitely wasn't ready to consider that again. Not now and maybe not ever. Everything was still so raw. Chloe knew she'd done wrong, and that she had to learn from this and move on. She kept striding forward, knowing each step took her closer to home and the chance to lock herself away in her little house and nurse her wounded soul in private.

The sound of rubber on the road behind her made her stop in her tracks, her fingers clutching her keys even tighter than before. A dark shape drew up beside her. Her heart hammered in her chest. The car's engine was soundless, which was why she hadn't even heard its approach until it was right there beside her, but she recognized the outline of the sleek machine. The driver's door was flung open, and the interior light of the car blazed on, revealing an all too familiar male figure before he alighted from the car and stood there, staring at her over the top of the roof. She felt his presence as if it was an emotional punch to her midriff. Seeing him standing there sent her already chaotic emotions into overdrive, leaving her conflicted and confused.

"We need to talk," Miles said in a low monotone.

She couldn't say why, but instead of leaping at the opportunity she'd been dreaming of, she just got mad.

"Why, hello, Chloe. How are you? Did you make it home from Royal, okay? Oh, lovely, I see you did. And how are you faring? Well, I hope." Fury mounted, replacing the miasma of misery she'd been dwelling on within. "We need to talk, do we? You wouldn't listen to me when I tried to talk to you before. Why the hell should I listen to you now?"

She turned her back on him and kept walking. There was a dull thud of a car door and then the creeping sound of tires on the road as he followed her. The car drew up beside her again and the passenger window rolled down.

"Chloe, please. I'd like to talk."

Every cell in her body was urging her to do as he

asked. To actually stop walking and get into that luxury status symbol that he drove, but a perverse imp of self-preservation made her keep putting one foot in front of the other. A couple was walking toward her, and she saw concern painted clearly on both their faces. The man stepped forward.

"Ma'am, are you okay? Is this guy bothering you?" he asked. "Would you like us to call the police?"

"No, it's okay. I know him, I just—"

She just what? She didn't know what she wanted. From the minute she'd left the Wingate estate, she'd wanted Miles. In fact, through every waking moment and almost every sleeping one since, she'd wanted him. She'd wanted what they had to be still in one piece, not shattered and bleeding all over the floor. She'd wanted to feel as if she was a part of him, the way he was indelibly a part of her. She dragged in another breath before speaking to her potential rescuer.

"Thank you for asking. I'll be fine."

And with that, she turned toward Miles's car and let herself into the passenger side. As he drove the car away from the curb, she forced herself to smile and wave to the couple.

"I appreciate you not making a scene back there," Miles said, keeping his eyes firmly on the road in front of them.

Chloe didn't know what to say so she opted for silence. The moment Miles pulled up outside her house she got out of the car and walked to the front door. She could feel Miles just a few steps behind her. Once they were inside, she gestured to the living room, and he went and sat down on the sofa.

"I'll be back in a moment," she said.

She probably needed more than a moment to gather

her thoughts together but with him right here under her roof right this minute, the least she could do was dump her things in her bedroom and then go and wash her hands and face. After leaving her bags on the desk she kept in the corner of her room, she scurried to the bathroom and quickly splashed some cold water on her face.

Chloe regarded her reflection in the mirror. She looked like a wreck. The light summer tan she'd accumulated during the break had faded and a lack of sleep had left her skin and eyes pale and dull. She quickly dried herself off and forced herself to return down the hall to where Miles awaited her.

He hadn't stayed seated. Instead, he was up and pacing the threadbare carpet.

"I thought you'd escaped out a back window or something," he said half-jokingly as she came into the room.

She'd been tempted, but she wasn't going to let him know exactly how much he'd unsettled her with his sudden reappearance in her life.

"You said we need to talk?" she answered.

Chloe lowered herself onto the single armchair she possessed and sat stiffly with her hands clasped in her lap, almost as if she'd been called before the principal and was expecting a reprimand. Nervously, she began to chew the inside of her cheek.

Miles moved past her, and the merest waft of the cologne he wore teased her nostrils. She breathed in sharply, then instantly wished she hadn't as her mind was filled with the scent of him and just how close she'd been to him to inhale that particular fragrance. A deep pull of longing dragged through her center and she felt a faint tremor ripple through her body in response. Darn it, how could she let him affect her so easily?

He finally sat down opposite her and leaned forward.

She drank in the sight of him, concerned to see that he looked about as rested and happy as she did, which was to say not very much at all.

"Are you okay?" he asked.

She stared at him. She'd betrayed him in the cruelest way and he was asking her if she was okay? Chloe dragged in a deep breath and let it go before answering.

"No, Miles. I'm not okay. How about you?"

The words bounced between them like a tennis ball in a grand slam tournament.

"Me neither. Look, I know I was abrupt with you when you left the estate and I'm sorry. The way I handled that was wrong. I was angry and I didn't listen to you. I owed you that much at least."

"What are you doing here, Miles?" she asked, her voice wreathed with the weariness that pulled at every muscle in her body, including her heart.

"We need to talk… No. Correction. *I* need to talk and I ask that you listen."

Chloe let her body relax against the back of the chair.

"Okay, I'm listening."

He looked at her then, his eyes clashing with hers, and in them she saw a world of hurt meshed with a world of longing. She recognized the look because she saw the same thing in her gaze every morning when she looked in the mirror. Her foolish heart ached for him and what he was going through—for what they both were going through.

"I won't deny that it crushed me to find out that you'd hidden your true motive. I have never in my life felt so betrayed by another person, and believe me, when you grow up with a man like my father, you get used to the feeling. But what you did, it cut me like nothing else I'd ever experienced. I felt as if you'd destroyed us. That you'd torn apart the very fabric of the precious relationship we were building together. I lashed out. And I apologize for that."

She let his words sink in, then parsed through them. Looking for a glimmer of hope that they could work this thing out between them. But so far, there was not so much as a kernel to cling to. Chloe blinked against the burn of tears that was starting at the back of her eyes and fought not to rub at the sharp pain piercing her chest.

"I'm so sorry I hurt you, Miles. While that might have been my intention— No," she corrected herself. "I have to own this. That *was* my intention—before I met you. But it didn't take me long to realize that you were not the man your father was. My anger and my family's betrayal began and should have ended with Trent Wingate, and I am truly sorry that my mom and I thought we had the right to visit that on you and your brothers and sisters."

She dragged in another breath. "But you hurt me, too. When you confronted me, I told you the truth. I told you everything. I opened up to you and you just slammed a metaphorical door right in my face. You refused to listen to me. You refused to even try to understand what I'd been through and what my life had been like since your father's treatment of my dad, or what motivated me to contemplate doing what I did.

"Choosing that path—revenge—wasn't easy, especially when I discovered exactly who you are on the inside. And knowing who you are and what you're like made it hurt all the more when you turned me away."

Miles's expression twisted, as if he was in pain, and he pressed his lips together as though fighting to hold back words that begged to be said. He closed his eyes briefly and drew in a shuddering breath before opening them again.

"I'm sorry for that, too, Chloe. Believe me, I've never known anyone like you before. The circles my family move in, the people I've mixed with all my life? None of them are like you. Not a single one. I couldn't believe that I could open up and feel about another human being the way I felt about you, right from the start. Do you have any idea what that did to me? You rocked the foundation of my life." Exhaling roughly, he scrubbed a hand across his face. "Yes, of course I know that people meet and fall in love and live happily together forever after. But I always thought that was a pipe dream. Hell, it wasn't even a dream for me. I had my work, I dated. I never expected to fall in love the way I fell for you."

Chloe felt cautious anticipation begin to grow deep inside. Did this mean there was still a chance for them to work through this? To find a way back to each other that had a solid foundation based on truth and love?

"Well, I didn't exactly expect to fall in love with you, either. All my life your family was held up in front of me as a target. As something to bring down. A group of people I didn't know or understand, but people that had destroyed the stability my family had been based on and who forced my father's hand to take his own life. Obviously, now, I understand that no one made that ultimate decision to end my dad's life but him. But that didn't lessen my anger at your family."

"What my father did was despicable, Chloe." Miles shook his head in disbelief. "Even now I can't begin to understand what he was thinking when he did that. *How* he could do that to another human being. But to him, the end always justified the means. When I reached the stage of my life where I understood how he operated was wrong on every level, I distanced myself from him and everything associated with him. I made my own way in the world. Without his support or approval or his money. I am not my father."

"I know, Miles, and I'm sorry I ever thought you were. Of course, when I got to know you, I knew you were not to blame. It made me think twice about what I'd hoped to achieve in hurting you, let alone hurting your entire family. It made me realize that I couldn't go through with it."

They both fell silent for a moment. Each awash in pain and regret. But then Miles shifted and looked at Chloe again. The expression on his face had changed. His eyes held something new. Hope?

"Chloe, answer me this."

"Anything."

"If you were being totally honest with me about your feelings, do you think we can get past this? You brought sunshine in my life in a way I've never experienced before. You blew out the cobwebs and you replaced them all with a breath of fresh air. I've never felt happier with anyone the way I felt when I was with you and, on the flip side, I have never felt as utterly bereft as I have since I ordered you out of my life."

"Of course I was being honest with you, Miles. I fought it. Yes, I'll admit that. But I couldn't help but love you as I started to get to know you. I know you're a proud man—a self-made man—and that you don't need anybody to complete you or your life on any level. But I hope there is room for me in your heart because you fill mine and I wouldn't want it any other way."

He abruptly stood and walked to her chair and pulled her upright.

"Do you mean that? I mean, I'm not doubting you,

but this depth of emotion is new to me. I feel like I have to second-guess myself all the time. Today, when I came to find you, I wanted to demand you give me the truth about why you did what you did, but then I realized you'd done that. It was my own stubbornness that refused to listen to what you'd already said."

She lifted her hands and bracketed his face. "Miles, I mean it. I loved you then, I love you now. I will love you forever."

He shuddered then, as if the weight of the world had lifted from his shoulders and he'd finally freed himself from his deepest fear.

"I love you, too, Chloe Fitzgerald. I want to be with you, always. I want to plan a future together with you, a life where we know we can rely on one another and to hell with the rest of the world. We can build our lives together, our own family together—and all of it on a foundation of truth and happiness. What do you say?"

Tears came to her eyes in earnest now, but she didn't blink them away. These were tears of joy. Of faith in a future she had only ever dreamed of.

"Yes. I say yes!"

He tightened his hold on her and drew her closer, angling his face to hers and capturing her lips in a kiss that imbued all the sweetness of this moment together with all the heat of his love for her and hers for him in return. They might not always have the smoothest road ahead and they still had so much to learn about one another, but Chloe knew in her heart and to the depths of her soul that they'd endure, no matter what.

* * * * *

INSATIABLE HUNGER

YAHRAH ST. JOHN

Thank you to my agent Christine Witthohn
for encouraging me to participate
in the Seven Sins series.

One

Falling Brook's country club had been given a face-lift, Jessie Acosta thought as she walked around the elegantly appointed ballroom. The Black & Silver Soirée theme was in full effect. Silver and black balloons hung from the ceiling and the tables were decked with black tablecloths and silver lamé runners.

Black and silver confetti had been sprinkled over the tables, giving them a festive touch, and on top of each sat either a glass vase filled with black tulips and silver-gray roses or a bowl topped with silver and black ornaments. Black plates sat atop silver chargers and held silver napkins and flatware. Reunion guests' names were in tiny silver frames next to each setting. The reunion committee had outdone itself.

Jessie herself had come prepared to dazzle in an eye-catching, sequined spaghetti-strapped gown with a plunging V-neckline and an open back with crisscross detail. Or at least, that had been her intention, but her long-distance boyfriend, Hugh O'Malley, was nowhere to be found. When she'd asked him if he was coming home from London for the event, he'd informed her he was too busy at work. So she'd spent most of her evening in the company of Ryan Hathaway, at one time one of her oldest friends.

That changed fifteen years ago when her parents had lost their entire fortune because of Black Crescent Investments. CEO Vernon Lowell had embezzled millions from his clients—her parents included—disappearing before authorities could catch him. That loss had led Jessie to always wanting to make her parents happy and to do what was expected. Instead of hanging out with Ryan all the time, she'd started dating Hugh O'Malley, who was from one of the richest families in town, just to please them, and she knew they expected them to marry. But lately she'd become increasingly dissatisfied with the direction of her life and their long-distance relationship. And then tonight happened and suddenly she was seeing the world through a different lens.

Ryan stood a few feet away, talking to several of their classmates, but he was head and shoulders above them. Ryan wasn't the sweet, shy boy next door who wore glasses and was slightly overweight she'd grown up with. The Ryan Hathaway she'd met tonight was confident, lean and trim, and wore contacts. There wasn't anything shy about him. He was sexy and carried it well in a black custom-fit tuxedo.

Jessie hadn't be able to stop herself from ogling. It had been several years since she'd last seen him. Ryan's once-curly black hair had been cut into a close-cropped fade along the sides with curly tendrils at the top. And since when did he have facial hair? It was just a smattering—a mustache and fuzz on the chin—but it gave him a hint of mystery and danger. His charcoal eyes had been trained on her for most of the night and, to Jessie's surprise, she kind of liked it.

When they'd talked, it was like the years faded away and

they were just Ryan and Jessie sitting in his tree house and talking about their dreams for the future. Ryan had done quite well for himself. He worked for a high-profile investment company in Manhattan while Jessie toiled away as an associate at a midsize firm in corporate law.

It amazed her that they'd been in the same city yet hardly seen each other. But how would they, when she worked sixty-hour weeks? Sometimes more. She wanted to make partner and the only way to do that was to get those billable hours.

"Penny for your thoughts?" Ryan asked, suddenly by her side. She'd been so engrossed in thought, she hadn't seen him wander over.

"Just thinking about how so much has changed," Jessie said, glancing up at him from underneath her lashes. "You, especially."

A large grin spread across his incredibly full lips. *Why hadn't she noticed how divine they were before?* "Me? I'm the same Ryan you've always known."

Jessie shook her head. "I beg to differ. You're different."

"Is that a bad thing?"

She smiled. "No, it's a *great* thing."

He regarded her silently for a moment, as if weighing his options. "Care to dance?"

"I would love to."

Any thoughts she had evaporated the moment Ryan pulled her against him. Jessie felt...well, sort of strange because they'd never danced together. Maybe when they were little and had been playing around. In his arms now, Jessie felt acutely aware of her body and the way her breasts crushed against Ryan's chest.

Raw masculine heat radiated from his close proximity, causing her heart to flutter uncontrollably. And when Ryan pressed his body against hers and slid his thigh between the softness of hers, Jessie nearly lost it. This was *Ryan*. It wasn't right she should be feeling these things…but she did.

He smelled so good. *Felt so good.* When he wound his arms around her waist, Jessie wanted to reach up on her tiptoes and sweep her lips across his. *What was wrong with her?* Ryan was her friend, but he didn't feel like a friend. She glanced up and peered into his eyes. He didn't look at her like one, either.

His ebony gaze raked over her face, his eyes trained on her mouth. He was going to kiss her. And she wanted him to. *Desperately.* She wanted to feel his lips crushed against her own, only then might it slake the hunger growing deep in her belly. She licked her lips in anticipation and watched Ryan's eyes grow dark with desire.

He wound his fingers through her shoulder-length bob, bringing her face to his.

"Ryan!"

"Tell me you don't want me to kiss you," he taunted.

Jessie opened her mouth to say no, but she couldn't get the word out. And it would be a lie because she did want Ryan's kiss. She closed her eyes, preparing herself for an unforgettable kiss, when suddenly there was commotion behind them.

Startled, Jessie glanced over Ryan's shoulder to see Hugh saunter into the ballroom amid much fanfare.

Hugh was her dream guy—all six feet of him. With his classic good looks, she'd been in love with him since she was a teenager. Wavy jet-black hair cut just above the neck, piercing blue eyes, a sculpted face and a square jaw encompassed by day-old stubble made Hugh O'Malley Falling Brook's hottest catch. He was the man she was supposed to marry.

The tailored white tuxedo he wore fit him handsomely, but he'd always looked good in a suit. The fact he was there was a big deal considering he hadn't been back to the States for months. Everyone at Falling Brook Prep had loved Hugh and she'd been no exception. *So why had she been falling over her onetime best friend?*

Jessie immediately pushed against Ryan's chest and stepped a few inches away.

"What is it?" he asked and then swiveled in the direction of her gaze. His expression turned from sexy and slumberous to irritated. Ryan glanced back at Jessie. "Now that Hugh is here, the party's over?"

"Ryan…"

He held up his hand. "It's okay. I was only a stand-in until the man you really wanted came along. If you'll excuse me…"

He didn't make it far because Hugh blocked his path. "Well, if it isn't Ryan Hathaway. How are you, man?"

"Fine."

Ryan tried to move past him but Hugh wasn't budging. Instead, he wrapped an arm around Jessie's shoulders. "Thanks for keeping my lady occupied until I could get here. My flight got delayed. It was a real bear traveling from London. How's my Jess?" He bent down and kissed her on the forehead.

Jessie glanced over at Ryan, who was fuming at her. "I'm…uh, good." She felt like a total heel to have her boyfriend in front of her when two seconds ago she'd been lusting after Ryan.

"I'm going to mingle." Ryan, not waiting for a response, made a hasty retreat.

Jessie watched him leave, feeling incredibly guilty for leading him on. If Hugh hadn't arrived…

"Never known you to be so tongue-tied, babe," Hugh responded, breaking into her thoughts.

Jessie blinked, refocusing on Hugh. "I'm shocked. I didn't know you were coming."

Hugh grinned broadly. "I wanted to surprise you. I know

it's been tough the last few years with our long-distance relationship, so I was trying to make an effort."

Jessie forced a smile. "I appreciate that."

"Do you? Because I could do with a better greeting after not seeing each other for months." Hugh wrapped her in his embrace and planted a long kiss on Jessie's lips, but all she could think about was the anger etched on Ryan's features as he'd departed.

Would he ever learn? Ryan wondered as he stared at Hugh and Jessie from across the ballroom. Hugh was in his element with a crowd of their Falling Brook prepsters flocked around him, Jessie standing by his side like an adoring girlfriend.

Of course, she hadn't been so adoring moments before Hugh's arrival…

When he'd looked at her, Ryan had been entranced by the bow of her slightly parted mouth, by her slender throat and the gentle swell of her breasts. Jessie had made his breath catch and he hadn't been able to take his eyes off her. Warning bells should have sounded in his head the minute she'd looked at him the way a woman looked at a man—*him*—like she wanted him to kiss her. He'd taken full advantage of her desire for him, sweeping Jessie into his arms and showing her just how good they could be together. He knew what he wanted and it seemed Jessie had finally, truly, seen him.

Not as a friend.

But as a man.

A man she wanted.

Had he mistaken the signs that she was interested?

Surely not, Ryan wasn't a novice when it came to women. He'd read Jessie's body language. The way she'd leaned into him, pressed her small but firm breasts against him, which had caused him to nearly erupt.

Ryan had had a crush on Jessie since he was six years old when she'd moved to Sycamore Street with her parents and brother, Pete Jr. The Hathaways and Acostas had been close neighbors once. Their fathers had played golf at this very same country club, while their moms had volunteered at the prep school. Both families had often met up at soccer games to see Ryan's two older brothers, Ben and Sean, or Pete Jr. play soccer.

Meanwhile, Ryan and Jessie had shared an easy rapport, often spending hours in each other's company, hanging out at one of their homes playing video games or riding their bicycles to the town square for ice cream. But Jessie had never seen Ryan as anything other than a friend. The situation had only worsened after Black Crescent's hedge fund tanked, leaving the Acosta family as collateral damage in its wake. Adversity hadn't brought him and Jessie closer. Instead, they'd grown further apart.

"Are you all right, Ryan?" one of their classmates asked. "You look like you're ready to blow your lid."

Ryan inhaled deeply and schooled his expression. "Sorry. I was deep in thought about a deal I've got going."

"Are you sure?" the man inquired. "Because your deadly glare was aimed at Hugh over there." He inclined his head toward the man of the hour.

Everyone was fawning all over Hugh and, while Ryan hated to admit it, he was jealous. He had to let go of the notion that he and Jessie would ever *be* together. Time and time again, he'd watched her choose Hugh over him and tonight had been no different. He needed to move on with his life for good this time. The time for looking back on what might have been was gone.

"Yeah. I'm good," Ryan replied. "I'm going to cut out, it's been a long night and I've seen all I need to see." Ryan turned on his heel and walked out of the ballroom toward the valet. Regardless of the kiss he and Jessie almost shared, they were over. He wasn't willing to play second fiddle to any man and certainly not Hugh O'Malley. One day he would find the woman meant for him. She certainly wasn't in this ballroom.

"Babe, I'm so happy I came," Hugh said after the crowd surrounding them dissipated, leaving him and Jessie alone. He swept her into his arms, but when he bent to kiss her, Jessie turned her head to the side. His eyebrows shot up in surprise. "What's wrong?"

Her lips twisted in a cynical smile. "What's wrong? Really, Hugh? You didn't even tell me you were coming and I'm supposed to welcome you with open arms?"

His blue eyes regarded her warily. "Actually, yeah, that's what I thought. Excuse me if I thought you might be happy to see me."

Jessie sighed. She *should* be happy to see him, but her reaction to Ryan tonight was a problem. She turned away from Hugh and walked swiftly toward the covered terrace. The committee had bedecked it with string lights and balloons. Since the night air held a chill, heaters had been strategically placed around the terrace.

Hugh followed her, catching up in two quick strides, and spun her around. "Jessie, what's going on?"

"Nothing." She looked down at the floor.

"We may have been apart for a while, but I can tell when you have something on your mind. What is it?"

After almost kissing Ryan, Jessie realized she was done with playing the "perfect couple." She was tired of living up to everyone's expectations. She knew her parents thought they would get married; expected her to be the dutiful daughter she'd always been. But Jessie didn't think so. If she and Hugh were meant to be, there was no way Jessie would have had such an intense and passionate encounter with Ryan. She had to do the right thing and end their relationship.

"I can't do this."

"Do what?"

"Be with you," Jessie stated. "*We.* Aren't. Working. We haven't been for some time because you're across the ocean. Besides, you and I both know that we've been together mainly because of our parents' wishes, not because it's what we both want."

"I'm sorry, Jessie. I know I've been caught up in my career, but surely you don't mean what you're saying. I've worked so hard for us—to build a better future."

"Hugh, we haven't lived in the same place, let alone the same country, for years. How are we supposed to get married one day if we never spend any time with one another?"

Hugh ruffled his hands through his dark curls. "I can't leave my job right now. I've got major deals in the works. It would ruin everything I've been working toward."

"I know. Your career has always been more important than our relationship, which is why I think we need to break up."

"I see."

"Please tell me you understand," Jessie pleaded.

"I do. I haven't been there for you and now you're evaluating if you want to continue our relationship. But instead of breaking up, why don't we take a break and think about what we both really want?"

Jessie lowered her head and tears clouded her eyes. She'd always thought they would be together forever, but she wasn't so sure now, not after tonight with Ryan. She glanced up at him through wet lashes. "Yes."

"Oh, sweetheart." Hugh pulled her into his arms, cradling her underneath his chin. "It's all right, take all the time you need and I'll do the same. But know I'm rooting for us."

Jessie wished she could say the same, but the way she'd felt tonight with Ryan showed her she wasn't as all-in on Hugh as she'd once thought. Otherwise why had she been thinking about Ryan the way she had tonight? She'd also come to realize that her *own* happiness came first, not what her parents or the citizens of Falling Brook expected from her.

"Can we keep the break private?" Hugh asked, glancing down at her. "I don't want to make it public or tell our parents yet in case..." His voice trailed off.

Jessie understood. Hugh had always cared about what people thought of him—how he was perceived. She was sure he thought there was hope they would get back together. And why wouldn't he? They were Falling Brook Prep's golden couple. "Of course. It will stay between us."

They left the terrace and went back into the party, pretending to be the happy couple in front of their peers. But deep down, Jessie knew it was over between them because tonight her eyes had been opened to not only stop living her life according to her parents' expectations, but finally to do what's right for herself.

Two

"It's good to see you, Ryan," Jessie had said when he'd strode into the famous restaurant in lower Manhattan near the financial district. He'd unbuttoned his suit jacket and taken a seat across from her. Within minutes, they'd ordered and received their meals. They had little to talk about other than the weather.

Ryan hadn't seen Jessie since their ten-year high school reunion and had been surprised when, out of the blue, she'd asked him to lunch. With her busy career, Ryan had assumed she hardly gave lunch a thought, while he, on the other hand, believed in eating small meals throughout the day. He supposed it had something to do with being overweight as a preteen and the endless bullying he'd received. He now religiously watched his weight, which was why he was eating a grilled salmon and spinach salad at the exclusive eatery.

Ryan sipped his club soda. "I was pleasantly surprised to get the invite."

Jessie released a long sigh. "You shouldn't be. We were close once."

"That was a long time ago, Jessie."

"And I'd like to rectify that," she stated.

Ryan peered into her earnest eyes and, damn him, he believed her.

Hadn't he told himself he was saying goodbye to the decades-old crush he'd had on this woman since his voice had begun to change?

He steepled his fingers together on the table. "I'm listening…" He measured his response. He wasn't about to rush to judgment. This could be nothing more than loneliness in the big city. Perhaps Jessie was in need of a dose of the familiar?

"Did you see the newspaper's fifteenth-anniversary article about Black Crescent?"

He was right. Jessie wanted a shoulder to cry on or someone to listen. In the past, he'd been all too willing to give an ear. Except this time, it was different. He wasn't the young, naïve teenager he'd once been, hoping for a scrap of her time. He was done with wishing and hoping Jessie would see him differently. He was a grown man and he had plenty of women he could call who were eager to spend time with him. "Yes. It's the same ole, same ole, Jessie. Why get rattled?"

"It may be old news to you, but not to my family," Jessie replied, dismay in her tone. "My father has never gotten over Black Crescent's hedge fund tanking. When Vernon Lowell disappeared, my father lost his job, his friends and his country-club membership. He nearly lost the house, too, but somehow Mama was able to hang on to it."

Ryan heard the wounded tone in her voice. He, too, had always wondered how the Acostas had managed to stay in their five-bedroom house when many of the other Falling Brook scions had fallen. He doubted Mrs. Acosta could have been making much in her receptionist job at O'Malley Luxury Motors, Hugh's father's company. "I'm glad your parents were able to keep the house. Otherwise, you and I wouldn't have remained friends."

Jessie pursed her lips. "Yeah, but it was never the same, was it? I know I pulled away from our friendship."

Ryan was shocked Jessie was owning up to it. As the years had gone by, he'd watched their relationship steadily fade into a shadow of its former self. "Why did you?"

Jessie was silent for several moments, then reached for her water glass, sipping generously. "When I learned that Jack O'Malley paid for Pete's and my tuition at Falling Brook Prep, I felt like I owed them my loyalty, you know? How could I forget what he'd done? Because of him, we were able to stay at prep school when most of our classmates had to withdraw and enroll in public school."

"I can understand your need to show your appreciation, but it didn't stop there, Jessie, and we both know why."

She arched a brow. "What do you have against Hugh?"

"Hugh? I don't want to talk about him." Ryan's mouth clenched tightly. "We were talking about Black Crescent and the impact it had not only on your family but our friendship."

Jessie took the bait and stopped talking about his rival. "That exposé brought to the surface all those old wounds. My mother said my father was beside himself after reading it and refused to come out of his study for the rest of the day. And then Joshua Lowell had that press conference to announce he was stepping down as CEO to live happily-ever-after. How dare he! He shouldn't get a happy ending after what his family did to the rest of us."

"I'm sorry to hear that about your dad," Ryan said. "Truly I am. And I get that Black Crescent has a black stain in your book. But what if someone could come along to revitalize it with fresh ideas to make the company better, more transparent?"

Jessie stared at him with a dumbfounded expression. "Why do you sound like a walking interviewee?"

Ryan took a forkful of salad and focused on chewing his food. This was a conversation he was not looking forward to. He'd known one day it would come, but it had come sooner than he liked.

Jessie's eyes grew large with expectation. "Well?"

"I've interviewed for the CEO position at Black Crescent. When Joshua Lowell made a formal announcement that he was stepping down to focus on his art career, that he'd gotten engaged and was currently in search for a successor, I tossed my hat into the ring."

"You've done what?" Her raised voice caused several patrons to openly stare in their direction.

Ryan wiped his mouth with his napkin. "Can you lower your voice, please?"

"I can't," she hissed. "You're making the worst mistake of your life! How can you even consider working for the family—the company—that destroyed mine? I thought we were friends."

"We are."

"Then how can you do this?"

Ryan reached across the table for Jessie's hand, but she shrank back in her chair, away from him. He took that one on the chin. He knew his announcement would come as a shock to her, but the position had also been a way for him to cut off feelings for her full-stop. He knew that working at Black Crescent, the company Jessie despised, was a surefire way to keep her away. She blamed Black Crescent for all her family's financial troubles and her father's inability to move forward with his life.

Her beautiful face was flushed bright red. "Why does it have to be you?"

"With my MBA and background, I'm uniquely qualified to take on the role. Who better to repair Black Crescent's damaged reputation?"

"Not you. When I spoke to Hugh, he thought—"

Ryan interrupted her, cutting off her sentence. "Wait just a minute. Hugh…hasn't been in Falling Brook in years. What would he know about the company?"

"He called me when Jack told him about the press conference."

When Ryan rolled his eyes, she pointed her index finger at him. "There it is."

"What is?"

"The animosity you always have whenever I bring up Hugh. Why do you dislike him so much?"

"I couldn't care less about Hugh," Ryan replied. "But you? You're giving this guy, who's been MIA for years, too much credit. I mean, how well do you even know him? When was the last time you spent any significant amount of time with the man?"

Was he pushing Jessie to admit her relationship with Hugh was a sham because he hadn't truly gotten over her? He'd stubbornly forced himself to forget about the almost kiss they'd shared at the reunion, but sitting across from Jessie now reminded him of how strong the attraction between them still was.

Jessie stared at Ryan in disbelief. The Ryan she remembered was always quiet, shy and even-keeled, yet the man sitting in front of her was anything but. In fact, she would say he was the opposite. He was confident with lots of swagger.

When he'd walked into the restaurant, Jessie had forced herself not to wag her tongue in delight. He'd looked resplendent in a gray suit, white shirt and skinny silver-striped tie, just as he had three months ago when she'd seen him at the ten-year reunion. She'd thought the heady, powerful feelings he'd evoked in her when they'd danced together had been a fluke.

A flare of heat had sparked within her on the dance floor, warming her in a way that surprised the heck out of her. If Hugh hadn't interrupted when he had, Jessie was certain Ryan would have kissed her and she would have liked it. That had been the most confounding thing of all. The unexpected desire she'd felt for her old friend.

So she'd pushed it down, spending the last few months purging her heightened emotions by working tirelessly at the law firm until well after dark. She'd tried convincing herself she'd imagined it, but she hadn't. The flame was there now, burning as bright as it had that night.

"Are you going to answer me?" Ryan asked, breaking into her thoughts. She saw the faintest clench of his jaw as his eyes narrowed at her. "Or can you not recall the last time you saw the great Hugh O'Malley? Was it the reunion? If so, that was months ago."

His tone brought Jessie out of her musings. "My relationship with Hugh is my business."

"You made it mine when you brought him into the conversation to pass along his advice. And I'm calling a spade a spade. You've been with the man on and off for years. Mostly off, in my opinion. Yet the consensus has always been that you're going to marry the guy. I'm pointing out that you might not know him enough to make such a monumental decision."

She knew that. It was why she'd agreed with Hugh to take a break. They'd texted frequently or FaceTimed and Skyped as often as they could for much of their relationship. And while Hugh attended Harvard and Wharton, they'd been able to maintain some semblance of being a couple, but it had been difficult with their demanding studies. However, when Hugh had decided to accept a job in London, straight out of Wharton, Jessie had been taken aback.

She'd thought Hugh would want to be closer, not farther apart. He'd insisted their relationship was strong enough to handle the distance and time apart. It hadn't been. Instead, Jessie had begun to feel restless, as if the life she'd carved out for herself was no longer enough. So she'd pushed herself harder at work, but that hadn't brought her the fulfillment she'd thought it would. She needed more.

"I admit marriage is a huge step," Jessie finally responded, "And we are not there yet." She had no idea where her relationship with Hugh stood at the moment. She didn't appreciate Ryan shining a light on it. "But, Hugh is a stand-up guy and the O'Malleys are good people."

"So you would marry him for his family? Because you feel obligated?"

"Of course not," she huffed. Though sometimes she felt that way, she couldn't tell Ryan that. "You're purposely misunderstanding me."

"Am I? Do you even know what you really want?"

Jessie narrowed her eyes. "Of course I do. There's no rush to jump into marriage. Hugh and I are focusing on our careers right now. It's been hard for me as an associate at my firm. I have to prove myself. It's the same for Hugh. We both have big dreams."

"Which is keeping you both on different continents. Sounds romantic."

"Don't presume to judge me, Ryan, when you don't have a relationship yourself."

"You don't know that," he countered.

Jessie stared into his dark brown eyes. Was he trying to get under her skin? Because if he was, it was working. Her nerves were frazzled imagining Ryan with someone else. Was it because she wanted him for herself? Her mind burned with visions of Ryan and another woman in an intimate embrace and she rapidly blinked to rid herself of the damning images. "Are you dating someone?"

He was silent for several beats before saying, "Not at the moment. But that's not to say I haven't enjoyed an active dating life. I've had girlfriends."

Girlfriends. Plural. "Bully for you."

Had she imagined Ryan was sitting home alone on the couch in front of the television waiting for her to acknowledge him? If so, she'd been wrong. He was a good-looking man and clearly finding someone to spend time with hadn't been a problem for him.

"Why should you care, Jessie? We're just friends, after all."

Jessie offered a bland smile even though she felt quite the opposite. She hadn't thought about Ryan like a friend since reunion night. "That's right. I want you to be happy."

"Good, then accept that I know what's best for me," Ryan stated. "And the opportunity to run Black Crescent and clean up its image is what I want."

Jessie frowned. "Are we back to that?"

"We never left."

Her eyes found his and his stare was uncompromising. He was digging in his heels. She sucked in a long-drawn breath. "I guess you can do whatever you want, but I can't support you on this, Ryan. It goes against everything I believe and against my family."

"I understand. Just don't fight me."

She chuckled. "Now you're asking too much. Fighting with you is one of my favorite pastimes." When they'd been younger, she would often give him the business to get a rise out of him.

"How about we stop fighting and have some fun?"

Jessie was surprised Ryan still wanted a relationship with her. Since the night of the reunion, he'd kept his distance. She suspected this potential job with Black Crescent was a way for him to create further distance between them. But until the reunion, she hadn't realized how much she'd missed him the past couple of years and the open camaraderie they'd always shared.

"Did you have something in mind?" she asked.

He grinned and her stomach knotted with a peculiar twisting motion. "Actually, I do. You remember my friend Adam?" She nodded, the name sounded familiar. "Well, with July Fourth coming up, he's invited a bunch of friends to his place in the Hamptons for the weekend. Would you be interested in going?"

"I would. You're sure he wouldn't mind you bringing a plus one? I haven't been to the beach all season. The city is so hot this time of year." Her roommate and bestie, Becca Edwards, had been trying to get Jessie to the beach, but she was usually working late, clocking in hours at her firm.

"Excellent. If you can get off early, I'll pick you up on Friday afternoon. Sound good?"

"I'm in," she told him. Despite knowing she was putting herself in the path of danger by going to the beach with Ryan for the weekend, she thought that, perhaps, she could put their relationship back into the box it had always been in. She would finally be able to stamp out his face, which had found itself floating into her dreams, both day and night.

She would do it.

She had to.

Although she was restless and dissatisfied with her life, she wasn't about to blow up her relationship with a dear friend over an attraction that would fade. Plus, if Ryan was considering a job at Black Crescent, it would be the antithesis of what her parents would want. She had to stay the course.

Figures danced on the screen in front of Ryan's eyes later that afternoon. He'd been staring at them for the last hour with little result of producing the report he'd wanted to complete by end of day. Leaning back in his executive chair, he glanced out the window from the forty-fourth floor of his office building.

Since his lunch with Jessie, he'd been out of sorts and unable to focus. At first, he'd thought it was because he'd finally spilled the beans about his job opportunity with Black Crescent, but that wasn't it at all.

It was Jessie. He'd thought going to lunch and telling her of his opportunity at Black Crescent would put a nail in the coffin of their already strained relationship. Instead, there was an awareness between them that hadn't been there before. When he'd peered into her beautiful brown eyes, he'd forgotten she was the next-door neighbor he'd known for nearly twenty years.

Instead, he was seeing a full-grown, woman with a wavy mass of thick black hair and a wide, generous mouth. And when her two dark orbs gazed on him, all Ryan had wanted to do was to sweep her into his arms and forget about everyone and everything. But he hadn't. This was Jessie. His friend.

Or was she?

Ryan had studied her during lunch, looking for signs Jessie felt the same vibes, and, if he wasn't mistaken, she had. There had definitely been a spark of electricity between them that'd had nothing to do with a dazzling evening underneath the stars. Ryan thought he'd ended that attraction. Pursuing the position with Black Crescent should have ensured any fantasy of being with Jessie was crushed, but the spark was still there.

Unfortunately, the attraction he'd felt for Jessie had become like an infection. One he was sure he could get rid of. He mustn't forget that Jessie had ignored him for years by choosing to be with Hugh and his family instead.

He squeezed his eyes shut trying to block out her image. If only he could block her out of his heart.

He hadn't lied when he'd told her he'd had girlfriends. Although the number was small—he was selective in the women he chose to go to bed with—he'd had lovers. None of which held a candle to Jessie, the woman he'd measured them all against. His last girlfriend had told him in no uncertain terms that until he dealt with his unrequited feelings for Jessie, he'd never truly move on with anyone.

Is that why he'd blurted out an invite to Adam's Hampton house? *Was he testing himself? Jessie?* To see if her relationship with Hugh as solid as she portrayed? To see if what they'd felt for each other on the dance floor was real or imagined?

And if he was testing, what result would the weekend produce?

Ryan supposed he would have to wait and see.

So why am I so excited at the prospect of finding out?

Three

"You're not coming home this weekend?" Angela Acosta asked when her daughter called her late in the evening from her office. Jessie was working late, as she always did, and apparently had only stopped to order some sushi for dinner.

"No, Mama. I have plans."

"But's it's July Fourth. I'd planned to have a big family BBQ. Your brother Pete is coming with his girlfriend, Amanda." Jessie could hear the pout in her mother's voice. "Surely, the firm can allow you to take some time off. You're working your fingers to the bone."

"I do have the long weekend off."

"Then why aren't you coming?"

"I have plans," Jessie stated.

"More important than your family?" her mother inquired.

Jessie didn't appreciate the guilt trip her mother was trying to lay on her. She was a dutiful daughter and came home more often than her big brother, so why was she being made to feel bad because she was taking time for herself? Plus, she wasn't too eager for a repeat performance of her last visit. When the Black Crescent article had come out, her father's mood had bottomed out, to say the least. Jessie had been dreading going home and this last-minute invitation for the weekend had provided the perfect excuse.

"I had these plans before I knew you had something planned," Jessie said. "I'm going to the beach with Ryan and some friends."

"Ryan from next door? What about Hugh?"

"What about him?"

"It's not right that you should be off gallivanting with another man when your fiancé is in another country."

"We're not engaged, Mama."

"But that's always been the plan—that you would get married."

"One day."

"Sounds more like no day," Angela said underneath her breath, but Jessie had heard her. And her mother had cause to be concerned. Jessie and Hugh were in trouble. If her weekend with Ryan took a turn, a permanent break might happen sooner than expected.

"Give Daddy my best," Jessie said, quickly rushing off the phone. She didn't want to feel guilty about spending time with Ryan. They were friends. But would they stay that way? She hadn't been able to forget how she'd felt when they'd danced, how her body responded in ways she could only contribute to its awareness of Ryan. His enticing scent had intoxicated her and she recalled feeling as if all the oxygen had been sucked out of her lungs. Her mind was telling her to follow the path she'd chosen, but her body was reminding her how completely dissatisfied she'd been over the years.

Jessie was curious. If they were alone again would she feel the same way?

The more important question is, if I do, will I explore those feelings?

* * *

"Do you really think it's a good idea to play with fire where Jessie's concerned?" Adam McKinley asked when Ryan told him he was bringing Jessie with him to the Hamptons for the weekend.

After settling down with a beer, Ryan had called his best friend once he'd finally made it home from work. "I'm not."

"Who do you think you're talking to?" Adam said on the other end of the line. "I'm the guy who listened to your sob story for years about how this girl never paid an ounce of attention to you. Who pretty much abandoned your friendship after her rich boyfriend's parents paid her high school tuition. Do you recall those conversations?"

"Of course I do." How could Ryan forget? He sounded pathetic. Like a real schmuck, hung up on a girl who paid him no mind. He wasn't that man anymore. "That's not what's happening here."

"Then you're lying to yourself," Adam stated bluntly. "You can't tell me there isn't some part of you hoping this weekend goes differently."

Ryan both hated and appreciated Adam's forthrightness. He was straddling the fence, so he spoke plainly. "I admit I've always wanted Jessie to see me in a different light. Not as a shoulder to cry or lean on, but as a man."

"And if she doesn't? I thought, after the reunion, you were done with wishing and hoping she would see you differently?"

"I was. Hugh came in and Jessie morphed right in front of me, but maybe away from our normal surroundings, she can be free to be herself."

"Free to be with you?"

"Yes."

Adam sighed. "All right, but don't say I didn't warn you."

Seconds later, Ryan looked at the phone in his hand.

Spending the weekend with Jessie was a gamble, but it would enable him to see if the sparks he'd felt weren't one-sided.

It was totally worth risking their twenty-year friendship.

"You realize you've been trying to pack a weekend bag for over an hour," Becca told Jessie as she stared at the pile of clothes on her bed in their two-bedroom apartment in Chelsea when Thursday evening rolled around.

"I know, I know." Jessie sighed heavily. She had left the law firm around 7:00 p.m.—a reasonable hour given she usually stayed until nine, sometimes ten, o'clock—so she could go home to pack for her weekend with Ryan. But it wasn't a weekend with Ryan, per se. It was more like two friends hanging out together. So why was she stressing out over what outfits to bring?

"Then what's the problem?" Becca asked, her eyes glinting with amusement. "I mean you're going with Ryan. I thought you guys were just friends?"

"We are." Jessie lied.

"Are you sure about that?" Becca, sitting on Jessie's bed, looked up at her. "I've never seen you act this way except when you were fretting about Hugh coming for a visit."

Hugh.

Truth be told, Jessie hadn't thought about him in weeks other than when he'd called her about the Black Crescent press conference. And when he'd tried to Skype last night, she'd avoided the call. Pushing the clothes aside, Jessie joined Becca on the bed. "Can I be honest?"

"If you can't be honest with your roomie and friend of nearly a decade, who can you?"

Jessie smiled at the lovable redhead with the brilliant green eyes. Becca had been her roommate since her freshman year at NYU. When they'd met, they'd hit it off instantly. There'd been none of the craziness she might have assumed based on Becca's hair color. Instead, they were like sisters, often trading clothes because they were both a size four. They'd lived together ever since. Becca was a fashion buyer for Bloomingdales and often came home with great finds.

"I've been struggling with some unexpected feelings that have come up with Ryan."

"Did something happen?" Becca asked.

"Not really. Nothing concrete. Except…at our ten-year reunion at Falling Brook a few months back, something changed between us."

"You mean you finally noticed how drop-dead gorgeous he is?"

Jessie stared into Becca's green eyes. "What are you talking about?"

"C'mon, Jessie. You seem to be the only one oblivious to how good-looking Ryan is," Becca replied with a smirk. "Don't you remember how all the girls in the dorm went crazy whenever he came to visit?"

"Really?"

Becca chuckled. "Maybe not. You were too busy making goo-goo eyes at Hugh to notice, but Ryan is quite a catch. And now that he's working at that big investment company, some woman is going to come and snatch him up at any moment. So, if you're just noticing him, you've had your head in the sand. Now is as good a time as any to make your move."

"Becca!"

"I know I mentioned Hugh, but let's be real. You guys have had a long-distance relationship for nearly a decade. You both haven't lived in the same city since you were at prep school. Maybe it's time to let him go and start looking at all your options, including Ryan, who's been right in front of your face this entire time."

"That's not why I'm going to the Hamptons."

Becca raised a brow. "Aren't you?" She motioned to all the strewed clothes on the bed. "The reason you're having such a hard time packing is because you're nervous. You want Ryan to like everything you're in. Or out of." She winked.

Becca was right in that Jessie wanted Ryan to find her attractive. *But did she want more?*

Maybe.

Ryan had invaded her dreams lately and she'd wondered how he'd looked outside of his clothes. The once chubby preteen she'd grown up with had thrown off the baby fat and was lean and trim. And very dangerous to her sensibilities.

Jessie stood. "Help me, then. I need to look my best." There was so much still unsettled. What if Ryan went to work for Black Crescent—the company that had caused her family so much pain and misfortune? And what about her own growing dissatisfaction with her life and wanting to step away from her parents and doing the expected? This weekend would surely be a test to see if she could break out of the mold of her life and embrace all life had to offer.

Ryan leaned against his Porsche 911 Carrera in front of Jessie's brownstone. It was a warm Friday afternoon in early July and, after working half a day, Ryan had returned home to change into a polo shirt and lightweight slacks for the trip to the Hamptons. Now he was waiting for Jessie to come down.

When the door opened to her building, it had been worth the wait. Instead of straightening her hair, Jessie had it in soft waves to her shoulders. She wore a pretty, yellow sundress with flowers all over it, showing off her olive skin.

He met her halfway up the steps and took her bag from her.

"Thanks." She smiled at him and his heart kicked over in his chest.

"No problem."

She glanced at his wheels and back up at him. "I like fast cars. How fast can it go?" she asked, following him to the back of the vehicle while he put her bag in the trunk.

"About 190 miles per hour."

Jessie grinned. "Then I can't wait for our two-hour drive to the Hamptons."

She didn't know the half of it, Ryan thought as he helped her into the vehicle. With the car so low to the ground, he watched Jessie try to climb in without showing too much skin. He closed the door behind her, but not after seeing a nice length of her smooth olive-toned legs.

When he climbed in, he looked over at her. "We aren't driving all the way there."

Jessie's brow furrowed. "Then how are we going to get there? Please tell me we are not taking the shuttle. If we are, I would have worn a more comfortable ensemble."

Ryan chuckled. "We are not taking a shuttle, either."

"Then how are getting there?"

"Helicopter."

Jessie's eyes narrowed as she regarded him. "So, you've been holding out on me."

"What do you mean?"

She eyed him warily. "You've always made it seem like your job was on the low end, yet you drive a Porsche and we're on our way to a helicopter?"

"Your point?"

"How wealthy are you?"

"It's indelicate to ask someone, Jessie," Ryan reprimanded, but he grinned at her. "But to answer your question, I do all right." He was more than all right, having already amassed his first million years ago, but he'd always held off bragging about his successes because he'd wanted to spare Jessie's feelings. He knew how hard it was for her and her parents to scrape by. He'd never wanted to flaunt his wealth.

"Clearly, it's more than that, while I will forever be mired in debt trying to pay off my student loan from law school."

"You'll get there," Ryan said, glancing quickly in her direction before returning his eyes to the road. "I know your work ethic. Failure is not an option for you."

"No, it's not," Jessie responded. "After seeing what happened to my father, I've always been determined to succeed at all costs. And once I make partner, my plan has always been to help my parents."

"And you will. I believe in you."

Jessie smiled and it lit up her entire face. "You always have. And I don't think I've ever told you, thank you."

"For what?"

"For your support. For your friendship. For never giving up on me when maybe I deserved it."

"You're being too hard on yourself. You deserve the best and then some."

They were silent for the remainder of the short ride to the Downtown Manhattan Heliport. After parking his Porsche 911 Carrera, he handed the keys to a gentleman wearing a polo shirt with the Porsche logo. He appeared to have been expecting him.

"What's going on?" she asked Ryan.

"They're going to service the car while I'm away and drop it back at my penthouse in Murray Hill. C'mon." Ryan picked up their bags and guided Jessie across the short distance to the helipad, where a bright red helicopter was waiting to take them to Adam's East Hampton beach house.

Jessie positively buzzed with excitement by his side. "Have you never been on one of these?" Ryan asked with amusement.

She shook her head.

"You've lived in Manhattan for nearly a decade."

"I know, but I've been too busy at the firm to have much time for extracurricular activities."

Ryan spoke with the pilot and, following the taking of several pictures that Jessie just had to have, their bags were loaded and they were ushered inside. After being given earphones so they could talk to each other, the helicopter soared into the air above the Manhattan skyline.

"It's stunning," Jessie said from beside him as they made a sweep around the city and got a view of the Empire State building and 911 Memorial. Soon, they were passing the Statue of Liberty and headed toward the Hamptons in Long Island. Ryan was excited for the weekend ahead and never more so when Jessie reached for his hand and gave it a squeeze.

"Thank you so much for this special treat." Her eyes were brimming with tears. "This is amazing!"

"You're welcome."

They landed at the Southampton Heliport located on the western end of the Meadow Lane peninsula in thirty minutes after taking off from Manhattan.

"I can't believe we flew here," Jessie said once they'd landed and taken off their earphones. "I feel like one of the rich and famous traveling to one of our summer homes."

"Glad I could oblige," Ryan said once he'd hopped out. Given she was wearing a dress and it was quite windy out, Ryan offered his hand so Jessie could hold onto her dress and avoid becoming Marilyn Monroe.

Unfortunately, she lost her footing. But Ryan was there to catch her. His heart raced triple-time as he held her in his arms. When she looked up at him, all Ryan thought about was kissing her pink and delectable lips, but he didn't go for it.

He'd promised himself three months ago that he was done waiting for her to come around to see that *he* was the man for her. One way or another, this weekend would either turn out to be a torture for him to stay away or a temptation he couldn't deny. Regardless, in the end, he would find out where he stood with Jessie.

Four

"Uh, thank you." Jessie's words came out in short, ragged pants. She could hardly think with the feel of Ryan's muscular body pressed so tightly against her own. It made her want to feel all of him. Squeezing her eyes shut, she counted to ten and then slowly disengaged herself. "I didn't realize 'knight in shining armor' was on your résumé."

She tried to make light of the sexual tension coming off Ryan in droves. Jessie was certain if she hadn't pulled away, he would have kissed her.

"Just one of many skills I have you're not privy to."

"Perhaps I'll learn more of them this weekend?" she purred.

Ryan grinned and Jessie realized she was flirting with him. Her *friend*. It seemed strange, yet crazy, sexy cool at the same time.

"Our ride is here." Ryan indicated the black SUV parked nearby, its door being held open. "After you."

Jessie moved toward the vehicle, marveling at how Ryan managed to afford all of this. She'd underestimated how successful he was. Ryan didn't automatically brag to make himself look better, unlike Hugh, who was always quick to tell her about his latest deal and how much money he made. Jessie knew she shouldn't compare the two men, but they were the most important people in her life other than her family.

Speaking of family, she reached inside her purse and shot off a quick text to her mother, advising she'd arrived safely. The next was to Becca, along with a picture of them in front of the helicopter with the line, "Our ride to the Hamptons."

Becca was going to be green with envy.

"Everything okay?" Ryan asked from his side in the SUV.

"Oh, yes." Jessie put her phone away. "I was letting everyone know we arrived. My mother isn't too happy with me."

"Why?"

"Because I'm not spending the holiday weekend with them."

"Oh, I'm sorry. I should have realized. I know you don't get to go home often when you work so hard."

"Do you?"

"Oh, I do," Ryan chuckled. "But probably not nearly as much as I should. There's something about sleeping in your old room with all your teenage posters that feels kind of wrong."

"Your parents haven't changed it?"

He laughed. "No, and I've no idea why. Maybe Mom thinks if she keeps them long enough, my brothers and I will revert back to children."

"I miss your mom," Jessie said. Marilyn Hathaway was an amazing woman. Jessie had always looked up to her because, not only was she a principal, but a mother of three boys. Mrs. Hathaway made the "being a working mother thing" look easy and had convinced Jessie that one day she, too, could have it all.

"You know you can call her or stop by anytime. Mom has an open-door policy."

"Thank you. I might have to do that."

"Here we are," Ryan said as the SUV drove up a cul-de-sac to the wide gravel driveway of a big, classic, shingle-sided home with a large wraparound front porch. Several cars were already parked on the drive, she noticed as Ryan exited first and helped her out.

Seconds later, the grand front door opened almost instantaneously and a tall man with dark hair and a wide smile, wearing board shorts and a Columbia University T-shirt, wrapped Ryan in a big hug. Jessie remembered Adam; he'd been Ryan's roommate in college. But given they'd been at separate universities, her and Adam's paths hadn't crossed much. Jessie regretted that. "It's good to see you, man," Adam said to Ryan.

"You, too," Ryan returned. "You remember Jessie."

Adam walked toward her with open arms and gathered her in a hug. "Jessie, it's good to see you again. Glad you could make it to my humble abode."

"Welcome!" said a gorgeous brunette as she bounced down the steps to join them. She had to be nearly six feet, matching Adam in height, and was wearing a bikini top and cut-off jean shorts. She had long, flowing, dark brown hair that Jessie would kill for. "Name's Tia."

Jessie accepted her hand for a shake. "Pleasure to meet you."

"Let's show our guests where they'll be staying, honey." She looked at Adam. "Then a refreshment after traveling."

"I would love a drink," Ryan stated, but Jessie wasn't so sure. Something told her she was going to need to stay on her toes.

* * *

"There's only one bedroom?" Jessie asked.

After the McKinleys had given them a tour of the house with its double-height foyer, dark polished-wood floors, white interior with moldings, bright, open floor plan with views of the beach, and a chef's kitchen, they'd led them up the grand staircase to a palatial guest suite with a coffered ceiling. The king-size bed was turquoise and white with starfish and a white shag rag.

"Yes, I'm sorry." Tia shrugged. "I assumed when Ryan said he was bringing a friend that you were 'together.'"

She saw Ryan glare at Adam. "Adam, a word outside."

"I hope this won't be a problem." Tia glanced at her husband's retreating figure and then at Jessie. "I mean… if you guys are platonic, I'm sure Ryan won't mind sleeping on the couch."

"We're friends," Jessie responded.

"Really?" Tia raised a brow. At Jessie's nod, she amended, "Why can't you share a bed?"

Because Jessie was having a hard time keeping her hands to herself. *How was she supposed to do that if the object of her affection was lying a few inches away?*

"Adam!" Ryan yelled as he followed his friend downstairs to the kitchen where Adam was headed for a slew of alcoholic beverages on the counter.

"What would you like?" Adam asked, ignoring Ryan's foul mood. "I've got vodka, rum, tequila and a darn good brandy I got from my dad last Christmas after I secured a big deal at the company."

"Are you going to ignore the elephant in the room?" Ryan knew his friend wasn't dense. "You knew Jessie and I would need two rooms. Yet you deliberately put us in one."

Adam pointed his index finger at Ryan. "Don't look at

me like that. I didn't do it on purpose. Tia wanted to invite another couple, so I figured since the two of you are—" he used his fingers to make quotation marks "—just friends, there really wouldn't be an issue. You told me you were done."

Ryan turned to make sure no one was listening and moved closer. "I am, but I don't need the added temptation of sharing a bed with her."

"And I'm sorry," Adam said with a devilish grin, "but all the rooms in the inn are full, my friend. You're just going to have to suck it up."

Ryan punched a fist into his hand and moved toward Adam.

Adam backed away. "Hey, look at it this way. I'm helping your cause. The close quarters will help you determine if you really are done with Jessie as you claim."

Ryan would have preferred not to chance his luck, but he was out of options. "Fix me a brandy, will you? I think I'm in for a bumpy weekend."

Ryan stayed downstairs drinking with Adam for half an hour until he thought it was safe to go upstairs.

When he did, he found Jessie in the bathroom with the door closed. Her weekend bag had been unpacked and was tucked away in a corner while the king-size bed loomed in the middle of the room.

He sipped his drink. He didn't know how he was going to sleep next to Jessie for the next three nights without kissing her, touching her, making love to her. The almost kiss a few months ago and that moment by the helicopter had cracked something open in him. On the one hand, he wanted to explore what they could have. On the other, he knew, like Adam said, he was playing with fire. Downstairs, Adam told him he and Tia had invited a few other singles to their dinner at a local restaurant. Perhaps he should keep his options open and not be too quick to leap into something with Jessie when she'd only given him some knowing glances and looks, but she hadn't exactly stuck her tongue down his mouth to show him she wanted him.

The bathroom door opened and Jessie emerged in the itsy bittiest shorts he'd ever seen and a halter top revealing a smooth expanse of shoulder and a deep V that revealed the swell of her small but round breasts.

Ryan swallowed. "What are you wearing?"

Jessie smiled and Ryan felt his groin swell. "It's hot out and I wanted to get comfortable. Dinner isn't for another few hours." She came toward him, took the tumbler out of his hand, placed it to her generous mouth and took a sip.

"Strong." She handed it back to him. "I think I need something sweet and fruity."

What Ryan saw in front of him could certain qualify as both. And if he had his wish, he'd be indulging all weekend.

"Are you coming?"

Ryan blinked and realized Jessie was standing in the doorway. "No, you go ahead. I'll change, as well."

"All right. I'll see you downstairs."

Ryan breathed a sigh of relief when the door closed. He sat on the accent chair on the opposite side of the room and inhaled deeply. He had to calm himself, because if he didn't, he'd be hauling Jessie back into the bedroom.

Jessie was thankful for a few moments to herself while Ryan stayed in the guest room. When he'd been downstairs, she'd taken a moment to gather herself. She'd talked herself off the ledge about sharing a bedroom with Ryan. Like Tia said, they were two adults. Surely they could *platonically* share a bed together for a few days.

But then Ryan had come into the room and the way his eyes raked hers, Jessie was starting to believe she might be in trouble.

"Jessie, come on over." Adam caught sight of her in the foyer. "Have a drink."

Smiling, she walked over to join him and his wife at the bar and slid onto a bar stool. Tia was busy putting out chips and salsa on the countertop.

"What can I get you?" Adam inquired.

Jessie motioned to the pitcher of red liquid with fruit. "Is that sangria?"

"It's my specialty," Tia answered. "Would you like some?"

"Would love some," Jessie replied. "This place is great." She spun around and looked over the expansive living room with its wood-burning fireplace. She also liked that she could see the hexagon-shaped breakfast room and high-backed chairs that went with the wood table. The kitchen was spectacular, complete with stainless-steel appliances.

"Thank you," Adam said. "Here's your sangria." He handed her a glass and then raised his beer to tip against her glass. *"¡Salud!"*

"¡Salud!"

The doorbell rang and Adam went to answer it. Another couple came in, waving as Ryan rambled down the stairs. While Adam helped them with their bags, Ryan waved Jessie over to meet them.

"Jessie…" Ryan slid his arm around Jessie's shoulders. It was a casual but somewhat proprietary gesture. "I'd like you to meet my good friends, Mike and Corinne."

The couple complemented each other with their pale skin and dark hair. Corinne was tall and willowy with striking gray-blue eyes. Mike had a slim, athletic frame, a bald head and brown eyes. Husband and wife were both casually dressed in shorts and T-shirts for the weekend.

"Great to meet you both," Jessie said.

"I'll show you your room," Adam chimed in. "Follow me." He led them up the stairs.

"What are you drinking?" Ryan asked.

"Homemade sangria." Jessie licked her lips and found Ryan watching the movement. She quickly stepped out of his embrace, toward the kitchen where Tia had set out some fruit and cheese. Jessie reached for a cube of cheddar cheese, desperate to do something to escape the sexual tension in the air.

"Great spread," Ryan commented to Tia, who was busy arranging hummus and veggies on a platter.

"Why, thank you." Tia smiled. "I love to entertain, but this will tide you over until dinner. Adam made reservations at his favorite spot in town."

Eventually Adam, Mike and Corinne joined them downstairs, and they all drank and nibbled on the munchies Tia had laid out.

"It's great to finally meet the infamous Jessie," Mike commented as they stood around in the kitchen. "Ryan has talked about you often, but were beginning to think you were a figment of his imagination."

The entire group laughed, but Ryan didn't appear as amused as the rest of his friends. "Oh, I'm very much real," Jessie replied. "But I admit I've been a bit busy trying to get my law career off the ground that I've taken this one—" she motioned to Ryan at her side "—for granted. But not anymore." She winked at him.

And she hoped he knew she meant it. Jessie had recognized that she'd turned her back on her oldest friend, who been there when she'd scraped her knee or fallen off her bike. Or when she'd cried when her parents had made her get braces, even though Ryan had soon been sporting a set, as well. He'd always been by her side and this weekend it was her turn.

"To friendship!" Adam held up his beer bottle and everyone raised their glasses.

Jessie glanced up to find Ryan's eyes on her and, once

again, her insides clenched. She bit down on her lip and forced herself to remain calm. Surely she could handle a few hours in his company at dinner, in a public place surrounded by his friends? Resolution filled her. By the end of the evening, she would have tamped down on her desire for Ryan, otherwise they wouldn't be able to share a bed together.

The trendy seafood restaurant they went to later that evening was great and so was the company. Their group of eight consisted of two couples—Adam and Tia, Mike and Corinne—and four singles—Ryan, Jessie, Dean and Lauren. Dean and Lauren had arrived shortly before they'd left the house. They were both blond and blue-eyed—Jessie could see why Tia and Adam were trying to hook the two of them up.

The food was passed family-style across the table and the wine flowed freely. Over dinner, Jessie discovered they'd gone to Columbia with Ryan, which was how they all knew each other. Despite her going to NYU, they didn't make Jessie feel like the odd woman out. She couldn't remember a time when she was so relaxed and at ease, but she supposed she'd always felt that way in Ryan's presence. He had a natural way about him that was reassuring.

Corinne commented on how Jessie and Ryan suited each other. "You say you're just friends, but you guys finish each other's sentences and you know what food the other likes."

Ryan hadn't even bothered passing the peel-and-eat shrimp appetizer to Jessie because he knew Jessie didn't care for shrimp, though she'd killed her king crab entrée. And when Tia had given Ryan the sautéed Brussel sprouts with bacon, Jessie commented on how he hated the vegetable.

"They're like an old married couple," Mike said from Corinne's side.

"Was that supposed to be a put-down?" Ryan asked with a laugh, placing his arm along the back of Jessie's chair, which she seemingly didn't mind. "I think there's something to be said for knowing another person, better than they maybe even know themselves."

Jessie turned to look at Ryan, but she couldn't read his expression. She glanced around the table and the others were exchanging knowing glances. *Did they know something she didn't?* She felt exposed.

"So how did your job interview go with Black Crescent?" Dean suddenly inquired of Ryan.

Jessie rolled her eyes upward. She was thankful that Dean changed the topic—she'd wanted to be off the hot seat—but didn't like the new focus of conversation.

"I'm surprised you want to man that damaged ship," Mike said. "I mean didn't the original owner, Vernon Somebody, run off with everyone in town's money?"

"Yeah, Vernon Lowell pretty much bankrupted the entire town," Dean replied. "What gives? Why would you want any part of it?"

Ryan looked at Jessie. Was her face burning because she could feel herself becoming flushed? He had to know she hated to talk about this. "Because I can change everyone's perception."

"If anyone can, it's Ryan," Adam said from across the table.

Jessie sensed Adam was trying to help by boosting Ryan's ego, but she didn't care. Vernon Lowell's machinations had left her family penniless and they were discussing it over dessert as if it meant nothing. Unsure how much more she could take, Jessie fidgeted in her chair, eager to move on to another topic.

"Why is Joshua Lowell leaving anyway?" Mike asked. "Or is he exactly like his father and turning tail and running?"

"Rumor is he has a lovechild out there somewhere. They could be worth a lot of money since his father probably has it all secretly hidden somewhere," Dean stated.

Ryan must have sensed her unease, because he said, "Does it matter? It's all conjecture, anyway, and shouldn't be believed."

Jessie had had enough. "If you'll excuse me." She pushed out her chair quickly and rushed out of the room. Instead of heading for the bathroom, she went to a side door. She heard footsteps behind her but kept going.

Once outside, she bent over and breathed in deeply. The door opened and she saw men's shoes. She didn't have to stand up to know Ryan had followed her.

"Are you okay?"

Jessie straightened and narrowed her gaze at him. "What do you think?"

He glanced beside him. "I'm sorry about that. None of my friends know about your family's past with Black Crescent. I've never broken your confidence and shared it with anyone."

"Not even Adam?"

"No."

Jessie had to admit she was impressed because, over the course of the evening, she'd seen how close the two men were. "Thank you, but I don't think even you get it."

"Get what?"

"How hard it is to one day to wake up and find all your money is gone along with all the dreams and hopes you had for yourself and your family. That's what my father felt. You have no idea what it's like to walk a day in my shoes, to endure the whispers and pitying glances from your classmates who know your family has literally been wiped out by the snap of a finger."

"Jessie…" Ryan made to come toward her, but Jessie held out her hand.

"Black Crescent changed the course of my life, my future, influencing the decisions I've made. And ever since that anniversary article came out, I've had to relive the most difficult time of my entire life. I thought I was behind it, but hearing your friends laughing and joking in there about how Vernon destroyed our town... Well, it didn't affect them. It affected me." She pounded her chest.

"I get it, sweetheart." This time, Ryan moved until he was a few inches away. She saw him hesitate for a second before putting his arm around her.

"Maybe a little." She leaned into him and accepted the comfort he was offering, "But haven't you wondered why I live in New York?" She pushed away slightly to look up at him and felt tears leaking from her lids. "Because I can be anonymous. Everyone in Falling Brook knows my sorry history, but in the city, I can be someone different. I've reinvented myself."

"Yes, you have," Ryan said, wiping the tears from her cheeks with the pad of his thumb. "But you have nothing to be ashamed of. What happened wasn't your fault. You were a child."

"I know that here—" Jessie pointed to her temple "—but not here." She patted her heart.

"You've accomplished so much, Jessie," Ryan stated. "Don't lose sight of that. Despite everything that happened to you, you finished college and law school. You're a lawyer for Christ's sake! I'm sorry to tell you, but not every one of our Falling Brook classmates fared as well."

Jessie thought back to their reunion. Ryan was right. Jessie had been surprised at the strides she'd made in the last ten years over her peers. "You're saying all this because you're my friend."

His expression was dark and serious. "No, I'm not. I'm saying it because you're *you*."

Before she could guess his next action, Ryan hooked an arm around her waist and pulled her tight against him.

Jessie looked up into his eyes and was lost. How could she have denied herself this magic when she wanted him? She pulled his head down so his mouth was just above hers. Then she pressed her lips against his and it unleashed a longing deep in her body. She grabbed his biceps as her overloaded senses took in that she was kissing Ryan. His mouth was smooth, questing with the right amount of pressure. Glorious, heady sensations took over Jessie, burning her skin from the inside out. Ryan devoured her mouth as if he was in the desert sand and she was his water.

When his tongue teased her lips apart and swept inside her mouth, her body took over and Jessie began kissing him back. She followed his lead as he delved deeper into the heat of her mouth. Their tongues slid along each other's in an erotic duel. Her nipples turned erect against the fabric of her dress and she restlessly moved against him, wanting more. Ryan pressed her tightly to him and she felt the swell of his manhood.

A loud cough from behind startled them, causing Ryan to suddenly release her. Jessie, embarrassed to see a restaurant worker had stumbled across them, immediately rushed through the doors until she found the ladies' room.

"Jessie, wait!" Ryan called after her, but she didn't stop. She needed distance. *Now.*

Ryan's head fell back against the wall of the restaurant as his brain struggled to process what had just happened.

He'd kissed *Jessie*!

He'd always felt that, if given the chance, they could be good together. He hadn't been wrong. The heat they'd created had been nothing short of sensational. He hadn't been thinking when he'd closed the distance between them and taken her mouth in an insistent kiss that left no room for hesitation. She'd responded when he'd slid his tongue inside her mouth and met his tongue with her own. The way she'd moved against him would have made a strong man weak.

The feel, the taste of her on his mouth, was like forbidden fruit in the Garden of Eden and he'd sampled. The irrational part of his brain wanted to know how far they would have gone if they hadn't been interrupted. But they had been and Jessie had run like her pants were on fire.

Where did they go from here?

Five

Jessie stared at her reflection in the mirror of the restaurant's bathroom and what she saw there scared her. Her pupils were dilated, her cheeks were flushed and her breaths were coming in shallow gulps. What she saw was desire. Pure and strong. She'd thought she was immune and could control it. *Had her desire for Ryan always been there waiting to emerge if presented the opportunity?* How else to explain that they'd made out?

She closed her eyes and attempted to calm her nerves, but she couldn't. No matter how hard she tried, she couldn't forget Ryan's mouth on hers. The *taste* of him. The scent of his cologne and the warmth of his skin through his button-down shirt. It was all right there in vivid high definition in her mind.

She wouldn't be able to put him in a box and tuck it away as she'd done with that almost kiss on reunion night. She'd done her best to act as if it had been an anomaly. A moment in time in which they'd both been carried away. But tonight was different. She'd willingly participated in the kiss and, if they hadn't been interrupted, she'd have asked for more because it was *that* good. The attraction she'd felt for Ryan blew her mind.

Jessie couldn't recall a time in which she'd felt that way when Hugh kissed her. She'd never experienced the all-consuming lust she'd felt in those few minutes she'd shared with Ryan in any of her encounters with Hugh. Hugh was the only man Jessie had ever been with. Although there been other opportunities in college and again in law school, Jessie had remained true to Hugh. Plus, the intimacy she'd shared with Hugh had always been pleasant enough, but there had never been fireworks like the kind she'd felt just now with Ryan.

She knew she had to go back to the table with Ryan and the other couples and feign that what had happened, hadn't. How was she supposed to act? *How would he?* She knew they needed to talk, but she wasn't sure what she would say. She would have to fake it until she made it.

Summoning all her courage, Jessie left the restroom.

Ryan was waiting for her in the corridor. His hungry eyes soaked in hers and her stomach wanted to melt in a puddle, but it didn't. "Are you okay?" he inquired.

She nodded. Her vocal cords were unable to speak.

"About—"

She stopped him and put her fingertips to his mouth. "Can we not analyze it right now and get back to the dinner?"

His eyes shuttered at her dismissal and she recognized that she'd hurt him. "If that's what you want."

"I do."

"Very well, then." He motioned for her to precede him. "After you."

When they returned to the table, everyone glanced up at them. *Were they all assuming she and Ryan had snuck away to make out?* Because they'd be right.

"We were wondering where you two had disappeared

to," Adam said with a bemused smile. "We're going to head back to the house, if you're ready?"

"We are," Jessie and Ryan said simultaneously.

The group laughed because once again they were in unison, like everyone had teased earlier. And maybe they were, but on that terrace, their relationship shifted and there was no going back.

The ride in Adam's Escalade was uncomfortable to say the least. Ryan didn't attempt to make polite chitchat. When he'd met Jessie in the restaurant corridor, he'd hoped they would talk. He'd known it was an inconvenient time, but he'd hoped that maybe she'd finally admit they should pursue whatever it was between them. But instead he'd been shot down. Jessie wanted to sweep the kiss underneath the rug and he was pissed off about it.

When they made it to the house, Jessie rushed off upstairs. Dean and Lauren went to their respective rooms while Mike and Corinne departed quickly. Ryan figured the married couples wanted to be alone, because Adam and Tia were right behind them, but he stopped Adam on the steps.

"I'll be right up, babe," Adam told Tia.

"I'll be waiting." She winked at her husband and left the two men alone.

Adam turned to Ryan. "What's up? As you can see—" he glanced up the stairs "—I have a hot date."

Ryan grinned. "I won't keep you. I just need some linens and a pillow. I'm going to sleep on the couch."

"Really? The vibe I got when you guys came back to the table led me to believe…"

Ryan rolled his eyes. "Nothing is going to happen. So, if you don't mind, I need those linens."

Adam stared at him for several beats. "All right, I'll be right back." He ran up the stairs and Ryan followed him.

He would only be in his and Jessie's room long enough to get something to sleep in and return downstairs.

When he arrived, Jessie was in the bathroom, brushing her teeth. She had already changed into some sort of matching pajama set with a camisole and shorts. Had to be some sort of record for getting undressed. Guess she wanted to be sure she was nowhere around when he came in. *What did she think was going to happen? That he would jump her bones the minute they were alone?* He'd gotten the message: their first kiss had been a mistake.

Ryan walked to the doorway. "I'm going to sleep on the couch downstairs."

Jessie eyes grew wide and then she rinsed and wiped her mouth with a towel from a nearby rack. "That's probably best."

He glared at her. So that's the way she wanted to play this? Had the kiss meant nothing to her? He most certainly was having trouble remembering why he'd insisted to himself and his friends any attraction he'd felt was over.

"All right. Well…good night. I'll see you in the morning." Ryan grabbed his toiletry bag and some shorts and a T-shirt from his suitcase, and left the room.

He ambled down the stairs and found a pillow and a blanket waiting for him on the sofa. He stared at the midsize sofa. It didn't look very comfortable and he was not excited to sleep on it, but what choice did he have?

After using the half bath to brush his teeth, Ryan came back to the living room and proceeded to prepare himself a makeshift bed on the sofa. He didn't bother changing. It was going to be a long night anyway. Lying down, he stared up at the ceiling, reliving the kiss with Jessie in his mind.

The kiss had warmed him. He'd felt the scorch of her lips on his and the taste of her on his tongue. Sleep would be a long time coming because he doubted he could rid his mind of the feeling of holding the woman he'd always wanted in his arms. Their first kiss was everything he'd dreamed of and more. Now his emotions felt pummeled because of Jessie's refusal to acknowledge they could be so much more.

Ryan sat upright. Maybe some ocean air would help him find peace and the sleep he needed. But first he was going for a glass of brandy. He found Adam's favorite sitting on the counter with the other alcohol. After pouring himself more than two thumbs in a tumbler, Ryan made his way through the French doors and out onto the wraparound terrace.

It was dark, but there were thousands of tiny stars in the sky and, with the full moon, it was enough for Ryan to see his drink. He leaned against the balustrade and sipped his brandy.

He didn't know how long he was out there, musing over the night's events, when the creek of the floorboards forced him to stand upright.

As if he'd conjured her up, Jessie was standing by the French doors. His eyes ate her up, loving the sight of her shapely legs in shorts that barely reached her lush thighs.

"Go to bed, Jessie." He turned away and stared back at the dark night sky. It was late and he wasn't in the mood to dissect the kiss, their relationship, or anything else. If she didn't go right now, he wasn't sure of his next actions.

"I can't. We need to talk."

The words every man dreaded.

Ryan turned to face her. "You first."

Jessie felt the anger emanating from Ryan and knew it was directed at her for not confronting the kiss earlier. She'd run because she'd been too afraid to face what had happened. She'd tried to put the mask on, layer by layer, but had failed miserably. Was it any surprise that when she'd tried to go to bed, she couldn't sleep? She'd tossed and turned until she'd finally given up the ghost and realized that until she settled things with Ryan, sleep would elude her.

Jessie had come downstairs to find him, but not before she'd shocked herself by taking the spare condom she kept in her purse and placed it in her pocket. Was she hoping for something more? Maybe. But when she'd seen the empty couch, her heart had lurched. She'd wondered if she'd pushed Ryan away enough to make him leave, but instead she'd found him on the deck looking out over the ocean, his button-down shirt nearly undone and still wearing his jeans.

"You're angry with me."

"Does that surprise you?"

She shook her head. "No. I suppose not. I deserve it for being a coward." The kiss had left her feeling vulnerable and exposed.

"Go on." He sipped the drink in his hand.

"The kiss caught me off-guard. We've always been friends, but everything has changed and…"

"That scares you," Ryan finished. "Do I scare you? Or is this because you're still with Hugh?"

"I—I'm not with Hugh anymore. We're on a break."

"A break?" Ryan asked, straightening. "Since when?"

Jessie walked over to him at the balustrade and glanced at the dark ocean.

"Jessie?"

She turned to him and his gaze focused on her. "Since the night of the reunion."

Ryan's eyes darkened and Jessie forced herself to swallow. "Why didn't you tell me?"

Jessie cocked her head to one side. "Do you really have to ask me? Because *everyone*, especially my parents, think Hugh and I are supposed to be together. But they couldn't be more wrong."

"How long have you been feeling this way?"

Jessie shrugged. "A while. I've been restless and unsure

of our relationship for some time… But I've felt so ruled by Black Crescent's fall and my parents' expectations to marry a guy like Hugh, from an established wealthy family, that I've pushed aside my own feelings. And when we nearly kissed at the reunion, it threw me for a loop. Just like tonight did. I couldn't continue seeing him if I had feelings for another man."

Ryan's gaze locked with hers and then he drew her to him. Pinning her against him, his mouth sought hers. Sky and earth tilted on its axis for Jessie as Ryan's lips parted hers in a kiss that was everything she'd ached for but hadn't realized she needed. And in that devastating moment, Jessie knew that she would die if she couldn't be with him. Is that why, in a spur-of-the-moment decision, she'd put a condom in her pocket?

When Ryan pulled away, he held both sides of her face and peered into her eyes. "Tell me to stop, Jessie, because I don't know if I can."

"I don't want you to stop, Ryan. I need you."

He leaned his forehead against hers, his lips a fraction away. "You're temptation for even the strongest man. You have no idea how much I want to make love to you."

She gasped and, that very instant, his mouth was back on hers. Jessie didn't have any doubts. She wanted Ryan. She didn't know if she always had. She did know that in this moment she had to have him. His fingers tangled in her hair and brought her forward to his mouth. Oh how she wanted that mouth. That beautiful mouth.

They kissed and kissed and then kissed again. He pulled away a few times to move from her lips to kiss his way down her throat to her neck, but then he'd return to her mouth as if he couldn't keep away.

Sensation engulfed her as she concentrated wholly on Ryan and vice versa. It was crazy to think she was on fire for her friend, but she was. The emotions she felt were

real. Jessie melted from the onslaught and didn't realize
he was walking them somewhere. With his hands framing
her face and without breaking the kiss, he'd moved Jessie
up against the wall of the house. Their mouths opened so
their tongues could taste each other deeply. His hand slid
up and down her body until Jessie found her pajama camisole being lifted over her head and tossed aside.

He jerked his head back to look at her and Jessie basked
in his openly hungry gaze. He wanted her and she wanted
his mouth roving over every inch of her. What had started
from a simple kiss on the dance floor three months ago
had turned into hot, heavy need. Jessie ached and the only
one who could soothe her was Ryan—and only if he was
buried deep inside her.

She wanted to shout in delight when his hands finally
encircled her breasts. Raw need ricocheted through her.
With a feathered touch, Ryan skimmed the undersides and
swell of her breasts before treating them to the touch of his
lips and fingertips. They turned to peaks with his sensuous
suckling and the cries echoing through the night weren't
someone else's, but her own. Never had her breasts received
such attention with a deliberate attempt to bring her pleasure. And he did. Ryan treated the other breast with equal
attention and Jessie was lost, but not for long.

It was her turn to seize the moment. When he lifted his
head, she quickly set about unbuttoning the last few buttons of his shirt. She heard Ryan catch his breath as she slid
the shirt down his shoulders and biceps until it fell with a
soft swoosh to the deck.

Jessie's greedy eyes looked their feel of his torso. Ryan
had an amazing body, broad at the shoulders and slim at
the hips, with defined, long muscles. They weren't overly
developed or bulging, but would be enough for her to hold
on to. He had an amazing ab eight-pack with a sprinkling
of hair that arrowed below his washboard stomach to his

jeans. Jessie couldn't help licking her lips. She wanted him in every way possible. She couldn't wait to feel him and to experience everything he could give her—release and completion.

She reached out and touched him. He was all heat and muscle, and she trembled with excitement at the feel of his skin on her hands. She ran her fingers through the hair on his chest and then lower to smooth down his abs. When she reached the waistband of his jeans, she fiddled with the snap until she could push his zipper and jeans down in one fell swoop, allowing his erection to spring free.

He stepped out of his jeans and her hand grasped his straining length. She stroked him gently. His nostrils flared and he choked a growl when she cupped and stroked him with both hands. "You're killing me, Jessie."

She wanted to do more, but her body was wet and damp and readying itself for his possession. She released him and, placing a hand on the back of his head, pulled him in for another dizzying kiss.

"I need you now," she murmured into his lips.

Ryan was spinning out of control. This was all moving too fast. Hell, he couldn't remember if he even had protection in his wallet. *Did he have one?* Think. But his brain was mush because kissing Jessie—the woman he'd adored from afar for nearly two decades—was making rational thought impossible.

He should regroup, slow the pace, but he didn't. Instead, reaching for her shorts, he quickly snatched them down her hips and dropped them to the floor. He was stunned to realize Jessie wasn't wearing any underwear. He had complete and unfettered access to her. For a second, his mind blanked. Luckily, Ryan knew his way around a woman's body and how to pleasure them. Satisfy them. Ryan was determined Jessie would be when he was done with her.

He dropped to his knees and, reaching for her curvy bottom, pulled her to his mouth. He teased the cleft of her sex with his tongue. He lifted his head and his eyes glowed when they connected with hers. "You're wet for me."

She nodded. "And you are hard for me."

Ryan grinned and then he made her even wetter. He used his fingers to tease, swirl and stroke her sensitive numb. He knew Jessie wanted more, but instead he worked her with his fingers, going faster and faster. She opened her legs, stretching for him and riding his hand until he replaced those fingers with his mouth.

Jessie cried out at the lick of his tongue on her clitoris. So he continued kissing, licking and flicking her with his tongue. When she bucked, he added his digits again and sucked so deep on her nub that she came almost immediately. He rode the wave with her, his breath coming in unsteady gasps because he'd been right there with her. The speed they were going left him no doubt on the direction they were heading, but he wasn't sure about protection.

He rose off his haunches to fasten his mouth on hers for a quick searing kiss and then lifted his head. "I don't have a condom."

"Check…my…shorts," Jessie said on an uneven breath.

"What?" He was stunned, but leaned down to grab up her pajama bottoms that he'd tossed aside and indeed found a single condom packet in the pocket.

"Jessie Acosta! Did you come down here with the sole intention of seducing me?"

She blushed and looked away.

"Don't do that," Ryan said, clasping her chin in his hand and forcing her to look at him. "You wanted me. Don't be afraid to admit that."

She nodded. "I do, so don't make me wait another minute. Or do you need my help putting that thing on?"

He smirked. "No, I think I got this." Within seconds,

he'd sheathed himself, placed her hands on his shoulders and lifted her off the floor.

"Hook your legs around my hips." He knew he was being demanding, but Ryan was at the edge of control.

When she complied and wrapped herself around him, clinging to his shoulders, he brought them together in one slow, deliberate thrust.

Jessie's eyes snared his and she didn't look away, not even as he went deeper with the second thrust all while his hands were under her bottom, supporting her. Instead, she moved to meet him and a shudder went straight through Ryan. "Yes, babe. Just like that," he said through gritted teeth as he righted his balance so he could bear his weight and hers.

God, she felt so good. So wet. So right for him.

She wiggled and slid until she'd taken him to hilt. *Sweet Jesus!* This was going to be over before it began. Sucking in air, he fought to hold back and kissed her again, but Jessie was in control now. She was riding him and his grip grew stronger, his kisses became more frantic, trailing her face and down her neck as she rocked against him. Her breath was coming short and fast—faster and faster until she was panting.

If this was the road to heaven, Ryan didn't mind being on it.

Jessie was having an out-of-body experience. Her legs were curled tightly around Ryan's hips in a viselike grip. She'd never felt so completely and utterly abandoned during sex before. With Ryan, she could revel in her desire for him and he allowed her to do so without claiming victory for himself.

She whimpered in delight when he pushed inside, further and further, until her entire body absorbed him and the tension snapped. Waves of pleasure radiated through her, threatening to swallow her whole. Yet still she wanted *more, more, more.*

She coiled tighter around him and Ryan growled as he pumped up to meet her, supporting them both. When her screams threatened to wake the entire house, he grasped her by her hair and pulled her mouth to his in a hard and hungry kiss. Jessie gave as good as she got, because she craved this man with every cell of her body. Her lips weaved around his and her tongue sought entry into his mouth, fusing them closer and closer together.

She took all she could while demanding more. She devoured him and in return she found the purest pleasure she'd ever had her entire life. The flames inside her erupted when Ryan reached between them to press his thumb on that sensitive nub between her legs. She gave up the fight when her third orgasm surged through her, tightening her muscles around him as a bright light exploded behind her eyes. She clutched Ryan's shoulders and heard his growl of satisfaction as he, too, reached the peak of the mountain and came tumbling back down to earth.

Six

Ryan awoke the next morning in the guest room he and Jessie were sharing. They were sprawled across the bed with the covers and pillows strewed across it. Ryan's entire body was effused with satiation. He slid his hand through the spill of Jessie's hair lying like a silken cloud on his chest. She was draped over him after he'd devoted the morning hours to exploring her delectable body. He'd been fascinated by her reactions and her unabashed responsiveness. Jessie wasn't afraid to show how much she enjoyed making love with him. In fact, she'd been as eager as he was.

He'd been shocked when she'd told him of the condom in her pocket. That meant she'd come looking for him last night with the express intent of taking their relationship to the next level. She'd wanted *this. Him.*

Being with Jessie had been urgent and explosive. Thinking about the way her breasts had jounced up and down against him as she rode him was a turn-on. She'd welcomed him, wrapping her tight little body around him until he'd detonated like a rocket. He was afraid he'd become addicted because the more they did, the more he wanted. He wanted to obliterate any memory of Hugh in her mind and he was sure he had. They'd made love so many times, they'd finished a second pack of condoms.

Was it because making love with Jessie had been the culmination of years of wanting? Being with her was the most satisfying sexual experience of his life, more than any other lover he'd ever been with. It felt different. *Had he always known that?* Is that why he'd run as soon as Hugh came back into the picture? Or why he'd purposely set his sights on the Black Crescent job to alienate Jessie and ensure they'd never have a chance?

Jessie shifted to roll away but Ryan stopped her. "You're awake."

She nodded shyly.

"You okay?" He didn't know if he was asking for himself or for her. All he knew was that the closeness and intimacy they'd shared in the wee hours of the night and into this morning was real. Yet he didn't want to get ahead of himself and think it was more profound than it was. Yet he couldn't deny that, spectacular sex aside, Jessie meant something to him and always would.

"Yes."

"Any regrets?"

Jessie slid up his chest and, to his surprise and delight, swept her lips over his. Ryan didn't realize he'd been holding his breath waiting for the answer. When she lifted her head, her palm caressed his cheek.

"Ryan, last night was amazing. Incredible. Wonderful. I don't know how many more adjectives you need for me to describe it. I mean…" She glanced down and played with several hairs on his chest. "I never knew it could be that exciting, fun, *explosive*." She grinned.

"Neither did I, but I guess it's based on chemistry."

"Which we seem to have in spades." Jessie glanced at

the clock. It read 10:00 a.m. "You realize we've been in bed for hours. What must your friends think?"

"They'll think we're grown adults who hooked up."

"Is that all we are?" Jessie asked expectantly.

"That depends. What do you want, Jessie?" Ryan asked. "I don't want to be your backup plan because things between you and Hugh have fallen apart and you need a soft landing."

Jessie sat upright, taking the duvet cover with her to cover her small breasts. "That's not what this is."

"I'm free, single and unencumbered," Ryan said.

"So am I."

He eyed her suspiciously.

"I admit, I may not be ready to jump into something serious. I enjoyed last night with you, Ryan, and I don't regret it. But we have crossed the line from friendship into something more."

"And?"

"I'm okay with seeing where this goes if you are."

He grinned. "I'm game."

"Good—" she threw off the duvet cover "—because I'd like to experience more of it."

Ryan raised a brow. "Oh, would you?"

She grinned mischievously. "Oh, absolutely."

Jessie stared at Ryan from behind her Guess sunglasses. He was playing football with Adam, Mike and Dean in the sand while the ladies—Jessie, Tia, Corinne and Lauren— were on their way to a great tan. He was bare-chested and wearing a pair of knee-length board shorts and all Jessie could think about was how soon they could go back to the bedroom.

It had damn near taken an act of God to get them out of there to begin with. They hadn't made it downstairs until nearly noon because they'd shared a long, hot shower wherein they'd both given and received pleasure. Jessie was on a natural high because sex with Ryan made her feel powerful, beautiful and bolder than she'd ever been in her life.

How was it that her supervixen urges were sky-high with Ryan, but nonexistent with Hugh? Hugh had commented on her lack of sex drive whenever they were intimate. Perhaps their lack of intimacy stemmed from Hugh symbolizing stability and her parents' wishes, not being her own, thus making their love life lackluster. Or was being with Ryan a rebellion against her parents and their expectations? Jessie wasn't sure if what was happening was for real.

"Must have had a great night," Tia commented from Jessie's side.

"Pardon?"

Tia looked at her incredulously. "C'mon, girl, we all know the two of you were getting busy all night and into the morning."

Jessie blushed several shades.

"The walls aren't soundproof," Tia commented, pointing toward the house.

Jessie was mortified that everyone in the house knew what they'd been up to, but Tia patted her thigh. "Girlfriend, don't be embarrassed. We were not paying you guys any mind because we were having fun of our own. I'm just saying that we are all adults here and you two are welcome to do what single adults who are attracted to each other do."

Jessie sighed. "I suppose."

"You like him, right?"

"If you heard us, then the answer is pretty obvious."

"Well then, enjoy him and forget about the rest. What's wrong with having a holiday fling?"

"Because it's Ryan," Jessie whispered. "He's my oldest friend. He knows everything about me."

"Including what turns you on." Tia winked.

"Tia!"

"Hey, don't be mad. I speak the truth. Sometimes it takes being with someone who knows you so completely, inside and out, that makes it so incredible."

Jessie nodded. "How are we going to navigate this outside in the real world? Because right now it feels as if we're a bubble and this is a moment outside of normal reality."

"Stop worrying about tomorrow and enjoy today," Tia said. "Or at least the next couple of days. Tomorrow's worries will be here soon enough."

Jessie supposed she was right. They could have this moment in time without her worrying about her parents' expectations, doing what was right or how their friendship might be impacted. But it was hard for her to do. She usually looked before she leaped, but last night she hadn't. Instead, she'd gone on instinct. The kiss at the restaurant had shocked her, leading her to believe Ryan was as attracted to her as she was to him. She'd take a gamble when she'd put the condom in her pocket, never imagining that they might really use it.

But they had.

She blushed, thinking about sex up against the wall with Ryan and how deep he'd buried himself inside her. It was amazing to think that, after all this time, it was Ryan who did it for her. Who made her feel sexy and desired.

As if he intuitively knew she was thinking of him, Ryan smiled in her direction and her stomach fluttered. Ryan gave her butterflies! Why had she never realized how great they could be together? Because she'd been so focused on Hugh, on her parents' choice, that she had underestimated Ryan. Hadn't given him a second look. But now she was giving him a first, second and third. And she couldn't wait for the evening to come so they could resume their activities.

* * *

"Someone is feeling himself," Adam said when they paused from playing tag football long enough to drink some Gatorade and wipe the sweat from their foreheads.

"What do you mean?" Ryan said, swigging the sports drink.

Adam laughed. "C'mon, bro. We all know you and Jessie got horizontal last night."

Ryan glared at him.

"Don't even try to deny it," Adam said in response to his look. "Tia and I found your makeshift bed unslept in this morning. And to make matters worse, you and Jessie didn't emerge from the guest bedroom until damn near noon."

Ryan sighed heavily. Adam was right. There was no denying his relationship with Jessie had turned intimate. "Okay, okay." Ryan admitted reluctantly, "Things between Jessie and I have taken an unexpected but pleasant turn."

"It's what you wanted, right?" Adam asked, glancing in the women's direction. "For Jessie to see you as someone other than a friend."

"Yes," he said, nodding. "I do. But you know sex always tends to bring complications."

"Exactly. You were hung up on this girl then you said you were done. Obviously, you're not over her, Ryan. Watch yourself. She'll be nothing but heartbreak."

Ryan understood what Adam was saying, but this was a temporary relationship and he was embracing the now and forgetting about tomorrow. What happens in the Hamptons stays in the Hamptons. They'd just fallen headlong into bed. He smiled. Well, the bed came later.

"What's so funny?" Adam asked.

"Nothing," Ryan said. "Let's head back to our women." He was going to take full advantage of every moment he had with Jessie this weekend. He wasn't going to waste a single minute.

* * *

Later that afternoon, while everyone else went back to the house, Jessie and Ryan stayed out on the beach, choosing to take a walk instead. She enjoyed being in the outdoors with the clear sky and blue water. Often she was indoors, whether in class, the library or at the law firm, that she had precious little time outdoors. Unconsciously, Jessie's hand slipped into Ryan's as they trudged through the sand.

Eventually they came to a sand dune and, after a short climb, Jessie realized there wasn't another soul on the small curve of private beach. No boats were in the distance, either.

"This is crazy, you know? You and me," Jessie said, swinging their arms.

"Is it?" Ryan asked.

"I never anticipated having these feelings for you," Jessie admitted. "I've always had a plan. Knew exactly where my life was going."

"And with whom?"

She stopped walking and turned to face Ryan. "I don't deny that I thought I was supposed to be in love by now. Me and Hugh. That was always the plan. Get married. Buy a house. Have two kids. Along the way, the pressure got to me and I got restless for something more. The anniversary article on Black Crescent didn't help and only reminded me of the fact."

"Am I a way for you to get out from under your parents' expectations and end your relationship with Hugh?" His eyes were earnest yet cautious as they searched hers.

"My parents, my friends…everyone keeps telling me what a great catch Hugh is and I believed the hype. I was so faithful, I wasn't even tempted in college to stray from the preordained path set for me. Even after I graduated, I didn't look at anyone else until the night of the reunion. That's when I really *saw* you."

"And I saw you."

"The desire in your eyes scared me," Jessie said. "It was so open, so honest. I knew then I couldn't stay committed to Hugh. Otherwise, I'd be tempted to cheat, and that's just not me. I want to just enjoy each other without any pressure."

"Without any commitments?" Ryan added.

She nodded. "Can you accept that while we navigate this?"

"I can. As we discussed, this is temporary."

"I don't want to lose our friendship, Ryan. That scares me most of all."

He reached for her, enveloping Jessie in his arms. "You won't lose me as a friend." He stroked her hair and looked deep into her eyes. "I'll always be here for you."

She smiled. "Now that we have that settled, why don't you be here for me another way…" She circled her arms around his neck and brought his mouth down to hers. At first his lips merely grazed hers—rubbing lightly back and forth until she parted her mouth and reached up on tiptoe to demand more pressure.

Ryan gave it to her. His hand shifted her head firmly in place so his tongue could delve into her hungry mouth. He stroked her with purpose that left no doubt as to the explicitness of what he wanted. It was the same for Jessie. It was like Ryan had pushed her On button and she'd come to life. Jessie hadn't known her body was capable of humming with so much pent-up desire.

She pushed her body hard against his, reveling in the impact of his muscular chest against her. He slid his arms tighter and, with one hand low on her bottom, pulled her even closer. He rocked them both, mimicking the actions of sex and bringing her to a flashpoint.

"Ryan," she moaned and, before she knew it, they were

sinking into the sand on their knees and falling backward, Jessie on top of him. They kissed greedily and possessively. His hands splayed across her back and her fingers dug into the nape of his neck until there wasn't a single part of their bodies not touching.

Jessie felt Ryan's arousal against her belly and everything inside her burned. When she stole a glance at him, his eyes pierced right into her soul and she knew it was the same for him, too. She felt his hand move underneath her cover-up, reaching for her bikini bottom and pressing his palm against her damp heat. She gasped into his mouth and reached for the band of his swim shorts. Caressing him, she kissed him hard.

Ryan grabbed her hand to steady her. "We don't have a condom," he said,

In that moment, Jessie wanted to say she didn't care because she was on the pill, but she'd always practiced safe sex and wasn't about to stop now.

"I'll still make it good for you," Ryan whispered. His hand went beneath her bikini bottom and touched her intimately.

Shamelessly, Jessie rocked against him and Ryan delivered his promise to make it good by kneading and massaging her breasts and catching his mouth with hers. She loved the way he took over. And when he pushed a finger inside her, thrusting in and out, she began to squirm. She was so hot and wet, she groaned, raking her fingers down his back.

"Easy, love." Ryan flipped them over until he was leaning over her and Jessie was in the sand. Somehow it didn't matter because he was pushing her bikini aside so his tongue could feast on her nipples. She gripped his shoulders for support as a rush of heat surged through her.

"Oh my God…" She moaned as every cell of her body came alive.

Ryan continued paying homage to her breasts while his

fingers gently yet ever so slowly found the swollen spot where she ached. With each stroke, Jessie became a live wire and when his thumb massaged her nub, Jessie couldn't hold back any longer. She shuddered, crying out as wave after wave of pleasure overtook her. As she floated back to reality, Jessie realized she felt languid and at ease.

"Feel better now?" Ryan asked softly in her ear.

It was the understatement of the year and she looked up at him, truly looked at him, and when she did, she noticed a sheen of sweat on his forehead. He was tightly coiled, all because he'd ensured she was satisfied first with no thought of his own needs.

"I do. But you—" She reached for his waistband, but he shook his head.

"Don't feel like you have to."

"But…"

"I wanted to give you pleasure. And you can return the favor tonight." He glanced at his watch. "We should go back, anyway. There's going to be a seafood boil tonight. And we don't want to be late again. Otherwise my friends will think we're sex addicts."

"If you're sure." She eyed him suspiciously. Hugh had always been about getting off first. Regardless of her satisfaction in the process.

He grinned. "I am." He rose and reached for her hand, pulling her to her feet as she adjusted her clothing.

"Where have you been all my life?" Jessie inquired.

"Next door."

Seven

Ryan stood on the porch holding a beer and watching Jessie as she cleaned up the dinner dishes. Adam and Tia had gone all out with good old-fashioned seafood boil complete with a beer base. It had been delicious and Ryan had the full belly to prove it. He couldn't remember when he'd had so much fun. He'd hung with his friends before in the Hamptons—Adam invited him all the time—but it was the first time he'd asked Jessie to join him. He thought he'd prove he'd conquered his attraction to Jessie, but he'd been wrong. Somehow this little trip had become more than he'd imagined. Yet it didn't change the facts. He wanted to run Black Crescent and Jessie…well, she was still as unsure of what she wanted as she'd ever been.

They'd gone from being next-door neighbors to friends to lovers in the span of less than forty-eight hours and he'd loved every minute. Yet he knew eventually their time together would come to an end. It had to. He might have a bright future ahead with Black Crescent and Jessie needed to do some soul-searching.

That's not to say that being with Jessie wasn't spectacular. She'd blossomed in front of him and his friends. She held her own with the likes of Mike and Dean, easily bantering and trading teasing barbs with that brilliant smile of hers. She'd come alive in front of him and the sweet girl next door had been replaced with a sexy siren who burned hotter than any other woman he'd ever known. She was proud and confident. How else to explain how she'd literally brought him to his knees in the sand and unleashed his hedonistic affinities where anyone could have seen him giving her pleasure?

He'd worked until she'd screamed into blissful satiation. He'd known she hadn't been happy leaving him unsatisfied, but in that moment he hadn't minded abstaining. In fact, he could hardly think at the time because the attraction between them was so intense. In the past, he would have pushed for more, but he wasn't going to do that now because Jessie needed to make some choices about what she wanted in life.

"If I didn't know any better, I'd think you lovebirds were on your honeymoon," Adam said as he joined him on the porch.

Ryan looked at him in surprise.

"I saw the look you sent Jessie from across the room. It was like you have eyes for her and her alone."

"Suppose that's true," Ryan said. The sexual tension between them was too fraught to ignore. He supposed it was because hidden, long-denied feelings had bubbled to the surface and he was indulging over and over and over again.

"Uh-oh, she's headed this way and looking at you like you're the tasty morsel she can't wait to have. If you'll excuse me, I'm going to find my woman," Adam said with a laugh.

Jessie joined Ryan, her gaze colliding with his as electricity arced between them. "Hey, you."

"Don't look at me like that." Ryan swigged his beer.

"Like what?"

Ryan raised an eyebrow. "You know how. If you don't stop, I'm going to take you upstairs and have my way with you."

"Would that be so wrong?" she asked, moving closer and wrapping her arms around his midsection.

"It is if the evening is barely over," Ryan whispered. "The group was talking about going to a club tonight."

"Sounds like fun. I haven't been dancing in ages."

"You want to go?"

She nodded. "Usually, I'm pouring over briefs and doing research until my eyes droop closed. This weekend is my time to relax and let loose."

Ryan wondered if that's all he was to her. Freedom from the strict regime she'd placed herself under. "Then let's do that."

Thirty minutes later, after changing into club gear, Ryan heel-tapped the floor, waiting for Jessie to come downstairs. She'd asked him to wait for her so she could make an appearance. When she did, his eyes traveled over every inch of her. The short skirt was nearly indecent because it reached her mid-thigh and the sparkly halter top wasn't much better. It was backless, which meant she wasn't wearing a bra underneath. Ryan was going to have a hard time focusing with Jessie looking like that.

"You like?" she asked, twirling in her four-inch heels.

"Yeah." He came toward her and traced the long stretch of exposed bare thigh. "But I would prefer it if you had on more clothes."

"Oh, don't be a spoilsport." She sidled next to him. "I promise I'll make it worth your while later."

"You promise?" he whispered.

"Absolutely." She winked. "You're guaranteed to get lucky."

Having Jessie on his arm made Ryan feel like the luckiest guy in the world. He was both jealous and proud of the envious looks they received when they made it to the popular Hamptons' club. Adam had ensured they were seated in VIP, but Jessie didn't care. She was itching to get on the dance floor.

"You don't dance?"

Ryan shrugged. He didn't usually, but for her, he could be compelled to make an exception.

"Don't tell me you have no rhythm?" she teased.

"I can hold my own, but I wouldn't mind watching you."

She grinned mischievously. "C'mon, girls." She grabbed Tia, Corinne and Lauren and corralled them onto the dance floor.

Ryan watched in amusement as she positively strutted onto the floor with the ladies and got her groove on. The music was loud and he loved watching Jessie move and gyrate. She was all fluid grace. There was a freedom to her as she swished and sashayed her hips. Ryan could feel himself getting turned on. Apparently he wasn't the only one because another guy came over and began dancing with Jessie.

Ryan's fists curled. He wanted to punch the guy in the face, but instead he unclenched them and walked straight toward her.

"Excuse me," Ryan said, cutting into their dance, uncaring of the other man and pulling Jessie into his arms. "The lady is with me."

Jessie had never seen this side of Ryan. His aura commanded respect. He was broader in the shoulders than the man she'd been dancing with and the other man had easily capitulated and stepped back. Despite herself, Jessie loved Ryan going totally caveman and capturing her in his hold. Her body instinctively turned to him, but his look was dangerous. His hand grasped a handful of hair and tilted her face up to his.

"For the duration of the night, you're dancing with me, got it?"

She glanced up at him and was mesmerized by the slightly dangerous look in his eyes. She nodded. His hand slid around her and pulled her that bit tighter to him. Now she was wholly pressed up against him, chest-to-chest and thigh-to-thigh.

Ryan didn't say anything else. He didn't need to because the close proximity of their bodies said it all. All she could do was move with him in a slow and easy rhythm. Just like he did in bed, Ryan guided her where he wanted her to go. When he inserted a jeans-clad thigh between hers, need slammed into Jessie. She was uncomfortably warm even though she was wearing very little.

That's what Ryan did to her. He made her hot and bothered, and she was powerless to fight it. Not when he used the setting and crowded dance floor to crush her to him. If he continued this dirty dancing routine, she'd been hiking up her skirt and begging him to take her on the dance floor.

Like you did at the beach?

Jessie blushed when she thought about how abandoned she'd been. If it hadn't been for Ryan thinking about protection and being safe, she would have allowed him to have her right there in the sand where anyone could have come across them.

"Tonight you're mine," Ryan whispered.

And he was right.

She had the damp thong to prove it.

Later, after they'd gotten hot and sweaty bumping and grinding at the club, they returned to the beach house. Mindless of the other couples, they'd gone straight to the room. Jessie was desperate for a shower, but also for Ryan to take her to paradise.

He must have been as frantic as she was because they both stripped on their way to the bathroom. She turned on the shower and stood under the steaming water, allowing the spray to pummel away her tension. At the sound of the shower door creaking, Jessie turned around in enough time to see Ryan sporting a massive erection.

"I'm calling in my marker," Ryan said with a wide grin as he came closer, joining her in the shower. "I'm ready to get lucky." He kissed her, deep and erotic, with slow yet firm kisses. His lips nipped and his tongue slid—it was an art form Ryan had mastered quite well.

As the water sluiced over his brown skin, Jessie slid her palms across his chest. She loved that he'd kept the lights off. Now Jessie could explore him by touch and not by sight. Blind to everything but him, she lowered her head to brush soft kisses against his wet skin. When she came to the dark disks of his nipples, her lips circled them, licking and flicking with her tongue. Ryan shuddered. That didn't stop her, Jessie sank to her knees and reached for his length. *She* was making the choice to please him because it felt right in the moment and because it was what she wanted.

She gripped the base of his erection and he groaned. She licked the head of him and Ryan's entire body tensed. So she did it again, swirling her tongue over the thick ridge. She opened her mouth and took him fully in. She pleasured him, pumping her hand to match the movement of her mouth. She loved the taste of him, the scent of him, and as his breathing became more labored, it turned her on.

"Jessie..." he gasped. "You have to stop..."

She lifted her head and looked up at him. "I'm not stopping." She wanted him to come as hard and loud as she had on the sand dune. His eyes were closed and she sensed he was fighting her, holding back, so she firmed her grip and increased her speed and suction. It didn't take long for Ryan to groan loudly as he came in her mouth.

Jessie, impressed she could bring this strong, exciting man joy, licked her lips. She rose and quickly found her back pressed against the cool wet tiles as Ryan returned the favor by licking down her torso.

"You enjoyed tormenting me—didn't you?—even though I was doing my best to keep you at bay," he inquired. His hands cupping her breasts, he lifted them to his mouth and began tonguing them generously.

"I did," she panted. The cloak of velvety darkness made it easy to soak up his watery caresses.

"I'm going to give it right back." He used his fingers and mouth to bring Jessie to peak, causing her orgasm to knife through her. Jessie lost her mind and screamed, but Ryan continued lapping her with his tongue through the spasms.

When the water became too cold from all their ministrations, they abandoned the shower. Not bothering with towels, they landed on the bed in a hot, damp tangle of limbs. Their mouths and hands spoke, kissing and touching and roving each other from head to toe until eventually Jessie couldn't take any more foreplay. With a firm grip, she grasped his length and guided him home.

He gasped, but didn't stop her. Instead, he let her climb on top and ride him hard. She kept it crazy fast until they were both teetering on the edge. She waited for him, eager to climax together, and they did in one harsh breath.

Eight

The Fourth of July came in with a bang. *Literally for Ryan.*
Last night with Jessie was nothing short of incredible. Usually he didn't care for women to please him that way, but Jessie? She was another story altogether. He enjoyed the way she'd used her mouth, tongue and hands to take him over the edge. And yet he'd still found the energy to make love to her after.

Now they were on the deck of Adam's father's yacht, enjoying the sun and great weather before returning later to attend a party. It was impossible not to notice Jessie in the sarong she wore over the gold bikini.

Ryan refused to let feelings that were trying to emerge for Jessie free. They'd made a pact that this holiday weekend was temporary and purely fun. He had to remember that and not let Jessie get under his skin. Had she always been there, just beneath the surface and he'd clamped it down?

At the stern of the yacht, he saw Mike taking one of two Jet Skis out and followed him. "Can I take one for a ride?" he asked the yacht crew member.

"Sure."

He was climbing on when Jessie came rushing toward him. "Can I come?"

He had hoped to use the fresh air and speed to help clear his mind of the woman who'd seemed to invade all his senses for the last couple of days, but he couldn't very well turn her down. "C'mon, hop on."

Jessie quickly tossed aside her sarong and stepped down to the docking platform to climb onto the Jet Ski. Feeling her snugly settled behind him, her arms held tightly around his waist, was the last thing Ryan needed. "Hold on."

He started the engine and opened the throttle, sending the Jet Ski skimming over the ocean. It was exhilarating feeling the wind whip around his face, and exactly what he'd needed. Jessie was enjoying it, as well, because she tapped his shoulders to point out several things of interest.

When they returned to the yacht, Ryan felt in control of himself. He had to be. Tomorrow they would be returning to the real world where Jessie wasn't wholly his anymore and he couldn't spend every waking minute with her. They would both go back to work, to their own lives. He would return to his quest to be CEO of Black Crescent and turn the small-town hedge fund into a household name. Maybe then he'd feel satisfied with his life and good enough that a woman like Jessie would want to be on his arm.

Would she go back to Hugh?

His anger deepened because Ryan wanted a relationship with Jessie other than sex. Sure, they were sexually compatible in ways he'd never been with another woman, but he wanted *more*.

She'd indicated a restlessness with her life and her family expectations and being obligated to marry Hugh. But would she really change? Or was being with him just a rebellion against her family? Ryan didn't know for certain, but one thing he was sure of was that he wouldn't settle for being second best. Once the weekend was over, he would dismiss her from his life again and focus on his future at Black Crescent.

"What's wrong?" Jessie frowned as they turned the Jet Ski over to a crew member.

"Nothing."

She carefully studied him as she put her sarong back on. "Are you sure? You looked angry about something. Didn't you enjoy the ride?"

Oh yes, Ryan had enjoyed the ride the last few days; he was afraid of what would happen when the weekend was over.

Jessie couldn't put her finger on it, but something was definitely bothering Ryan. Since their return from Jet Skiing, he'd been more reserved, even standoffish. The last couple of days, he'd always been by her side with his arm casually wrapped around her. And she hated to admit it, but she kind of liked it. Hugh hated to show public displays of affection. So she'd gotten used to keeping her emotions in check. But with Ryan, he was so warm, so open, she rather liked the way he kissed her in front of his friends. He was unapologetic about his interest in her and she dug that about him.

She would get to the bottom of whatever was troubling him. Although tomorrow loomed, signaling the end of their three-day fling, she didn't want anything to spoil the perfect weekend they'd shared.

She reached inside the bucket of beer by the bar, pulled one out for him and one for herself, and joined him as he looked out over the water. "Everything okay?" she asked, handing him a beer.

"Thanks." He tipped his beer to hers. "I'm fine. Why do you ask?"

She shrugged. "I don't know. You seem *off* today."

"I was thinking about tomorrow when this all comes to an end."

She stared up into his brown eyes. "Don't do that. Don't let reality seep in yet. We're supposed to enjoy our time here without a care or worry. Remember?"

"It's not that easy."

"Yes. It is. We'll deal with tomorrow when it comes. Now, c'mon." She pulled him over to where the rest of his friends were gathered in the hot tub. Jessie threw off her sarong. She knew the tiny gold triangles of material that made up the top of her gold bikini barely covered her breasts.

Jessie had to admit she like how his eyes gleamed when his gaze dropped to the swell of her breasts. Heat surged through her and her nipples puckered. She was glad to be sinking into the hot, bubbling water because then Ryan wouldn't know the potent effect he had on her. Hugh was dead wrong. She didn't have a low sex drive. It just took the right man to bring it out of her.

She watched Ryan whip his T-shirt off and set it beside her sarong before joining her in the hot tub. Her eyes were hidden behind her oversize sunglasses so no one could tell what she was thinking. Jessie supposed it was a good thing because it gave her time to think.

Being with Ryan was everything she hadn't known she wanted and her feelings for him were growing exponentially. He was handsome, strong and kind. When she was with him, she felt herself anchored by his strength in way she'd never been with Hugh. She could learn to let go with other lovers, right? She closed her eyes because the very idea of being with anyone else was repulsive. Yet she had so much more to figure out because her fun in the sun with Ryan in the Hamptons had showed her that she and Hugh would never make it. But could she and Ryan? If he accepted a position with Black Crescent, there was no way they could ever be together.

It was so much to think about. She'd thought sleeping together would ease the tension between them, but instead it had become an ache she couldn't erase. Her emotions were complicated by the feelings Ryan evoked in her and, once they were back in reality, Jessie was going to have to figure it out one way or another.

The rest of the afternoon was a blur for Ryan. He'd made sure to keep some distance on the yacht between him and Jessie. And when they'd returned home, he hadn't joined her in the shower—no matter how much he wanted to. Their time was ending and he was preparing himself emotionally as well as physically for when they would no longer be together.

He'd succeeded.

Even after she'd come out of the bathroom, in a sexy romper for the barbecue at a friend of Dean's that evening, Ryan kept his composure despite the tug of desire in his groin. Instead, he'd slid her arm into the crook of his and led her out of the bedroom.

They joined the rest of the gang downstairs and were driven to the party on the other side of the Hamptons in a party bus big enough for eight so no one would have to drink and drive. This beach house was bigger and more grand than Adam's. After checking in at the security gate, they'd driven through a compound to an oceanfront estate.

The house was a split-level, but it was the features that stuck out in Jessie's mind. The soaring ceilings, marble floors, transom windows and coffered ceilings were miles over anything she'd ever seen. Even the O'Malley house. Partygoers were on all levels, milling around with drinks and canapés from a five-star chef in their hand.

"How did you score an invite to this?" Ryan asked Dean.

Dean shrugged. "My firm worked a big case for the

owner. Invited the entire firm. Didn't think he'd mind a few extra guests."

Ryan laughed. "The more, the merrier." He tugged Jessie's hand forward. They mixed and mingled throughout the evening, but Ryan disguised his feelings behind a wall of bravado. He made sure to keep Jessie's wineglass full, but the lady herself at a distance.

He must have been doing a good job because Adam commented when Jessie went to the ladies' room, "Everything all right with you and Jessie?"

"Yeah, why do you ask?"

"Because you've been decidedly more measured in your interactions with her today."

Ryan frowned. He was hoping no one would notice. But Adam had, which meant Jessie had, as well. "I'm taking this for what it is."

"Which is?"

"Two people having a good time."

"But that's not what you want?" Adam asked what Ryan had been trying his best not to.

"Doesn't matter what I want. Jessie has to figure out what and *who* she really wants. Not to mention, the Black Crescent job is still on the table. If I were to accept, it would cause Jessie and her family a lot of grief and tear open old wounds. So, if it seems like I'm pulling back a bit, I am. It's called self-preservation." He wasn't going to put himself out there when he wasn't sure if she felt anything for him.

"I hear you, but perhaps you should talk to her first," Adam said. "Clear the air? And far as Black Crescent goes, the job isn't a done deal yet."

Ryan grinned smugly. "Sure it is."

"A little cocky, eh?"

"More like confident," Ryan responded as he left. The first interview had gone well and he would be called for the second any day now.

When she didn't return immediately to his side, Ryan went in search of her and found Jessie outside on the terrace looking over the beach. Despite the party around her, she seemed a million miles away. "Penny for your thoughts?"

She turned and studied him and then led with a whammy. "Why have you been avoiding me today?"

Oh, she was going straight to the point.

"I haven't been avoiding you."

She cocked her head to one side and regarded him with an angry glare. "Did you think I wouldn't feel you pulling away? Was it something I did? Are you already bored with me now that we've slept together?"

Ryan's eyes filled with horror and he placed his beer on a nearby table. He reached for her, but she stepped away from him. "Of course not. How could you think that?"

"I don't know what to feel, Ryan," she said, folding her arms across her chest in a defensive posture. "You've kept me at a distance all day."

"I'm sorry."

"Don't be sorry, for Christ's sake. Just tell me what's going on."

"I don't know how to do this." He pointed between them. "You and me."

Jessie grinned. "I beg to differ. I think you've been *doing* this quite well."

If he could have blushed, Ryan would have. "I'm not talking about how compatible we are in the bedroom. I'm talking about the fact that you're my friend and we crossed the line this weekend. And don't get me wrong, I don't regret it, Jessie." He looked into her eyes. "I wanted you. I always have. But I'm also wondering what will happen when we go back to the real world."

"I thought we were going to take this one day at a time?" Jessie asked.

"We were. I mean we are."

"I feel like you want an answer from me on what's going to happen between us after this weekend and, if I'm honest, I can't give you one. Not yet, Ryan. I'm confused about a lot of things. But what I'm not confused about is my decision to be with you this weekend."

Ryan released a heavy sigh and looked down at Jessie. The stubborn tilt of her chin as she looked into his eyes made him burn with mortification. He shouldn't have stayed away from her today. Thinking about the obstacles they faced with his possible job at Black Crescent and her family's oppressive expectations made him waste time. Plus, his pride had gotten in the way and he'd begun to think about her casting him aside to go back to Hugh. Envy that Hugh would have his woman after sharing such a passionate weekend with him had his stomach churning.

He brushed her cheek with a single finger and tucked a strand of her shoulder-length hair behind her ear. He felt her pulse quicken at his touch, because when they were together that's all it took. A spark for them to burn bright. His finger continued a path to her mouth and he marauded it back and forth over her lips. When she opened her mouth and took his finger inside and began sucking, Ryan felt his groin harden in response.

Damn minx could turn him on with the snap of her fingers. She looked up at him as she sucked his finger deep into her mouth and Ryan knew in that instant that they needed to get out of there, otherwise he would lose his grip.

He pulled away. "We need to go," he groaned hoarsely.

She nodded her agreement.

It didn't take long for them to call an Uber and say their goodbyes to the group. The short drive back to the house was fraught with sexual energy as they gave each other hungry looks. Ryan was thankful when the car came to a stop and they rushed through the front door like two randy teenagers. They quickly raced upstairs to their bedroom and began stripping, eager to get naked.

Ryan couldn't wait to please her in all kinds of ways. And he did. She trusted him to do anything and she enjoyed every minute of it. They were so amorous, they ended up on the floor, but neither of them seemed to care. After putting on protection, he allowed Jessie to sit astride his lap and set the pace.

"Take what you want," he urged her softly. "Whatever you want."

She kissed him long and deep, stroking inside his mouth with an intimate exploration. Then she lifted her hips, allowing him to slide through her feminine folds.

"Good…you feel good," he couldn't resist murmuring.

"So do you." She began rocking her hips and he tightened his arms clasping her to his chest. She rode him hard and he pushed up to meet her. Again. Then again and again. Every time she moved, he moved. She gave him everything and he claimed it. He wanted to claim all of her and when he gazed into her eyes, he could see the same sense of wonder, pleasure and need that were mirrored in his.

It wasn't just sex for her, either.

Those were his last thoughts as she feverishly clutched him, digging her fingernails into his biceps. He roared in satisfaction.

Afterward, a flash of light caught his attention. Ryan realized it was Fourth of July fireworks, but he didn't need the real-life ones because he and Jessie had made some of their own.

Nine

After a goodbye-lunch with the entire gang the following day, Jessie and Ryan headed back to Manhattan. Rather than take a helicopter to the city, Ryan had a limousine pull up to the beach house.

He was shaking Adam's hand when Tia whispered in Jessie's ear, "You've got that man around your pinky. Enjoy."

Jessie laughed as she moved toward the vehicle.

"You like?" Ryan asked.

"A limo?" Her voice rose a pitch. "Pretty fancy."

"Only the best for you."

Jessie's heart kicked over in her chest as Ryan handed her bag to the driver who'd exited the vehicle. Then he helped Jessie into the luxurious comfort of the interior and watched with amusement as she surveyed her surroundings with its plush leather seats and bottle of champagne chilling in a bucket of ice.

"Would you like a glass?" Ryan asked as the limo pulled away from the curb. They waved at the McKinleys as they left.

Jessie turned from staring out of the window. "Yes, please. A limo? Do you do this often?"

Ryan shrugged. "I often take them for business."

Jessie shook her head. "You continue to surprise me, Ryan Hathaway."

He laughed as he reached for the bottle of bubbly and popped it open. He quickly poured flutes for him and Jessie. They toasted and Jessie let the champagne course through her veins.

"I think you're sitting too far away," Ryan said as he raised the privacy glass between them and driver.

"Oh really?"

"Oh yes." Ryan took her flute from her hands and placed it next to his on the console. Then he proceeded to show Jessie that after last night and this morning's lust-filled haze, they were not nearly done with each other yet.

By the time they arrived at Jessie's brownstone after navigating the NYC traffic, they'd steamed up the windows pretty darn good.

Jessie hated to leave Ryan, but she had an early day tomorrow. She exited the limo first and Ryan joined her, helping take her bags up the stairs to her apartment.

"I had a really great time," she said awkwardly at her door. She didn't have the words to express how being with Ryan had changed her life and totally flipped the script on what happened next.

"So did I. I'll call you later."

Jessie nodded and watched as he started down the stairs, but then he must have thought better of it because he came running back up. He swooped her into his arms and pressed his mouth to hers. He took full advantage, sliding his tongue deep to taste her, tearing a soft moan from her lips. Jessie wound her arms around his neck and melted against him. Her body softened to accommodate the steel of his.

His mouth ravaged hers. How was it possible they could

still be as hungry for each other when they'd just gotten busy in the back of the limo? Jessie couldn't deny that somehow Ryan had taken hold of not only her body but her soul. He'd unlocked parts of her she hadn't even been aware of.

Eventually they lifted their heads and pulled away to take in large breaths.

"Get some rest," Ryan said. "I'll call you soon." Seconds later, he was gone.

Once inside her apartment, Jessie found Becca curled up on the couch with a bowl of popcorn. "Thought I heard voices outside the door, but then when I looked through the peephole…" Becca began, "all I could see was you and Ryan going at it like rabbits."

Jessie flushed, lowered her head and began swiftly walking to her room. She could hear Becca's footsteps behind her as she followed Jessie to her bedroom.

"Don't you even dare try to hold out on me," Becca stated, flopping down on Jessie's bed. "We have seen each other through all kinds of crap. No way are you going to hold out on me that you and Ryan—*Ryan*, of all people— hooked up over the weekend."

"It wasn't a hookup," Jessie said as she emptied the majority of contents from her suitcase into the laundry hamper.

"No? Then what was it?"

Jessie shrugged. "I have no idea, Becca." She stopped unpacking. "One minute, I'm hanging out with my best friend and his friends. The next minute, I'm up against the wall and we're having the most amazing sex I've ever had in my life."

"Better than Hugh?"

"Doesn't even compare." Jessie sat beside Becca on the bed. "Ryan is…commanding and powerful when I want it and soft and gentle when I need it. He's so in tune to my every need, my every desire. I couldn't get enough of him."

"Wow! That's saying something. And this is the first time you've ever felt this connection to him?"

Jessie rose from the bed, unable to meet Becca's querying eyes. "I didn't say that."

"What does that mean? What aren't you saying?"

Jess spun around. "Three months ago at the reunion… There was a moment when Ryan and I danced that I thought there might have been a spark, but I dismissed it. Hugh came and I got caught up in the excitement of his surprise appearance."

"Clearly, you weren't wrong about that night."

Jessie nodded. "No, I don't suppose I was. This weekend was a complete revelation. I had no idea Ryan and I were so—so sexually compatible. We were together *all* weekend."

"Sounds hot! I can hardly believe it. I mean you've never once said you were interested in Ryan in that way. He was always the boy next door."

"Yeah…well, he's still that, too, but he's also got a sexy body and a wicked tongue," Jessie said with a grin. When she thought about how he used his tongue to turn her inside out, Jessie felt her skin turn crimson.

"Are you going to continue seeing him?" Becca inquired. "Isn't Ryan still applying for that job at Black Crescent?"

"Yes." Except for his friends mentioning it Friday night, Ryan hadn't spoken of the job the entire weekend. Jessie was certain that had been deliberate because they'd wanted to keep the real world out of their Hampton bubble, but it was still a real possibility.

"Could you accept him working there?"

Jessie shook her head. "I couldn't. It would hurt too much. Black Crescent cost my family everything and changed our lives forever."

"So where does that leave you? What about Hugh?"

"Hugh and I have had a long-distance relationship for

years and I'm tired of it. I have been for years. We decided three months ago to take a break to figure out what we wanted."

"Why didn't you speak up and tell me sooner?"

"Because… I've always tried to do what's expected of me, what my family wants, but I'm coming to realize that it's overshadowed my life and stifled me from making my own choices."

"A choice like Ryan?"

"It's not tit for tat."

"No?"

"Of course not. I'm not using Ryan because Hugh is no longer in my life. Our attraction surprised both of us."

"Maybe you, but Ryan has always been into you, Jessie. He's always been jealous of your relationship with Hugh. You just refused to acknowledge the obvious."

"That's not true."

"It is. I knew it the moment I met him. But you'd always had him in the friend's zone and seemed content to have him there, so I never questioned it."

"Well, I'm questioning everything. So to answer your question, Ryan and I didn't really discuss what comes next once we got back home."

"What did you talk about?"

Jessie blushed. There hadn't been a whole of talking going on. Just kissing, touching, licking and lots more.

Becca fanned herself. "My apologies, my love life has been on indefinite pause. No amount of Match, eHarmony or Tinder can resuscitate it."

"You'll find someone, Becca. You're an amazing human."

"Not someone as fine as Ryan. I mean, when did he get so good-looking all of a sudden?"

Jessie chuckled. She'd thought the same thing. One day he was overweight. The next he was lean and trim and had become a man. All man. And through the years, she'd see him here and there, but she supposed she'd never really *seen* him until the reunion. And now that she had, there was no way they could go back to being only friends.

But she also wasn't sure she was ready for a full-blown relationship. There were too many obstacles she had to get through first. And they began with figuring out what she wanted and how to stop doing her parents' bidding and finally live for herself. In an ideal world, she and Ryan would be able to make their Hamptons tryst into something more, but how could they if he took the job with Black Crescent? Jessie didn't see a way forward for them and that was the most disappointing part of all.

"Well, look who the cat dragged in," Sean Hathaway, Ryan's older brother, said when Ryan joined him and their brother Ben for drinks later that evening. They were at a local pub in Murray Hill that specialized in craft beer and burgers, and was not all that far from his penthouse. He'd forgotten his brothers had come to the city after the annual Hathaway barbecue for a Yankees' game and he was to meet them beforehand for a drink.

"Don't give me a hard time," Ryan stated. "I've been busy."

"Too busy to hang out with your bros?" His younger brother, Ben stated. Ben had inherited their father's wiry frame and salt-and-pepper hair. Poor guy had started graying in his twenties. But that hadn't stopped the ladies from fawning over his light brown eyes, which was a trademark of their mother's family, even though his brother dressed like a preppie in trousers and a button-down shirt. Though tonight it appeared he'd made an exception and had traded his trousers for jeans, but still the button-down remained.

"You didn't even come home for the Fourth," Sean chimed in. "Mom was none too pleased. You know she looks forward to having us all home." His eldest brother, on the other hand, was the exact opposite of Ben. He was broad-shouldered, with a football player frame, and wore jeans and a Yankees jersey. He had dark brown hair and deeply set brown eyes.

Like Jessie's parents, Marilyn Hathaway hadn't been happy when Ryan had told her of his plans to spend the Fourth of July with his friends. His father's barbecue was one of the biggest parties on Sycamore Street and everyone in their Falling Brook neighborhood usually came out to sample Eric's ribs, brisket and pulled pork.

"Yeah, it couldn't be helped." Ryan shrugged.

"Why not?" Ben inquired. "What's so important?"

"I was hanging with some friends in the Hamptons. You remember my roommate Adam from college? He invited several of us to his place."

"By friends, do you mean Jessie Acosta?" Ben teased.

"Ah." Sean grinned and pointed at Ryan's guilty face, "Now that makes sense. There's only one person that would make Ryan abandon his family and that would be a certain beautiful Latina."

"Don't start," Ryan admonished.

"Tease you about the crush you've had on the girl next door for decades?" Sean stated, wrapping his arm around Ryan's shoulder. "No way, bro. You've got it coming and then some. I'm friends with Jessie on Facebook. I saw the pictures she posted. You can't hide the look of absolute adoration on your face."

Ryan rolled his eyes. "Adoration? That was in the past. I stopped pining for Jessie months ago when I realized at the reunion that she was never going to choose me."

"Yet you took her with you to the Hamptons?" Sean quipped.

"That was different. It was just a temporary fling."

Both his brothers laughed, but it was Ben who piped

up next. "You're so sprung on that girl. Always have been and always will be."

"Agreed," Sean stated. "But what was more interesting about the pics posted was the look in her eyes." Sean pulled out his IPhone and showed a picture of Ryan and Jessie with his friends. "Finally, after all these years, little Jessie is feeling you. Isn't that right?"

Ryan rose from the high-top table they were seated at and moved over to the bar. He motioned to the bartender and quickly ordered a beer. He needed a minute to collect himself before he faced his brothers. If anyone could read him, they could. He didn't want them to know how much he wanted that to be true. How much he wanted Jessie to be as into him as he was into her.

The bartender slid a beer across the bar and Ryan accepted it, taking a swig. When he returned to the table, his brothers eyed him.

"Well?" Sean asked. "Are you going to fess up now? Or are we going to have to beat it out of you?" He glanced at Ben who nodded his agreement. When Ryan was younger, his older brothers loved razzing him.

Ben held up his hand. "I vote to beat it out of him. It's been a while since we gave our little brother a proper whooping."

"As if you could take me," Ryan snorted. "I'm not that chubby kid you guys could push around. Like Popeye, I've been eating my spinach," He showed off his biceps "And I can take either of you. Any time of day."

Sean threw back his head and roared with laughter. "Is that right? You are definitely full of yourself because Jessie Acosta finally gave you the time of day."

"C'mon, spill," Ben said, staring at Ryan.

"I admit I invited Jessie to the Hamptons with me and our relationship went to the next level."

"Okay, I want my twenty bucks." Sean held out his hand to Ben.

Ryan glanced at his brothers. "Did you guys make a bet on me and Jessie?" he asked incredulously.

"Sure did," Sean said as Ben pulled out a twenty-dollar bill and handed it to him. He tucked the money into his jeans. "I told Ben that Jessie finally opened her eyes to what's been right in front of her the entire time. He told me no way. He was wrong."

"How could you tell?" Ryan asked. "That picture was of all of us at the party."

"Yeah, but if you look real close, you can see your hand was around her waist, real proprietary-like, and you had a look of absolute happiness," Sean replied. "So, are you happy?"

Ryan took a swig of beer. "Why wouldn't I be?"

"Because you're here with us instead of your new lady love," Ben responded.

Ryan laughed at his euphemism. "It's a bit early to start calling her my lady."

"Well, she's certainly not O'Malley's anymore," Sean said with a smirk.

Ryan frowned. Hearing his nemesis's name always irked him.

"I don't want to talk about Hugh."

"Why not?" Ben asked. "He's been your competition from the start to win Jessie. Is he out of the picture?"

Ryan shrugged. "I think so."

"But you don't know for sure?" Sean finished.

Ryan shook his head. And that bothered him. He didn't know exactly where Jessie stood with Hugh or anything. She'd said they were on a break, but Ryan wasn't so sure. Hugh was still formidable opposition standing in the way of his finding true happiness with Jessie. There was also the possible job at Black Crescent to contend with.

"You need to find out," Sean stated. "You can't stay in limbo. I know how you've felt…" he began and then corrected himself. "How you *feel* about Jessie. You should have an honest heart-to-heart talk and find out where you stand."

Ryan put down his beer and looked at both his brothers. "In due time." He didn't want to fall back into bad habits, not after he'd done such a good job of pushing down his feelings after the reunion. He didn't want to take a step back.

"All right, but that's the only way you'll have your answer," Ben said. "If it doesn't work out, you'll have the memories to look back on about your one hot weekend together in the Hamptons."

Ryan frowned. He didn't like Ben's honest assessment, but he knew his brother was right. He and Jessie needed to clear the air and come to an understanding. He needed to know if what they shared was just a fling for her. Because it sure as hell wasn't for him. He'd begun thinking of the end game because, in his mind, he wanted her to be Mrs. Ryan Hathaway.

Ten

Ryan was in a bad mood. After getting up at 5:00 a.m. to complete his workout regime to keep his body fit and trim, he'd checked the overnight news to see if there were any relevant market movements. Finding none, he prepared himself for the firm's morning meeting. He had some investment ideas he wanted to discuss with upper management before making a presentation to his institutional clients.

The morning meeting went as expected and they loved his ideas. So he'd gone back to his office to set up appointments, including an investor visit to a distribution center. The only bright spot had been Allison Randall, the recruitment specialist, calling him to advise Black Crescent was interviewing other candidates, but was very happy with him and she hoped to have the second interview set up shortly. Ryan had expected as much. His credentials spoke for themselves.

Yet by midmorning, Ryan still felt unsettled and he knew why. After sharing brews and burgers with his brothers last night, he'd gone home full of purpose and expecting to have a serious conversation with Jessie about the state of their relationship. Instead, all he'd gotten was silence. His calls, voice mails and texts had gone unanswered for the entire evening.

If Jessie was trying to tell him what happened in the Hamptons stayed in the Hamptons, he'd received the message loud and clear. He supposed he shouldn't be surprised, it had been her idea to keep the weekend light and strings-free. He'd gone along because he'd wanted her so badly, he'd been willing to compromise. When in fact, he wanted it all—marriage and babies—with Jessie.

He knew to tell her would be suicide and send her running in the opposite direction. But at the very least, he'd hoped she'd want to continue seeing him to see where they might lead.

He'd been wrong.

Instead, he'd gotten his hopes up only to have them dashed and he had no one to blame but himself.

"Hey, Ryan, would you mind looking at some of my research?" Mark Bush, a junior analyst at his firm, said from his doorway.

"Of course." Ryan motioned him inside. He liked the kid. He was young, straight out of Trinity and a little green, but he had tremendous promise. Ryan wasn't like some of the other senior analysts who treated those underneath him like the bottom of their shoe, making them work hard like an intern. He believed in paying it forward.

Ryan peered over the figures Mark presented. "These are good. Really good."

"Thanks, Ryan. I appreciate you taking a look."

Ryan smiled. "You're welcome."

Helping others had always brought Ryan joy, which was why he wanted to run Black Crescent Investment. The company had bounced back under Joshua Lowell's leadership, but if Ryan became CEO, he was certain he could get rid of the tarnished reputation once and for all. Many in Falling Brook thought the Lowells were still secretly in contact with Vernon. That's why Ryan felt he was the right choice to lead the company.

With someone new at the helm, the fund wouldn't be accused of financial malfeasance and could finally be the leader in investments it had once been.

Black Crescent, however, wasn't Ryan's only opportunity to move into upper management. He was pursuing a couple of other interesting initiatives—though none of them had the personal impact of working in his hometown. Working at Black Crescent had been Ryan's way of cutting ties with Jessie and exorcising her from his life *permanently*.

Maybe he'd been onto something a few months ago. Jessie's lack of communication was a blessing to show him he needed to focus on himself and his career. Or at least, that's what he told himself as he continued working until the sky darkened outside.

"You still here?" Mark said.

Ryan glanced up from the report he'd been reading. It's not like he had anyone to go home to. "Yeah, I'll be here for a while. I'll see you tomorrow."

"Sure thing. Have a good night."

Ryan returned to studying the facts and figures in front of him until a silhouette at the door captured his attention. He sucked in a deep breath.

Jessie.

Jessie stared into Ryan's dark brown eyes and let out a sigh of relief. It had been too long to go without seeing him. She'd had every intention of calling him last night, but after drinking a couple of glasses of wine with Becca, she'd drifted off to sleep and hadn't awakened until Becca alerted her she'd overslept because her phone was dead.

She'd barely had enough time to shower before catching the subway to work—leaving her phone at home on the charger. Jessie hadn't realized how exhausted she'd been from the weekend, but she supposed it was because she'd stayed in bed with *this man* and hadn't gotten much sleep.

Though she didn't like the frown currently marring his features. "Ryan, listen… I'm sorry," she began as she walked into his office and shut the door.

"What for?" he asked, closing the folder he'd obviously been reading.

"Because I told you we'd talk last night and I fell asleep."

"And this morning?" he queried. "Heck, the rest of the day, for that matter. You mean to tell me, you couldn't bother to pick up a phone?"

"I overslept and left my phone at home, and you know I'm terrible with remembering numbers. That's your forte not mine."

He eyed her suspiciously, as if he didn't quite believe her, and a funny ache began to develop in her chest. She wasn't used to Ryan being this cold toward her and she didn't like it. Not one bit.

"C'mon…" She tossed her purse and briefcase on the chair in front of his desk and walked around to sit on top of his desk. "Don't be mad. I really did mean to call you, but I was exhausted and, quite frankly, it's all your fault."

"My fault?"

"If you hadn't kept me awake for nearly three nights straight, I might have gotten some rest."

Her statement finally produced a smile and the pain in her chest began to subside.

"All right. Well, you're here now…what did you want to talk about?" Ryan asked.

"Talk?" Jessie said with a grin. Standing, she sashayed over to the door and locked it. She was thankful his office wasn't all glass or had a sidelight. They would have all the privacy they needed for what she had in mind. "I wasn't exactly thinking about talking."

"Oh really?"

"Oh yes. I'm sure there's another activity we could come up with." She walked back to him and, before he could move, she covered his mouth with hers. The kiss was every bit as ravaging as it always was between them. Tongues seeking, tasting, taking everything. Jessie hadn't thought about what she would say when she'd come to Ryan's office. She'd assumed they would discuss their future. But when she'd seen the frown on his face and obvious displeasure with her, she knew one way to put him in a better frame of mine.

She'd thought she would be in control of the situation, but she quickly found out she was wrong as his fingers deftly unfastened the buttons on her pink silk blouse and tossed it to the floor. "Ryan..." she began, but he was already disposing of her black bra to expose her breasts.

"I thought we weren't talking," he said, quickly spinning her around so she was bent over his desk.

Any thought of her being the one to establish the rules and boundaries of their affair quickly vanished when his roving hands were everywhere. When he came to the hem of her black pencil skirt, he pushed under and up. His warm palm slid across her buttocks and over the panel of her thong. Jessie trembled and her breathing quickened when he began kissing her neck and his fingers rubbed the place where she ached for his touch.

But he didn't reward her with what she wanted. Instead, he tipped her head back and his tongue plundered the cavern of her mouth. He was dominant and claiming her, and Jessie yielded to the passion he evoked in her. She wanted him. *Now.*

"Please." She knew she was begging, but she had no control when she was with Ryan.

Ryan's fingers pushed the silk scrap of material aside to probe her damp, hot sex. Jessie gasped as delicious sensations curled through her. She arched into his erection and shamelessly rubbed her bottom against him, desperate to get off. That only seemed to aggravate him and she heard the rip of material, rustle of a packet and the tug of his zipper. Then he was there. Right there. Nudging her thighs apart and surging inside her.

Their lovemaking was wilder and hotter than anything Jessie could imagine. She was bent over and Ryan was holding her hips while he established a devastatingly fast, hard rhythm that had her moaning in pleasure as any element of control she thought she had was shattered. And when Ryan thrust again, his harsh groan was mingled with her orgasm as they both climaxed together.

Afterward, he spun her in his arms and claimed her mouth in a slow, deeply sensual kiss that made what they'd shared even more profound.

When their breathing finally returned to normal, Ryan pulled away to discard the protection, asking, "Was it good for you?"

Jessie smiled as she rebuttoned her blouse and pulled down her skirt. The thong, lying in tatters on the floor, meant she would have to go without underwear, which felt even more sinful. "What do you think?"

"I hope I wasn't…"

She blushed. She'd never been as uninhibited as she was than when they were together. "You were just right."

After zipping up, Ryan sat in his chair and pulled Jessie into his lap. "I suppose we should have that talk now."

"You mean the one where I was going to tell you I wanted to see where this goes? You mean that one?"

His face lit up as if he'd won the Super Bowl. "Yeah, that one."

Jessie stroked his cheek with her palm. "I like you, Ryan.

I think you know that. I like you a lot and I'm not exactly sure where this is leading, but I'd like to find out."

He grasped both sides of her face and brushed his lips across hers. "So would I. So would I."

Eleven

Ryan couldn't believe he and Jessie were an item. They weren't exactly boyfriend and girlfriend, but they'd definitely crossed the threshold of being more than just lovers. He'd been so angry when he'd thought she'd stood him up, but then she'd come to his office to apologize. His emotions had been somewhat high if the way he'd taken her from behind on his desk was any indication.

However, what came after was even more precious. After packing a bag at her apartment, much to Becca's obvious approval, Jessie had returned to his penthouse that evening and had rarely left since. And that had been two weeks ago.

They'd both agree to keep their relationship private and to not tell either of their parents. Ryan's motives were clear because he didn't want the Hathaways getting their hopes up until he was sure exactly where they were headed. Jessie's parents, he wasn't so sure of. Was she still not ready to stand up to them and all their expectations to tell them she'd made a decision for herself and chosen Ryan over Hugh? That rankled him.

Ryan wanted Jessie to say she was completely done with Hugh, but he supposed it was hard, given she'd been with the man for over a decade. He was having to exercise patience when it came to Jessie. He didn't want to move too fast or to rush her into something she would later regret.

Instead, he was enjoying how easy it was for them to be together. After work, they'd usually congregate on the sofa with their laptops and work. He'd whip up dinner in his superb chef's kitchen, which was outfitted with a Bosch electric cooktop stove, Fisher & Paykel refrigerator and microwave, and chrome appliances. He was a pretty good cook having learned to survive after college.

Sometimes they sat out on his private terrace with a glass of wine. Other times, they'd get takeout and catch a Netflix movie on his built-in concealed television on the wall and make love until the wee hours of the morning until they were both spent yet fully satisfied.

Their relationship wasn't always sunshine and roses. They'd argued once when she'd heard him calling Allison Randall for an update on scheduling his second interview with Black Crescent. Jessie had made it very clear she was vehemently opposed, but then she'd backed down when he'd told her he had no news to report. Ryan knew it was just a matter time before they both had to take a stand, but he was enjoying their relationship until then.

One day last week, he'd surprised her with front-row Broadway tix that one of his clients had given him. But tonight, Ryan had planned something special.

He would whisk her away to an enchanted garden for a private dinner. He'd arranged it with a friend who had a membership at the garden. A client of his, Theo Morales, was a local chef who owned a farm-to-table restaurant and he was preparing a feast for them to enjoy. Ryan was already dressed for the casual evening in dark jeans and a black button-down sport shirt.

When Jessie arrived at his penthouse that evening, she was still dressed in a suit and wearing heels. Her usually straight hair had started to wave up because of the humidity from the hot July evening.

"Hey, babe." Ryan took her briefcase from her and handed her a glass of wine.

"Thank you," Jessie said, kicking off her heels and plopping down on his leather sectional. "It's been a long day. I'm so glad we can just kick back and relax."

"Actually—" he sat beside her on the sofa "—I was thinking we could go out tonight."

Jessie glanced at him. "Do we have to? I was hoping for a quiet evening in."

"We do. It's nothing fancy. But I promise you, you'll enjoy."

She eyed him suspiciously.

"Trust me."

After showering, Jessie changed into slim-fitting jeans, which had Ryan salivating at her pert bottom, a floral-print blouse and espadrilles. He could tell she'd flat-ironed her hair because it was back to being bone-straight. She looked cute and sexy as hell, but then again, he always thought that. Although it had taken them a long time to go from friends to lovers to a couple, it was so natural and felt so right, it was like it was always meant to be. He didn't want to think that it could all go away if he accepted the job at Black Crescent.

"You ready?" he asked, snatching his phone and wallet off the console table.

"I am, but I'm curious as to where you're taking me."

"You'll see." Ryan grabbed her hand and they took the elevator down to the first floor. A cab, waiting outside, whisked them away to the East Village to the Sixth Street and Avenue B Community Garden.

When the cab pulled up outside the black wrought-iron gates, Jessie turned to look at him. "What's going on?"

"Wait for it." He paid the cabbie and slid out of the back-seat to stand on the pavement and helped Jessie from the cab. Theo was waiting for him at the entrance.

"Ryan!" Theo grabbed his hand and pulled him into a one-armed hug. "It's good to see you. Welcome to 6 & B Garden."

"Thank you, Theo. This is my lady—" he circled his arm around Jessie's waist and pulled her forward "—Jessie Acosta."

Theo grasped her hand and placed it to his lips. "A pleasure." He released her hand and looked at Ryan. "Are you ready for a feast for the senses?"

"Absolutely." Ryan smiled, glancing down at Jessie. "Lead the way."

Theo opened the gate and led them through a maze of ornamental shrubs and lush evergreen trees, past the garden plots for many of its members. On the way, Theo pointed out the different variety of fruiting trees, flowering shrubs and innumerable herbs, flowers and vegetables.

"This is amazing," Jessie said. "And the members keep this all up?"

"Year-round," Theo commented. "But now we're part of a nonprofit corporation comprised of a board of directors, many of whom are garden members, along with some community leaders. Everyone wants to lend their expertise and support, and because of that we've been going strong for decades."

"I never knew," Jessie commented.

"Wait to see what your man has in store for you."

Several minutes later, they'd come to a beautiful decorated trellis with string lights, lanterns and large urns of colorful seasonal flowers everywhere. And in the middle of it all was a candlelight dinner for two.

"Well, what do you think?"

*   *   *

Jessie was overcome. She couldn't believe Ryan had gone to all this trouble for a Wednesday night date. They'd been spending so much time together, she hadn't spent much of the last weeks in her own bed. She hadn't wanted to be separated from him—and that scared her. Was she getting in over her head? She'd pretty much ignored calls from her folks in Falling Brook and Hugh in London. She was sure they all wanted to know what was going on and hoping things would return to normal. But they wouldn't. Couldn't. At first, she'd felt guilty for abandoning her family, but for the first time in her life, Jessie felt free and liberated. Able to do what she wanted and be damned with what her parents or anyone else thought about it.

Instead, she and Ryan had only grown closer. They spoke everyday on the phone whenever she could take a break at work and texted often. And at night…well, that was off the charts. Ryan made love to her with such passion. He knew her body so intimately, probably better than Jessie ever did.

And now he'd done this. Something so romantic but yet completely Ryan. "Thank you. I love it." She couldn't resist smiling from ear to ear.

"Come." Ryan held out the chair for her. She sat and he joined her, sitting across from her. A large cloche covered both place settings.

"I've quite the meal planned for you lovebirds," Theo stated, "but for now, enjoy the salad, straight from the garden." He lifted both their domes. "It's a shaved trumpet mushroom salad with a truffle vinaigrette. Hope you enjoy." He quickly left the area, leaving them alone.

"Ryan, how did you manage this?" Jessie said, glancing around. "It's magnificent."

He shrugged. "I rented the garden out for the night so we could have privacy and enjoy the surroundings."

Jessie's heart sang with delight and she blinked away the tears at the backs of her eyes. "Thank you. No one has ever done anything like this for me."

His gaze met hers and traveled over her face, searching her eyes. "You deserve it, Jessie. I hope you know how much the last couple of weeks have meant to me. And I wanted to do something meaningful."

She nodded, overcome with emotion. "You did. You did."

The rest of their dinner was nothing short of superb. Theo went all-out with the second course of duck à l'orange with glazed turnips picked straight from the garden. The dessert was a delicious lemon meringue tart with a compote made from the fruits in the garden. Jessie dabbed her napkin at the sides of her mouth.

"Theo, dinner was magnificent. Thank you so much."

"You're welcome. I hope we'll see you both soon?" He glanced at Ryan. "Maybe at our next public event we're hosting?"

"We definitely won't be a stranger," Ryan said and looked over at Jessie. "Care for a stroll?"

"Would love one."

They took a leisurely walk through the gardens, taking time to admire the different species of plants and vegetables while smelling flowering lilacs and sunflowers. When they ended back up at the front gates, Jessie stopped and spun into Ryan's arms. She tilted her head back and pressed her lips against his. He grasped her to him, claiming her lips languidly as if they had all the time in the world, as if she belonged to him. And she did because with each stroke of his tongue, Jessie couldn't bear to tear herself away from him.

Eventually, Ryan lifted his head. "Let's get back to my place," he murmured.

"Yes."

Jessie didn't remember the cab ride to Ryan's. All she could think about was getting Ryan alone and naked. Naked being the operative word. As soon as they were in his private elevator, riding to his penthouse, they were all over each other, kissing and touching. When the elevator dinged, they didn't even separate, they just continued kissing.

Shoes were kicked off and shirts began flying everywhere, followed by their jeans. By the time they reached Ryan's bedroom, there was a trail of clothes behind them, but they were both thankfully naked. They joined together with such intensity in a mass of limbs on the bed that Jessie felt she would pass out from the excitement. Instead, she heard a purring sound in her throat when Ryan slid inside her and they became one. She writhed, clinging to him as the entire world fell away and Ryan was her anchor. When their release came, Ryan shouted and Jessie cried out because they'd reached paradise and it had never felt so good.

Those were her last thoughts as she drifted off to sleep.

Could life get any better? Although Ryan hadn't heard any more about the Black Crescent opportunity, he knew he was still in the running, so he was taking it one day at a time. He also knew that, at some point, he would have to make a decision, but for now he was enjoying the ride. He was discovering new things about Jessie each day. She was breaking out of her parents' shadow and doing what was best for her.

It was an attractive quality, Ryan thought the next evening when he and Jessie attended one of his favorite activities. They were volunteering at a local school's food bank, stocking shelves with peanut butter, jelly, canned goods and snacks. After learning many children didn't eat after they left school, Ryan had wanted to get involved and had been donating money as well as giving his time to help stock groceries for children to take home with them for the weekend.

Ryan's special treat last night had really touched Jessie and she'd showed her appreciation when they'd gotten home. Ryan smiled when he thought about her hands and mouth on him. He'd thought he'd worn her out and, with her hard day at work, he'd assumed she'd want to stay in tonight. Instead, she agreed to accompany him.

"Why wouldn't I come? Do you think I'm that much of a diva?"

"Of course not," Ryan replied. "You've never talked about giving back, is all."

"I should," Jessie replied. "Our family was one paycheck away from needing their services after Black Crescent went bust. We almost left Falling Brook and moved in with my grandparents in Brooklyn."

"I'm glad that day never came," Ryan said.

"It wasn't easy. Although my dad was employed after the crash, ultimately, it was my mother who put in long hours at the dealership, often working overtime until eventually she was made office manager."

"Does she resent your father for never recovering from the disaster?"

Jessie stopped filling up the food bag and looked at him. "That's a fair question, but one I've never asked her. My parents' marriage has always been somewhat of a mystery to me."

"Why is that?"

"They sleep in separate rooms. She has her job and clubs, while he stays at home and broods. I've always wondered why they're still together. I suppose it led to my trying to be helpful after Black Crescent collapsed. I just wanted them to be happy again and they were when my exposure to the O'Malleys led me to date Hugh. And so I've continued fulfilling their expectations for my life and future, but

I've been unhappy and dissatisfied for a long time. I want what your parents have. I've never seen two people as in love with each other as your parents are."

Ryan smiled. "Thank you." He was proud his parents had celebrated thirty-five years of marriage and were still going strong. He wanted to emulate them and have the same kind of solid foundation they had one day. "Speaking of my family… My mom's birthday is coming up this weekend. I know we said we'd keep our relationship between us, but I'd really like it if you could make it."

Jessie's brow quirked questioningly. "Are you sure I should come to a *family* gathering? I mean… I haven't spent time with your mother in years. Won't she suspect something?"

"You're still my friend. There's no reason you can't join us, if you 'happen' to be in town."

"I don't know."

"C'mon, it'll be fun. And I'd really like to have you there."

"If I go, I'll have to stay at my parents'," Jessie said. "There's no way I could come home and not make an appearance. My mother would roast me over the coals."

"Of course."

They continued boxing and bagging up groceries for the school, but in the back of his mind Ryan knew that any day now, when his second Black Crescent interview was called, their relationship could come tumbling down.

Jessie didn't know why she was nervous as she sat in the passenger seat of Ryan's Porsche 911 Carrera as he drove them to Falling Brook for the weekend. It wasn't like he hadn't given her a lift before, but this time was different. They were an unofficial couple and hadn't yet shared this detail with any of their friends or family, except Becca and Adam.

This weekend would be the first time she accompanied him to a public outing where his family and anyone else in the community would see them. Was she afraid of the blow-back? Absolutely. Although she and Hugh were on a break, she didn't want to hurt him, either, and if anyone gossiped about her and Ryan being together, he could feel betrayed.

Not that she owed him anything. She'd been honest nearly four months ago when she'd shared with him that their decade-old, long-distance relationship wasn't working. They were on two different paths. But she wasn't looking forward to her parents' disappointment on learning that she and Hugh were no longer an item. Sometimes the weight of living up to their dreams was almost too much to bear.

"You okay?" Ryan asked, reaching for her hand from across the gearshift. "Your hands are like ice. Are you nervous about coming home?"

She shook her head in denial.

"Liar."

She turned to face him. *How could he tell?*

"I'm one of your oldest friends, do you think I can't tell when you have something on your mind? Anyway, you're like me—you're very expressive and whatever you are thinking shows on your face."

"You know me so well. And yes, I'm a bit nervous, but not about your family."

"About yours? Hugh's?"

She nodded. He'd hit the nail on the head.

"We agreed to take this as slow as you need," Ryan said.

"I know. It's not easy coming back here sometimes. All the expectations and obligations overwhelm me."

He squeezed her hand. "Don't let it. You have me and I'll protect you."

She couldn't resist smiling at him, because Ryan did have a way of easing her anxiety. He'd always been a shoulder she could lean on, the man who listened to her troubles without judging her. "I'm extremely lucky to have you."

He kissed the back of her hand and then released her as he pulled into the Falling Brook city limits. They passed the coffee shop, dry cleaner's and post office on the way to oak-tree lined Sycamore Street. Jessie's anxiety increased when they passed O'Malley Luxury Motors and she had to remind herself to breathe.

Finally, Ryan pulled into her parents' paved driveway. Her family's five-bedroom home was once the talk of the neighborhood with its traditional Spanish red-tiled roof, wrought-iron work and manicured lawn. But over the years, newer more modern homes had been built, making theirs a shadow of what it once was.

She hopped out of the car without waiting for Ryan. Her mother's Maserati was in the driveway, so she wanted to beat her to the punch before she came out to meet them. "Thanks for the ride."

"Jessie, for Christ's sake, relax!" Ryan exclaimed as he walked around to the trunk to get her bag. "I can walk you to the door without your parents or anyone else for that matter seeing alarm bells."

Jessie offered a tentative smile. "I'm sorry."

The front door opened and her mother did exactly as she thought and rushed to greet them, launching herself at Jessie. "Honey, I'm so glad you're home. It's been ages."

Angela Acosta matched Jessie in height. Her complexion was fairer than Jessie's, but they shared the same jet-black hair and small curves as many of their ancestors. "It's only been a few weeks," Jessie replied, pulling back. "Mama, you remember Ryan."

"Ryan!" her mother exclaimed and came forward to wrap him in her embrace. "How are you? Now, you haven't been home in a while. Your mother was sorry you couldn't join her for their annual Fourth of July barbecue. My Jessie couldn't, either."

Jessie glanced at Ryan and they both had to resist a smirk.

"Well, I'm here now, Mrs. Acosta. We're celebrating Mom's birthday." Ryan handed Jessie her bag. "I'll see you later."

Jessie couldn't resist watching Ryan walk away. She waved as he got back into his car and drove to the house next door.

"It was so nice of Ryan to bring you home this weekend." Her mother grasped her by the arm and led her inside.

"We've been getting close again," Jessie said once they were indoors and she'd dropped her bag in the foyer.

"That's wonderful, dear," her mother said, releasing her arm. "And you're sure Hugh won't have a problem with that?"

Jessie frowned, folding her arms across her chest. "Why would he? Ryan and I are friends."

Her mother shrugged. "I don't know. You know what they say—men and women are rarely just friends."

"You and Mr. O'Malley are," Jessie commented. "You've been working for him for years and he's always been so kind to us. Helping me and Pete stay at Falling Brook Prep."

Jessie was surprised to see her mother blush, "Uh, yes, we have been friends—I mean colleagues for some time."

Was her mother flustered? Her skin had become pink and Jessie could see the entire topic was making her uncomfortable.

"Is that you, buttercup?" Her father's voice rang out.

"Yes, it's me, Daddy." Following the sound of his voice, Jessie found him in the living room watching a golf tournament. She frowned when she saw a glass of brown liquid beside him. Plastering a smile on her face, Jessie walked over to give her father a kiss.

"It's good to see you, sweetheart." Her father had been her hero. Well under six feet, Peter Acosta was normally average weight, but it looked as if he'd dropped some pounds recently. And his once jet-black hair, like her own, had grayed at the temples. He'd also grown a salt-and-pepper beard since the last time she'd seen him. And why was he still in his pajamas in the afternoon?

"You, too, Daddy. I thought while we were home we could go to the golf range and you could help me with driving?" She knew how much he'd enjoyed the sport before he'd been kicked out of the country club for nonpayment of dues.

As soon as she'd made enough in the firm, she'd paid for a membership for him again, but her father adamantly refused it. He didn't take handouts, certainly not from his daughter. Furthermore, he didn't want to hang around fake people who ditched their friends. Because that's exactly what had happened to her parents. Friends they'd known and socialized with for years had ostracized him and made him feel small after the loss of their wealth.

"Oh, I don't think so," Pete Acosta replied. "I could never go back there."

"We don't have to go the country club, Daddy. A fun spot just opened in the nearby town. It's called Top Golf. You can practice your swing on their range. It even shows replays and your stats on the display, which helps you make adjustments to your swing. What do you say?"

"I say it sounds like a lot of fun, Pete." Her mother concurred, patting his shoulder, which was the most contact Jessie had seen from her mother toward him in years. Why had she not noticed it before? Was it because she and Ryan were so affectionate and touched each other often? "Did you ask your brother and Amanda if they could join us?"

"Already on it. I couldn't get reservations for tonight…" Jessie added because once she told her mother she was going out with Ryan, it was going to be a big deal. "So I made them for tomorrow. Could be a family affair. What do you say?"

Her father smiled. "It sounds wonderful, buttercup. Thank you."

Jessie released a sigh of relief. She would get her father away from the television and finally living again with the rest of the world. She wanted to do the right thing for her family, but for them that meant salvaging her relationship with Hugh, even when Jessie's heart was starting to lead her in a different direction.

"How's my baby boy," Marilyn Hathaway said when Ryan had come strolling into the family home minutes earlier. His mother was in the kitchen baking his favorite chocolate-chip cookies.

Ryan swiped one as he swept his mother into a whirlwind hug. "Good now that I see you. You're as beautiful as ever."

"Oh stop!" She patted his chest. "And put me down."

He did as instructed and continued munching the cookie in his mouth. "Have Sean and Ben arrived?"

"Ben and Daphne are on their way. Sean and Monica will be along shortly. Monica had a bout of morning sickness, so they'll be a bit behind." His sister-in-law, Monica, although past her first trimester, was still suffering during her pregnancy.

"That means I get you all to myself," Ryan said, reaching for another cookie.

"I don't mind that at all," his mother replied. "So tell me what's new with you? Seems like we haven't chatted much the last few weeks." Ryan and his mother were close and usually spoke a couple of times a week, but since Jessie, his attentions had been focused elsewhere.

"Um, that's because I've been real busy."

His mother folded her arms across her chest. "Do I look stupid? A young woman has turned your head and that's who you're spending all your time with."

Ryan chuckled. "Mom, that's getting awful personal."

"And since when do you have a problem telling me you're dating?" she inquired. "Unless—" she paused and eyed him "—you think this one is someone special? Someone you could get serious with?"

"Aww, Mom. Don't go marrying me off just yet. I'm still in my twenties. There's plenty of time."

"That's what you young folks always think." His father, Eric, joined them in the kitchen. "How are you son?" He gave Ryan a one-armed hug.

"I'm good, Dad. You're looking well."

"That's because I have your mom by my side and she takes good care of your old man." He flashed his wife a smile.

His father was the picture of health. He'd been diagnosed with Type II diabetes and had to adjust his diet, losing thirty pounds in the process. Over six feet tall, his father now looked slim and trim in the Nike tracksuit he wore. They were similar in that Ryan and his father had the same brown complexion. "You need a good woman by your side."

"Just because Sean and Ben have coupled up doesn't mean I'm ready to join in."

"But you are seeing someone?" his mother inquired. When she wanted something, she could be persistent.

"Yes."

"I knew it." His mother pointed her spatula at him as she took another tray of cookies out of the oven. This time they were peanut butter, Sean's favorite. She spoiled him and his brothers rotten, always making treats when they were home. "A mother knows these things."

"How's that job opportunity with Black Crescent coming along?" his father inquired.

Ryan's brow furrowed. He was hoping to not have to think about it because he knew it would draw a line in the sand in his relationship with Jessie. "Slowly, Dad. Black Crescent's interview process is moving at a snail's pace. I know I'm not the only candidate, but you would think I would have heard something by now."

"Are you sure you want to move back to town?" his mother inquired. "You've lived in Manhattan since you left home."

"I know. I wanted a change of scenery."

"It's your choice," his father said, "and we'd love to have you close by. But be sure you can live with the decision. Black Crescent caused this community and the Acostas, our neighbors, a lot of heartache. I know Joshua Lowell has done a lot to fix things, but to some people it will never be enough."

"I will, Dad," Ryan replied because, quite honestly, he was having a hard time justifying his reasoning for choosing Black Crescent. At the time, it had seemed like the right choice to put distance between him and Jessie. But the more time he spent with Jessie, the more Ryan realized the company played a huge role in shaping her life. Could he live with himself if he was the cause of Jessie backsliding and going back to living by her family's expectations?

Twelve

"I can't believe you're leaving us to spend time with Ryan and his family," her mother wailed. "I thought you were here to be with *your* family."

"Oh, Angela, don't make the girl feel bad," her father stated. "It's one night and she's been with us all day, helping you in your garden."

"I know that, Pete, but we get to see her so infrequently."

"It's only a few hours. I'll be back in no time. It's Mrs. Hathaway's sixtieth birthday." Jessie had already texted Ryan to meet her outside.

"I didn't know you were close with the Hathaways anymore."

Jessie didn't bother commenting. "I'll see you later. Don't wait up." She waved and quickly left the house. She didn't want any more comments or questions from her mother. No, she hadn't been close with Ryan's mother for some time, but she was *very close* to Ryan and it meant a lot to him that she came tonight.

She'd dressed with care for the evening, choosing a little black spaghetti-strapped dress with hints of silver, which hit

below the knee. It was the perfect complement to the black
suit and silver tie Ryan planned to wear. Modest makeup,
silver earrings, kitten heels and a black clutch completed
her look. Jessie was satisfied Mrs. Hathaway would not
have a problem with her ensemble.

Walking the short distance between driveways, Jessie
was nearly to the Hathaway house when an arm encircled
her waist, bringing her into the shadows.

"Ryan…"

She didn't get another word out because he cupped
her face in his hands and kissed her. She wound her arms
around his neck and opened her lips to his invading tongue.
He plundered her mouth, kissing her deeply and reminding
her of exactly what he could do to her. Make her on fire for
him so that every part of her was hungry for more contact.

Ryan pulled back. "Easy, love."

"Then don't start something you don't plan to finish,"
Jessie replied with a groan.

"I'm sorry. I missed you," Ryan whispered.

"So did I." And she had. Because Ryan made her feel
special. So special, it scared her. Could this be real? She'd
never felt this closeness with Hugh or even with her own
family.

"C'mon." He grabbed her hand to lead her inside, but
Jessie stopped him.

"No." She wrenched her hand away. "You've just kissed
me senseless. I need a moment to repair the damage to my
makeup." She pulled her compact and lipstick out of her
purse and quickly touched up her face. When she was done,
she said, "Now I'm ready."

Jessie took his breath away.

Ryan was certain his entire family could see how absolutely he'd fallen for her. Tonight she'd sparkled. His parents hadn't said a word when he'd brought Jessie into the

house. Instead, his mother had enveloped her in a warm hug and welcomed her back into the fold.

Soon his brothers, in black tie, arrived with their wives and they'd all hopped into the limousine Ryan had procured to take them to the country club where they were to have dinner.

He knew his mother didn't like big displays of wealth, but this was different. It was her sixtieth birthday and she'd already done so much for him and his brothers, they'd all agreed she deserved something nice for her birthday.

They enjoyed a glass of champagne on the drive to the country club and once there, were led into a private dining room where the chef had prepared a special menu for his mother.

"Honey, you didn't have to go to all this trouble," his mother said, looking at Ryan. *How did she manage to know he was the instigator of the plan?* Like she'd always known when they were up to no good. Once, he and Ben had been playing ball in the house and broken her favorite lamp. They'd tried to superglue it and hoped she wouldn't notice. But Marilyn Hathaway had known instantly and they'd gotten the punishment to prove it. A week without video games.

"You're worth it, Mom," Ryan replied.

"I'm happy to have all my boys here," she said, glancing around the room. "And my daughters." She glanced at her daughters-in-law and then at Jessie. "You, too, Jessie."

Ryan felt Jessie clutch his hand from underneath the table. He could see she was touched by his mother's words.

The dinner went exactly as planned. The food was delicious, and his mother was genuine happily to be surrounded by her sons and their women. Later, they retired to the main dining room where a table had been set aside so they could listen to the solo artist for the evening.

Ryan was on his way to sit down when he ran into a

familiar Falling Brook couple, Joshua Lowell and Sophie Armstrong. He'd met Joshua Lowell at his first interview for the CEO position. There was no way to forget him. With his angular face and stone-hewed jaw, the six-foot, broad-shouldered, dark blond with sharp hazel eyes looked more like a model than he did the CEO for an investment firm.

"Ryan?" Joshua was the first to speak.

"Mr. Lowell."

"Joshua, please. I didn't realize you were in town," Joshua said.

"I don't live here. It's Mom's birthday." Ryan glanced behind him to see that his parents were already seated. "We're—" he inclined his head to Jessie at his side "—here to celebrate."

"I'm sorry, I don't believe we've met." Joshua extended his hand to Jessie.

Her eyes narrowed and she didn't accept his hand. "I know who you are, Joshua Lowell."

He frowned. "My reputation. Or shall I say, family's reputation, precedes me."

"It's a small town," Jessie responded.

Ryan glanced at Jessie and her expression was not one of warmth, like it usually was. Did she blame Joshua for what his father had done? It wasn't like her to be unfair. Changing the subject, Ryan opted for happy news. "Congratulations on your engagement." He smiled at Sophie.

Joshua beamed down at the petite reporter whose wavy, highlighted brown hair fell in waves to just below her shoulders. She was in a tailored dress that suited her slim figure. "Thank you," Sophie responded. "I was certainly surprised when he announced to the world we were getting married, but I couldn't be happier."

"That's quite a ring," Jessie commented, and Sophie was eager to show off her diamond ring.

While Sophie gushed about her ring, Joshua whispered,

"I want you to know, I was very impressed with your credentials, Ryan. You are very high on our list of a few select candidates. I look forward to our next interview."

Ryan grinned. "Thank you. I appreciate you saying that."

"No, I absolutely mean it," Joshua said. "You have a passion for what you do, more than I ever did. Although I majored in economics in college, art has always been and will always be what wakes me up in the morning."

"Why did you stay so long at Black Crescent?"

"I felt responsible to clean up the mess my father made. To try to make amends as best I could. And I've done that. Or at least, all I can. It's time for me to hand the baton off."

"Are you men talking shop?" Sophie inquired.

Ryan could see the wheels of her journalistic mind churning, thinking up another story.

"C'mon, honey, let's leave these two to their evening," Joshua said. "Ryan…" He shook his hand. "We'll talk soon."

The couple left, but Jessie was still staring at them. "Omigod. *She's* the reporter who wrote the Black Crescent anniversary article."

"One and the same."

"I'm surprised he could forgive her, given he didn't come out smelling like a rose in the story."

Ryan shrugged. "Opposites attract, right?" He and Jessie were certainly at opposite ends of the spectrum when it came to him accepting a job at Black Crescent. He wanted the challenge and she wanted him to forget about it. They were never going to agree, so he held out his hand. "Let's dance." She accepted and took his hand.

On the dance floor, he pulled Jessie into his arms. "I know this is rather public," he said. "You okay?"

She tilted her head to look up at him.

"I've never had a more fantastic night. Your family…" He saw tears in her eyes. "They're amazing. So warm and inviting. They made me feel like I belong. I've never felt that way with my family. I've always felt like I had to put on a show and do what's expected. It's a relief to just be myself."

"That's because you belong with me." And before he knew what he was doing, he was kissing her. He hadn't meant to, but she was looking at him so adoringly and with the songstress crooning "At Last," Ryan forgot where he was.

When he lifted his head, Jessie was staring at him intently. It was a turning point. They'd just announced to everyone in the country club that they were a couple.

Jessie was overcome and immediately excused herself to go to the ladies' room. She hadn't expected Ryan to kiss her like that, out in the open where anyone could see them. But now that he had, didn't she feel a little bit relieved?

They were no longer a secret. And soon everyone in Falling Brook would know. Jessie was under no illusions word wouldn't get around. It was a town of two thousand people and many of them knew the O'Malleys and would no doubt be telling them they'd seen her kissing Ryan Hathaway. Although she and Hugh were on a break, their parents didn't know that.

Once again, Jessie was repairing her lipstick in the mirror when the door to the restroom opened. Ryan's mother entered. "There you are. I was wondering where you'd escaped to."

Jessie laughed nervously. "I needed to use the restroom."

"Aww, honey, we both know that's not the real reason you're in here. You're running away from what's going on between you and my son."

"I'm not running away."

"I'm not blind, Jessie. You and Ryan used to be so

close, the best of friends, but then your father fell on hard times. There were rumors you and your brother received a scholarship from O'Malley Motors. Suddenly, you and that O'Malley boy were thick as thieves and you and Ryan were no more. And I never understood how that could happen because I always felt you and Ryan might grow into more one day. And I was right."

Jessie shook her head. "Mrs. Hathaway, you don't understand..."

"Oh yes, I do." His mother reached for both of Jessie's hands and clasped them in hers. "I understand you've been fighting your own heart for some time and doing what others expect of you because you think you owe them. When are you going to allow yourself to do what *you* want to do? Life is too short, Jessie. You have to grab your happiness when it comes. *With* whomever it comes."

"Thank you, Mrs. Hathaway." She squeezed her hand. "I appreciate your sage advice. And let me say, happy birthday."

"So the cat is out of the bag," Ben said when he and Sean found Ryan outside, interminably pacing the terrace.

"I was wondering how long you were going to be able to resist telling the whole world."

Ryan chuckled. "Whoever knew my brother could be a comedian. I crossed the line out there. I told Jessie we would keep our relationship private until she was ready to go public, and I go and blow it."

Ben came toward him and grasped his shoulder. "Don't be so hard on yourself. You dig the girl. And you wanted to show it. There's nothing wrong with that."

"And the idea of you two staying private was ridiculous," Sean stated, "when it's so obvious by looking at the two of you that you're crazy about each other."

"You're seeing things," Ryan responded. "Jessie doesn't feel that way about me. We're compatible in the bedroom."

"TMI," Ben said. "And we both have two eyes. If we can see it, so can everyone else in that room." He pointed to the ballroom.

Ryan stared through the double doors. Could he believe Jessie was developing feelings for him? He was afraid to think it, let alone believe it. For months, he'd vowed to keep his distance after pining away for years, but now he was getting in deeper than ever.

No, he had to keep his feelings to himself. Act as if he didn't care until Jessie was ready to say those three words.

The return limo drive was a bit more subdued. Jessie didn't mean to be a buzzkill, but she'd listened to what Mrs. Hathaway'd had to say and knew she had a lot of thinking to do.

When they made it to the Hathaway residence, she wished them all good-night and walked in silence with Ryan the short distance to her parents' front door. She fumbled her keys out of her clutch and dropped them on the front step.

"I've got it." Ryan bent to pick them up. He handed them to her and a fizz of electricity sparked between them. "Jessie, I'm sorry about tonight. If I embarrassed you in any way."

She shook her head. "Well, you did. I thought we agreed to keep our relationship between us? I thought you understood that. Now everyone in Falling Brook will know. Word will get back to my parents, to Hugh."

"Is Hugh all you care about?" She could see he was visibly angry at her mentioning his name.

"I've told you how hard it's been living up to my parents' expectations, and I intended to talk to them in my own time, but you've forced the issue."

"Maybe it needed to be forced, so you can finally make a choice."

Jessie ran her fingers through her hair. "Why do you do this? Why do you always push me?"

"Because if I don't, who will?" he responded hotly. "You'll keep doing as everyone expects instead of being true to you. Wake up, Jessie!"

"I have to go," Jessie said, turning on her heel. "Are you still going to give me a ride back into the city?"

He nodded. "Of course. That hasn't changed. Have fun with your family at Top Golf."

She glared at him. She didn't know how that was going to be possible when word would get back to her parents that she was dallying with Ryan.

Using her key, she opened the front door, stepped inside, closed it and leaned against it.

"Is something going on between you and Ryan Hathaway?" She heard her mother's voice in the darkness.

"Not now, Mama."

"I thought you were with Hugh." Her mother moved out of the shadows. Her arms were folded across her chest, looking as if Jessie had disappointed her. She was in her pajamas, which meant she'd waited up after Jessie told her not to. "I got a call from one of my friends that she saw you and Ryan kissing at the country club."

"I said not now, Mama," Jessie bit out and then rushed up the stairs to the guest bedroom. She wouldn't stand being Twenty Questioned about her love life by her own mother. She had a right to make decisions for herself. To choose whom she wanted to love.

Love.

Was it possible she'd fallen in love with Ryan?

If so, she'd done it unconsciously. She'd assumed their sexual chemistry was why she'd felt so close to him, but perhaps she was wrong. Perhaps Mrs. Hathaway was right and Ryan was who she was supposed to be with all along. But it had taken the reunion to show her that the man of her dreams was right in front of her face the entire time.

Thirteen

Ryan worried Jessie would be upset with him when they drove back to Manhattan, but she wasn't anything other than her usual self. When he'd picked her up, he'd thought he'd glimpsed something resembling a frown on Mrs. Acosta's face. But in an instant it was gone, so Ryan figured everything had gone well. "Did you have a good time at Top Golf?" Ryan asked once they were out of Falling Brook and settled on the interstate.

"We did. Daddy absolutely loved it," Jessie said. "It was the first time I'd seen him animated in a long time."

"That's great."

"Yeah, it was nice to go out as a family and not be about doom and gloom. Today was about the Acostas having a fun day out. We need more of them."

"If there's anything I can do to help, let me know," Ryan stated. "The Hathaway clan was very excited to have you share Mom's birthday with us."

"I'm glad I went."

"Are you sure about that?" Ryan asked, glancing in her direction. "We haven't had a chance to really talk about what happened at the country club other than a few minutes last night."

"You mean the kiss you planted on me?" Jessie's cheeks pinked.

"I was completely out of line. All I can tell you is that I got caught up in the moment. Having you in my arms, it seemed like the most natural thing to do."

"But we'd agreed to keep our relationship between us," Jessie responded evenly. "Do you have any idea what you did? My mom cornered me last night, then again at Top Golf about us, wanting to know when we became more than friends. She suggested the kiss was you staking your claim so everyone in Falling Brook knows we're together."

Ryan frowned. That's the last thing he'd been thinking. "That wasn't why I kissed you. How could you think that?"

"When you say one thing and then do the opposite, it does leave me to wonder."

Ryan tensed and his fingers clutched the wheel. He hadn't realized how upset Jessie would be, but he supposed it was naïve on his part to think this would blow over. "So you're okay to be on my arm as a friend, but nothing more. Heaven forbid anyone sees us as anything else and upsets the apple cart."

"Don't put words in my mouth." Jessie mouth firmed in a straight line. "We'd agreed on this before we left Manhattan and you blatantly went against my wishes."

Ryan glanced in her direction and found her gaze focused on him. "I didn't do it *blatantly*."

Her eyes narrowed as if she didn't believe him.

"How long have you known me? Have I ever given you a reason *not* to trust me, Jessie?"

"No."

"Then don't pick a fight. I said I'm sorry and I am. I would never want to put you in an awkward situation. You know that."

She nodded, folding her arms across her chest.

Ryan wanted to know what she was thinking, but she was closed off and doing a good impression of ignoring him. And he hated it. He wanted her to feel like she could talk to him about anything, like she always had. "Whatever is bothering you, you can talk to me about it."

"I can't." She turned her head and stared out of the window. Jessie wished she could talk to her dearest friend about what she was feeling, but she couldn't. *He* was the reason she was in such turmoil.

She suspected she'd fallen in love with Ryan.

She'd never expected their relationship to take the turn it had and it scared her. She'd only ever been with Hugh and theirs hadn't been a normal relationship. And her parents' certainly wasn't an example. Their lack of affection or passion couldn't be healthy. Jessie didn't know how to do this love thing, which made it difficult to confide in Ryan. If she wasn't sure of how she felt, how could she possibly talk to him?

Her mother already recognized their relationship wasn't what she'd led her to believe. She'd cornered Jessie at Top Golf when they were in the restroom, asking her when their relationship had become romantic, but Jessie had remained mum. Not only was she trying to keep her word to Hugh, but she'd pointed out to her mother that their relationship was none of her business. Her mother hadn't been happy with her answer.

Jessie had never had a close relationship with Angela Acosta. She'd always been a daddy's girl, which was why she'd always wanted to do what her parents asked—to please him. She's supposed that's why it hurt so much to see her father in such pain over what happened fifteen years ago. She wanted him to move on with his life, but he was mired in the past. No matter how well she did as an attorney and gave back to her parents, in her father's mind, it would never be what he once had.

That was why she didn't want Ryan to take the job at Black Crescent. The company's legacy was painful for so many people, her father included. Jessie was certain when the time came, Ryan would do the right thing.

"We're here," Ryan said, turning off the engine and jumping out of the vehicle.

Jessie glanced up and saw that Ryan had parked in front of her brownstone. She hopped out and found him pulling her overnight bag from the trunk. "I've got it."

She tried to take the bag from him, but he glared at her. "I'll walk you up."

They were quiet as they climbed the stairs and Jessie opened the door to her apartment. Ryan deposited her bag in her bedroom and turned to face her. "Whenever you want to talk, I'm a phone call away."

"You're leaving?"

"That's what you want, isn't it? You're clearly still upset with me, so I'm giving you some space."

"Ryan…"

He held up his hands. "It's okay. Take some time, but then call me later."

Jessie heard his footsteps on the hardwood floors and then the door closing on his way out. She wanted to stop Ryan, to tell him to stay, but she didn't. She couldn't when she was so conflicted. And then it hit her: she had some unfinished business to sort out before she could move forward with Ryan.

"Ryan, we can stop at any minute," Dennis, his trainer, said after he'd completed two grueling hours of physical activity.

"It's all right. I can keep going."

"Well, I can't," Dennis said, laughing. "I have another

client coming in. I agreed to come in early because you said you needed to burn off some excess energy, but you've done enough for the day."

He tossed Ryan a towel, which he caught. Wiping the sweat from his face, Ryan reached for a Powerade and drank the entire bottle. He'd pushed himself physically as far as he could go because he hadn't wanted to think about Jessie. But it was hopeless. He'd fallen hopelessly, irrevocably, in love with her. He'd known it since the Hamptons, had tried to fight the inevitable, but there it was.

Last night he hadn't been able to sleep because, in the few weeks they'd been together, Ryan had begun to get used to sleeping beside Jessie each night. He loved having her behind curved against his front and his arms wrapped around her slender frame.

Needless to say, he was cranky. But it was a new day and he had much to look forward to. He anticipated hearing from Allison Randall, the recruiter from Black Crescent any day now. He'd interviewed nearly a month ago. She'd told him they were taking their time selecting the right person with a vision on how to move the company forward.

Ryan was no longer sure it was him. He and Jessie were already on thin ice. If he accepted the position, their relationship would be over. He was certain Jessie wouldn't appreciate her boyfriend working for the company that ruined her father. That put Ryan between a rock and a hard place. Go after success, which was in his reach, or choose the woman he loved? If he was chosen, he would be required to make a decision and Ryan hoped he would make the right one.

Ryan was in her head too much. She'd been at work for hours and had missed a court filing for a case one of the senior partners was working on. She'd had to beg the court clerk for an extension, which thankfully had been granted.

Otherwise, her boss would have her head on a stick if she hadn't managed to correct her error.

Now she'd been staring at a brief she needed to finish for another partner and had only written a few paragraphs. *What was wrong with her?* Work had always been her respite. Her refuge from the storm. She'd never had a problem focusing, but then again, she'd never had Ryan Hathaway as a lover.

Whenever she was around him, any idea or thought she had flew right out the window. But she hadn't seen him last night. In an effort to gain some perspective, she'd spent the evening apart from him, though her body was revolting in protest. She literally ached to be with him. To see his handsome face light up when she walked into a room. To hear him laugh at one of her corny knock-knock jokes. To feel him buried so deep inside her she didn't know where she left off and he began. To taste the spiciness of his cologne on his brown skin.

Jessie wanted all of it, but on the other hand, she felt as if she was on a dangerous precipice and if she fell the wrong way, she'd fall headlong into disaster. One road led her on the path her parents envisioned for her with Hugh. The other less-known road led her to Ryan, who was always pushing her to live her life on her own terms. But Jessie was afraid of taking the road less traveled. If she revealed her feelings—that she was falling for Ryan—and their relationship didn't materialize into more, she would have ruined the greatest friendship of her life.

And what did more mean? Marriage? Babies? For years, all she'd had to keep her warm at night was her dedication and focus on her career. On achieving success, so she would never end up like her father. She'd been on the well-known, expected path for years and was on her way to making junior partner. But the victory had begun to seem hollow with no one to share it with. She'd thought that person was Hugh, but over the years had realized it didn't feel the same.

He was the upstanding guy everyone thought he was, and their relationship had always been one of mutual respect, but he didn't make her heart skip a beat or make her ache for him. The times they'd been intimate had been perfunctory and certainly lacking the passion she shared with Ryan. It only took one searing look from Ryan to make her panties damp. Or a drugging kiss like the one he'd given her at the country club for her to lose all thought as to where they were.

Ryan was in her blood. She was weak and defenseless when it came to him. The last few weeks certainly made Jessie believe they could have more, but she was afraid to take the leap. Look at her judgment when it came to Hugh. She'd allowed the relationship to go on much longer than she should have. She should have ended it years ago, but she'd used him as a crutch to keep Ryan at arm's length.

But she did owe Hugh the respect of having a heart-to-heart conversation and finally tell him there was no hope of resurrecting their relationship—so she could have a future. A future that may include Ryan.

Ryan knew he should give Jessie the space she asked for, but it had been over forty-eight hours since the kiss at the country club. Surely, Jessie had calmed down by now? That's what he told himself as he waited outside her apartment door.

Becca answered, fully dressed, her hair done up and her makeup flawless. "Hey, Ryan. C'mon in. I was just leaving for a date, but Jessie's in there." She inclined her head down the hall to Jessie's bedroom. Then she flew out the front door.

Ryan took the pizza box and six-pack of beer he'd brought with him and placed it on the counter. He was looking through the cupboard for some paper plates when Jessie came padding through the kitchen in a tank top, running shorts and her favorite pair of fuzzy bunny slippers. Her face had been wiped clean of makeup, but was bright and clear. Her eyes, however, grew wide when they saw him. "I thought I heard the door, but assumed it was Becca leaving."

"Yeah, I kind of caught her on the way out." Ryan paused from shuffling through her cabinets and pulled a bottle of beer from the carton. He unscrewed it and handed it to Jessie.

"Thanks," She tipped it back and took a swig. She wiped her mouth with the back of her hand. "What are you doing here?"

"I brought dinner." He pointed to the pizza box. "I hope you don't mind? I have cheese and pineapple."

That he still remembered her favorite pizza brought a smile to her face and he released a sigh of relief. Showing up unannounced was a gamble, but he had to do something. They couldn't go on like this.

"Thanks. I am kind of hungry. I skipped lunch." She opened the pizza box without getting a plate and began eating.

"Why?"

"Struggled writing this brief for the senior partner and it was due by six. I think he purposely gives me these deadlines to screw with me." She finished the slice in record time.

"Did you finish?"

"Barely." She swigged her beer. "Today was not my best day."

"Because you're still angry with me?" Ryan surmised.

Jessie shook her head. "I'm not angry. Not anymore."

Ryan brushed a hand across his forehead. "Thank God.

I hope you know I got carried away. It's no excuse for not keeping my word. And I'm sorry."

"I believe you," Jessie said. "I always did. The problem isn't *us*. It's that no one knows Hugh and I broke up."

Ryan frowned. "I don't understand."

"We discussed going our separate ways in private, but hadn't quite had the nerve to tell our families and friends."

Ryan digested this information. "So anyone who was there Saturday night thinks you're cheating on Hugh with me?"

Jessie nodded. "But I don't care about any of that. Or what people think about me. I stopped caring a long time ago after my family and I were ostracized when we lost everything. I worry about my parents and what they think and how they feel. You know my father hasn't been in a good way for years. This could derail him. He's been depending on me to do what's expected and I feel bad because I told Hugh we would tell everyone when the time was right."

"The *time* is right," Ryan stated. He didn't understand what the holdup was. Or perhaps he'd been fooling himself. He thought back to the conversation he'd had with Jessie on the deck of the Hampton beach house. She had said they were on a break and he'd gotten it in his mind that it was a breakup. That's certainly what Jessie had led him to believe. But maybe she was holding out hope that, with time apart, Hugh would see the error of his ways and come crawling back. *Was this all part of some elaborate power play to get him to heel? To get Hugh to finally put a ring on it and stop procrastinating?*

"It's going to have to be," Jessie said. "I left him a message last night that we needed to talk."

"I see."

She eyed him suspiciously. "What's wrong?"

Everything. He'd gotten in too deep with Jessie, even though he'd vowed not to, and she was walking away, doing what her family expected by choosing Hugh. It was beginning to appear that Ryan had been the fool to believe it was truly over between Jessie and Hugh and he finally had a chance of winning her heart when the deck was stacked against him. His phone vibrated in his pocket. He saw the display with the caller's name and knew what he had to do. It was time he finally pursued what was best for him. He couldn't let Jessie or her reaction influence his decision.

Swiping left, he answered.

"Ryan. Hi, it's Allison Randall."

Ryan glanced down at his watch. It was rather late for her to call, but he was happy nonetheless. "Hi, Allison. It's good to hear from you."

"I apologize for the late hour, but I wanted you to know how impressed we were with you and we would like to bring you back for a second interview so you can talk with Joshua about your specific ideas for replacing him as CEO."

"Did Joshua tell you I ran into him in Falling Brook?"

"Yes, he did," Allison replied. "Which is why he told me not to waste any more time. You made a great first impression."

"Thank you, Allison. When would he like to meet?"

"I'll email you a couple of date/time options."

"That would be great. I'll clear my schedule."

"Wonderful," Allison responded. "We'll talk soon. Take care."

"You do the same." Ryan ended the call and, when he did, the somber expression on Jessie's face told him she was not happy about his decision to move forward with the interview process.

"I thought you had forgotten about Black Crescent," Jessie said, placing her beer bottle on the counter.

"Why would you think that?"

Jessie glared. "I don't know." She shrugged. "Maybe because we discussed how taking this position would be an awful idea. Not just for you, but for me and my family. Heck, the entire community. Black Crescent needs to fail so we all can move on with our lives."

"I understand your position, Jessie. But it's not your decision to make. It's mine. Whether I do or do not pursue Black Crescent is my choice. I don't appreciate you trying to dictate my future."

"That's not what I'm doing."

"Aren't you?" he inquired. "Would you be making this same request of me if we weren't sleeping together?"

"How dare you?" She huffed, pushing away from the counter. "One thing has nothing to do with the other. It's a bad move. And I would think, after everything that's happened, everything you witnessed me and my family go through, you would be more sympathetic. But clearly I was wrong. You can only see what *you* want and forget about everyone else."

"Christ! I really can't believe you, of all people, would say that to me," Ryan replied. "I've always been there for you, Jessie. Always been an ear to listen or a shoulder to cry on. Look up the word 'empathetic' and you'll find my picture. It's you who's being unfair."

"Me?"

"If the shoe fits," he returned. "I would never ask you to give up on your dreams. Instead, all I've ever done is champion your goals. Yet that's what you're asking me to do—to give up something I feel strongly about. When you won't compromise yourself. You're not willing to go after the life you want, to break away from your family, but I am, especially if I can't have you."

Jessie's phone rang and she stalked away from him and pulled it out of her purse. "Hello?"

Ryan couldn't hear anything because she turned her back to him. His antenna went up. "Who's on the phone, Jessie?" He stormed toward her.

She held up a finger, telling Ryan to give her a minute, and stepped away to talk in her bedroom. "I'm sorry now isn't a good time to talk, Hugh."

So Hugh was on the line?

Was it fate that the man who was standing between them would call when they were in the middle of their fight? Ryan didn't like that Jessie had turned her back and tried to hide it from him, not wanting him to hear their conversation. If nothing else, he thought they had trust between them. He was wrong which meant they no longer had a future—Jessie wasn't willing to take a risk, to defy her parents and to choose him.

Hugh's timing was the epitome of bad. Why did he have to call her now? She and Ryan had never fought like this before, but this was big. He wanted Jessie to break away from her family, but she couldn't do that. So their entire relationship was at stake and not just their romance. If he took that job with Black Crescent, it would end their friendship, as well.

"Are you listening to me, Jessie?" Hugh asked on the other end of the line.

"I'm sorry, what did you say?"

"Did I catch you at a bad time?"

"Yeah, kind of…sort of." Jessie didn't want to give away that she was with another man. Hugh had never taken kindly to her friendship with Ryan. He'd never forbidden their association, but he'd been uneasy of Jessie's openness with Ryan.

"All right, well, I wanted you to know that I'm coming home to Falling Brook."

"You are?"

"Yes, these last several months apart have really made me see some things differently and I'd like to talk to you in person about some realizations I've had after I did some serious soul-searching."

"Hugh, I don't think that's going to change anything." She had to end things with him once and for all. There was no going back, not after the last month she'd spent with Ryan. It was time Jessie found her own way. She needed to stop doing what Hugh or her parents wanted. She needed to do what she wanted. She and Hugh had a superficial, surface-level relationship at best. They would never truly make one another happy.

"C'mon, Jessie. After everything we've been to each other, don't I at least deserve that much?"

Guilt ate at Jessie's insides. He was right. She owed him enough to let him speak his piece. "Of course. When are you coming in?"

"End of the week."

"All right, I'll see you then."

"And, Jessie…"

"Yes?"

"I miss you." He ended the call, not waiting for her response. And thank goodness he hadn't because she didn't feel the same. She'd hardly given Hugh a thought unless she was comparing how different he and Ryan were.

She returned to the living room and found Ryan with his back to her. She didn't need to be a genius to notice the tension in the set of his shoulders. He was angry. Not just about her stance on his taking the Black Crescent position, but about her call with Hugh.

"Ryan."

He didn't move. Instead, he faced forward, staring out her window as if it had all the answers. "Are you running back to Hugh now because you and I are having a disagreement? Is that what this is?"

Jessie fumed. "Of course not. Why would you think that? Because I took a call?"

He spun around to face her and the dejected look on his face broke her heart. She hated that she was the cause of Ryan's distress. "It's me, Jessie. The man who has been by your side for over half your life listening to you fawn over Hugh O'Malley."

"And you've always been angry about that."

"Yes!"

"You don't like Hugh."

"No, I don't."

"And you resent our relationship?"

"Yes!"

She stared at him and finally saw the truth. "How long have you felt this way?"

"Are you blind, Jessie? I've always wanted you," Ryan stated. "But you never saw me—" when she started to speak, he cut her off, shaking his head "—not until the reunion when we had a moment on the terrace. That's when you recognized the attraction between us. But as soon as Hugh showed up, you walked away. That's when I knew I should move on. But now I've been with you, I want you to stay, but you have to want it, too."

"Don't do that. Don't you make me out to be the bad guy."

"I'm not. I'm stating *I'm* the man for you, Jessie. I always have been and I always will be."

Ryan stared at her expectantly and Jessie's breath caught in her throat. She'd never been as honest and forthright with her feelings as Ryan was being now. He was laying it all on the line, baring his soul to her. And what could she do? She hadn't sorted out all of her feelings yet.

He sucked in a harsh breath. "I guess I'm completely alone in my feelings and clearly misguided." He started toward the door.

"Ryan, wait."

"Why? You don't know what you want. And if you do, it isn't me. It's Hugh."

"Stop putting words in my mouth. You have no idea what's going on here. I…" Jessie didn't know how to verbalize the thoughts rumbling around in her head. How she didn't know how to escape the confines of following her parents' expectations that were so ingrained her. That she'd only just begun to find herself the last few weeks, but was afraid of taking the leap. Hugh and Ryan deserved so much better than she was giving either of them at the moment.

"Yes, I do. You're never going to choose me," Ryan responded quietly. "So that's my cue to leave." His footsteps were sure and strong, and when he reached her front door, he turned to her. She wanted to tell him to stay. She wanted him to wrap his arms around her and tell her everything was going to be okay and they would work through this. But he didn't. He merely opened the door and walked out.

Jessie feared he was walking out of her life for good. And she couldn't bear that. Rushing to the window, she caught sight of him jumping into his Porsche and speeding off into the night. Had she done the right thing letting him walk away? Or had she just made the biggest mistake of her life?

Fourteen

"Jessie!" Hugh picked her up off her feet and wrapped her in a hug the moment she stepped foot in the guesthouse at the O'Malley residence on Friday evening. She'd come straight from work, taken the train and then an Uber from the station. The journey had been tumultuous and not because of the ride. Jessie had been thinking about Ryan and how angry he'd been with her. She'd needed his understanding while she figured out what to do next, but patience wasn't Ryan's virtue. Instead, he kept pressing her to decide, decide, decide. She would in her own time. And she had. On the train ride, Jessie had known she needed to end things with Hugh. They couldn't go on in limbo, not when she was in love with bullheaded, sexy Ryan. Why wasn't life easy?

"Hugh—" she patted his shoulders while peering into his brilliant sky-blue eyes "—put me down."

He laughed and did as she asked, but didn't let go of her. Instead, he kept his arm circled around her waist. "It's so good to see you, babe."

"You're looking well." Jessie politely removed his hand

and moved further into the house. "How does it feel to be back in the States?"

Hugh's handsome features had grown sharper and more defined since the last time she'd seen him. He was clean-shaved and didn't have rugged stubble like Ryan. His dark hair was expertly cut, stopping just above the collar of his tailored three-piece charcoal suit with its frosted-gray tie.

"Better now that you're here," Hugh said, following her into the living room. The room was immaculately decorated in soft creams and pastels with furniture Jessie knew was custom made. An Impressionist painting hung on the wall, showing how well off his family truly was. "Come sit beside me." He patted the empty spot on the sofa.

It seemed rude to resist, so reluctantly she sat beside him, but on the far side of the couch.

"I don't bite, Jessie. Or at least not unless you want me," he chuckled. When she didn't smile, he frowned. "Surely, we haven't been apart so long we can't joke with one another?"

"We've been apart for our *entire* relationship, Hugh. What do you expect?"

"Ouch." His eyes darkened as he held her gaze. "I guess I deserve that, but that's why I'm here. I've recognized I've put our relationship on the back burner and focused too much on my career."

"Yes, you have," Jessie said, running her fingers through her straight hair, "but I can't put it all on you. I never said anything or required more of you. I've been content to be put aside because I always thought one day we would find our way back to each other."

"But you don't feel that way now?"

Jessie shook her head and he placed his hand over his heart.

"I'm sorry. I'm not saying this to hurt you, Hugh, but when I look back, we haven't been in the same city since we were in prep school. That's no way to start the foundation for a relationship, much less a marriage."

"I know that, Jessie. Truly I do. It's why I'm here. I'm glad you told me we needed to take a break and figure out what it is we really want. Because it made me see that it's you I want. It's always been you, but I've been too blinded by my own ambition and lost sight of what's really important. But I'm ready now. I'm willing to find a job in Manhattan so we can work on our relationship. I've already sent my résumé to some executive recruitment specialists and put out some feelers."

"That's great, Hugh, but I've thought about it and I don't want you to move here. You don't really want to, and you're only doing it because you think it's what you *should* do. You should come back because you *want* to."

"I do want to," he stated more firmly.

"Are you trying to convince me or yourself?" Jessie inquired.

"What's gotten into you?" Hugh asked, hopping to his feet. He began pacing the marble floor and then spun around to stare at her. "You've never spoken to me like this before."

"We need to be honest with ourselves about what it is we truly want, Hugh. Do you really want to be with me? Or are you with me because it's the right thing to do? Or what your parents expect of you? Are you even in love with me?" Jessie knew she didn't have those feelings for him. "So much so, you can't see your life without me? That's the kind of love I'm talking about. That's the kind of love I want."

"I don't think now is the right time to talk to you," Hugh said, shaking his head. "Clearly you're not in the right headspace to have such a serious conversation about our future."

"What do you expect our marriage to look like?" Jessie persisted. She wasn't dropping this conversation. "A white picket fence? Two kids? Live in Falling Brook or Connecticut and have the perfect life?"

"Yeah, Jess. Maybe that is what I want," Hugh snapped back. "Is something so wrong with that? Because, correct me if I'm wrong, but I thought that's what you wanted too. What you and I have been working our butts off to achieve?"

Hugh had a point. That's what she'd *thought* she wanted. The O'Malleys had done so much for her during her youth. If it hadn't been for the scholarship Jack O'Malley had given her and Pete, she would have never gotten into a good university. And Hugh…well, he'd always been a constant. The good-looking, popular boy every girl in Falling Brook had wanted, including her. She'd thought herself lucky he'd given her the time of day. But as the years had gone by, she'd become increasingly dissatisfied with her life, and Hugh hadn't been around to see that.

"Dreams change, Hugh. And maybe, if you'd been around, you'd know that. I no longer want this perfect life where we are slaves to our careers and making money. Not to say there's anything wrong with being ambitious and striving for success. I've learned that love and passion are equally as important."

She didn't love him and never would. She loved Ryan. And she may have lost him because she was too afraid to take a chance, but she wouldn't compound the mistake by making another.

It was time she took control of her life. She'd lived too long under the shadow of her parents' expectations. She was taking the first step, ending it with Hugh because she was in love with another man.

Ryan.

"You've found love and passion with someone else, haven't you?"

A tear slid down Jessie's cheek. "I have. And you deserve someone who can love you with her whole heart and without reservation. And I'm not that woman."

Hugh lowered his head and Jessie felt terrible for hurting him, but it couldn't be helped. They could no longer go on like this, not when her heart belonged to someone else.

When Hugh finally lifted his head, Jessie was surprised to see unshed tears in his blue eyes. "I understand it's for the best. I should never have taken you for granted, assumed you would be there when I finally got my act together."

Jessie gave a half smile. "I didn't try hard enough, either." Because she'd been unhappy and restless for years. "Anyway, we're going to need to tell our families that we're no longer together. I know it'll be tough on your family, but I hope they know how grateful I am for everything they've done."

Hugh frowned in exasperation. "You never owed us anything, Jessie. I hope you know that."

She hadn't, but she did now. "I do. I do now."

"Can I ask who it is—the man you're in love with? Or do I already know?" Hugh inquired.

"What do you mean?"

"It's Ryan. Isn't it?"

Jessie wanted to end their relationship with a clear conscience. She was done with the lies. She owed Hugh the truth. "Yes."

Hugh shook his head and a wry laugh escaped his lips. "I guess I should have known. I'm surprised he waited this long to make a play for you."

"It wasn't like that…we just sort of happened."

"Jessie, Jessie, Jessie." Hugh released an exasperated breath. "Open your eyes, it's always been Ryan. He's loved you from afar for years. Even I saw it. I've always been jealous of the friendship and easy camaraderie you two shared."

Jessie frowned. "You were? I never knew."

"I hid it well underneath bravado because I thought I was the best man for you. I can see I was wrong." He leaned in for a hug. "I wish you all the best, Jess. I truly do. All I've ever wanted is your happiness."

Jessie reached out and stroked his cheek. "I want the same for you, Hugh. And one day you will find the person that completes you, like I have."

Hugh offered a wry smile and inclined his head to the door. "Go on. Get out of here. Go get your man."

Jessie grinned. "I intend to do just that, I just have to wrap up some family business first." She gave Hugh one final squeeze and quickly rushed out into the night.

Professionally speaking, Ryan's life was soaring. He'd had a great interview with a Manhattan investment firm that was looking for new leadership since their founding member was retiring. The meeting had gone well and Ryan felt confident he would be called back. Black Crescent wasn't the only show in town.

But they hadn't forgotten about him, either. Joshua Lowell wanted to meet him for a second interview. The former CEO appreciated Ryan's résumé as well his ideas for Black Crescent's future. Allison had called to confirm a Monday meeting in Falling Brook. However, he would be remiss if he didn't admit his thoughts had strayed to Jessie during the call with Allison.

What would she think about him going through with the interview? He knew she was adamantly opposed to his working for the enemy after the pain the firm had caused her family, but Ryan strongly believed he could make a difference.

Quite frankly, he wasn't sure there was a relationship to fight for because she couldn't break away from her parents. Ryan wanted all or nothing. He hadn't heard from Jessie the last several days and it was driving him crazy. No amount of late hours at the office or working out with Dennis was going to ease the tension he felt. He wanted to call her, but what would he say that he hadn't said earlier in the week?

He'd bared his soul to her. Shared how much he cared for her, and she'd stared back at him with her doe eyes and hadn't said a word. What was he supposed to think, let alone feel about her silence? Was she afraid to tell him "thank you for the orgasms and take a hike"?

Ryan was desperate to get away from it all and decided to go to Connecticut for the weekend to visit his brother, Ben. He certainly wasn't going to Falling Brook early so his parents could hound him about Jessie. They'd already inquired about her and wondered if she might be the newest addition to the family. Ryan hadn't had the heart to tell them that they couldn't be further off track. Jessie would much prefer to be with the O'Malleys.

Instead, he would spend some quality time with his brother to see if he couldn't put Jessie Acosta in his rearview.

"Hey, baby bro. Come on in." Ben greeted him with a hug when Ryan rang the doorbell later that evening. He'd driven through Friday rush hour to the stunning mountaintop city of Bethel and was treated to some breathtaking views on his way, but now Ryan was ready for a drink.

"Thanks, man," Ryan said, stepping inside the contemporary three-bedroom town house. "Where's the missus?" He'd never been to his brother's new place and appreciated the open floor plan and well-equipped gourmet kitchen with its large center island and plenty of counter space.

"No offense, but you don't come to Connecticut often. She figured we might want some male bonding time, so she's hanging out with her girls tonight. So take a load off." Ben motioned to the leather sectional in the spacious family room Ryan had followed him into. "Can I get you anything? Beer? Wine?"

Ryan's face pinched. "You got something stronger?"

"I've got a nice Scotch if you're interested?"

"Yeah, I'll have that."

"On the rocks?"

Ryan shook his head. "Neat." He relaxed his head against the sofa and tried to let the week's events roll off him, but it wasn't working.

"Looks like you need this." Ryan heard Ben's voice behind him and turned to find his brother extending him a glass of brown liquid.

"I do." Ryan downed the two thumbs. "Another please." He handed the glass back.

"Uh, are you looking to tie one on?" Ben asked.

"Maybe." Ryan rolled his shoulders, but the tension wouldn't leave him. "It's been one crazy week."

Ben joined him on the couch after he'd refilled his glass and brought along the entire bottle of Scotch. "Thought you might need this." He set the bottle down on the coffee table. "So, fill me in. What's been going on? Last I saw you, you and Jessie were hugged up pretty tight on the dance floor."

"And if you recall, she wasn't too happy about that."

"But she's happy to be more than friends when no one's looking. Is that what's got you so riled up?"

"That and then some," Ryan replied, sipping his Scotch. "I learned Jessie didn't exactly break up with Hugh, not officially anyway. So, in essence, it was more of a break than calling it quits. I think she did it to keep up with the expectations her family had for her and O'Malley. She led me to believe we actually had a chance when she was merely biding her time until O'Malley got his act together."

"Do you really think that's true?" Ben inquired, staring at him intently. "As long as I've known Jessie, she's been a good kid." At Ryan's scowl, he amended, "A good woman. I can't imagine she would string you along."

"Well, what am I supposed to think?" Ryan inquired.

"Wait. Be patient."

"I'm done waiting," Ryan said. "Hell, I've waited for her for nearly two decades, but it eats me up because I know she's probably not alone."

"What do you mean?"

"Hugh called her during our argument earlier this week. And since then, I haven't heard a peep from her."

"And you think he's the reason why?"

"Partly. It's also her parents' expectations and her obligations to the O'Malleys," Ryan said, throwing up his hands and rushing to his feet. "I've been competing against him my whole life. And right when I thought it was a fair fight, I find out my hands have been tied behind my back the entire time and she was never really *free* to be with me."

"Ryan, you need to settle down. You're making a lot of assumptions without talking to Jessie."

Ryan didn't think so. Her silence spoke volumes. She wanted nothing more to do with him. It had been fun while it lasted, but now that Hugh had come calling, she was running back to the familiar. When Ryan knew for a fact her physical relationship with Hugh didn't hold a candle to theirs.

He plopped down on the sofa. "As much as it pains me, I can't sit around waiting for Jessie to decide she wants to be with me."

"What are you going to do?"

"Move on, as I'd intended to do before taking her to the Hamptons."

"Can you do that?" Ben asked, watching him intently. "This woman has been an important part of your life. Are you sure you can just cut her off, cold turkey?"

"You act like I'm an addict or something."

Ben chuckled. "I wouldn't go that far, but you have been hooked on her to the detriment of some of your other relationships."

Ryan supposed his brother was right, because none of those other women had ever measured up to Jessie. Whenever his previous relationships started to get serious, he would withdraw. He'd told himself it was because he wasn't ready to commit, but that wasn't the truth. Maybe, deep down, he'd been holding out hope one day Jessie would come around and see him as her Prince Charming. What a fool he'd been.

"You're right," Ryan said. "I have to break the cycle and I will, but I have to talk to Jessie. I need her to tell me to my face that this entire month has been a lie. That it's been nothing more than a summer fling. Only then can I move on."

"I agree. Now, can we please stop bemoaning your woes and watch some baseball? The Yankees are playing tonight and I'd much rather watch them than you cry."

Ryan chuckled. "Sounds like a plan."

"I'm so happy you're home again," Jessie's mother said as they walked through the farmers' market in downtown Falling Brook, perusing vegetables. "I hear Hugh is also back in town."

As if on cue, Kathleen O'Malley appeared from one of the stalls, carrying a basket of fruit. She stopped when she saw Jessie and her mother standing nearby, selecting tomatoes.

"Jessie! It's so fabulous to see you. Hugh told us you were in town."

"Mrs. O'Malley, a pleasure." Jessie air-kissed the woman and inclined her head sideways. "You remember my mother?"

The brunette smile. "I do." Her eyes narrowed as she

surveyed her mother for several beats. Jessie wondered why Hugh's mother was giving her such a close inspection. Had the two women had a quarrel?

"It's good to see you…" Jessie said and began to turn away. "If you'll excuse us?" She was eager to get away from the negative vibes emanating between the two women.

"I was hoping you might join us for dinner tonight?" Mrs. O'Malley's invitation dangled in the air. "We'd love to have you."

Jessie inhaled deeply. Hugh hadn't told his parents about the breakup and neither had she. She was working up to it. "Of course." Jessie offered a smile. She would attend the dinner for old times' sake. She would have to text Hugh later to give him a heads-up.

Fifteen

"Mrs. O'Malley, dinner was delicious," Jessie told the older woman she'd come to admire. Kathleen O'Malley was the epitome of class. She wore a sleeveless floral sheath that flared out at the hips matched with a pair of stylish pumps. Her dark brown hair was swept up in a sophisticated chignon while her makeup and jewelry were subtle yet noticeable.

"Thank you, dear," she responded. "I'm so happy Hugh came home. It was in the nick of time, don't you think?" she whispered as she led Jessie to the sunroom.

"Pardon?" Jessie asked, looking up.

"I was disappointed to hear about your dalliance with the Hathaway young man." Her eyes glinted when she spoke and there was no mistaking that mama bear was out in full effect.

"I didn't tell him," his mother whispered conspiratorially. "He's back now and I believe ready to do right by you. So we'll keep this between us and never speak of it again." She glanced down at Jessie, who could only nod her agreement.

By the time they arrived at the terrace where Mrs. O'Malley had tea and mini-desserts waiting, Jessie had lost her appetite. The lies and deception had to come to an end. She was ready for both of them to come clean with their parents.

"You can come visit us anytime, Jessie," Jack O'Malley stated as he and Hugh joined them. "No need to wait for this one—" he pointed to his only son "—to make an appearance."

"I appreciate that, thank you," Jessie said, sucking in a breath. She was doing her best to be cordial, but she felt like she couldn't breathe. She felt like the walls were caving in all around her and this lunch with Hugh's parents had done little to alleviate her anxiety.

"I hope your visit means you're finally getting serious about your future?" Jack questioned, his piercing gray eyes finding his son's as he waited for a response.

Hugh smiled good-naturedly. "No need to be so heavy-handed, Dad. If you must know, there are big changes, starting with… Jessie and I broke up."

His father roared. "You did what?"

"Hugh!" Jessie rose. "A word, please."

He lifted his shoulders in a shrug. "It's okay, Jessie. I appreciate you keeping up with this charade, but I've got this. Go find your happily-ever-after."

Jessie looked into Hugh's baby blues for the last time and smiled. "Thank you." She inclined her head to his parents. "And thank you both for everything. I'll never forget it."

It was time she took a page from Hugh's book and was honest with her parents. When she made it to her rental car, she quickly started the engine and sped away.

Jessie found herself pulling into her parents' driveway fifteen minutes later. She noticed her father's car wasn't there and she was thankful. She could start first with her mother and smooth the waters before talking to her father.

She was such a daddy's girl and would hate to disappoint him, but she had to live her own life. Dragging herself from the car, Jessie used her key for the front door. "Mama?"

Her mother came in from the kitchen, wiping her apron. "I was making some *ropa vieja* for your father for supper. I'm surprised to see you. I didn't expect you until much later this evening,"

"Oh, Mama, where do I begin?" Jessie released a long sigh.

"Honey, what is it?" Her mother circled her arms around Jessie's shoulders and helped her to the couch. "Whatever it is, you can tell me. Surely, we can figure it out."

Jessie shook her head. "Nothing has to be figured out, Mama. It's as simple as this. I'm not marrying Hugh because I'm in love with Ryan," Jessie blurted the words out. As soon as she'd said them, she felt as if she'd been set free. She hadn't realized that trying to deny her feelings was making her heartsick.

"Ryan?" The stricken expression on her mother's face told Jessie she'd shocked her.

Jessie nodded.

"But I thought you said you were just friends."

"We were. I mean, we are. Or then again, maybe not, because I've royally screwed this up. I was so conflicted about wanting to do what's right. What's expected…"

"Darling, you're talking in circles. Why don't you take it from the top and tell me what's going on?"

Jessie took a deep breath and gathered herself together. "Hugh and I… I know it's what you wanted and I did, too, but not anymore."

"I thought he was coming home now to repair your relationship."

"Yes, that's why he's here," she cried, "but it's too late."

"Why? Can you explain?"

"Four months ago, at the prep school reunion, something changed. I don't know why, but it did. Suddenly, Ryan wasn't just my friend. He was a good-looking man who looked at me like he wanted me. But then Hugh surprised me by showing up. When I realized I was having feelings for Ryan, I knew Hugh and I couldn't possibly continue seeing each other. Hugh and I agreed to a break because he understood distance hadn't made our hearts grow fonder."

"So you broke up then, not now?"

Jessie nodded. "Four months ago, we decided to take a break and we chose to keep it private. Tonight we ended it officially."

"Why didn't you say something?" her mother inquired. "I wouldn't have pushed you so much if I'd known your relationship status."

Jessie shrugged. "You didn't do anything wrong, Mama. I did. I thought I'd imagined the attraction I felt for Ryan because he was the boy I grew up with next door, so it couldn't possibly be real. I suppressed my feelings for him for three months until the July Fourth weekend. That's when our relationship changed and we became *more than* friends."

"I see."

"Ryan and I have been seeing each other the last month. And it's been wonderful, Mama. Honestly, it's been the best month of my life. But I struggled with my decision because it wasn't right for our family."

"What do you mean breaking up with Hugh isn't the right thing for us?"

"Because I owe them. We all do. Everything Mr. O'Malley has done for me, for Pete. Because of him, we were allowed to continue at Falling Brook Prep. Keep the house."

The horrified look on her mother's face startled Jessie. "You owe the O'Malleys nothing. You've already paid enough. Your brother working at the dealership during school breaks. And you? You've been devoted to the family, to Hugh, for years. But that doesn't mean you owe them your whole life. Your happiness."

"Oh, Mama." Tears of joy sprang to Jessie's eyes at her mother's words.

"Jack didn't give us the money out of the goodness of his heart."

"Why else would he give us that kind of money?"

Her mother lowered her head. "It's complicated, Jessie." She glanced at Jessie and her expression was haunted.

"Mama?"

"Jack and I have been having an affair for years."

"What do you mean? I don't understand." Jessie didn't want to believe the words coming out of her mother's mouth.

"I'm saying I've been lonely. Losing all his money made your father depressed and withdrawn. You've seen it. Think about it. If you feel that way as his child, imagine how I feel as his wife. I was distraught. I didn't know what I was going to do, how I was going to keep our family together. We were going to lose everything. The house. The cars."

"So that justified you having an affair?"

"No. No, it didn't." Her mother shook her head. "And I never meant it to go that far, but Jack was kind and he listened and one thing led to another, just like it did for you and Ryan."

"It's not the same! You're *married*. Ryan and I are single. How could you do this?" Jessie's head fell into her hands and she cried softly.

"I don't know," her mother said tearfully. "Jack was offering support at a time when I needed it most. I didn't mean for it to happen, but once it did, I didn't know how to stop."

"You should have never started in the first place! But thank God you realized it was wrong."

Her mother looked away and Jessie stared at her in disbelief. "Mama." She grabbed her by the arm. "Please tell me this affair with Mr. O'Malley stopped? Please tell me you came to your senses and realized what you were doing was wrong?"

Angela Acosta shook her head and Jessie clasped her hand over her mouth in horror. "You're still seeing him?"

"We never stopped. I tried, but Jack wouldn't let me go."

"What do you mean he wouldn't let you go? He's married. You're *both* married." Maybe.

"I know how this must sound but, like you, I felt beholden to him because he helped me out by giving me a job at his company and paying me an exorbitant salary, which helped us keep this house. Then he offered to pay for your and Pete's education if we stayed together, and I wanted the very best for you both and I saw it as a win-win. I know it is cliché. Lonely married woman has an affair, but I guess I enjoyed the attention Jack bestowed on me because your father hasn't been interested in me in years."

"That doesn't give you a license to cheat."

Her mother was quiet at the reprimand and Jessie fell into silence. She couldn't believe her mother had been having an affair—at a minimum, fifteen years—with Jack O'Malley. Half her life. It had all been a lie.

"Does Daddy know?"

Angela Acosta shook her head.

"Kathleen O'Malley must know. I saw how she looked at you today."

"Then she must turn a blind eye because she's happy with the life and privileges she has being Mrs. Jack O'Malley."

"This would kill Daddy if he found out. He looks at Mr. O'Malley as his best friend, all the while he's been cavorting with his wife behind his back."

"I did what I had to do to ensure you and your brother's

future wasn't limited by the losses your father suffered at the hand of Black Crescent. You know as well as I do, your father was never the same after he lost his fortune. And when he lost his job a few years after, he had a hard time finding another one. We would have lost the house if Jack hadn't intervened."

"All right, say for instance I believe the pile of hogwash you're giving me. Pete graduated years ago and I've been out of college for six years. Law school has been on my own nickel and I have the student loans to prove it. So why are you still with Jack O'Malley?"

Her mother shrugged and Jessie could see she didn't have a pat answer. "Convenience? Companionship? Familiarity? What? Why have you continued this affair after your kids were gone?"

"Because I didn't want to be alone!" her mother yelled passionately, meeting Jessie's eyes without flinching. "If I stayed here with your father, without any companionship or affection, I would shrivel up and die."

"Finally, we're being honest with one another," Jessie retorted with cold sarcasm. "But if you're so unhappy, why don't you divorce Daddy?"

"If I did that, it would break him," her mother responded. "It would be the final nail in his coffin of failures. Do you believe your father could withstand the blow? Because I don't think so."

She was right. Jessie doubted her father could take knowing his best friend and his wife were together. It would kill him. Of that, Jessie was sure.

"My whole point in telling you all of this was that I don't want you to feel obliged to the O'Malleys. You owe them nothing."

"What if there are repercussions from breaking things off with Hugh? We told his parents tonight. Will Mr. O'Malley retaliate and tell Dad the truth?"

Her mother shook her head. "Jack would never do that, not if he wants to continue having a relationship with me. He would never hurt me that way. Plus, it would ruin his marriage."

Jessie's eyes grew large. "You're going to continue seeing him, aren't you?"

"I care for him a great deal," her mother said. "It's not that simple."

"And Daddy?"

"I care for your father and love him in my own way, and you're just going to have to accept that answer."

Jessie glared at her mother. She didn't know what to make of any of this, but knew she wouldn't be like her mother, staying with a man when she clearly wanted to be with another. Jessie started for the door, but stopped in her tracks, spun around and faced her mother.

Angela Acosta looked older and wearier in the recliner by the window. *Why had she never seen how unhappy her mother was?* Maybe she hadn't wanted to look too hard.

"Does Hugh know about you and his father?"

"No. Jack has never told him. He wouldn't want Hugh to know the truth. Hugh looks up to his father. It would tear their family apart."

"This has been too much," Jessie said, shaking her head. "I'm leaving and I'm not sure when I'll be back. I need some time to digest this, and to make peace with everything you've laid in my lap and how I'm going to be able to live with myself keeping this from Daddy. Because you're right, knowing this would devastate him."

"Thank you."

"I know you told me all of this at great risk to your marriage and our relationship, but I have to tell you, Mama, I'm disappointed in you and I don't know if I'll ever get past this."

Tears trickled down her mother's cheek. "I know. And

I understand. I wanted *you* to know that your future is your own."

As Jessie closed the door behind her, she planned on heeding her mother's advice and taking her future in her hands.

Starting now.

Ryan was ready for his second interview with Black Crescent. After spending the weekend with Ben, watching baseball and playing pool, Ryan felt positive about the day ahead. He'd left his brother's town house early, with enough time for the scenic drive into Falling Brook.

He arrived half an hour early for his interview and stared up at the notorious Black Crescent building. The angled roof, exposed concrete and wall of windows made it everything a modern midcentury office should look like. Parking his Porsche 911 Carrera, Ryan buttoned the jacket of his Armani suit as he walked inside.

A receptionist greeted him. "Good morning."

"Good morning. Ryan Hathaway to see Joshua Lowell."

"Yes, he's expecting you. You can take the elevator to the second floor." She motioned to the bank of elevators across from the desk. "They'll take you to Mr. Lowell's office."

"Thank you."

He followed her instructions, but when he stepped out of the elevator, no one was there to greet him. Instead, he found a tall, athletic man leaning over a large, circular desk. As he moved forward, Ryan caught sight of Haley Shaw, Joshua Lowell's assistant, sitting behind it. The man was murmuring something to her that Ryan couldn't hear, but Ryan suspected he was trying to come onto her. *Why else would he be looming over and in her personal space?*

"Is everything all right over here?" Ryan asked, moving forward. He glanced at Haley and then again at the man. He instantly recognized Chase Hargrove, one of the other candidates for the CEO position. Ryan had met him by accident at his first interview. "Perhaps you can give the lady some space?"

Chase's eyes narrowed and he rose to his full height. He was a few inches taller than Ryan, but Ryan didn't care. Ever since he was a kid and had been picked on, Ryan hated bullies. Once he'd gotten fit, Ryan vowed no one would ever take advantage of someone smaller or helpless again. It's why his Krav Maga classes were so important. This guy might outweigh him, but Ryan could take him down if needed.

"Everything is fine, Ryan," Haley said. "I've got this under control. Chase, make yourself scarce. I have work to do." Then she was sashaying down the corridor, leaving Ryan to follow behind her.

"Does he do that often?" Ryan asked, stepping in line beside her.

She grinned. "Yes, but he's harmless. No need for you to defend my honor. I'm a big girl. I can take care of myself."

"That's good to hear." Ryan stopped when she reached a closed door and knocked. When she heard the occupant's voice, Haley opened the door. "Mr. Lowell, Ryan Hathaway is here for his interview."

A pair of hazel eyes trained on Ryan as he entered the conference room "Ryan, thanks for coming in. Have a seat."

Haley closed the door behind her and took a seat next to Allison Randall.

The conference room was all glass with sleek, modern furniture done in muted gray and white. A large Sputnik chandelier hung over the table while the elongated acrylic back panels and white padded chairs were minimalist in their design. The man in the midst of it all, Joshua Lowell, looked the picture of a CEO today in what was no doubt an expensive charcoal suit and blue tie.

"Appreciate the invitation," Ryan said, taking a seat across from them.

"We've only extended the invite to a few candidates who I feel would be the best fit to lead this organization when I'm gone," Joshua said. "It's important I find someone who understands Black Crescent's history, so we're not destined to repeat the mistakes of the past."

"Understood," Ryan said. "And the strategies you've used for your investments have been traditional in the approach, but I do believe there are times some risks are worth taking. Like hiring the top talent in our industry to provide our clients with a more robust return while giving Black Crescent the management and performance fees."

"I'm eager to hear more," Joshua replied.

Over the next hour, Ryan discussed his ideas and vision for Black Crescent's future. When it was over, Joshua reached across the table and shook his hand. "You just might be exactly what this company needs."

Ryan chuckled softly. "I believe that's true and, if given the opportunity, I can show you what I can do. Is there anything in my qualifications that you see as lacking?"

"Your résumé is stellar. And you know that my only surprise is your willingness to leave behind a large Manhattan firm in favor of a small-town company like Black Crescent."

"Like you, I grew up here. My family is here. And I could see myself planting roots in Falling Brook."

Allison rose and walked Ryan to the door. "We'll be in touch, Ryan."

"I look forward to it."

Ryan marched out of the conference room full of swagger and feeling on top of the world.

He was nearly to his car when he unsilenced his phone and looked at his text messages.

Several were from his mother.

Hugh O'Malley is back in town.
Rumors say he's planning on proposing to Jessie.
Did you know?

Ryan's heart stopped. Now he knew why he hadn't heard from Jessie. She was here in Falling Brook. With Hugh. And ready to become a member of the O'Malley family. He was done with Jessie. He refused to allow her any more space in his head, but his heart was another matter entirely.

Opening the door, Ryan hopped inside, but once he did anger fueled him and he pummeled the steering wheel with his fists. Why couldn't Jessie have told him? Been honest and not let him believe what they'd shared was something special?

Well at least now he knew rather than hold out hope on something that would never be. What they'd shared was over. If he was lucky, Jessie would go back across the ocean with Hugh and he wouldn't ever have to see her again.

Would that hurt any less? Ryan doubted anything hurt this much. Because Jessie had just ripped his heart out and he would never be the same.

Sixteen

Ryan appreciated Adam allowing him to use the Hampton house for the night. He knew he was pouring salt in the wound by coming back to the scene of the crime, but there was a part of him that wanted to relive happier moments he'd spent with Jessie. He knew it was twisted, but he couldn't help himself. He certainly hadn't wanted to stay in Falling Brook to see Jessie and Hugh reunited. No thank you.

He would stay here and lick his wounds in the privacy of Adam's beach house. When Adam had asked if he wanted company, Ryan had declined. He needed time to think. Think about the direction of his life and figure out how he'd veered so far off course.

Getting involved with Jessie when she was not over Hugh had been an epic mistake, but looking back, Ryan doubted he'd do things differently. The month he'd shared with Jessie had been exciting, thrilling and very *passionate*.

Sitting on the terrace, Ryan thought back to the night he'd looked out on this very same beach. He'd been wondering if he'd gotten his signals crossed when he'd kissed

Jessie in that restaurant, but then he'd turned around and seen her silhouette in the moonlight as she'd stood at the doorway. He recalled sucking in his breath at the significance of the moment. He remembered what it had felt like to hold Jessie in his arms and to know she'd wanted him as much as he'd wanted her.

And she had.

For that one moment in time.

Ryan's cell phone rang, prompting him from his musing. The display read Joshua Lowell. He was surprised to hear from the CEO of Black Crescent directly, but instantly knew the reason for his call.

"Ryan Hathaway."

"Ryan, it's Joshua Lowell. Is now a good time? I was hoping we could talk."

"As good a time as any," Ryan responded.

"Excellent, well…" There was a pause on the other end of the line. "I wanted to call you personally and tell you that you made a quite an impression on me. You're exactly what Black Crescent needs, which is why I'm offering you the job of CEO. What do you say?"

Ryan inhaled. He'd wanted this position so badly and had worked hard his entire life to get to the point in his career to make this shift, but it didn't hold as much appeal as it once did. Being in Falling Brook wouldn't give him the distance he craved, not if Jessie was back with Hugh. Given how small the town was, Ryan would surely run into them and he couldn't stomach it. Why did she always go running back to Hugh when they not only lacked chemistry, which Ryan and Jessie had in abundance, but had absolutely nothing in common other than the fact that his father, Jack O'Malley, had helped her and Pete when they'd been younger. She didn't owe them her life, but Jessie *couldn't* or *wouldn't* see beyond the past. And so she was destined to repeat her mistakes.

Ryan was certain he was the only man who could truly make her happy. He'd never seen her as alive and vibrant as she'd been with him. And because he loved her, there was no way Ryan could take a job that would hurt Jessie and her family. Even though they weren't together, he couldn't do it. He owed her his loyalty if nothing else than for their twenty-year friendship.

"Ryan, are you there?" Joshua asked. "Did you hear me?"

"I did. And the answer is no. I can't accept the position."

After calling in sick to work, Jessie sat parked outside the Hathaway house for several seconds. She had no idea where Ryan was, but she had to find him. It wouldn't be easy. She'd put her and Ryan's relationship on pause while she'd *finally* dealt with her past. But she had and now she was ready to move forward with the man she loved.

Her call to Ryan went straight to voice mail, as had the others all morning. She wasn't surprised. *Had she honestly expected him to pick up because she'd suddenly had an epiphany?* So she texted him. Again.

No response.

Damn.

She had to tell him she'd realized he was the only man for her, but she couldn't do that if he wouldn't pick up the phone. She had to tell him she'd made her peace and put Hugh and the past firmly behind her. Glancing up the driveway, she recognized Mrs. Hathaway's Audi and breathed a sigh of relief.

Jessie raced across the short distance, climbed the steps of the porch, pressed the doorbell and wrung her hands as she waited.

Marilyn Hathaway answered the door with a smile. "Jessie!" she cried. "What are you doing here?"

"I'm sorry to disturb you so late, Mrs. Hathaway, but

I… I was hoping you'd heard from Ryan? I haven't been able to reach him and…" Her voice trailed off. She wasn't ready to spill her feelings to his mother on their front porch.

"Do you want to come in, dear?" his mother asked, but Jessie shook her head.

"No, ma'am. It's important that I find him. I have something to tell him."

"That you love him?" his mother asked quietly.

Had everyone realized her feelings before she had? "I… if and when I say the words, Mrs. Hathaway, they have to be to Ryan first."

"I completely understand, but I'm afraid I haven't heard from him. All I know is that he visited his brother Ben this weekend before his interview this morning at Black Crescent."

So he was still pursuing the job? *That* stuck in Jessie's craw but they would have to figure it out somehow. She wouldn't let that dissuade her from speaking her truth, which was that she was madly, deeply, in love with him.

"Do you have Ben's number?" Jessie reached inside her purse and took out her iPhone, ready to dial him. "Perhaps I could speak with him?"

"Absolutely." Marilyn Hathaway pulled her phone from her back pocket and rattled the number off.

"Thank you so much." Jessie moved a few steps in and gave Ryan's mother a warm embrace. "You're a lifesaver."

"I wish you luck."

Jessie nodded. "I have a feeling I'm going to need it." She raced down the steps to her rental. Once inside, she called Ben immediately, but he wasn't much help, either. He informed her that Ryan was over being jerked around and had gone away to get some peace of mind from the roller coaster ride she'd taken him on. He also told her that he had no idea where Ryan had gone.

Jessie sat in the Hathaways' driveway, racking her

mind on where Ryan could have gone to clear his head. She thought back over the last month and when Ryan had been his most happiest. And she knew where he would go.

It took her two hours to get to the Hamptons from Falling Brook, but Jessie was determined that this night wouldn't end without her telling Ryan how sorry she was for putting them through the paces. She would tell him how much she loved him and wanted a future with him.

But was she too late?

Would he even hear her out after she'd hurt him?

Thankfully, she had Tia's cell and after speaking with Adam, he'd given her the address to his Hampton beach house and even told her where to find a second spare key. Following the instructions Adam had so graciously given, after she'd promised him she was going to make amends with Ryan, she pulled up the gravel driveway. When she saw Ryan's Porsche 911 Carrera outside, she damn near wanted to weep with joy.

He was here.

She would get a chance to make things right. It would be the toughest sell of her life. Probably harder than any case she'd ever tried in mock court during law school, but Ryan was worth the fight.

Girding her loins, Jessie walked up the steps and found the planter that held the other key. Ryan would be out back on the terrace, watching the stars, with a beer.

She was right about the terrace.

But not the beer.

He was on the terrace, his eyes closed and head leaned back. He was wearing the same open shirt he'd worn that night she'd found him and had had the most exciting sexual encounter of her life. *Stop it. Focus.* That's when she saw a bottle of dark liquid sitting on the side table along with the empty tumbler beside it. Half the bottle was empty.

"Can I have one of those?" she asked softly.

Ryan jerked upright. When he saw her, he blinked several times as if to be sure she was really there. "You don't usually like dark liquor," he finally said.

"I feel like I need it."

He poured some from the bottle into his glass and handed it to Jessie.

She downed the two thumbs in one gulp, coughing slightly.

"That was meant to be sipped."

She shrugged. "Liquid courage."

"What the hell are you doing here, Jessie? The more important question is why." He raised an eyebrow. "I assume Adam told you where to find me?"

"Don't be mad at him. He was only trying to help."

"He should have stayed out of it."

Jessie ran her fingers through her hair. This was going to be more difficult than she'd thought. Ryan's eyes weren't glassy but they were cold as ice. It was like he was looking right through her.

"I'm sorry." She didn't know what else to say.

"Exactly what are you sorry about?" Ryan asked, folding his arms across his broad chest.

"For ignoring you this week. I was so conflicted about so many things and I needed time to figure it all out. It was wrong of me not to return your calls or texts."

"But you're not *conflicted* anymore?" He snorted.

She nodded. "That's right."

He threw back his head. "Really, Jessie? You figured this all out and it's back in a nice, neat box? Well, guess what, life isn't that easy."

"It is when you know what you want."

"And what's that?"

"You."

Seventeen

Ryan had waited a long time to hear those words. For Jessie to tell him it was *him* she wanted. That it was *him* she hungered for. But that time had come and gone. Sitting out here in the dark, he'd picked up the pieces of his heart that she'd crumbled.

He was never going to be the man she chose. He was always going to be second best. For his sanity and his pride, he'd accepted she was with Hugh O'Malley—and now she was here telling him exactly what he wanted to hear? It couldn't be. Clearly, he'd had too much to drink tonight.

"Don't lie to me, Jessie. It's cruel. What did you come here for? A roll in the hay? That's all I was good for the last month, so are you ready for a repeat? If so—" he stood "—I think I can recreate our first escapade on this very same terrace."

"Stop it!" Jessie moved a few steps closer to him. "Don't do this, Ryan. Don't cheapen what we meant to each other. I mean, what we *mean* to each other."

"Me? I'm the one that's been fighting for us this entire time while you've been *conflicted, confused* or whatever other adjective you want to use. I've been very clear from day one *who* I wanted. And that was you. But you made it abundantly clear that you are with Hugh."

Jessie shook her head. "You're wrong. I'm not with Hugh. We broke up."

"Again?" Ryan laughed uproariously. "How many breaks is this now?"

"Stop being so pig-headed, Ryan. This wasn't a break. It was a breakup. I told my mom. And he told his parents. It's over. It has been for a long time. I think Hugh and I were content to have each other as a backup plan, but that's no way to live, and Hugh realized that, too."

"Bully for him." He reached for the bottle and poured himself another drink. "But what's that got to do with me?"

"Everything. Ryan, I'm bungling this, but what I'm trying to say, very badly, is that I love you."

Ryan's eyes blazed with anger. How dare she say those three words to him! "No, no." He pointed his finger at her while holding on to his glass. "So suddenly you're not with Hugh and you're running here to me because you love me? Do you honestly expect me to believe that?"

"Yes."

"Well, I don't. I don't believe you. Do you have any idea what you've done? I'm broken, Jessie. You broke me. You gave me everything I'd always wanted, allowing me to be with you, and then you snatched it all away in the next heartbeat."

"Ryan, please—" Jessie moved toward him, but he stepped away from her. He couldn't let her get any closer. It would be his undoing. He might falter and then where would he be? The sap who'd carried a torch for this woman for nearly two decades.

Ryan shook his head. "No way am I going to go through this again. I'm not giving my heart to you again and end up broken."

"I—I never meant to hurt you, Ryan. I thought I was doing what was right for me. For my family. You know I've felt beholden to the O'Malleys. They'd helped my family so much. Mr. O'Malley gave my mom a job, which ensured we were able to keep the house. It was because of him Pete and I had a future worth dreaming of. Staying with Hugh seemed like the right thing to do—to... you know, honor him, and thank him.

"Hugh was an O'Malley," she continued. "He was going places, which meant I would never end up nearly destitute like my father. It made sense on paper. But Hugh and I never had any sparks or passion between us. As the years went by, we grew further and further apart, but I was afraid to let go of the safety net he represented. So I stayed instead of opening myself up to the possibilities of what was right in front of me."

Ryan pointed to himself. "Are you talking about me?"

"Of course I am. The reaction I had to you on reunion night shook me to my core. It threw everything on its head about what I thought I wanted. Showed me I'd fooled myself into thinking love and passion didn't matter. And then we came here to the Hamptons and I could no longer deny the obvious. I wanted you. And the attraction was mutual and so hot, I wasn't ready for how powerful it was."

"Why are you telling me all this?" It hurt to hear and Ryan moved to the terrace sofa. His chest felt tight as he placed his drink on the table and took a seat.

"Because I need you to understand that I was mixed up about my family and Hugh, and it colored my thinking. But what I have never been confused about is you. I love you, Ryan. I fell in love right here—" she pointed downward to the deck "—in the Hamptons. I knew it wasn't just an affair, but I didn't really know what love was, so I didn't recognize it. Or maybe I was too afraid to, but I'm not anymore."

Jessie came forward and knelt in front of him. She took

his hand in hers. "You're not second to Hugh, Ryan. You're second to none. You're the only man I want. I know I've been foolish for turning my back on the precious gift you gave me—your heart. But I promise you, if you give me another chance, a chance to make this right, I will show you in every way imaginable that I'm yours."

Ryan slid his hand out of hers and cupped her face. Jessie rested her face in his palm. She prayed she hadn't left it too late to tell him how much she loved him.

"I'm yours, too," Ryan stated. "I always have been, Jessie. No other woman has ever, or will ever, measure up to you. You're it for me."

"Are you saying…?"

"I love you, Jessie."

She smiled through her tears and lowered her head. "Oh, thank God. I haven't lost you."

He lifted her chin and his brown eyes bore into her. "You haven't lost me, but I did try to forget you. I tried to tell myself not to love you, but I was fighting a losing battle. From the moment you stood inside the doorway of our tree house when you were six years old and asked me if you could come play, you've bewitched me and I've been yours ever since."

Jessie couldn't stop herself. She flung herself into his arms and he fell backward on the sofa. She sealed her lips against his and it was pure magic, sending the pit of her stomach free-falling into a wild swirl. She gave herself freely to Ryan because he was the only man she'd ever loved or ever would. There was a rightness in his kiss and it sang through her veins.

When his lips left hers to nibble at her earlobe, Jessie couldn't resist a low moan. When his lips returned to capture hers, he was more demanding. They kissed madly and deeply. It was wet and hot—so hot that Jessie surrendered any defenses she might have. Ryan took her weight, adjusting their position until she was sitting atop him and she could feel the press of his erection underneath her.

Jessie rocked her hips back and forth, teasing him, but it was her body that reacted swiftly and her inner thighs tightened around him in anticipation.

"If you keep doing that, I'm going to have to have you now."

"Go ahead," she murmured. "Have me." She lifted off him long enough for Ryan to reach underneath her dress and snatch the scrap of silk she'd been wearing. He tossed it on the deck. Then he was unbuttoning her shirt dress and pushing aside her bra. Jessie felt a gust of air on her nipple just before Ryan sucked it into his mouth. She shivered and moaned.

When he lifted his head, he stopped long enough to admire her breasts. "God, you're so beautiful."

"You make me feel beautiful." And he did. She felt like the sexiest woman alive in his arms.

"I don't have a condom."

"It's okay," Jessie slid one from the pocket of her dress.

"You naughty nymph." Once again, she'd come prepared to play.

Jessie grinned wickedly. "I hoped it wasn't the end of us. And I'm so glad I was right."

She helped him don the protection and then she guided him to where she wanted him. She impaled herself and rode him while Ryan sucked her nipples, taking his time to worship them with his mouth and tongue. Jessie melted into Ryan's hard chest and, though she wanted to ride him to swift peak, he was caressing her where they were joined.

He explored and incited her until a wave of pleasure so mighty and all-consuming engulfed Jessie and she broke while Ryan shouted his culmination. They tumbled back to earth, clinging to each other in the aftermath.

* * *

Ryan awoke with Jessie spooned tightly against him. Last night had been extremely gratifying and it was because they'd reinvented the Kama Sutra into the wee hours of the morning. They'd been so greedy for each other after a week apart, they'd stayed up half the night devouring one another. But eventually, he'd fallen into a peaceful sleep.

Awakening this morning, Ryan realized he had everything he could ever ask for. The woman he loved, loved him back. She'd *chased* after him, tracked him down to the Hamptons and revealed she was truly, madly, deeply in love with him. He couldn't ask for anything more. He'd wanted this for so long, for a moment he'd thought it had been a dream. But after closing his eyes tightly and reopening them, Jessie was still there wrapped in his arms.

It meant everything to him that Jessie made him a priority. It was a heady thought to think this beautiful, smart, independent woman was truly his. He stole a kiss, but when he did, her eyes popped open.

"Good morning," he said, glancing down at her sleep-deprived face.

"How long have I been asleep?" She rubbed the sleep from her eyes.

"Not long. I think I tired you out." He kissed the side of her neck then took her earlobe between his teeth. He reached for her breasts and they swelled in his hand.

"No fair, you know that's my sweet spot," she said breathily.

"Really? I thought this was…" He slid himself down her body so his face was between her moist folds. Then he swiped his tongue back and forth.

"Oh God," she cried out, but Ryan continued sucking, prodding and kissing her intimately until shudders racked her body.

A few moments later, Ryan moved upward, utterly satisfied with his handiwork, and looked at Jessie. He liked seeing her satiated and completely uninhibited. He knew how lucky he was and he wasn't going to do anything to jeopardize what they'd built.

"I got the job with Black Crescent."

Jessie sat upright, pulling the sheet to cover her breasts. "I see." She nodded. "I know how important this is to you and that you need to do what you think is right. So I want you to know, I'll support you in whatever you decide."

"You will?" Ryan was taken aback. From the moment he'd mentioned it, Jessie had been dead set against his taking the job and he'd understood. Vernon Lowell's greed, and therefore Black Crescent, was the cause of her family's hurt and pain.

"Yes. Part of loving you is loving all of you, including what's important to you. And if you feel strongly that you can make a difference and turn the company around, then I'll stand by you."

"Jessie, you've no idea what this means to me, but I turned down the job offer."

Jessie's eyes grew bright with unshed tears. "You did?"

"I turned it down as soon as they made the offer last night."

"Last night? We weren't even together. Why would you do that?"

He gazed at her tenderly. "Because I will always put you first, Jessie, whether we're together or not."

Jessie caressed his cheek. "How did I ever get lucky enough to find you?"

He shrugged. "I don't know. Maybe thank your parents for moving next door?"

Jessie laughed at him. "I love you so much, Ryan. But I only want you to turn down this job offer with Black Crescent if you want to. I'd never want you to look back and resent me for holding you back from your dreams."

"You're my dream," Ryan stated swiftly. "And I don't want to spend another moment apart from you." He lowered himself to the floor by the bed in front of her.

"What are you doing?" Jessie asked, clutching the sheet to her chest.

Ryan knelt on one knee and reached for her hand. "Jessie Acosta. I have loved you since I was six years old. I love your beauty, spirit and passion and there's no one else in the world for me, but you. Will you do me the honor of being my wife?"

"Yes, yes!" Jessie leaped into his arms and Ryan fell backward onto the floor, taking Jessie with him. "I love you, and I can't wait to be Mrs. Ryan Hathaway."

Epilogue

"Welcome to the fold," Marilyn Hathaway told Jessie when she and Ryan arrived at the Hathaways' annual July Fourth barbecue the following year.

She and Ryan had been married three weeks ago. It had been a small, intimate ceremony on the beach at Adam's Hampton house. His best friend had not only allowed them use of the house for the wedding, but had stood as Ryan's best man. Jessie's bestie, Becca, had been her maid of honor. Both Ryan and Jessie's parents had been in attendance. They'd only recently come back from honeymooning in Hawaii.

Ryan had booked them a villa with an infinity pool and stunning lagoon. Most of their time had been spent making love in the palatial master bedroom. Though they had, eventually, ventured out into the resort to eat delicious tropical meals, drink wine, swim in the pool or snorkel in the ocean.

"Thank you, Mom," Jessie said, responding to his mother before she departed to tend to other guests. Marilyn Hathaway had refused to allow her to call her anything else and Jessie didn't mind it one bit, especially since she wasn't close with her mother at the moment.

Since her mother's revelation of her long-standing affair with Jack O'Malley, their relationship had been strained. It was hard for Jessie to come home knowing everything she'd ever believed was a lie. She did visit, but they usually stayed with the Hathaways to avoid any awkwardness. If her father had noticed, he'd never said anything. Jessie suspected he knew something was wrong between her and her mother, but he didn't pry.

Jessie was thankful because, although she didn't agree with her mother's behavior, she refused to be the person who broke up their marriage and forced her father out of the only home he'd ever had. And so she'd kept her mouth shut. Though her mother had recently shared with Jessie that she'd ended her affair with Jack O'Malley, much to his chagrin, Jessie didn't know whether she had done it for Jessie or for herself. Regardless, she'd taken her at her word that it was over.

"Is everything okay, babe?" Ryan said from her side. "You looked like you were somewhere else."

"I'm sorry. I zoned out for a minute." Jessie shook her head, trying to shake off any negative vibes. Today was a day for enjoying her new family—and, besides, there was one more in the Hathaway clan now. Monica, Ryan's older brother Sean's wife, had had a baby girl a couple of months ago, and everyone in the family was excited and fawning over the newest addition. The seven-pound baby was a pure delight.

It made Jessie want to make some babies of her own with Ryan someday, but only after they had a couple of years to enjoy each other.

"Well, whatever is troubling you, you know you can talk to me, right?" Ryan whispered.

"I know." And she did, Ryan had always been her rock.

That would never change. In fact, Jessie would say their connection was stronger because he was her husband. She knew he would protect her and vice versa. On the beach in the Hamptons, when she'd said her vows to love, honor and protect him, she'd meant them.

"Good, so let's join the family. I think everyone's ready for a game of charades."

"Sounds like fun."

Jessie grabbed his hand as he led her toward her new future; a fulfilling life with a loving husband and his family. It was a life she hadn't known she wanted, but now that it was here, Jessie couldn't think of any place she would rather be.

* * * * *

COMING SOON!

We really hope you enjoyed reading this book.
If you're looking for more romance, be sure to
head to the shops when new books are
available on

Thursday 9th July

To see which titles are coming soon, please visit
millsandboon.co.uk/nextmonth

LET'S TALK
Romance

For exclusive extracts, competitions
and special offers, find us online:

f facebook.com/millsandboon

🐦 @MillsandBoon

📷 @MillsandBoonUK

Get in touch on 01413 063232

For all the latest titles coming soon, visit
millsandboon.co.uk/nextmonth

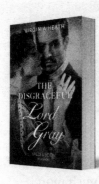

MILLS & BOON

THE HEART OF ROMANCE

A ROMANCE FOR EVERY KIND OF READER

MODERN

Prepare to be swept off your feet by sophisticated, sexy and seductive heroes, in some of the world's most glamourous and romantic locations, where power and passion collide.
8 stories per month.

HISTORICAL

Escape with historical heroes from time gone by. Whether your passion is for wicked Regency Rakes, muscled Vikings or rugged Highlanders, awaken the romance of the past.
6 stories per month.

MEDICAL

Set your pulse racing with dedicated, delectable doctors in the high-pressure world of medicine, where emotions run high and passion, comfort and love are the best medicine.
6 stories per month.

True Love

Celebrate true love with tender stories of heartfelt romance, from the rush of falling in love to the joy a new baby can bring, and a focus on the emotional heart of a relationship.
8 stories per month.

Desire

Indulge in secrets and scandal, intense drama and plenty of sizzling hot action with powerful and passionate heroes who have it all: wealth, status, good looks…everything but the right woman.
6 stories per month.

HEROES

Experience all the excitement of a gripping thriller, with an intense romance at its heart. Resourceful, true-to-life women and strong, fearless men face danger and desire - a killer combination!
8 stories per month.

DARE

Sensual love stories featuring smart, sassy heroines you'd want as a best friend, and compelling intense heroes who are worthy of them.
4 stories per month.

To see which titles are coming soon, please visit

millsandboon.co.uk/nextmonth

MILLS & BOON

HISTORICAL

Awaken the romance of the past

Escape with historical heroes from time gone by. Whether your passion is for wicked Regency Rakes, muscled Viking warriors or rugged Highlanders, indulge your fantasies and awaken the romance of the past.

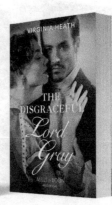